Praise for Emily Barr's writing:

'Emily Barr is carving out a successful niche combining fiction with travel writing – and this latest novel is no exception . . . An exciting read with some evocative description' *Sunday Mirror*

'A warmly engaging novel of genuine quality' *Publishing News*

'Emily Barr has pulled off this compelling story of what happens when things become too Single White Female so effectively, we're thinking maybe her best friend should start to watch her back' *Heat*

'Barr is a fresh new talent in literature and this novel certainly packs a punch' *Glasgow Evening Times*

'Honest, sharply observed, funny and sad' *List*

'Her light touch allows her to make some obviously heartfelt points, and she manages to keep the momentum going with some very funny twists and turns of the plot' *Oxford Times*

'A highly evocative read. It has all the ingredients of pure escapism . . . and a pace that never slackens' *Eastern Daily Press*

'Superb characterisation and edgy style' *Glasgow Daily Record*

Also by Emily Barr

Backpack
Baggage

Cuban Heels

Emily Barr

review

This Edition published in 2004 by REVIEW
First published in Great Britain in 2003 by
REVIEW

An imprint of Headline Book Publishing

10 9 8 7 6 5 4

ISBN 0 7553 0192 7

Typeset in Garamond Light by
Palimpsest Book Production Limited,
Polmont, Stirlingshire

Printed and bound in Great Britain by
Mackays of Chatham plc, Chatham, Kent

Papers and cover boards used by Headline are natural,
recyclable products made from wood grown in
sustainable forests. The manufacturing processes conform
to the environmental regulations of the country of origin.

HEADLINE BOOK PUBLISHING
A division of Hodder Headline
338 Euston Road
London NW1 3BH

www.reviewbooks.co.uk
www.hodderheadline.com

For James and Gabe

Thanks to Jessica Yudilevich for being so happy to help with the Spanish, and to Fefita, Luis, Ricardo and Dianelli for welcoming us to Havana and making us feed malanga to our baby. Many thanks, as ever, to Jonny Geller, and Jane Morpeth, Flora Rees and Alice McKenzie at Headline for all the encouragement, support and advice. Finally, thanks to Gabriel and James for coming to Cuba with me and for providing the most charming distractions possible during the writing process.

chapter one

Maggie

Dear Mark,

I just thought you might have mislaid my new address, which I sent you a couple of months ago. I know how absent-minded you can be – particularly without me there to keep an eye on you. So here it is again: 17a Sixth Avenue, Hove, East Sussex, BN3 3QU.

I'm sure you're busy – me too! American Express is a demanding place to work – but as we said all along, we'll be friends for ever. Hope you're looking after yourself. You know you're welcome here on the south coast any time.

With love,

Mags x

I put a copy of the letter inside the cover of my new diary, reading it again, as I do so, to check that the tone is right. It's too late now; I sent it this morning. I always keep copies of letters. I photocopy them at the corner shop before I send them. That way I can fill a few minutes from time to time, looking back at the entire correspondence, not just the half of it I didn't write. My half is normally the better component.

I must admit, the correspondence with Mark has been one-sided lately. In fact, without my side of it preserved, there wouldn't be anything at all. But I know I'll hear from him one of these days. I am pleased with this letter. I think one sole exclamation mark conveys the appropriate degree of nonchalance, the coolness that might lead him to respond. I have not said that I will love him for ever, that I want to marry him, that if he has ever felt anything for me, he must catch the next train to Brighton and take me away from this laughable excuse for a life. It does not beg. It does not ooze desperation. It is a masterwork of understated poise.

I put the diary back into the desk drawer, and wander into the kitchen to make a cup of tea. I have four hours until I go to work, and in that time I will think only of Mark. I will not think about the evening's work ahead of me. Only Mark.

I never felt like this about him when we were living together. It was only after we split up that I realised that in welding my life to his, I had lost myself entirely. We were together so long that all our friends were joint friends, and no one was loyal to me. When I saw that I had to leave Edinburgh, I left them all behind. It seemed that these people all belonged to him. Mark is the charismatic one, and I was his appendage. No one would bother to stay in touch with me, on my own. I have no friends left from school. I don't want anyone who knows me from that far back.

If they saw me now, those Edinburgh people I thought of as my friends might laugh. My school friends might do the same. They might be horrified. They'd all feel sorry for me.

The kettle blows steam towards my face, and I search for a peppermint tea bag. I don't drink normal tea any more, because I can't be bothered to keep milk in the fridge. The smallest carton goes rancid before I finish it, and I don't feel that foul globs glistening on the surface of perfectly good drinks are an essential component of my diet. Peppermint suffices. Even though it's unseasonably warm, I shiver, and go to fetch a cardigan, leaving the tea to infuse. One of my many spinsterish habits, acquired since my exile began, is a tendency to walk around my life agreeing with myself in my head. I'll put on the black cardy, I tell myself, because it's baggy and cosy. That's a good idea. Well done. I find it crumpled on my bedroom chair, and snuggle into it. Mmmm. That's better. Now you'll be nice and warm.

I miss Mark. I miss Ivan, my first serious boyfriend, stolen by my best friend when I was eighteen. I miss that best friend. I miss someone to whom I could say: 'Hmm, I'm a bit chilly. Aren't you?' I never offer anyone a cup of tea. I never share my food, never check whether the other person wants a bath before I run my own, and never huddle over the TV page conferring about what to watch that evening. I watch what I like, when I like. I never argue with anyone. Nobody cares what I do for a living. When I go out, I fight my way along the seafront through a gale, and watch the pebbles being washed up on the esplanade. I do not comment. Once, a fish was stranded, large and dead, over the back of a bench. It had been a wild night. I looked at the fish, with its bared teeth, and wanted to tell someone.

I live in an inhospitable basement, in a big old house that is inhabited by three couples, a baby or two, and me. I don't know any of the neighbours. I wouldn't recognise them if I passed them on the street, except for a man with a ginger beard. My flat is deceptive. When I first saw it I thought it was lovely. The ceilings are vaulted, as befits a cellar. The doorways are arched. There are funny nooks and crannies all over the place. It had, I thought, character and quirkiness. In my desperation for a home, I overlooked the fact that cellars are traditionally cold and damp, and have no light.

I have a large bedroom, an open-plan living-dining room and kitchen, and a small bathroom. My floors are wood-effect laminate, and I have no need for curtains. This flat graciously receives natural daylight between ten and eleven on mornings when climatic conditions oblige. The bathroom has no windows whatsoever – all the better to avoid looking at the avocado suite – and the windows

3

in the other rooms are close to the ceilings. They look mainly at blank walls.

I ache for my old life. I wish I had fought harder to keep it. Now I struggle to get it back, but in my heart I know that the battle is futile. Mark and I lived in a first-floor flat in Edinburgh. It was everything this place is not. The living-room windows stretched from floor to ceiling. Everything was bathed in natural light. We had a spare bedroom, and a roof terrace. The bathroom was white and blue, and was flooded with sunlight through frosted glass. We had friends, and we had each other. The rent was less than it is on this place. I loved Mark, and I love him even more now I haven't got him. All the same, I knew all along that the relationship was doomed. I felt it physically, from time to time, and I could never imagine what I would do without him. I never admitted it to myself, let alone to him or to anyone else, but I knew I needed him desperately, whereas he only quite liked me. I knew that one day he was going to walk away.

I put my hands to my waist. This has become something of a compulsion lately. I feel my jutting hip bones and smile. Your waist is tiny, girl. Why, thank you. Mark was an enthusiastic eater, and we used to go to restaurants more often than not. When we did eat in, it was usually a takeaway. The fridge was always stocked with full-fat milk, and there was often a tub of ice cream in the freezer. As a result I was too curvaceous for my height, and bordered on the dumpy. Mark constantly told me not to be so stupid.

'Christ's sake, Mags,' he'd say irritably. 'It's women that care about that stuff. I don't give a shit. Baby, I don't notice whether you're a bit chunky or not. Give it a rest! It's boring.'

I don't give a shit. That sums Mark up perfectly. I clung desperately to him, and he didn't give a shit. He was the sort of man who pulls away, the first time he kisses a woman, to inform her brusquely that he doesn't want a relationship at that particular time. It doesn't matter what his situation is: he will say that as a matter of course, as an insurance policy against future trouble; a get-out clause. I met him at university, where I made him laugh by being mean about everyone around us. He appealed to me because he was straightforward and I fancied him. It never went any deeper than that. I needed company – I needed my time to be filled – and he was too lazy for courtship.

Six months into our relationship, I told him I loved him, and waited for him to reciprocate. Against my better judgement, I tried to force him a couple of times over the years. Cornered and irritated, he'd insist, 'I do love you, Maggie, you know that. Don't make an issue out of it.' I'd turn his words in my head all night, until I'd convinced myself that 'I *do* love you' was heartfelt and passionate (if you say it in a different tone of voice, it can be quite convincing), and eventually I persuaded myself that I was happy and lucky and, best of all, that I was 'in love'.

I pace around the flat, switching lights on as I go. Maybe I'll watch the telly, I decide. Yes, you may as well see what's on. I press the red button. My sole extravagance with my considerable wages has been a wide-screen television. Luckily, it's time for *Countdown*. I settle back to stare at the screen.

I don't even like Mark very much, but I have no alternative but to get him to have me back. He worked as manager of a coffee franchise. I had a job in human resources for a software company. I had friends at work, but they were day-to-day companions, and certainly not the kind of people you stay in touch with if you move to the other end of the country. We rarely socialised outside the office. Mark's shop had a constant turnover of low-paid workers, many of them young female foreigners who came to Scotland to learn English. Sometimes they unnerved me a little, with their perfect skin and long, slender limbs, but I knew Mark was too lazy to embark on a torrid affair, or even on a lacklustre one.

We were settled. I assumed that the way we lived suited us both, that we would trundle along for the foreseeable future. Then, four months ago, it changed. It was early in the evening, on one of those busy week nights after the clocks go back. My sister, Emma, had just told me that she was pregnant, and I was unsettled. I popped along to the Coffee Café to share the news after work. It had been dark for ages when I left the office at six. I did not want a baby in the family. The vehemence of this conviction surprised me. I was close to tears when I pushed the door open.

Mark looked up at me, and smiled half-heartedly. He was as good-looking as he'd ever been, with his almost-shaven head and big brown eyes, but his body was beginning to lose its definition. He used to take care of himself, but now he was complacent. He had grown a belly, and his face was changing as his jawline softened and his cheeks began to sag. He winked at me, and carried on counting the contents of the till while Svetlana, a Russian student, cleared the tables.

I'd met Sveta before, and found her singularly unthreatening. She was shorter than me, dumpier than me, and spottier than me. She smiled all the time. Despite possessing a Russian soul, she had the inbuilt happiness that I lack. I often wonder whether I might have grown up with a sunny disposition if things had been different, but I will never know. I pulled myself together, smiled, and sat down at a big wooden table, to chat. The light bulb immediately above us blew out at the moment I sat down.

'Sveta,' I asked her, 'how do you say "Can I have another light bulb, Mark" in Russian?'

'Dayt-ye drooguyu lampach-koo, Mark,' she said, earnestly.

I laughed. 'That sounds so beautiful. How about "My name is Margaret"?'

'Myen-ya zavoot Margaret.'

'I hate my name, Sveta. I hate it so much. Margaret. Bet there are no Margarets in Russia.'

'Why do you hate your name?'

I twisted in my seat and looked at her in the half-darkness. I was distracting myself. 'You'd heard the name before you came to Britain, hadn't you?'

'Of course. Everybody in my country knows Margaret Thatcher, the lady of iron.'

'Lady of irony, more like,' interjected Mark, meaninglessly, as he locked the front door and prepared to let us all out of the back. That was typical of him: he would always say something that he thought sounded amusing, just for the sake of it.

'Well, exactly,' I said, ignoring him. 'That's one reason why I hate it. She was called Margaret and she was called Maggie. The only version of my name that doesn't have Thatcher after it is Mags, so that's what I call myself. I tried Meg at one point but it didn't catch on. Everyone thought my name must be Megan.'

'Don't worry,' said Sveta with a sweet smile. 'I call it a pretty name. I like it very much.'

Mark threw his apron down and grabbed his leather jacket.

'Come on, Thatch,' he ordered. 'Stop gossiping. Time to go.'

I raised my eyebrows at Sveta, and followed him out of the shop. I never went there, or saw Svetlana, again.

I can see him now, sitting in the smoky pub that night. His big jacket was over the back of his chair. His hair was at the right length, the one where it was soft and fuzzy to touch. I didn't touch it. He was wearing a blue shirt with a small coffee stain next to the third button down. And he was baffled by everything I said.

'*I* don't want a baby,' I insisted, when I saw his face. 'Christ, don't think that. That's not the problem, at all.'

'So what *is* the problem? You're not up the duff as well, are you?'

'No, I am not up the duff. I'm fine. I'm just, I don't know, not feeling great. You know, it makes me think of stuff. From the past. I don't want Emma to have a baby. I really, *really* don't.'

Mark put his glass down and held his head in his hands.

'Oh God, Mags,' he said, peering through his fingers. 'Please, I beg you, don't do the crazy thing. Everything that happened – that was years ago. I thought you were over it.'

'Well, it's not the kind of thing that exactly goes away,' I told him angrily. He knew I didn't talk about what had happened, and on the rare occasions when I alluded to it, he was supposed to be sympathetic. He knew that. He was breaking the code.

I make an effort to regulate my breathing. I'm not supposed to be thinking about Grace. I sit back and let *Countdown* flow over me. You could clearly make the word 'arse' out of these letters, though I'm sure no one will mention it. With a bit of concentration, I form a seven-letter word: lathers. This is good.

I take myself back to that last night with Mark.

I remember putting my glass of wine down and looking at him in exasperation.

'Well, no, whatever,' he said, sounding distinctly uninterested. 'Sorry. Look, Mags, I can see you're unhappy. And I don't think it's because of Emma's baby. That's too easy. You always imply some bullshit about how everything bad stems from your other sister. I know your game. It gives you an easy way out.'

I was outraged by that. 'But I never mention her, ever ever ever.'

'I know. You don't actually say it but it's always hanging there.'

'It is not!'

'And I'm sick of it. You know what's really wrong with you? Us. We've been hanging on to this thing we've got even though it's crap. It's not fun any more, is it?'

I was astonished. 'It is!' I remember grabbing the edge of the table, for support.

'It's not,' he replied calmly. 'I've been giving it some thought, and it's really better all round if we give it a break for a while.'

'A break?'

'OK, not a break. Call it a day, that's what I mean.' He didn't look me in the eye. 'Six years, Mags. Time to move on.'

The panic began to overwhelm me. I tried to take control. 'Mark,'

I told him firmly, 'there is no way on earth that I'm going to let you leave me.'

As it turned out, I couldn't stop him. Mark left me so I left Scotland. A week after I moved, when I had just decided to catch a train to Edinburgh and woo him back, he sent me a text message to let me know that he'd moved in with Freya, one of the Norwegian students.

I slide off the sofa and on to the floor to sip at my cup of peppermint tea. I perform the necessary sums with the *Countdown* numbers, and reach the target of 489 without difficulty. Both contestants do the same. Today is Friday. I'll go for a walk along the seafront, buy a bottle of wine on my way home, and write a letter to Emma before I go to work tonight. I must make a huge effort to keep up the myriad of pretences as I write. There are many things that Emma doesn't know. Number one: I wish she wasn't pregnant and I'm fairly sure that her baby will die. The thought of that happening turns me inside out. Number two: I have not a single friend in Brighton. Number three: I have no fat cells left. I am skin and bones and my skin is dead and grey. Number four: I do not work at American Express, but, rather, at a dancing establishment named Vixenz. Apart from those minor details, I can be completely honest.

I washed up in Brighton like that dead fish. I chose it randomly. Mark came here on a stag weekend once, and returned proclaiming: 'it was full of way cool stuff – we should live there, one day.' I thought that moving here was a stroke of brilliance. I expected him to follow. I imagined Brighton to have a better climate than Edinburgh. I liked the confident way I told my workmates: 'I'm moving to Brighton.' I liked the envy in their reactions. In my head, Brighton became paradise. I would, I imagined, be happy here. This is a holiday town. I would walk along the sandy beach and clear away my cobwebs. If Mark didn't come after me, then I would find someone else: a man who would love me back. We would walk along the esplanade hand in hand. I would take him to

France to meet my parents. We would have a small perfect wedding, and no children. We would be wrapped up in each other, for the rest of our lives. He would take care of me.

In real life, the beach is stony. Sometimes it's so windy that I can walk and walk without getting anywhere. The lovely-looking men who might save me from myself are gay, or else they're married. I should have gone to London, instead, where all the other lonely people are also watching *Countdown*, and feeling empty.

'I'm going out,' I tell no one. I know, now, why lonely women surround themselves with cats. They give you a reason to speak. I have been tempted, but I'm not allowed pets under the terms of my lease, and besides, I don't want to succumb to the craziness. I am not going to be like this for ever. Soon, I will come back to life, get a new job, and move on. I squeeze my big cardigan under my jacket, and wrap a scarf three times round my neck. Then I shut the door, and step out into the salty air, under the pale January sun.

chapter two

Maggie – Friday evening

Dear Sir or Madam,

I am writing regarding my council tax bill, which I received yesterday. Although I have spoken to the department on numerous occasions about the fact that I live here alone, I have still not been given the relevant discount. I am entitled to 25% off. You know that and I know that. I am therefore enclosing a cheque for the correct sum.

Yours faithfully,

Margaret Wilson

I posted the letter on my way to work, and as I change, I'm running through it in my head. I'm glad I signed it 'Margaret'. It makes me sound formidable. I write a lot of letters. If I had a computer at home, I'd send emails instead. Maybe I'll buy one this month. There has to be some compensation for this work I do.

I'm changing in the crowded back room, jostling with the other girls. It smells of sweat, in here, and hairspray. I don't know any of my colleagues very well. Most of them are younger than me. They range from Tina, a single mother of two who lap dances to feed her babies, to Amy, a student with a background even more middle class than my own. Amy claims to think this is, in her own

11

words, 'a fun way to supplement my loan!' I give her one more week. She clearly has self-esteem issues. I expect we all do. This is not fun, and we all know it.

Vixenz is not the most upmarket establishment. It is basic, and small. Drinks, laughably expensive ones, are served at a brightly lit bar. There are stages, walkways and poles. Spotlights and disco balls. The music thuds relentlessly. Topless women look at the punters with feigned lust, or undisguised contempt. Men push notes into the tops of our stockings, into our thongs. They do not, however, lay a finger on us. They would be out on the street in seconds. That is why I stay. That, and the novelty of never having to worry about money.

I nudge Tina out of the way to get a look in the mirror. My ribs look like piano keys. The shade between them is deeper every time I look. My breasts have all but vanished. I don't think I am remotely sexual, but the other girls envy me.

'Christ, Mags,' says Tina. 'You look amazing. Do you do carbs or fat?'

I look at her, and frown. 'Do I what?' I shake my hair loose, and assess its state tonight. It's wild, as ever. I start smearing it with gel.

'Carbs or fat? I cut out carbs once, and the weight just fell off.' Tina is curvy and dark-haired. She takes off her bra and looks critically at her body. 'Trouble is, I couldn't keep it up. Couldn't keep my hands off the kids' chips.'

'I don't do anything. I suppose I just don't eat much.'

She makes a face. 'I hate people like you. Don't stand next to me.'

'I look horrible. I'm scrawny. I'm amazed anyone will pay to see me naked.'

But they do. I stand in front of about a hundred men, and rub my barely noticeable breasts. The music thumps through my body. Friday nights, like tonight, are among the worst. The place is full of stag parties. Copying what I've seen the other girls do, I tilt my chin back as if I'm in the throes of passion, and moan slightly. Mark probably came here on that stag weekend. I hold the pole, and rub myself against it. *Oh*, I mouth, *this is amazing*. I hope Mark doesn't come down here again. Imagine if he saw me. I must remember to buy the baby monitors for Emma. Only my practical little sister would allocate useful items she wants to be given before the birth. Most people just settle for teddies when the baby arrives. I wonder if Amy wants to share a cab back to Hove later. She doesn't live far from me, and occasionally I pass her in the street, but we don't stop to chat. We just look at each other, smile wanly, and look away. I rub myself a bit more. I wonder whether letters to the council signed 'Margaret' are more effective than they would be if I had a normal name. It makes me sound much older than twenty-eight. Margarets are over fifty. They are staid and respectable. No other pole dancer is called Margaret. I wish they'd called me Emma or Grace. The first-born should get the best name, not the worst.

A man beckons me over and pushes a note into the top of my stocking. His hand hovers for a moment, then he retracts it. I stand in front of him, inches from him, and slowly remove my knickers. I can't think about what I'm doing. I used to wonder whether these men's wives knew they were here, but now I don't care. I concentrate hard on remaining in my head.

I hope I don't have to do many private dances later. Often I don't. I'm too skinny to be particularly sought after. There's nothing on me to fantasise about; nothing to grab hold of. This is one of the reasons why I don't eat. I like it that way. It's easy to ignore an audience, but when it's one on one, I am being paid to look them in the eye and feign desire. I hate the pretence of intimacy. I know, at times like this, that I am completely and utterly degraded, that I can barely sink any lower. I'll drink the rest of the wine when I get home. I have to drink half a bottle to get me to work every evening, and the rest to relax me when I get back.

The music is louder, now. I wriggle around, like I do every night. This isn't the career move I was planning. I thought I'd find something interesting here. Brighton is supposed to be hip and lively. I applied for a human resources job at American Express, and told Emma I was confident they would offer it to me. I didn't get an interview. I couldn't bear to relay this news to my sister, so I pretended they had complimented me on my interview manner and my interesting CV, and asked how soon I could start. I almost think it's funny, now, when I tell people I work for American Express. I'm sure a percentage of my audience hails from those quarters, so in a roundabout way I am telling the truth. My lies do no one any harm, and at least, this way, Emma and Jeremy respect me.

So do Mum and Dad. As I step away from the pole for a minute and look longingly at a few misogynists in the audience, I feel a familiar jab of pain. If I could phone my mum and wail about the crap turn my life has taken, I'd almost feel all right. Normal women can do that. I'd love to tell her about Mark, about my miserable flat and the job that's too awful to be acknowledged. It would be the beginning of the end of the horrors. Mum would be warm and comforting. She would insist on my leaving Brighton immediately. She would call me back within the hour to tell me she'd bought me a Eurostar ticket, which I could pick up at Waterloo first thing tomorrow morning. They know I love the train. Once I arrived at their stone house overlooking the most beautiful valley in Provence, I would be nurtured and cosseted. We would go to markets and for walks. Mum would want to buy me clothes at agnès b., and take me to look at art with her. They'd want me to stay for weeks, and months, and for ever. In a way I can't imagine anything more seductive. I can picture them now. Mum in her baggy linen, Dad with his sleeves rolled up, in the garden. They both look sad.

I have no right to make them fear for another of their daughters. That is why I can't let them know that I'm not coping. I can't let them worry about me, at all.

I slink off stage, and immediately feel naked and vulnerable. I rush to the changing room and put on a T-shirt. Amy is sitting in a corner, her dark hair sprayed into a solid helmet, her make-up garish and grotesque. She is staring at her reflection.

'Want to share a cab afterwards?' I ask, perching on the table next to her.

'I can't do this,' she replies. 'I feel like a lump of meat.'

'We are lumps of meat.'

'How long have you been here?'

'Three months.'

She looks up. 'How do you do it? I want to keep at it. I need the cash. I thought it would be a laugh, but it's *so* not. I wish I could do it, because the money's so great, but I just can't.'

I touch her on the shoulder. I rarely get to touch anyone, these days. My whole life is about not touching. 'So leave,' I tell her. 'Amy, you don't have to do this. Fuck the money. No amount would be enough, you know that. Get dressed now and walk out.'

She smiles sadly. 'Come with me?'

I consider it. I could easily live off my bank account for months, but the prospect of idling around without even my vile job to break up the days is horrific. 'No,' I tell her, with a degree of regret. 'I think I like the money more than I hate the work.'

The next morning, I wander around the shops, buying random items. I pick up a couple of scented candles for my bathroom; a scarf; a selection of non-gender-specific baby clothes and the set of monitors. Brighton is busy, and I lose myself in the crowd. For a while, I sit in the window of a café in the North Laine and watch people passing. I am invisible. I watch boys with piercings and girls on huge platforms, which I thought went out of fashion five years ago. I see chic mothers pushing babies who are covered by zebra-print blankets. I follow the progress of a couple of swaying alcoholics down the street. I enjoy being an observer. I look nondescript enough to be ignored. I don't look anything other than normal. Everyone has brown hair. Everyone is five foot four. No one would look at me twice. I blend in, and I love that feeling.

After two cappuccinos, I wonder whether to go to Jigsaw and buy myself some quality clothes, but decide that I can't be bothered. I'll only end up taking them off. The only clothes I buy are work clothes, and I haven't the stomach for that, right now. I do, however, call in at Debenhams to stock up on make-up. I never wear it except when I'm working. Then I plaster on as much as I can. I paint my own mask.

I walk home, along the busy main road, enjoying the tang of salt in the air. The clouds are gathering, but I think I'll make it back before it rains. I am almost contented, when I see a man pass by, look at me, and do a double-take. I accidentally make eye contact, and he smiles gleefully, and winks. I hate it when that happens. I speed up my pace, and dodge into Waitrose to make sure he's not going to follow me home. After five minutes in the vegetable section, I leave, empty-handed, and hurry to the flat. I have no friends, but that man has seen my breasts. I may well have gyrated, nude, inches from his face. I always wonder who my audience are in real life. Do they think I'm enjoying it? Can they really not see?

I run down the stone steps and through my front door, slam it shut, and double-lock it. Then I walk from room to room, blinking back tears. This has been happening a lot, recently. I don't know what's wrong with me. In a blurry fuzz, I thrash around for something to do. I decide to take the baby monitors out of their packaging. Why don't you check they work? I ask myself. Then, if they happen to be faulty, you can take them back to Mothercare tomorrow. You're desperate, I add. There is nothing on the telly, you don't want to phone your sister and pretend to be happy, and you've got nothing to read. You don't feel comfortable or safe in your own home. Your life is crap.

I have to create some kind of task for myself, because otherwise I'll call Mark's mobile and beg him to have me back. To give me a job in the Coffee Café, if nothing else, and to let me move in with him and Freya as a lodger. I have no dignity. Strippers don't.

I open a can of Stella, and take the monitors, still in their box, to the bathroom. With my drink balanced on the loo, I try to follow the multilingual instructions. Eventually, I switch on the 'baby unit'. My little kitchen radio goes next to it, tuned to Radio 4, which is offering the news. I used to listen to music stations, but I find speech more soothing, these days. It gives the illusion of company. Sometimes I hope the neighbours hear voices through the floorboards in the mornings, and assume I have company. Mark and I always had a CD playing, with the volume turned up. He kept them all, as well as the stereo. Men like stereos a lot more than women do. Keeping the stereo was a huge issue for him, but I couldn't have cared less. I picked up a fifteen-pound radio from Argos, and I was fine.

I close the bathroom door carefully, and take my Stella and the 'parent unit' across the living room and into my bedroom. When I switch it on, I am greeted immediately by the rather crackly information that 'To address any of the topics raised in this week's *Any Questions*, call *Any Answers*.' Great, I tell myself. It works, then. Before I conclude the experiment, I flick a switch on the side, changing to Channel B. I don't know why I do this. Just to keep me away from the TV for a few more seconds.

'Yeah, no, you're right,' says a woman's voice, loud and clear. 'A great big smelly poo.'

I freeze, my can of lager halfway to my mouth. The first, absurd, thought I have is 'Grace.'

'Here, I'll do it,' says a man. He sounds as if he's in my bathroom, but I don't think he is. 'Look, my darling, it's going to be all right. It's going to be brilliant. Look at it this way – we can make this situation the best thing that's ever happened to us. It is up to us. Can you imagine? South America? It's just so cool. I can't wait.'

'You stupid tosser,' says the woman. 'We've got a bloody baby here, in case you hadn't noticed. We can't go backpacking around the Inca Trail, can we? Hey?'

'Of course we could. We need to do it now, while he's so portable.'

The woman moves out of range and I can't hear what she says.

'Peanut allergy?' the man replies. 'Since when has your peanut allergy ever stopped you doing anything? Take an epi-pen. We'll talk later. Want to go to Pizza Express, or is that too adventurous, too? Ooh, they might have nuts.'

I can hear him clearly, but I know he's not in my bathroom. This is not a radio play. Why are these people talking about babies and peanuts and the Inca Trail? It makes no sense. They are not on the radio, because they would certainly not feature on either *Any Questions* or *Any Answers*.

I cannot stop myself getting excited. For a few seconds I am convinced that I have strayed into some magical realm, that I am listening to Grace in the parallel universe where she is still alive. I am certain of it. I am breathing rapidly, and I shiver with excitement and shock.

I don't move, in case she can hear me, too. I barely breathe. I am hearing my sister through the baby monitor.

Within moments, I realise what has happened. I forgot myself for a few seconds. Someone nearby has the same type of baby monitor tuned into the same channel. I have been eavesdropping on an innocent family, inadvertently, but they have no idea that I'm here. Of course I couldn't hear her. I am mad. The monitor crackles, and is silent. I sigh.

Then I am intrigued. I might leave it switched on, in case they come back after lunch.

While I wait, I try to picture these neighbours. I am fairly sure that the man with the ginger beard lives with another bloke. Beyond that, I cannot differentiate people who live in this building from any of the other happy, fertile couples I see on the seafront. Brighton and Hove are full of them. They are in their thirties, trailing little girls in stripy tights and boys clutching wooden toys. Often, they are calling 'Daisy!' or 'Josh!' at the tops of their voices. These women have never stripped to pay their rent. Occasionally, couples like this will turn up at Vixenz together, under the misapprehension that they can have fun in some kind of ironic and open-minded way. I find those dances the most demeaning of all. Dancing for a horny man at least allows me to feel that, to some degree, I'm in control. We both know the real score, but I allow him to pretend that I'm doing it for pleasure. Dancing for a man and a woman, so that I can be a dinner table anecdote, disgusts me. It makes me feel utterly degraded and filthy. I used to be a guest at dinner parties. Now I am the entertainment.

I knock back the rest of the lager, and wonder whether I should seek out these people and warn them that they are vulnerable to surveillance. It would, I realise, be a ridiculous idea. I do not have a baby. I had no reason to be using the monitors. I was bored, that was all. I was taking my mind off the fact that it's about to be Saturday night, the very worst night of my week. I will pack the monitors up again, and post them to Emma in the morning.

On the other hand, she's not due for eight weeks. I want to know whether they're going to go travelling or not. Going backpacking with a baby seems like a ridiculous idea. The baby's bound to get ill. I hope they don't go.

Listening to my neighbours a bit more would be harmless, and I'm sick of watching the television.

chapter three

Libby – the following Monday

Libby hasn't thought of herself as happy for a long time. She lives in a flat in a good street in Hove, with the sea at the end of it. Before they had Charlie, she and David oversaw its complete renovation, and they now walk on stripped and polished floorboards, and watch their widescreen television against pale blue walls adorned with original artwork that has been selected to fit the colour scheme. Watching television is something she does rather a lot. When it gets dark, she closes the shutters. She doesn't like the idea of the people coming home from work idly looking through the window, and seeing her in all her sloth. It is, she has discovered, important, stylistically, to have shutters rather than curtains.

The flat is, in estate agents' terms, a maisonette. It has an upstairs. Three bedrooms and a tiny bathroom upstairs, living room and large kitchen downstairs. Until he was given a compulsory year's sabbatical on the grounds that his firm had no work for him, David was pushing her to let him put the flat on the market. He wanted to move to a house. But Libby, unhappy, lonely, bored, likes the presence of neighbours above and below. Even though she doesn't know them, has never said more than a cursory 'hello' to any of them, she finds their presence reassuring. From time to time she hears voices or the muffled sound of the television from downstairs.

A woman moved in there a couple of months ago, but they've never met. There are often footsteps overhead. Two men live there. They come home at six in the morning on Saturdays and Sundays, and put music on. As she lies awake, waiting for Charlie to wake up for the day, Libby hears the thud thud thud of the bassline. She ponders a life in which six o'clock is a time to finish the day, rather than to begin it. Her life was like that, once. Not so long ago, really.

The Monday after the fights began, Libby is sitting, as usual, in the living room. She is parked solidly on the sofa, wearing a designer silk kimono over a grey nursing bra and a pair of big bobbly knickers. She was dressed earlier, but then she had a bath during Charlie's nap, so she didn't bother to put her clothes back on. She'll dress for when David gets in. Alternatively, now that she's so angry with him, perhaps she won't. Maybe she'll allow him a glimpse of the real Libby. Show him the monster he married.

She hates herself as a housewife. She is fat and self-indulgent and humourless. Her son, Charlie, is gorgeous. She still rolls that phrase around her head. 'This is my son,' she says aloud. She doesn't feel eligible to have a son. 'My son, Charlie. Charlie, say hello.' Charlie will not, of course, be saying hello for some time yet. He is not a conversationalist. He sleeps, eats puréed vegetables, and sits in his chair. Whereas Libby sleeps, eats chocolate, and sits in *her* chair. Charlie sucks Libby's nipples. She has attempted the same manoeuvre herself, purely to see how breast milk tastes. To her amazement, she was successful (such is the size of her breasts these days) and, to her further surprise, the milk was sickly and sweet. It didn't taste like milk, at all.

Charlie, Libby suddenly sees, has brought her down to his level. Before he emerged, she was a lawyer, and a remarkably successful one. She was dedicated. She was happy to sit at her desk from seven in the morning till eleven at night. She loved the way her earning power made her feel. Shamelessly competitive, she felt she was better than almost everyone else. More successful, prettier, thinner, richer. She loved spending money on herself, and making herself look stunning. She suffers from many allergies, and covering rashes was a part of her daily routine. Now she slaps on a little foundation if she's going to the shops, and that is all. The days when she turned heads wherever she went are gone. She is thirty, and that part of her life is over.

Libby throws down her magazine, and puts the television on. It's *Countdown*. She hates everything about being a housewife. It was David's idea. She would be back at work if it was up to her. She would have been back in the office, in new, larger suits, the moment the baby hit three months. A nanny would be far better at this than she is. But David didn't think it was right for both of them to commute to London. 'Our child should be cared for by its parents,' he said soon after she discovered she was pregnant. 'Don't you hate the idea that it might think some nanny is its mother? And that we'd be sixty miles away if there was an emergency?' When he put it like that, she did hate it, and so she agreed with him. David has always occupied the moral high ground. He forced her to become a full-time mother, and just as she'd decided she couldn't possibly get any more miserable, he decided they have to move to Latin America. Moving to real America she could cope with. Moving to Brazil or somewhere like that is unthinkable.

She sits up straight. 'Unthinkable!' she says. It's such a dreadful idea that she laughs. On the screen, Richard Whiteley laughs with her. Of course they won't move to Chile, or Paraguay, or Mexico. They live in Brighton. David wants to learn Spanish. He is fixated by the idea that it will help his career. Libby knows that his firm has recently opened an office in Madrid, and suspects that his bosses have been hinting that David could be posted there when the year is up. They know David too well. They are, she is sure, taking advantage of his unsuspecting nature to sedate him with unsubstantiated hints. David has lapped it up.

No. Libby will go back to work, they will find a nanny, and David can go to Spanish classes in Hove. If he wants to practise, they will spend three weeks in Spain over the summer. It is obvious.

Cuban Heels

Bumming around Latin America is something that a single guy could do with his enforced holiday. Not a married father. David is being immature. He's refusing to grow up, and her job is to rein him in.

She sighs. It is always her job to rein him in. Without fail, he comes home on Friday night with a plan.

'Listen to this!' he said last week as soon as he stepped across the threshold. 'Eurostar are doing a special deal. I saw a poster on the Tube. We'll go up to Waterloo in the morning, get to Paris by lunchtime, and we don't have to come back till Sunday afternoon. What do you reckon?'

She kills his plans every single time, yet he retains his enthusiasm. 'What about Charlie?' she said blankly. 'What about his routine? How are we supposed to do anything in the evening if he's in a hotel room? It'll only mess him up.'

'But he'll see Paris!' David remonstrated. 'He'll be the most cultured baby in Brighton. And they love kids in Europe – the hotel will provide a babysitter.'

'No they won't. It'll be one of those listening services. I don't trust them. Charlie doesn't need to see Paris until he's old enough to remember it.'

The same is going to happen with this Latin plan. It is inevitable. She just hopes it happens soon.

The baby monitor sits on top of the telly, so it's usually in her line of sight. She sees the lights flickering before she hears the wail, and gets up to fetch her son. She takes the stairs two at a time in a futile effort to regain her former slender thighs. They never felt slender enough at the time. If she ever gets them back, she will appreciate them. She will tend them with the finest moisturisers, and she will keep them sleek and hairless. She will worship them.

Charlie has rolled on to his stomach. He is trying to push himself up with his arms. His fine blond hair is ruffled at the back. Libby is suffocatingly proud of the way he learned to roll so early, but worries about him sleeping on his front.

'If you're strong enough to roll,' she tells him in a baby voice, 'you're strong enough not to suffocate.' She thinks that's probably true. He grimaces at her, and puts his head back down, resting his rosy cheek on the sheet.

By the time David gets home from work, Libby is wearing a forgiving pair of wide-legged trousers and a loose white shirt. She has pulled some gel through her hair, applied copious layers of lip gloss, and poured them both a glass of wine. Charlie has surpassed himself by eating a whole pot of organic sweet potato and courgette, washed down with breast milk. He has had his bath and is lying on the hearth in a white babygro. His cheeks are pink and his blond hair is drying in tendrils that have sprung away from his head. He is sucking contentedly on a towelling frog. The television is off, and Morcheeba are on the stereo. She has, she hopes, created a mellow atmosphere. The whole ensemble is designed to remind David of his priorities.

When she hears the key in the door, Libby stands up, but doesn't go to the hall to meet him. She lets David find them, so he appreciates the tableau she has prepared.

David stands in the doorway, a quizzical expression on his even features. She stands and looks at her husband. He shrugs off his overcoat. Libby feels suddenly shy.

'You look gorgeous,' he says, putting an arm where her waist used to be. She squirms. She hates it when he feels her fat.

She points to Charlie. 'So does he.'

'I know. Come here. Give me a kiss. Are we speaking?'

She pecks his cheek, then pushes him away. 'The first thing is, we need to get this thing sorted out. Don't we?'

David rolls his eyes. 'Where's your spirit of adventure?' he demands, deliberately provoking her. 'We always said that having a baby wouldn't stop us.'

She laughs, and kneels next to Charlie. 'You said that. And we also said that having a baby wouldn't affect our social life. Or our sex life.' She picks Charlie up. 'Things change, my love. Babies affect everything. And talking of things changing, your son needs a new nappy before he goes to bed.' She is aware that she's barely controlling herself. She wants to shout at him, shout at him not only for making such a preposterous suggestion, but for everything else, as well. For making her give up the thing she was good at to devote herself to something which she cannot do at all. The fact that she is an excellent lawyer and a terrible mother does not, she fears, make her a very nice person.

David obediently unpops the babygro and takes Charlie's nappy off, wincing at the smell as he does it. Libby passes him wipes and a new nappy.

'But the thing is,' he says suddenly, turning to her, 'it would just be so brilliant. Don't you see that, even a little bit? People have children in those countries. Diplomats go there, and expat workers. We'd have enough money. We could give Charlie clean water and safe food. He only eats vegetables anyway.'

Libby takes over the nappy. 'But he's got such an excellent routine—' she begins. David cuts her off.

'For once, please will you shut up about his bloody routine!' he says bitterly. 'We never, ever do anything at weekends, apart from walk along the seafront, because anything else is going to mess up the holy routine. Routine is boring! He really doesn't have to sleep in his cot three times a day. He can doze in the car, or the pushchair. Let the lad live a little. Christ, let *me* live.'

Libby looks at Charlie, who is staring at his father with an unfathomable expression. While she watches, he sprays an arc of urine across the room. It hits the far wall, and droplets cover her hand. Without thinking, she lifts it to her mouth, to lick it.

'What the hell are you doing?' David grabs her fingers. They both look at her hand, and laugh.

'Blimey,' she says. 'No one tells you that motherhood fucks your brains.' She watches David giggling, and is suddenly struck by how handsome he is. He has honey-coloured hair and big eyes with thick black lashes. She remembers that she does love him. But on this issue she cannot compromise. It is another of David's whims. She will not give in.

chapter four

Maggie – the following Friday

Dear Mark,

Thanks – I suppose – for the postcard. I was glad to hear from you after all this time, although clearly you are still upset by the end of our relationship and the fact that I moved away.

Look, I am getting on with my life. You have no right to suggest that I'm not. I am very happy here and have a good job and plenty of new friends. I just wanted to keep in touch with you. So don't you dare tell me not to contact you any more. I was trying to be friendly! I know you have a new relationship. As it happens, so do I, but I don't force that fact down your throat, do I? In fact, you wouldn't believe the amount of attention I get from men these days.

You were the one who insisted that we'd always be friends. I made the mistake of thinking you meant it. Sorry for believing you were more mature than you actually are. I won't be in touch again. Believe me, this is your loss, not mine.

Margaret

I am fuming. It is beginning to rain, and I notice the sea rising up over the railings. The wind is fierce. I ram the letter into the postbox, and reconsider giving up work. I press the button on the pedestrian crossing, and wait for the lights to change. I'm going to walk along the seafront, rain or no rain. My life wouldn't be empty, any more, without work. I could stay indoors on my own all day, and listen to Libby going about her business. It wouldn't take much for me and her to become friends, I'm sure of that. I could create a pretext. Even a one-way relationship with her is the most rewarding thing in my life. She is the closest thing I have to a friend, and I've never even met her.

The cold air hits my lungs. I am pitiful. No one cares. Mark thinks I'm some kind of crazy stalker. Libby doesn't know I exist. Amy has not been back to Vixenz, so I know I'll never see her again. Mum and Dad think I work at American Express and enjoy a lively, fulfilled life by the sea. Ivan is long gone. Emma is the only person I have left.

That's why I've invited myself to stay with her and Jeremy. I felt empowered when I demanded Friday and Saturday off work. We are supposed to take time off during the week. I suddenly realised, however, that since I didn't care, I would get away with it. They want me working more than I want to be there. Women are not exactly beating on the door pleading to be allowed to replace me. This means that they have to let me do what I like. I wonder whether they'd let me keep my knickers on, too.

I cross the road, turn the corner, and am hit by the full force of the gale. It takes all my strength to walk into it, and I barely cover any ground. I will miss my neighbours. I am gripped by their lives, and particularly by the ongoing argument over South America. I wish my life contained those sorts of dilemmas. Neither one of them has any concept of how lucky they are to be agonising over whether to live as expats for a bit, or whether to get a nanny. I hope they don't go, because I'll miss them. I hope Libby goes back to work. Then, as long as she keeps leaving the listener on, I'll be able to monitor the nanny. I'm sure that will be more than amusing.

I try not to think of it as spying, though frankly I don't care that much. Nothing I do is normal, or socially acceptable. I love huddling over the monitor and following their arguments. I generally get a good half-hour in before I go to work, because that's when David comes home, and they get together in the baby's room for a quiet, yet vicious, argument. Poor Charlie seems to have a regimented life. He goes to bed on the absolute dot of 7.45, every single night. One day I might leave my monitor on all night, by my bed, to find out whether he wakes up.

I am a spy. It is harmless. I like it. It is an unexpected, and immensely rewarding, turn of events. I haven't brought the monitors away with me, because I have no intention of surrendering them before I absolutely have to.

My weekend bag keeps being flung into the backs of my knees. It contains the little baby clothes, and my own bits and pieces. Emma and Jeremy are expecting the monitors. I really should grow up and go back to get them. Emma will fuss. She'll end up buying some herself. She already thinks I'm unreliable. I hesitate.

I can't face turning back. I have made some hard-won progress along the seafront, and if I go back, I'll end up giving up and catching the bus instead. I want to be out here in the elements. Emma's due in less than two months, so I'll have to give up my compulsive new habit by then. I'll post them to her next week.

I'm starving. Nothing is going right. I didn't have any breakfast, because the bread was covered in fluffy green mould. It looked fragile and rather beautiful. All I had in the cupboard was a tin of chickpeas. I bet David and Libby have cupboards full of Alpen and Frosties, plus a bread machine. I bet David cooks a fry-up at weekends. I'll get something at the station, probably. I'm walking as fast as I can, in an attempt to work off some of my feelings about Mark, and about my life. I am stamping my lack of joy into the esplanade.

The tide is high. From time to time a wave spills across the wide esplanade, but I know I'll manage to dodge them. There is something a little exhilarating about the mass of churning water; I can see that, through my fury. The wind whips against my cheeks, and I put my hands into my pockets and lean into it. Feathery clumps of spindrift pull away from the water and dance in the wind before settling gently on to the tarmac. Gulls shriek, almost inaudible in the gale. I can see the cars moving on the main road, across the grass, but I can't hear them. The wind is making the tips of my ears cold. My nose is beginning to run. My hair flies across my face, and I reach into my pocket for a band and tie it roughly back. I pull my bag higher on my shoulder, and head for the route out of town. I'll be a state by the time I get on the train, but I don't care.

At times, I can see myself building a life in Brighton. Living so close to the sea can be wonderful. I love the fact that I can see the horizon any time I want. If I only had a couple of friends here, I know I'd be all right. Libby would be a great friend to me. We are both around all day. I wouldn't be able to tell her that I work at American Express. I'll have to think of a night job. I couldn't ever be friends with anyone from work. Amy was the only one I felt I could relate to. I don't want to move in a social network of strippers. I don't want anyone to know about it. So Libby is it. I have no other options.

They leave that monitor on the whole time, thank God. It took me a while to realise that they use it to check the temperature in Charlie's bedroom. Occasionally, Libby will fret. 'It's only sixteen degrees,' she says. 'Should I put an extra blanket on him, do you think?' I want to put my hands to my mouth and shout through my ceiling: 'Babies don't die of cold in houses like this. He's fine! Don't bloody fuss!' But I know that wouldn't be fair. Christ knows, if I was in charge of an infant, I would be constantly obsessing. Luckily, that will never happen.

Last weekend I listened to them almost all the time. They spend a reasonable amount of time within range of the monitor. I heard them preparing to go out. Then I hurried to my door, and waited.

I knew Libby would be blonde. It never crossed my mind that she could be anything else. I knew she would be tall. She isn't as fat as she thinks she is. She's soft and pretty, and about a size fourteen. She's much taller than I am, and a little bit older, I imagine. I hope she's older than me, anyway. Otherwise the contrast between the two of us is too stark.

I realised that I have seen her around, pushing that trendy buggy by the sea with countless other women of her ilk. David was all-right-looking. I might or might not have danced for him. Nothing about him was particularly distinctive. He's about the same height as she is, or even a little shorter. They were both dressed casually, as befits Brighton parents on a Sunday.

I pretended I'd just put some rubbish out.

'Hello!' I said, cheerfully.

They both looked round and said hello back. David didn't flinch when he saw me, so either he is on the straight and narrow, or he didn't recognise me in my tracksuit bottoms.

'Lovely day,' I added.

'Won't last,' David replied, and with a smile, they turned back to each other and carried on with the argument they didn't know that I knew they were having. I watched them push their three-wheeler towards the seafront, and went back inside.

I look around now, just in case Libby is out with the pushchair. It seems to be compulsory, round here, to have three wheels rather than four. I don't need to ask Tina how many wheels support her children. She lives in Whitehawk, and I know she will have the sturdy four. Three-wheeler pushchairs are the environmentally friendlier equivalents of the Land Rovers that take the older children round the corner to school. We always walked to school. If I had children, I'd make sure they did, too.

The wind whips past my cheeks. I hope it's giving me a little colour.

Before I can stop myself, I'm remembering my childhood. There were a few years when everything was all right. Dad made us laugh. We used to wait to hear him open the door at half past six, and then we'd all run at him, giggling. Mum was a happy housewife, as far as

I am aware. She took us to school and picked us up, and drove us to ballet and gym and music lessons. The three of us were no closer than any other sisters. We liked each other and hated each other. We were best friends and worst enemies. We had the same friends and different friends. We walked hand in hand, and we fought. People were always telling us and our parents how pretty, and how different, we were. I had the wild dark corkscrew curls that blight my life to this day. Emma has the same but in yellow. Grace was completely different. Her hair was silky and white. I wince as I suddenly see Grace exactly as she was. I don't have any photos.

Emma was rosy-cheeked and shy. She used to seek me out in the playground in her first weeks at school, and hang on to my clothes. She wanted to be clutching Mum, and I was the next best thing. Emma was universally acknowledged to be 'a darling', 'a little love' and 'an angel'.

I stop my reminiscences there. It is painful not to be able to remember any more, but I have accepted it. There were three of us, and then there were two. I accelerate my stride and wipe the back of a hand over my nose. I have been coming far too close to thinking about Grace, lately. From the day she went, I tried to forget her. I often wish she'd never existed. I have always tried to convince myself that I've only ever had one sister, but it never quite works. There is a gaping hole where she used to be. Mum used to tell Emma and me that Grace was an angel, that she'd only been lent to us for a few years because she was too good for this world. I took this to heart as concrete fact. Grace looked like an angel. She played the angel in the Nativity Play. I don't ever picture her; I don't let myself remember her, but if I did, I would remember her in a shapeless white dress with paper wings attached to the back, with a tinsel halo resting on her hair.

I walk on, past a man sitting in a shelter, drinking beer from a can. He shouts something as I pass, and I ignore him.

I redirect my thoughts towards my neighbours. They are having the nastiest fights I have ever heard, including ones on TV. Listening to them is opening my eyes to the deceptive nature of appearances. Mark and I never fought like that. We never bothered to argue at all. We'd nag each other sometimes, but we never had full-blown rows. Full-blown rows would be better than the sniping and bitching that Libby and David are consumed by. They look like a normal happy couple, the kind that embitters me with their apparent bliss. In fact, when the doors are shut, they address each other with poisonous whispers. When Charlie's older, they will speak through him. 'Tell your father he's a tosser and I wish I'd never married him.' That sort of thing. I wish they would have a proper fight. I want to hear screamed obscenities. I can't listen to their sniping without wanting to go upstairs and tell them a few things. Number one: what they are arguing about is essentially a holiday. They are both being pathetic, particularly her. Number two: they have no idea how lucky they are in every single aspect of their lives. Number three: I would really, really like to be their friend. I could help them, and they could help me.

They are my only distraction. I have to become a part of their life.

I put my head down and quicken my stride. As I pass the old pier, it starts to rain.

By the time I reach Norwich, I am starving. I bang on the red front door, and hope she's got lots of biscuits. We had a red front door in the house where we grew up. Trust Emma to have recreated that. The house is a red-brick terrace, with a tree in the front yard. It is the epitome of middle class suburbia.

The door opens, and my sister rushes at me.

'Hey – you made it!' she squeals. 'Jeremy! Maggie's here!'

Emma pulls me close, and as her stomach squashes mine, I feel the baby kick me. I feel a certain amount of distaste. Mother and child are both, it seems, excessively excited by my presence. Emma has pink spots on her cheeks, the ones she used to get as an overtired, excitable child. Her hair is cut short, the curls close to her head. She's wearing an enormous red jumper and a pair of black drawstring trousers, and her bump is huge. She tries to usher me in from her doorstep, but I can't get past her stomach, so she has to reverse into the living-room doorway to let me through. I look over my shoulder at her.

'Emma,' I say, drily, 'you are massive.'

'Cheers. I feel it. But you are *tiny*. Fuck me, Mags. How much weight have you lost?'

'No idea,' I say briskly. 'I'm fine. I needed to lose it, anyway.'

'Not that much! Diet or exercise?'

I smile. I am tentatively relieved to be here. I am normal, all of a sudden. I am not a nude dancer, not a friendless weirdo who lives her life through other people's marriages, but someone's sister, someone's sister-in-law, someone's aunt. Emma and Jeremy have painted the hallway light green since I was last here. The house smells like home used to smell, too. It is almost spooky, how closely she has recreated it.

'Both,' I tell her, 'but not intentionally. Mark was such a pig. He was the king of stuffing his face. Now I'm on my own, I eat a lot less, and I usually walk to work along the seafront. That's a mile or so each way, at least. You've painted the walls. It looks great.'

Emma grins. 'Well, don't fade away. Not that I'm jealous or anything. Christ, Mags, do you know what I weigh now? Eleven sodding stone. Can you imagine? Five foot two inches tall, and eleven stone wide? I keep misjudging spaces, thinking I can walk through them, and then discovering I can't. I'm like a cat without whiskers.'

'How are you feeling?'

'Oh, fine.' She looks up and smiles at Jeremy, who is lolloping down the stairs three or four at a time, grinning and apparently genuinely happy to see me. I've always liked my brother-in-law. He is tall and fair and skinny, with pointed features. He lands next to me with a thud, and kisses my cheek.

'Welcome to our humble and somewhat chaotic abode, Margaret,' he says. 'Has Emma told you about her piles yet?'

'I think she was just about to.'

'Well you try it! Bloody hell, I tell you, pregnancy's a thankless task.' Emma, I realise, is deliriously happy.

We sit at the heavy pine kitchen table, and I ease my shoes off and put my feet up on the edge of Emma's chair. Jeremy hands me a mug of tea, and asks politely about my journey. I'm relieved to be able to start off with easy questions.

'It was great,' I tell him, leaning forward and reaching for a handful of biscuits. 'I love trains. I love sitting back and watching the landscape go by. It's funny coming into Norwich. I know the station so well, but there's always something slightly different about it.'

'Like?'

'Well, for instance, this time they've changed the clock to a digital one. I always liked the old one. It was a proper station clock.'

Jeremy looks at his watch. 'And they actually got you here on time? That's a rare honour. Did you get a cab?'

'Yep.' I pause for a moment, hating myself. 'I'll probably be able to claim it on expenses.'

Jeremy nods. 'Job perk,' he says knowingly. I nod, and look down at my tea.

Jeremy and Emma got married last year. Everyone said they were too young, and Mark almost left me that day because he was so freaked out by the fact that every single person at their wedding addressed us with exactly the same words: 'So when are you two going to be tying the knot?' Emma's twenty-five, now, and Jeremy's my age. We've all known him for ever. He was one of the boys at the village school who were slightly intimidated by the three of us. When I was eight, I thought he loved me. I think I even kissed him once, with pursed lips. Now he loves my sister. He adores her. Lucky, lucky Emma.

I wonder, sometimes, how the same childhood has created two lives as different as mine and Emma's. The Brighton lap dancer, versus the Norwich housewife. I've tried to ask her, once or twice, but she pretends not to understand.

'What do you mean, why did I want to settle down?' she'll ask, wide-eyed. 'Because I love Jeremy, of course. Why else?' Their house is comfy and chaotic, with five bedrooms. I feel too much at home here. It is claustrophobic.

'What do you think for the nursery, Mags?' asks Jeremy presently, handing me two cards of paint samples. 'We thought either Sugared Lilac, which would be great for a girl but maybe not quite right for a boy, or Silken Sky, which would be good for either but not quite so special.'

I stare at the colours. 'I'd go for the lilac,' I say, randomly. 'It's pretty, and it's fine for a boy. God, you've got so much space here, you could do one room in each if you liked.'

'No, we're having the nursery right next to our room,' Emma explains seriously. 'That way, there won't be far to go in the night, and when the baby's in with us for the first few months, all its stuff will be nearby.'

'Have you thought of names?' All this baby talk is making me feel strange. None of my former friends had babies. It's alien to me. First I have to listen to my neighbours fussing over their boy, and now this.

Emma and Jeremy look at each other, and I see Emma nod slightly but meaningfully.

'We have, actually,' Jeremy confides. 'If it's a boy he's going to be Harry Thomas, and for a girl we've got Madeleine Grace.'

'Madeleine Grace?' I echo, looking at Emma. She is staring at the table.

'It's only right, isn't it?' she says, then looks me in the eye. 'Don't tell anyone about the names,' she adds. 'We're keeping them secret until the birth. You're the only one that knows.'

'Sure,' I tell them, and drain my tea. 'I won't say a word.' I imagine myself breaking off from a pole dance to tell my punters about my sister's pregnancy. Most of them are probably fathers. They could chip in with some helpful advice. 'They're lovely names,' I add.

Emma rests her hands on her bump and smiles her dimply smile. 'Aren't they perfect?' she says.

The weekend passes relatively happily. I appreciate having company. It makes me wish Mum and Dad still lived here. I would love to run away to be loved and cosseted every weekend. Emma, however, must provide my sanctuary instead, without realising she's doing it. We were both amazed, and rather offended, when Mum and Dad emigrated two months after Emma left home. I can see, now, that they had longed to leave for years.

Mum and Dad did their best for Emma and me, through all the years when we were growing up. They tried to make everything normal, and they were patient when I went through my teenage rebellion, and relieved when Emma didn't. But nothing could ever be even one hundredth as happy and carefree and ordinary as an ordinary day had been before. Mum got lines on her face, and stopped dyeing her hair. Dad had a drink as soon as he got home at night. They did their best, but they were falling apart. Their best was never going to be very good.

On Saturday afternoon, Emma and Jeremy insist on showing me the new city library. The old one burned down years ago, and I have yet to see its replacement. We walk, extremely slowly, along their road, past the Catholic cathedral and through Chapelfield Gardens, where we used to play as children. It is a sunny day, and the city smells of spring. Jeremy is wearing an old green cardigan with leather patches on the elbows. Emma is formidable in a floral dress. They could be ten years older than they are. Twenty, if it wasn't for Emma's obvious fecundity. Norwich is closing in on me. I struggle to appear lighthearted, not to let it show.

'The cathedral hasn't fallen through the ground yet, then,' I observe, looking up at it towering against the pale blue sky. It is built on chalky, unstable earth, and we've been waiting for years for the drama of its collapse. A bus fell through the road outside it, years ago.

'Nope,' says Emma. 'But the library and the theatre both burnt down.'

'That was forever ago.'

'It's the best we can do. What drama can Brighton offer?'

'The Grand Hotel bombing?'

Jeremy jumps in. 'Yes. 1984. Before the fires. Even before the bus, I think.'

'Party conferences.'

'Oh, fascinating,' he counters.

'The highest heroin overdose rate in the country. Over to you, Norwich.'

Emma looks prim. 'We can't compete on that front, thank you.'

'Although the drugs problem is serious here,' Jeremy adds. 'I read that in the paper.'

'Yeah,' I tell him. 'Bored kids like we used to be, getting stoned in fields. Not really the same thing, is it?'

The new library is big and airy, and I am vaguely impressed. It incorporates a branch of Pizza Express and a café serving types of coffee that, I imagine, are normal for Brighton and exotic for Norwich. Libby and David would like it here. It takes me a while to spot any books. The walk – the interminable dawdle – has exhausted Emma, and we sit in the lobby café. Jeremy and I drink coffee. Emma has camomile tea. Typically, she has cut out all caffeine, including tea, including Earl Grey, for the sake of the foetus.

'So,' I say, looking around, 'what else is on the great Norwich itinerary?'

Jeremy puts down his cappuccino. 'Sorry, Mags, but you wouldn't come to Mothercare with us, would you?' he asks. 'We want to get the cot, but we're not sure whether to go for a regular cot or a cot bed.'

I stare at him. 'And you think I might be able to help?'

'Of course you can help,' says Emma. 'Your input will be most valuable.'

'Ems, Christ, I know nothing about cots. I don't even know what a cot bed is.' I bite my tongue to stop myself adding that I don't care. 'I'd be useless!'

'Sometimes it takes a fresh pair of eyes to see what's obvious,' says Jeremy. 'And we're going to get bed linen too. So you can help with the colour scheme, once again. You were in favour of the Sugared Lilac, weren't you, but we can't go for pink sheets in case it's a boy. So we need something that looks good, but is non-gender-specific.'

I stare around the room. I am a fucking stripper, for Christ's sake. My life does not incorporate baby bed linen. That is not my thing.

'Maggie!' calls a voice. All three of us look round. I can't see anyone, and assume some other Maggie is being addressed, probably a woman in her sixties.

'Okay,' I tell them, reluctantly. 'Count me in. Mothercare it is.'

'Maggie!' someone shouts again, closer this time. I scan the people in the café, and suddenly recognise someone. A tall blonde woman who looks like a model is heading towards our table. It takes me a moment to realise who she is.

'Hey, wow!' says Emma before I get my thoughts together. 'It's Yasmin! I didn't know she was around.'

When I realise that Yasmin McLeod is standing in front of me, I can't stop grinning. One should probably play it cool with boyfriend-stealing former best friends, but I cannot view her as anything other than my ticket out of Mothercare. I stand up and look at her. She is tanned and glowing. She puts a hand on each of my shoulders, then leans down and kisses my cheeks. I am immediately conscious of my pallor, my wild hair, my scruffy clothes. Yasmin smells of expensive moisturiser.

She is wearing a short red skirt, black tights, and a black moleskin jacket, unzipped over a tight white T-shirt. I haven't seen her for a decade, but she could almost pass for eighteen now. She's willowy and tanned, with long shiny hair and legs that are probably taller than I am. She is wearing about eight little metallic necklaces, which tinkle gently when she moves. No one but Yasmin would have carried them off.

'Look who it is!' I say, and pat her, somewhat inadequately, on the arm.

Yasmin grins broadly.

'Mags,' she says, 'what the fuck are you doing in Norwich? I was thinking about you the other day. Heard you were up north somewhere, moved there for lurve?' She pulls up a chair and sits down, a mass of legs and hair. Yasmin and I were inseparable for years, until Ivan. She destroyed me. I don't think I need to mention it: I can probably forgive her, now. I look at her. She is radiant, happy, and beautiful. I need someone like that in my life. Yasmin might drag me up, closer to her level.

'Just in town for the weekend,' I assure her. 'And I used to live in Scotland, but these days I'm in Brighton. What about you?'

'Got back from India last week,' she sighs. 'Come to think of it, you look like you've been there too. How skinny are *you*? Anyone mind if I smoke?'

'Actually,' say Emma and Jeremy, together.

'Oh right. Hey, Emma, having a baby? Good stuff. So, Brighton, then? What are you up to?'

'Working,' I say. 'American Express. No boyfriend. I split up with the Scotland bloke last year. I've just come to stay with my dear sister and brother-in-law this weekend. And my future nephew or niece. Are you living with your parents, then?'

She nods. 'It sucks. Brighton, that must be cool, yeah?'

I nod. 'Come and stay.' I try not to sound as if I'm begging.

She puts her head to one side. Her hair falls over the side of her face, and the necklaces clink together. 'You know, I might just do that.' She smiles. 'Travelling's one thing. Coming home is another. That bloody house – it does my head in. The same bedroom I lived in when I was five. You know how it is. Your folks still here?'

I shake my head. Emma jumps in. 'They've been living in France for the past seven years,' she says, eagerly. Emma was always scared of Yasmin. I never told her why Yas and I stopped being friends. She probably thinks Yasmin was simply too cool for me. That's what everyone else believed, too, all along. Now Emma is desperate to impress her big sister's friend, and all her pregnant serenity has vanished.

'France?' says Yasmin, without interest. 'Cool. Good luck to them. Emma, how can you bear to live here? I get back, and I'm running into our old teachers round every corner. They're all like, "Yasmin, dear, would you come and talk to the sixth form about whatever it is you're doing these days?" So I'm like, "Sure, if they want to hear about dossing with the folks and collecting the dole." They can't get away fast enough.'

'Oh, I like it,' Emma beams, as I try to imagine telling my former teachers first of all how much I earn, and then what I do to get it.

Jeremy has been sitting silently, staring at Yasmin. I don't think he's ever met her.

'Yasmin,' I say, interrupting. 'Sorry, this is Jeremy, Emma's husband.'

She slaps her head. Her necklaces clash and jingle. 'Jeremy!' she says. 'I *knew* I knew you. Christ, going back a bit, or what?'

He forces a smile. 'Indeed. Can I get you a coffee?'

Yasmin laughs, delighted. 'Sure. Skinny latte, cheers.'

I watch the back of Jeremy's neck, which has flushed a deep red, as he queues at the counter. Then I remember, quite vividly, Yasmin's description of the day she lost her virginity, at the age of fourteen.

No wonder he's mortified.

chapter five

Libby

Libby has a bad Saturday. She sticks more rigidly than ever to Charlie's routine, and withholds as many of David's paternal privileges as she can. As soon as she hears Charlie whimpering, at five past seven in the morning, she gets out of bed and throws on her kimono. David barely stirs. Normally she makes him get up on Saturday, and enjoys her lie-in. He usually brings her a cup of tea and two slices of toast, butter and honey. Today she spends half an hour in Charlie's bedroom, feeding him, changing his nappy, and dressing him.

The baby monitor in Charlie's room is switched on all the time. Neither Libby nor David ever bothers to turn it off, because they are both obsessed with the temperature at which Charlie sleeps. The monitor lets them know that it is within the acceptable range, sixteen to twenty degrees. Thus, as Libby talks early-morning nonsense to Charlie, that same nonsense is relayed downstairs to Maggie's empty flat, since Maggie has left her monitor switched on.

Charlie's bedroom is bright green. This seemed like a good idea before he was born, since they didn't know their baby's gender. Now it gives Libby a headache. She can no longer see why they felt unable to leave it white. White is a much better colour for walls. No wonder Charlie often wakes up screaming. His bedroom must glow in the dark. Toys are scattered around the room, as are nappies, muslin squares, and assorted other paraphernalia. From time to time she has a cursory tidy of the rest of the house, but that only happens when Charlie's asleep. His bedroom is always left out.

Today, though, things are going to be different. Libby opens the curtains, and looks out over the backs of houses. It is only half light. A tabby cat walks along the wall at the back of their tiny square of grass. The wind blows the bare branches around. Libby shuts the curtains again. She will never have curtains open and the light on, because she hates the idea that someone could be watching her. Today, she is going to keep Charlie to herself for as long as she possibly can. She sits him in his chair, and tidies the toys away, then tackles the immense pile of clean washing that has been growing against his chest of drawers for over a week. This forces her to empty the drawers completely, sort and fold everything, instigate a new pile of 0–3-month clothes that have long been outgrown, and replace everything. After ten minutes, Charlie is decidedly cranky. Even her monologue doesn't calm him.

'It's you and me, isn't it, Charlie?' she says, turning and giving him a wink. 'You and me against the world. And no one messes with us, do they, mister? No one forces us to go to South A-bloody-merica.' His whingeing becomes a full-blown cry. In a moment he will be wailing. Libby leaves the sorting, and picks him up. She walks around the room a few times, holding him close to her shoulder and smelling his baby smell. He is divine. She has many friends with babies – at least, she has two close friends with babies – and occasionally she tries to imagine Jenny and Natalie feeling this level of adoration for their offspring. She's pretty sure it's not possible. Charlie, with his fair hair and his rosy cheeks, is perfect. He is everything she never realised she was missing. He has a button nose, and big blue eyes, and his elbows and knees are dimpled. Charlie has the ability to reduce her to a cooing imbecile, and he utilises that capacity, in his own interests, every day.

'It's all right, my petal,' she tells him softly. 'We won't go to Uruguay, or Paraguay, or Venezuela. Daddy can't make us.' Worried that David might be waking up, she takes the baby downstairs.

Downstairs is not an inviting place. Last night's dishes litter the surfaces, there is a red wine puddle on the table, and the air is heavy with stale arguments. It is not actually raining outside, and Libby suddenly decides to take her baby for a walk in the gloom of the winter dawn. That, she decides, will show him. David will get up and stumble downstairs, to find them gone. She will leave her mobile behind, switched on. If he calls her, he will hear her phone ringing in the living room. She knows he hates that. And afterwards, she will be able to tell that he's tried to ring, from the number of missed calls. She won't leave a note. He will have to consider the possibility that she has left him. She giggles. Let him worry. The thought of actually leaving is not in the least bit tempting. It is the thought of winning that motivates her.

Luckily, there is another mountain of clean, unironed washing on the kitchen table, next to, but not touching, the wine pool. She dresses in tracksuit bottoms, a long-sleeved T-shirt, and David's fleece, puts Charlie into his snow suit and straps him into the unwieldy buggy. She closes the door quietly behind her, and bumps the pushchair down the front steps.

It is surprisingly mild. The big houses of Sixth Avenue loom in the dawn greyness. They look demure by day, all cream stucco and roof terraces, but now they are threatening. Libby looks up and down the street. She checks her watch. It is eight o'clock, and nobody is up. The road is empty. She turns towards the sea.

'Breakfast meetings!' Jenny has been up since six, and is thrilled by the unannounced visit. She sits Milly on her hip, and flicks the kettle on. 'I can't believe we haven't done this before,' she says over her shoulder. 'Christ knows, we're all up in time. Tea?'

Libby smiles. She sits at the table and unzips Charlie's suit. 'Please.

Cuban Heels

On Saturdays it's usually David that does stuff with him, but today I just wanted to, like, make a point, you know?'

Jenny sits down. She is wearing a threadbare towelling dressing gown which was white until she put it into the wash with a red jumper which, it transpired, should have been hand-washed. 'Take his child away until he gives in? How is all that going?' She pulls her hair back, and ties it with an elastic band. Jenny looks as dishevelled as Libby feels. As a single mother, she has a better excuse, but she does not care at all. She rations her caring energy, and for now, anything that doesn't concern her bald, big-eyed daughter is dismissed.

'Crap. I can't believe it hasn't blown over. David never used to be like this. How come it all changes, Jen? One minute it's all, "Oh, you're my princess, I'd do anything for you," and the next it's "Who cares what you think? I want to learn Spanish so we're all going to live in the slums of Rio and that's final because I'm the head of the household and you don't have a career any more."'

'Actually,' says Jen, 'they speak Portuguese in Brazil. So I don't expect he wants you to go there. Not to learn Spanish, anyway.'

'You know what I mean.'

'I do. Poor thing.' Jen strokes Libby's hand. 'So, let's talk about the way things used to be. Tell me again how you two met, and then I'll tell you about me and Martin, and then we can slag them both off.'

Libby laughs. 'All right. Could I put Charlie in Milly's chair? Will she mind?'

'She's just about ready for a nap. Help yourself.'

Libby met her two best friends, Jenny and Natalie, at Active Birth classes. She blanked them, initially. Libby used to form instant assessments of other people's worth in relation to her own, and both Jen and Nat came below her in this hierarchy. Natalie seemed rather suburban, while Jenny dressed like a student, and was clearly young. Too young for motherhood, Libby remembers thinking when she saw her. Lib aspired, instead, to be friends with a couple of women who wore designer maternity clothes and talked about the exceptional sweetness of Armani's children's range. They ignored her, and eventually, desperate to speak to someone, she smiled at Natalie.

They began talking, and started going out for cups of tea after the classes. Jenny and Natalie had already chatted a little, so Jenny began to join them. Before they knew what was happening, they were going into labour one by one. Nat had Alfie, then Jen had Milly, and finally Libby discovered that the daughter she had been convinced she was carrying was, in fact, Charlie. They became closer when they realised that the only people they wanted to talk to were other women going through precisely the same experience. Now they see each other most weekdays. Libby can't imagine herself thinking that Jenny wasn't good enough to be her friend. She is in awe of the way Jen tackles single motherhood. She genuinely seems, to Libby's astonishment, not to spend her evenings bemoaning her victim status. Libby knows that were she in Jenny's situation – had David walked out during the last month of her pregnancy, muttering about commitment and not feeling ready – she would have crumbled.

She likes having two friends, equally close. Jen and Nat are completely different. Natalie is enviably energetic and chic. She has sleek black hair and green eyes, and lost all her pregnancy weight in the first two months. She is married to an American Express IT manager whom Libby has never met, and gratefully stopped work as soon as they'd signed the marital register. She has devoted herself, for the past two years, to trying to conceive, then pregnancy, and now motherhood. Natalie is effortlessly good at all of it.

Libby now firmly believes that her two friends are better people than she is, and hopes they don't look down on her.

'We've never talked about our blokes much, have we?' she says, putting four slices of bread into the toaster. She held Jenny in her arms as she wailed when Martin left her. She remembers Charlie and

Milly kicking each other, through the double walls. 'Well, okay,' she continues. 'David and I met at a party. It was a leaving do. This girl I worked with was going travelling with her boyfriend, who it turned out was a friend of a friend of David's. I didn't really like the bar it was in, so I was about to leave.' She was actually wheezing because of all the smoke, and a search of her handbag had not produced her inhaler. This does not sound glamorous, so she leaves it out. Libby cannot stop censoring herself, even with a friend like Jen who would not think badly of her. 'He came over to me and said, "Hello, Libby." It turned out he'd asked my friend what my name was because he thought I looked nice.'

'He fancied the pants off you, in other words.'

'You could put it that way. That was in my thin days, when I bothered to get my roots done. He wasn't my usual type. To be honest, my usual type was a right bastard, a commitmentphobe, you know all the clichés. I'd been single for a couple of months after a particularly terrible break-up with someone who I still hope is going to die a long and lingering death. I was living in a shared flat in Battersea and working really incredibly hard. It was a big firm, and I was working my way up, but it was so competitive, I really did have to put the hours in. Christ, it could be boring, but I loved it. I adored the edginess of needing to be the best.'

'So did he ask you out then and there?'

Libby laughs. 'He did, actually. We went to dinner that night. You know David. Well, you don't, but you know what I say about him. He's very straightforward. He wouldn't see the point of liking me but pretending not to. I thought he was harmless and generous. He seems so sweet on the surface, but he has this really steely core. It took me ages to get to that. For ages I thought he was more of a friend than a potential lover.'

Jenny sits Milly on Libby's lap, and refills their mugs from the teapot. 'How long before you snogged?'

'A couple of dates. I surprised myself. He was madly keen on me but I was looking out for someone more fiery. I used to laugh about him to my friends. He lived in a terraced house in Kentish Town, and he actually grew his own vegetables in the garden. We thought that was hilarious. He cycled to work. He never took taxis. He had two work suits and a pair of jeans for weekends – he hated shopping. And he stopped me plastering myself in make-up.'

'So one day you suddenly decided you were in love with him.'

Jenny puts a plate of toast in front of Libby, and arranges butter, Marmite and peanut butter on the table.

'Help yourself,' she says, as she takes Milly back.

Libby shudders. 'Oooh, take the peanut butter away! Seriously, would you mind? I'm allergic and just looking at it scares me. I'm sure I'd love it, too.'

'I didn't know that.'

'I don't exactly shout about it. But it's why I never have proper slices of cake when we're out. Just the packaged-up biscuits with the ingredients written on the side. You never know what's got nuts in.'

'And I'd never even noticed you doing that, either. Sorry.'

Libby laughs. 'Don't apologise. I'm sorry for being so fussy. So, with David, I suppose what happened was that I gradually got happier and happier, and came to like the healthy life I was living. I really do have lots of allergies, you know? And my way of dealing with them has always been mainly to ignore them. I was feeling so much better through things like drinking water instead of Diet Coke, and eating vegetables instead of crisps. Then I realised I was truly happy. After that I couldn't wait to marry him.'

'And you don't regret that? Don't you feel that he made you into someone?' Jenny chews the end of her hair. 'Not someone you're not, but someone you wouldn't otherwise have been?'

Libby thinks about it. She tries to imagine herself as she would have been without David. She is thirty now. She might have been with a man who liked the look of her on his arm. It is conceivable that she might have got pregnant, that she could have a baby. She would have employed a live-in nanny, and started going to the gym at six weeks. She would have been back at work a few weeks after that. She would see her little Charlie, who wouldn't be Charlie but some other baby entirely, mainly at weekends. On the positive side, she wouldn't be staring at the prospect of Latin America.

'No,' she says. 'I can't regret anything, because I love David and we've got Charlie. But I do feel that there's a thin ambitious woman inside me. And right now she is feeling mightily pissed off.'

They look at each other, and smile. Then they look at their babies.

'Better put madam here down for a nap,' says Jen.

'And then you can tell me about Martin. Have you got any real coffee? Sorry, here I am being fussy again, and this time it really is personal taste. Sorry, I've just about finished the Marmite.'

An hour later, they call Natalie. She appears on the doorstep, with Alfie, half an hour after that. Libby is immediately aware of the contrast between her old tracksuit bottoms and Nat's Joseph jeans. Natalie's hair has obviously been blow-dried this morning. It is loose and layered. Her suede jacket is like one that Libby had five years ago. She feels terrible. She has let herself go.

The six of them walk along the seafront, through the weekend crowds, which are thin on a dull February morning. They wander around the Lanes, stopping for coffee and to stare into shop windows. The babies all sleep most of the way. Natalie buys a pair of boots from Jones. Libby gets the others to mind her buggy while she pops into Jigsaw, but she remembers David's sabbatical, and emerges empty-handed. They walk through the Pavilion Gardens, and emerge into the North Laine. As usual, people get out of the way when they see three women with large pushchairs approaching. They walk all the way back to Jenny's house and sit down, exhausted.

'So, Lib,' says Natalie, as her phone beeps loudly. 'Going home yet?' Natalie picks up the phone and reads a text message. 'Oh, Graham is outside. He's come to get us because we've got that lunch with his work people. On a Saturday! And it's at a country pub, which means I'm driving.'

'Graham's outside!' Libby is excited. 'Bring him in! We have to meet him.'

Natalie wrinkles her nose. 'I haven't met David. Not fair. Graham's scared of the idea of you two. He'd be embarrassed if I made him come in.'

Jenny picks Milly up. 'Then we'll help you out to the car.'

Libby puts her fleece back on. 'And I'll go home. That's our excuse for coming outside.'

Graham is sitting at the wheel of his Audi, listening to Radio Two. Libby sees him look round, with some surprise. He puts down his mobile phone, and steps out of the car. He looks older than Libby expected. Despite his thinning hair and bulging waistband, he is handsome, with the air of a man who knows it. He is wearing expensive jeans and a rugby shirt, and even though Libby knows that neither she nor Jenny looks as if they've stumbled from the catwalks, he is instantly charming.

'Hello, girls,' he says. 'Finally, we meet! Let me guess.' He takes Libby's hand and holds it for far too long. 'You must be the lawyer. Libby, the lawyer. Every bit as gorgeous as Natalie said. And this is Jenny. You're just a slip of a young thing! Far too girlish to be a mother, surely?' He winks at them both. 'In fact, it's a mistake, isn't it? You two aren't the mothers – you're the au pairs!'

Jenny and Libby laugh politely. Natalie is bundling the pushchair into the boot and ignores her husband. As she pushes Charlie in the direction of home, Libby tries to recover her good spirits. Graham is slimy and horrible. Martin left Jenny when she needed him most. David is intent on taking her and Charlie away from everything they know. What, she wonders, is wrong with men?

By the time she turns the key, she is scared. On balance, she probably should have taken her mobile, after all. David must be frantic with worry. He's probably packed all her things into plastic bags and piled them by the door. She wouldn't be surprised if he'd called a family lawyer. He might even have phoned the hospital. He is most definitely going to be angry.

When David hears the key turn, he looks at the woman sitting next to him on the sofa and puts his finger to his lips. Then he rushes to the hall and flings the door wide. He watches his wife, who is clearly stressed and feeling extremely guilty, pretending to be casual.

'Hi,' she says breezily, avoiding his eyes. 'Been over to Jen's.' In fact, she's surprised he didn't phone Jen. He can't care that much, after all.

'Must have been fun,' David replies lightly, 'since you went for breakfast and stayed for lunch.' Surreptitiously, Charlie's parents race to unstrap him from the buggy. They both want to hold him, to bring him on to their side. David takes him out, with a tiny smile.

'Have I?' asks Lib, in mock surprise. She wonders whether she can grab her son from her husband's arms. 'Well, there we go. You weren't worried, were you?' David sees her looking at him with big innocent blue eyes, and knows that the games must stop.

'Not really,' he says. 'I know when my pumpkin is making a point, and I know that, as the best mother in the world, you wouldn't have legged it without Charlie's dinner, or his bibs, or his pyjamas.'

Libby is a little disappointed. 'Fair enough,' she says, tossing her hair behind her shoulders. 'You're right, I guess. I *am* the best mother in the world. And that is why I want stability for my son.'

David squeezes her bottom, which makes her wince. Her bottom is disgusting. 'We'll talk about that later. Over dinner.'

'What, over a bowl of yesterday's pasta and pesto?' This is all they can be bothered to cook these days.

'I was thinking more of something like vegetable rosti with asparagus spears and a tomato coulis.'

'Go out, you mean? And take Charlie? Another of David's fabulous schemes.'

David walks into the living room before she does, and ushers her in with a flourish. 'Ta-da!' he says. 'I present the babysitter.'

Libby looks around the door in trepidation. Then she relaxes.

'Oh,' she says. 'Mum. You didn't say you were coming.'

Petra puts down Libby's old copy of *Heat* magazine, and stands up. 'Lovely to see you too, Liberty,' she says, and takes Charlie from David's arms. Petra is a former hippy. These days, she wears her hair cropped close to her head, and dresses in flowing layers bought at great expense from Ghost and Hampstead Bazaar. Today, she is attired entirely in purple. She models her look on Dame Judi Dench, but she's beginning to wonder why she bothers, and whether anyone would mind if she started going out in saggy tracksuit trousers and men's T-shirts. 'David rang me yesterday,' she continues, stroking Charlie's cheek. 'Aren't you just Grandmama's adorable boy? Yes you are. *Yes you are.* You never told me, darling, that you had a full-blown crisis on your hands. He's bigger, you know. Three weeks, and he's definitely bigger.'

'It's not a crisis,' Libby mutters, feeling like a sullen teenager. She hates her mother being involved in her marriage. It feels exactly the same as it used to when she was caught between her parents, with her mother asking her, casually, what her father was up to, how he was, what exactly he said in the letter she was holding. She knew her mother went into her bedroom to read them while she was at school. Now that she is married herself, she finds she no longer blames her. In any case, her father dropped all contact after a year, and she hasn't heard from him since.

'Dear heart,' says Petra, 'if you stay out from morning till half past two, holding your precious son to ransom, it is a crisis. You two are going to that divine vegetarian place, on me, and while you're there, I'm going to enjoy this little angel boy.'

'Mother, you are not! He goes to bed at half past seven. David, what time did you book it for?'

'Eight fifteen.'

'Perfect. Mum, if you get him up when we're out, I will know! I will.'

Petra laughs. 'Keep your hair on, darling. David, run the girl a bath, won't you? Geri Halliwell wouldn't get stressed like that. Did you know, she does six hours of yoga, every day?'

'Mum, you are ludicrous. She doesn't do that any more. And Geri Halliwell is far more screwy than I am. Stop reading bloody *Heat*.'

Petra laughs. 'Leave *The Economist* lying around your living room, my dear, and I will read *The Economist*. David, remind me, I have to give you something later.'

'If we went abroad, your mother would be a lot further away,' says David, as they sit at a window table and sip their wine. Terre à Terre is bustling, and they are both feeling happier than they have for months. Libby is wearing make-up and a dress which, despite the fact that it is a size fourteen, makes her feel good. David is wearing a new blue shirt. He shaved before they came out, and has two nicks on his chin.

Libby frowns. 'I like my mother.'

'In which case, I'm sure she would be delighted to come out on an extended visit. She would find it *divine*.'

'She'd be too busy. Christ, hon, the woman has three geese, a pig, an MA and two blokes on the go. She makes me feel like shit with all her energy. And she's post-menopausal.'

'She'd drop the pig at a moment's notice for her little girl, as you very well know. Why do you think she's here today?'

'Not for me. For her *divine* grandson. Oh, I know, what was she on about earlier, when she said she'd got something for you?'

'Oh, nothing. She wants me to teach her to use the computer. She'd cut out a Dell ad from the paper, wants me to advise her.'

'Why you?'

He shrugs. 'I'm a man?'

When Libby looks at David, she sees, for the first time in weeks, the man who used to worship her. He is gazing at her with huge brown eyes, and she needs it all to stop. David is infinitely more pleasant than either Martin or Graham. She is lucky. Libby feels the fight draining out of her.

'My darling,' she says, 'what are we going to do?' She reaches across the table for his hand. He takes hers.

'Will you hear me out, for a minute?' he asks, smiling nervously. At that point, the waiter arrives with their main course. They sit in silence as he tops up their wine.

'Go on, then.' Libby is worried.

'Right.' He picks up his fork, then puts it down again. 'Okay. Well, first of all, my darling, I had no idea how strongly you felt about going back to work. That is all true, isn't it? You do want to go back?' She nods, and eats a mushroom. 'So I propose a compromise. I've got this year off whether we want it or not. For the second half of the year we can live right here, and you can work full time or part time or whatever you want, and we can get a part-time nanny or a childminder, and I'll do some courses and do things with Charlie as well. It's going to be your time, so you can call the shots.'

Libby nods, guardedly. 'And for the first half?'

David grins. His cheeks dimple, his eyes light up, and he jigs in his seat.

'Cuba!' He says it so loudly that a couple on the next table turn and laugh. 'Lib, I've done so much research into this. Cuba is just the *best*.' He shovels a forkful of potato into his mouth, and talks through it. 'Right, it's in the Caribbean, so it's obviously very beautiful, and they have the most remarkable health service, which touch wood we won't need but it's nice to know it's there. There's no malaria. There's next to no dengue fever. Life expectancy is the same as in the US. I can learn Spanish at the University of Havana on a normal tourist visa. We just have to leave the country every two months and then fly back in again. When you're in the Caribbean, how much of a hardship can *that* be? They'll love Charlie, who wouldn't? We'll experience life under a communist dictatorship, before Castro dies and they start getting McDonald's and Starbucks.

And think of all the music and the dancing. It'll be incredible. Please, my darling. Please please please say you'll think about it.'

Libby puts her head to one side. She is largely reluctant, but a small part of her is intrigued. David's passion has always been infectious.

'What's dengue fever?' she demands, and tries to hide her smile.

'Mosquito-borne. Rarely fatal, and as I said not really a hazard.'

'And you promise it would be okay? What about the weather? They have hurricanes in Cuba, don't they?'

'Mmm, but hurricane season is September to November. We'll just miss it. Average temperature in Havana in March is twenty-seven degrees. Perfect, in other words.'

Libby looks at the raindrops coursing down the window pane. She looks down at her thick tights and suede boots. Twenty-seven degrees sounds acceptable.

'What about food?' she demands. 'They have a trade embargo. The shops are empty. I'm sure I've read about that.'

'But there'll be plenty of locally grown fruit and veg for the lad.'

An idea is forming. 'No McDonald's, like you said. No chocolate.'

'No Twixes or Mars bars, for sure. If you wanted, though, we could surely find you some kind. It might have to be quality chocolate though.'

Libby pinches her stomach. She is shallow, but she is tempted to treat the experience as a fat camp. Six months in Cuba dancing and getting thin. Then she'll be back at work.

'I'll think about it,' she says, because she desperately wants to be friends with David again. She doesn't want to be a single mother.

David is grinning broadly. 'Is that a yes?'

Libby shakes her head. 'No it is not. It's a maybe.'

David holds up his glass. 'To maybe,' he says, triumphantly.

Libby clinks glasses and smiles back. 'To maybe,' she repeats. They both know what it means.

chapter six

Maggie

Dear Mum and Dad,

How are things in France? I hope it's all *très bien*, and that *vous buvez du vin rouge sur la terrace*. Is the weather okay? We have had storms every day for the past week. I huddle in my little flat, feeling snug. It really is wild out there. As I write I can hear intermittent thunder.

I'm sure Emma told you that I spent a weekend with them recently. Emma really is blooming. She looks like she's got triplets in there! Are you going to be coming over around her due date? While I was in Norwich, I bumped into Yasmin McLeod! As you can imagine this was a surprise as I haven't seen her since we left school, ten years ago. She's looking very well and has just come back from India. In fact she's coming to stay with me today. I think she's finding it hard living with her parents, and glad of a chance to escape, but she's looking very well.

Life in Brighton is good. I've made friends with a few of my neighbours, a couple with a young baby. They live immediately above me, and I've been doing a bit of babysitting for them, as well as going out for the odd girlie drink with Libby once Charlie's asleep (that's the baby, not the husband!). Work is going well, too – Amex is a good place to be and it looks like there should be plenty of opportunities for promotion. All in all I am enjoying life here and moving on from my Edinburgh days. It's been nice to have a bit more daylight over the winter. I'm sure I'll see you before too long, when you come over for the baby. Take care.

With lots of love,

Mags xxx

I file the letter away and wish some of it were true. When I write my stilted lies to my parents, I almost manage to convince myself that, for example, my flat is 'snug', my job is 'great', and Libby is my friend. She can be irritating, for sure, but she and I would be good for each other. Sometimes I think she needs someone like me to put her so-called problems into perspective. She would feel better once she accepted that she has never experienced pain and loneliness in her life. I would feel better for having a friend.

Yasmin is coming to stay – that much is true – but I'm beginning to wish she wasn't. I have been glued to the baby monitor every evening. It is the main focus of my world. I'm not harming anyone. I'm not stalking. The last thing I am is any sort of a danger to Libby or David. I like them. I like it when she stands up for herself. I like it when she talks to her friends, occasionally, during the day. They're not often near the monitor, but when they are, I cannot tear myself away from my 'parent unit'. That, I think, is when I find out what she's really thinking. She puts on a charade for David. That marriage will not last five more minutes unless she starts being upfront with him. She thinks she's done so well to tell him that she wants to go back to work, but he has no idea how she really feels. She only has marginally more self-esteem than I do, but, unlike me, she has numerous reasons to feel good about herself.

I keep it switched on all the time, so I'll always know when there's anything to listen to. I sometimes hear Charlie waking for a feed when I get in from work. I love the illusion of company, when that happens. It's quite odd to realise that I'm not the only person in the building who sees three o'clock in the morning. But now they're going to Cuba. I can't believe she bloody agreed to that.

I pour myself a glass of water, and ponder the important question of what to wear for Yasmin's arrival. Apart from sequinned underwear and easily discarded gauzy dresses, my wardrobe is dull. When I'm not working, I hide my body under jeans and baggy jumpers. I don't wear make-up. I keep my nails nice, and shave my legs, but I look as dull as fuck.

I put a few contenders on the bed. Yasmin was wearing daring, chic clothes in Norwich. I have nothing like that red skirt in my everyday wardrobe. Perhaps I should dip into my tarty stuff. I could wear jeans, because jeans would look great on Yasmin, but mine are all too big. I was wearing outsized jeans in Norwich, and they didn't make me feel foxy. I put out a red long-sleeved T-shirt that I picked up in Hennes the other day, and some black trousers that are nothing special, but show off my bony hips. Then I assemble an alternative outfit next to them: a crocheted gold bikini top, a white shirt to be worn undone over it, and a gold skirt so skimpy that it makes Yasmin's red one look like a burqa. I think I'll go for the trousers, and pack up the other stuff for later.

The monitor buzzes into life. I hear Charlie's bedroom door creak open. She keeps saying she's going to oil it, but she never will. She wants David to do it, but she doesn't actually ask him.

It's nap time.

'Here we are,' says Libby's soothing voice. 'Close the curtains. Now it's time for your nap. You'll feel so much better afterwards. When you wake up we're going to the shops with Nat to buy you some clothes for Cuba. So you have a lovely rest. Night night, darling boy. We love you so much.'

I am growing to like the way she talks to him. It's soothing and soppy but stops just short of cloying. If I sometimes find myself looking after Emma's baby, I'll talk to it just like that. I am, however, perturbed by the whole Cuban development. It seems that the bastards are actually going to go. My flat will be a dungeon after they leave. I will miss them horribly.

I may as well follow them into town, since I'm going anyway. I might even try to strike up a conversation in Mothercare. I can use Emma's baby as a starting point, and ask their advice. But I know I won't dare.

'Yasmin!' I call, when I see her striding down the platform, holding her umbrella easily above the heads of the crowd. I don't possess an umbrella, partly because the rain here is normally accompanied by vicious winds that yank it from your hands, turn it inside out, and deposit it in the middle of a busy road. Also because I tend to poke people in the eye with the spokes.

She looks up and greets me with a broad smile. 'Mags,' she shouts, startling the man in front of her. I see him look round, and up. I see his expression change as he takes her in. Yasmin would make a magnificent stripper. The man smiles ruefully as he realises she will never acknowledge his existence. I wave. She waves back. The man looks at me, the small, unassuming girl in the studenty clothes, and wonders how I've managed to become the friend of the tall beauty. I catch his eye, and smile triumphantly.

Yasmin strides through the barriers, and envelops me in a hug. She is wearing her moleskin coat. I smell the expensive toiletries again.

'How are you?' she demands. 'So this is Brighton. Would you believe, I've never been here before? I mean, fuck, I've been to little settlements in the Himalayas, I've been to bloody Peshawar and Goa and fuck knows where else, but I've never even made the trip to little old Brighton.' She pauses for breath.

'It's probably not as exciting as all those places,' I say duti-fully, wondering just how impressed I'm supposed to be by her place-name-dropping. I hope I'm not going to have to listen to backpacking stories all day long. I steer her to the front of the station. 'But,' I continue, 'I can safely say it's got more going for it than Norwich. How heavy's your bag? We could walk back along the seafront, if you like, but it takes about forty minutes. Or we could jump on the number six bus.'

'If we walk, can we get chips?'

'Of course. This is the English seaside. Chips are actually compulsory.'

'It's a deal, then. Fuck, I missed chips. I missed them so much that I went into McDonald's in Delhi to get some a couple of weeks ago, if you can believe that. Those Maccy D fries weren't exactly what I had in mind, but they're fucking addictive. I went back three times on the same afternoon. You know, going to McDonald's is a status symbol there. It's full of rich young couples on dates.' My heart sinks. She notices. 'So,' she says abruptly, 'tell me about you. Now Emma's not with us you can give me all the saucy details. God, sitting with those two was like being with the vicar and his wife. What's your sister like? Twenty-five going on fifty-five?'

I laugh, feeling somewhat treacherous. 'Tell me about it,' I say lightly. I look up at her and wonder how honest to be. 'Where do I start?' I wonder aloud. 'Well, I went to Sheffield, as you know, and then after I graduated I moved to Edinburgh with Mark. My twat of a boyfriend – I met him at uni. We lived there until we split up last year, and then I came down here. You know, to "make a fresh start".' I mime quotation marks with my fingers, feeling braver for being self-deprecating.

'Good woman. So, have you reinvented yourself in Brighton?' She looks around. 'I must say, after being here five minutes, I'm still waiting for the famous hipness to show itself.'

I follow her gaze. The road that leads down to the sea is lined with greasy takeaways and nightclubs. Cars edge by, slowly, with their windscreen wipers swishing in the drizzle. Halfway down the road, the old clock tower has been hidden by scaffolding for as long as I've lived here. At the bottom of the hill, the sea forms a grey line between an ugly cinema and a hotel. The horizon is fuzzy with rain.

Cuban Heels

The sky is heavy with black clouds. My workplace is in a side street off this road.

'There is a certain seedy side,' I say, with feeling. 'It's an odd mixture. It's swarming with smug couples who move here from London to have their kids. But it's also got massive problems with homelessness, drugs, gangs of lads rampaging around on Saturday nights. All the stag dos come here from London.' I look around. 'We'll get some chips when we get to the seafront,' I add.

'And you're happy here?'

I look at her. 'Kind of.'

'Meaning?'

'Oh, I'll tell you later. I've got to be somewhere at nine – is that okay? We can maybe go for a drink and some early food beforehand, if that's all right. I'll tell you everything when we get to the flat. I got the wine in, specially.' Not to mention the milk, the bread, the tea bags, the normal accoutrements of a household.

I catch sight of our reflections in the opaque window of the old casino. Yasmin is swinging her bag from her shoulder, and holding her umbrella over us both. She looks like a model. She's wearing tight jeans, today, and a floaty blue blouse that looks as if it was purchased on her travels, under that beautiful jacket. She is slim, but not scrawny. Next to her, I am insignificant. I see myself walking with my shoulders hunched, and my hair frizzy. I wash the gel out of it every morning, and leave it to dry naturally. Six months ago I wouldn't even let Mark see me before I'd used straightening irons.

I search my pockets for a band with which to tie it up, but I don't have one. My clothes are too loose, but I don't look fashionably thin in them, just gaunt. I look a wreck. I look like one of this city's celebrated drug addicts.

'But you've got a good job, by the sounds of it,' Yasmin says, halting a car with an imperious wave so we can cross the road. 'That must count for a lot.'

'Actually,' I say, and then stop. I know I have to tell her the truth, and luckily, I think she'll be a little bit impressed. She is the sort of woman who thinks strip clubs are cool in an arch, ironic way. The kind of woman I hate to meet when I'm working.

She looks at me, only half interested. 'Mmm?'

'Nothing.'

We are sitting on my living-room floor, drinking red wine from pint glasses, when I finally take a deep breath, and tell her.

'Yasmin?' I say, catching her between anecdotes.

'Yeah?'

'I'm actually a lap dancer.'

She flicks her hair back. I see her looking at me, trying to work out whether or not I'm winding her up.

'You are kidding,' she says.

'Nope,' I tell her, forcing a smile. 'It's the truth. I take my clothes off and writhe around in people's faces, and I am paid handsomely for it.'

Yasmin splutters. 'Margaret Wilson! Serious?'

'Absolutely.'

'But . . . You've got three A levels and a degree in English literature! Why would you want to take your clothes off? And gyrate in someone's face?'

Her expression has changed. She looks concerned.

I shrug and try to convince us both that it is not a big deal. 'I don't *want* to,' I tell her. 'I did try for American Express, but they didn't want me. The only jobs around here are shitty ones earning minimum wage. It was a choice between Vixenz or a retail establishment called Everything's A Pound. I went where the money was.'

I look at Yasmin, and she looks at me. We burst out laughing. I don't think either of us is greatly amused.

'You're amazing!' she says through her forced giggles. 'You are so, so hilarious. So, now you have to tell me all about it. Can I come and watch?'

I panic for a moment. If Yasmin came to watch, I would die. 'No,' I tell her, firmly. 'Women aren't allowed.'

She lifts her glass. 'To you, Maggie, and your undiminished ability to surprise.'

We go out before work. I have my work clothes and make-up and hair gel in a plastic bag.

'Where's a good restaurant?' Yasi asks, as we walk up my road. We pass David on his way home, but I don't say hello. I force myself not to turn round and watch him. 'I take it that you do eat, occasionally?'

'Not really,' I confess. 'I cook a vat of pasta and sauce from a jar, usually pesto, about once a week and just get a bowlful when I remember. And I have toast for lunch. I bought new bread because you were coming. Hope you appreciate that.'

'You pushed the boat out for little old me? Cheers. So, where are we going?'

'I read the reviews sometimes. There are tons of restaurants up here. You can't go wrong.'

We settle for one of the many Italians on the main road at the top of my street. Having found out everything she can think of to ask about my job, Yasmin begins to tell me about herself. She talks incessantly, and I struggle to say anything at all. I check my watch every few minutes. I don't want to be late, or I won't be able to sort my hair out.

'You remember Hugh Davies?' she says, pushing away her starter plate and offering me a cigarette. 'I went out with him after the Jeremy fiasco, when we were, God, about fifteen, I think? Thin lips and no chin? Well I ran into him the other day, and he's lost his hair already. He looks fifty. Still living with his folks.'

I take the fag she offers. I never used to smoke before I moved here.

'The one that got away, huh?'

'Mmm, what a catch.' She reaches over and lights it for me. 'And then I see Jeremy looking all smug, having impregnated your sister. I have the weirdest collection of exes, and I seem to be running into all of them.' She leans back and exhales. Twin plumes of smoke come out of her nose.

'Are you still in touch with Ivan?' I ask her, because one of us has to mention him.

She looks up quickly. 'No. Why, are you?'

I laugh, convincingly I hope. 'Of course not.'

Yasmin stubs out her cigarette. 'Last I heard he was engaged, and living in London. But that was a few years back.'

I nod. I can't think of anything else to say. 'I've seen so many people in Norwich,' she says, 'still living there, never quite got around to leaving. It's so depressing. Fuck. And now I'm one of them. I keep going away, and then when I come back I have no idea what to do next. So I end up getting a shitty job – not even flamboyantly shitty like yours, just mindfuckingly dull – and saving up and going away again. It's cool, but I mean, fuck, I'm twenty-eight years old, and I can't carry on like this for ever, can I? I should have a career by now. Or I should be wanting to settle down, like your sister.'

She taps ash into the ashtray. I realise I'm supposed to say something.

'No you shouldn't,' I tell her. 'You're fine.' I want to ask what happened between her and Ivan, how long it went on for, why they split up. I don't say anything.

Yasmin nods. 'Yeah, in some ways, but what's going to happen when I'm forty? I'll be looking a bit sad then, won't I?'

'You'll be great when you're forty. And you will look stunning. What will I be doing? Not what I do now. That would be tragic.' I can't even bear to imagine it. 'Anyway, you must have had relationships along the way?'

Yasmin smiles wickedly. 'Well, travelling is great like that, I must admit. I've had tons of them. Honestly, sometimes I am the queen of casual sex. The mistress of it. Germans, Israelis, Indians, the lot. A hotel manager in Laos. A Japanese pilot. No offer I won't consider, when the muse strikes. I'm a shameless slapper. What about you? Do you see much action? I bet you do. All in a day's work, right?' Her eyes are gleaming. She is dying to know.

'Yeah, right,' I tell her. 'The only guys I meet are paying to look at me. It's not exactly the foundation for a healthy relationship.'

'You mean you never . . . ?'

She is seriously annoying me. 'I am *not* a prostitute,' I say crossly. 'If one of them laid a finger on me he'd be out on the street.'

Yasmin looks embarrassed. She scans the room. 'Those guys there,' she says suddenly. 'They look okay. They'd be up for it. Let's go over.'

I follow her gaze to two men of about our age, wearing suits. There is nothing striking about either of them. Yasmin starts to get up. I grab her arm and push her back into her chair. 'No, Yasi, let's not.'

'Why? Nothing to lose. You said you don't meet anyone normal: let me prove to you that you can. Your confidence needs bolstering. They will have our numbers before our pizzas arrive, and that's a promise.'

'I've got to go to work. And anyway, they'll both want you. I don't want to be the ugly friend. Believe me, that wouldn't bolster anything. I want to talk to you. Not to some bloke I don't care about.' Yasmin is looking at me sceptically. 'We can go out properly tomorrow, if you really want,' I tell her desperately, 'and you can find me someone then. You've got to tell me all about India.' I stop, and then continue on impulse. 'And then you can give me some advice. There's something I really want to ask you.'

I don't completely trust Yasmin. I don't even know if I like her. But I don't have anyone else to talk to. It is a luxury to be sitting in a restaurant, having a conversation.

She frowns, annoyed at my reluctance to let her boss me around like she did when we were teenagers. I wonder if, by trying to help me find a mate, she is trying to make up for stealing Ivan. If so, she has a strange way of doing it.

'What advice?' she asks, frowning.

'I'm thinking about going travelling,' I tell her, liking the sound of the words as I say them. 'To Cuba.'

She drains her glass, slams it on the table, and smiles brilliantly. 'Well, why the heck didn't you say so?' she asks, and orders a second bottle.

When I come in, at half past two, I hear David and Libby's leaving party winding down. A couple of people stagger out of the porch as I come in. They spot my cab, and run to halt its departure, marvelling loudly at their luck. I stride purposefully to my front door without saying hello. I was going to gatecrash the party, but I don't have the strength. I can't be bothered with drunken revellers. They're playing Robbie Williams. All around my house there are happy people without a care in the world. I despise them.

I have had a terrible night's work. My conversations with Yasmin made me see what I do through new eyes. I can't bear it. I watched the men, tonight. I saw the way they looked at my bare body. I wanted to curl up and die. I wanted to run as far from Brighton as I could get. I could barely believe that I, Margaret Wilson, the sensible, high-achieving older sister, am reduced to this. There is nothing cool about it. There is no glamour. There are sad men who want to leer, and there are women without self-esteem, or women who can disconnect themselves from what they do sufficiently for the money to outweigh the horror. I don't think any woman can do this for fun. The woman who gets turned on by writhing for strangers is more of a myth than the tooth fairy.

I am exhausted. I open the door as quietly as I can, and take off my shoes. I creep through the living room, where a bundled-up sleeping bag presumably represents Yasmin. In the kitchen, I open the fridge door wide and locate the gin on the shelf by its light. I pour myself a tumblerful, and take it to the bathroom with me. I sit on the edge of the bath, and blink back tears. I am not one of life's criers. I am hard, tough. I have to be, to live this life. I am a loner. I am not the sort of woman who bursts into tears when the phone doesn't ring. I didn't cry when Mark left me. I didn't cry when my sister died. There is nothing else to cry for, after that.

I knock back my drink and remove all my make-up. I note that Yasmin has been experimenting with my many eyeshadows and liner pencils, this evening. I would have done the same. My palest pink lipstick has fallen behind the loo. It would have suited her better than it suits me. I scrub hard at my face, removing all traces of the vice girl, and revealing a tired and fed-up woman with blotchy skin and saggy eyes.

In my bedroom, I take the monitor from its hiding place under the pillow, and switch it on with the volume down. I hold it to my ear. Nothing happens. They have had a fabulous party, no doubt, and now everyone's going home, and Charlie is sleeping peacefully.

I realise that I feel more for the family above me than I do for anyone else I know. They pull me in two directions. I hate them, because they have everything that I lack. I love them, because they have everything that I want. I am drawn to them. I can't bear to see them go.

I don't know why I think it, but I know they are my only chance. David and Libby and Charlie are, in some weird way, the people who are going to save me.

Silence. The temperature in Charlie's room flashes reassuringly green at nineteen degrees. A few seconds later, he makes some snuffly noises, and then it all goes quiet.

chapter seven

Libby – the next morning

Libby rolls over in bed and clutches her head with both hands.

'Ohhhh,' she groans, and grabs hold of David.

'Mmmmm?' he demands, almost asleep.

'Charlie's crying,' says Libby. She wishes she could block out the sound and carry on sleeping. They went to bed at half past two. It can only have been five minutes ago. 'Been crying for ages.'

David rolls towards her. 'I know,' he says, sleepily. 'Wasstime?'

They both raise themselves on their elbows, so they can see the digital display of the clock radio.

'Half seven,' Libby says. She is feeling slightly better already. Breastfeeding moderates her alcohol intake so effectively that she might carry on feeding Charlie for longer than she had planned. She might breastfeed him till he's three or four. 'Half seven?' she repeats. 'That means he slept through the night!'

'Slept through the party,' says David.

'Wish I had. He must be starving.'

Libby jumps out of bed, takes a slurp from the glass of water on the bedside cabinet, and pulls on the closest garment to hand. This turns out to be David's shirt from last night. She used to love wearing boyfriends' clothes, because they swamped her and made her feel petite and cute. This morning, she can barely button David's shirt over her tender breasts. The shirt doesn't really fit her. The truth is, she is fatter than her husband. She has, of course, known this for months, but it is unpleasant to be reminded this starkly when she is this tired. She glances at herself as she passes the mirror. Her hair is a bird's nest. Her eyes are ringed, panda-like, with smudged eye make-up. She thought she had taken it off last night, but clearly she didn't do a particularly thorough job. Her face is puffy with tiredness.

Her baby is screaming for her. She steps out on to the landing, wobbles slightly, and begins to remember the night before. It started off as a good party, a great one. She and David are both consumed with nerves about going to Cuba, and that restless energy made them excellent hosts. Having friends over – people they hadn't seen, in many cases, since before Charlie was born – made it all suddenly official. Libby dressed up carefully, aware that when her old colleagues saw her, they would probably reel in shock at how fat she was. She was always the smuggest woman in the office, the one who delighted in informing people that 'the only way to lose weight is to burn up more calories than you take in'. It had been easy for her to say that, when she was a small size ten. Last night, in her bias-cut black dress, she was a generous fourteen, and would have happily punched her old self.

'Now that we're having a party,' David told her, when the doorbell rang and the first guests arrived, 'we actually have to go away. You do realise that.' She nodded. She still didn't want to go, but she was happy to bask in the attention that their reckless decision had brought them.

'We have to go anyway,' she reminded him, as they walked to the front door together. Libby was trying to convince herself that her dress hid all her flabby bits. 'We've got tickets. We've got visas.'

David held the latch, and paused for a second. 'And we've got friends who have come all the way from London to make sure we're really leaving,' he said, winking at her, and he opened the door. One of his old university friends was standing there, with a bottle of wine in each hand and a glamorous woman by his side, shivering in the cold night air.

Libby takes Charlie into their bed, and lies him next to her. She shrugs off the small shirt, and positions herself on her side, with her nipple in her son's mouth. While he sucks hungrily, she lets her mind drift off.

The party had been going far better than she imagined. Lots of people turned up, including some neither she nor David recognised, which she took to be a good thing. Everyone was drinking, talking and dancing. Libby loved the spotlight. Everybody told her that she looked well and that motherhood clearly suited her, and she accepted it as a compliment without demanding to know whether 'well' meant 'fat'. Then, sometime after midnight, a terrible thing happened. She remembers it suddenly, and feels sick.

Natalie and Libby and Libby's old colleague, Anna, were chatting in the living room when Graham stumbled in, drunk. He looked at them, laughed, and turned and walked out. His face was smudged with pink lipstick. Natalie's lipstick was brown.

Natalie stared after him. Then she muttered, 'Excuse me,' and left the room. Anna and Libby looked at each other.

'Is that her husband?' Anna asked. She was dressed in black, and clearly made daily visits to the gym. Libby had just begun to realise that Anna, despite being svelte, was actually jealous of her baby, jealous of her marriage, and jealous of their trip to Cuba. 'I was talking to him earlier. He was a bit creepy. I can't believe she's married to him. He told me he was "single-ish".'

'I know! He's horrible. I mean, I don't know him very well, but he seems it.'

'And she's gorgeous and lovely and stunning. She could do so much better for herself. Bit late now, though, I suppose, with the baby and all. God, Lib, I can't believe you live in baby land now. It seems so responsible. And you're friends with people like Natalie, and she's fab. You've got a whole new life, haven't you?' Anna was drunk. 'And I'm just left behind, where you used to be, same old same old in the office, while you go off to have adventures. Bloody hell . . .'

She tailed off as Natalie came back into the room. Behind her, Libby saw a woman she had seen earlier in the evening, but didn't know, slipping away towards the front door.

'Nat!' said Libby. 'What's wrong?'

Natalie collapsed into her arms, sobbing.

Charlie is still sucking noisily and contentedly.

'David?' says Libby, quietly.

'Mmmnh?'

'I'm going to get up with Charlie. You stay asleep. I'll call Natalie, see if she's okay.'

David rolls over and curls himself towards her, with Charlie between them. He pats Charlie's soft hair. 'She won't be.'

'I know. You saw that woman too, didn't you? Are you sure you didn't know her?'

'Positive,' says David. 'Do you think they actually shagged?'

'Unfortunately, yes. You saw the way his face was covered in lipstick. Apparently his pants were inside out.'

'Do women sign some kind of agreement whereby they are compelled to tell each other absolutely everything? So where did she spring from, this gatecrasher?'

Libby smiles at him. 'She's not your fancy woman, is she?' she asks wickedly. 'You didn't invite her on the sly and then she was pissed off that you were ignoring her, so she went off with Graham?'

'Oh yes, that'll be it. Rumbled at last.'

'Poor Nat.'

'Married to a twat.'

'That rhymes. Did you see that girl properly? She looked gorgeous, what I saw of her. Which doesn't make Nat feel any better.'

David props himself up and laughs. 'That's a trick question, isn't

71

it? A woman question. If I say yes, she had long blonde hair and she looked like Barbie or a porn model, but Barbie and porn models are not really my type, then you'll just call me a liar.'

'So say she wasn't gorgeous.'

David rubs his foot up her leg. 'She wasn't gorgeous.'

'Good. Although she looked it. Who was she, though? Anna didn't think she'd seen her before, so she wasn't with my work people. She must have come with some of your mates. Ask them.'

David yawns. 'What, now? At seven forty-five?'

'If you're not doing that, you can make us a cup of tea.' Libby fixes David with a sharp stare. 'I would do it, as you very well know, but I've got a baby on my nipple.' Today, and for as long as she can manage it, Libby vows that she will appreciate her husband and his fidelity. She knows that she is extraordinarily lucky to be able to trust David implicitly. Natalie is devastated. Libby wanted her to stay here last night, but she insisted on escorting Graham into a taxi. The party lost its momentum after that.

David stumbles out of bed. 'For you, my princess, anything.' He remembers the guests who crashed out in the living room, and struggles into a pair of pants. 'Cup of tea coming right up.' He stops outside the bedroom door, and comes back. Libby looks at him, with his floppy hair and his honed body. 'You know something?' he asks her.

'Mmm? What?'

'That party was the last thing that stood between us and Cuba. We're flying in three days.'

Libby laughs. 'Three days. Let's not go. It's too scary. David, when we're in Cuba, I don't want us to talk about me going back to work. It's all too much to get my head round. We'll just take each day as it comes. All right?'

David nods. 'Three days,' he repeats.

They look at each other, and neither of them knows what to say.

chapter eight

Maggie, three days later

Dear Sir or Madam,

   I am writing as per the terms of my lease to let you know that my flat, 17a Sixth Avenue, will be empty for approximately three months as of the end of this week. I will continue to pay the rent as normal. My possessions will be there but I will be away taking a compulsory course in Cuba as part of my job.

   If there are any problems in my absence, please contact my sister, Emma Austin, on 01603 129890.

   Yours faithfully,
   Margaret Wilson

'So,' says Yasmin, bundling up her sleeping bag and pushing her long hair out of the way. 'That's me trailing back to Norwich, and you jetting off for Cuba. Why does that not sound fair? Can I come with you?'

She pushes the sleeping bag under my bed, and hands me the pillow. She is smiling too brightly. Her eyes are full of worry. I can't understand her expression, at all.

'Of course,' I say listlessly. I don't mean it. I cannot wait for Yasmin to leave so I can get on with my new life.

'What are you writing?' She peers over my shoulder. 'Oh my, very organised. Now, how are we doing with everything else?'

I hate the way she says 'we'. Cuba is my project. It was my idea. Yasmin has, naturally, been helpful, but I don't want her muscling in on it. I wish she would leave.

'Well, I've got a ticket,' I tell her, flatly. 'That has to be a start.'

'And you'll come with me on the ten twenty to London and get your visa.'

'Yes. So that's it, really.'

'Clothes? Tell me, Mags, I bet you haven't even got a backpack, have you?'

'I have, actually.' I take out the black rucksack I bought for putative weekends that were to be spent walking in the clear Scottish air, Mark and I told ourselves and each other that healthy blasts of oxygen would keep our lazy lives in balance, and bought matching rucksacks. We only said it because all our friends were saying the same thing. We even mentioned sleeping in youth hostels. The idea of Mark in a dormitory bed makes me snort, even now. It was never going to happen.

Yasmin pulls my empty bag on to her back, and turns sideways to the mirror to inspect herself. 'Not bad,' she says, head on one side. 'And clearly never used. Well done, Mags. I thought I was going to have to point you in the direction of the YHA shop in Covent Garden.'

'You're familiar with London, still, then?' I ask. Yasmin talking about London can't be any worse than Yasmin telling me about Goa. I want her to start one of her monologues so I can switch off. David and Libby have left, and the only word I ever said to either of them was 'hello'. I am bereft, and I can't wait to get going, to catch them up. Everything else is irrelevant.

'Uh-huh,' she says. 'Ever so slightly. I went to uni there, didn't I? So I know most of it like the back of my hand.'

'That's just great.'

'You know, I'll probably end up back there, as soon as I get my shit together. I'd like to get a good job. If the travelling's out of my system. Not sure it is. But I think I might like to become, you know, a travel writer, or something. Or maybe present one of those holiday programmes. I really reckon I'd be good at that. Don't you reckon? Can't you see me doing it?'

'Yes, Yasmin, I can see you on TV.'

'Mmm. Me too. That doesn't sound big-headed, does it?'

'No,' I tell her, bored.

I remember the day Yasmin found she had a low offer from University College, London. It had been her first choice, because she was dying to live in the big city. Looking back on it, I think she had an idea that London, like LA, was somewhere you could go to become a star. I am certain that she imagined a model scout, or a casting director, stopping her in the street and promising her the cover of *Vogue*. Yasmin, at eighteen, could have pulled it off.

During the summer before we went to university, Yasmin hung around Norwich impatiently, working in the café at Cinema City, ostentatiously flicking through books from her course reading list, and failing to hide her desperation to move on with her life. She and I had promised to visit each other for weekends, even though I was probably going to Sheffield and would thus be hundreds of miles away from her. I knew I would be spending as much time as I could in London, anyway, because Ivan was going to the LSE. We thought the three of us could get together when I was down, and see London's sights.

It doesn't take much effort for me to recapture the feeling of that summer. I was optimistic. It was the last time I have ever been optimistic. I really thought it was going to be all right. I thought that Ivan and I could make a long-distance relationship work. Then I decided that I didn't want to risk it, and looked into going to university in London instead of Sheffield. I couldn't bear the idea of living so far from Ivan.

I had adored Ivan from afar for two years before we were introduced, at a house party in the Easter holidays before our A levels. He had curly black hair and rosy cheeks. He doubtless still has them, wherever he is. He played rugby. He was big and strong and kind, and he went to the local boys' school, the Cathedral School. My stomach would turn over whenever I saw him, and I never imagined that he would notice me. I never imagined that I would be able to speak to him.

Ivan lived with his mother. He was an only child whose father had died before he was born. When we met, properly, we fell into conversation astonishingly easily. In no time, he was telling me how guilty he felt about the prospect of leaving his mother on her own.

'She's going to be so lonely, Maggie,' he told me, looking at me with his big brown eyes.

I remember daring to reach for his hand. 'I know she is, but you can't stay in Norwich for ever to look after her.'

He looked miserable. 'You know, I should. I should go to UEA and be done with it.'

'Would your mum want that?'

He looked at me and smiled. 'Of course not. She's never wanted to hold me back. She's so proud that I've got a place at the LSE. The offer of a place,' he corrected himself. 'Mustn't make assumptions.'

'You see?' I told him. There was something about Ivan that brought me out of myself. I felt I could say anything to him. I couldn't believe that we were actually having a conversation. 'She wants you to go. Ivan, your mum must be so proud of you. Look at you. You're tall, dark and handsome. You're easy to talk to and you've got loads of friends, and you're going to one of the best universities in the country. In the world. You've got nothing to feel bad about.' I remember stopping, worried that I'd said too much.

I looked at him. He was smiling down at me. 'Thanks, Maggie,' he said. 'You're a star. Do you know that?'

To my amazement, Ivan and I fitted together perfectly. I felt as if I'd always known him, and he said he felt the same way. I've never experienced the thrill of getting to know another person since then, and I'm sure I never will, unless Libby and David turn out to be the soulmates I want them to be. Ivan was my only chance. We started going out for pints of lager at old pubs around the city, and seeing films, and riding our bikes out to the countryside. We had picnics. We went to each other's houses and I was polite to Ivan's mum, who didn't seem suspicious of me, as I had feared, after all. When Ivan held me in his muscular arms, I felt safe.

Towards the end of the summer, I started to tell him about Grace. He already knew that I'd had a sister who'd died, and he remembered the blanket coverage that had been carried by the local paper, so he knew the details. I was glad about that: I would have found it hard to talk about it, otherwise.

I remember us sitting together in the corner of a dark coffee shop, on a hot afternoon when everyone else was outside. We had been talking about Grace that day, and I suddenly felt myself able to say the words that I'd never been able to utter before.

'I really miss her,' I told him. As I said it, I crumbled. He held me.

'It's all right,' he said into my hair. 'It's okay, Maggie. It's good that you miss her. You have to talk about it. You're eighteen. You're strong. I'm here to look after you.'

My second choice of university had been King's College, London. Tentatively, I began suggesting that I might see if they would have me, instead of Sheffield.

'If I get the grades, that is,' I added, and watched Ivan nervously. We hadn't spoken about the immediate future; hadn't acknowledged the fact that, within six weeks, we would both be moving away, one to the north, the other to the south.

He squeezed my hand. 'Maggie, that would be amazing. I don't want you as far away as Sheffield. King's is just down the road from the LSE. Only if you want to, though.'

I could not imagine my life without him. He was looking after me, just like he said. I needed him. King's told me that as long as I got three Bs, I would be welcome. I began to look at Grace's photograph from time to time, to say her name to Mum and Dad and Emma.

On the day that our A-level results came out, we opened the envelopes together, in the park. My mother had shouted after me, as I snatched it from the doormat and ran to my bike. Ivan said his mother had tried to block the doorway, but he'd lifted her out of the way. We wanted to face the future together.

We sat on the grass. I opened mine first.

'An A and two Bs,' I said, delighted, and watched his face.

'Two As and a B! I can't believe it! Mags, my angel, we're going to London.'

I kissed him. I was in love. I couldn't believe that my life was looking as if it might turn out all right, after all.

That night, Yasmin had a party. It seemed as if every trendy eighteen-year-old in Norwich was there. We were all drunk, either celebrating or drowning sorrows. When Ivan and I arrived, the Shamen were playing loudly on the stereo and everyone was dancing badly and singing 'Es are good, Es are good, e's Ebenezer Goode,' and laughing at their own subversiveness. Yasmin was mixing a cocktail in the bath. We handed her two bottles of cheap red wine, and she opened both and tipped the contents into the mixture. Then she took two plastic cups, filled them with 'punch' and handed them to us. I noticed her winking at Ivan, but thought nothing of it at all.

There were people everywhere, smoking cigarettes and joints, at various stages of incapacitation at the hands of Yasmin's punch. I can picture her now, the star of any party she went to, and the queen of her own gathering. She was wearing a tiny denim miniskirt, with bare legs, white sandals, and a white boob tube. Her hair was loose down her back, and she was wearing little enough make-up to allow her clear complexion to shine through.

At one point, I lost Ivan in the crowd. I was talking to some girls from school, shouting above Take That to make them hear all about the romantic gesture I had made in changing universities to be near my boyfriend. We got into a discussion about long-distance relationships, and the fact that they rarely worked. I looked for him, wanting to bring him into the conversation, to show him off. He was nowhere around, but I didn't worry. The house was big, and crammed. I drank some more punch, talked to some random people, and, after a fourth cup, I ran out to the back garden to be sick. I stumbled down the back steps, and wished Ivan was with me to hold my hair back. I threw up copiously and inelegantly into a flower bed, splashing my hair, and my shoes. Then I sat down to recover, and wished I had a glass of water. I looked vaguely around the long garden, noticing that I was not the only person who had succumbed to the nausea. I could hear many of the party guests singing along with Right Said Fred inside the house. It sounded muffled and distant out here.

They were halfway down the lawn, leaning on the fence. They hadn't seen me. They were too wrapped up in each other to see anything. I didn't believe it could be them, at first. It must be Yasmin with someone else, I told myself. Someone else with curly black hair and long muscly legs.

There was a full moon, and it was a hot night, and my best friend was kissing my boyfriend.

I wanted to turn and run, but the punch forced me to walk over to them. I stood above them and looked down. I wanted to die.

After a few seconds, Yasmin pulled away from him and looked round.

'Oh,' she said. 'Hi.'

Ivan saw me and quickly looked away. 'Maggie,' he said. 'Shit. This wasn't planned, you know. It kind of just happened.'

'That's all right, then,' I said quietly, and walked away. Out of the house, out of Ivan's life, away from Kings' College, and as far as I could possibly get from my former best friend.

Ivan phoned me several times the next day. On the fourth call, at my mother's insistence, I agreed to speak to him. I desperately hoped he'd be able to say something that would make it all all right. I had lost my lover and my best friend, and I needed at least one of them back.

'I'm so sorry, Mags,' he said awkwardly. I had never heard him sounding like that before. 'Look, I feel terrible. I never wanted to be a bastard to you. You deserve more than that. You need to be cared for and looked after. You don't need someone like me buggering up your life.'

'Did you fancy her all along?' He didn't say anything. 'Be honest, Ivan,' I told him. 'Nothing to lose now, is there?'

'Okay. Well, of course I did. Everyone fancies Yasmin. I never thought she'd look twice at me. She was going out with a twenty-five-year-old, last I heard.'

'So you settled for me, instead? Second best?' I wasn't even angry. I couldn't believe I'd ever seen our relationship in any other light.

'Not second best, Mags. First best. You're too good for me. Way too good. Look, I'm not a very nice person. When she came on to me I was drunk and I just couldn't say no. Yasmin's not a very nice person either, is she, to come on to her best mate's bloke. Yasmin and I are suited to each other. You will meet someone far better, Mags, you really will. That's what you deserve.'

'I won't.' I knew I wouldn't, and I was right.

I went to Sheffield after all. I met Mark in the first term, and he seemed safe, so I stuck with him. I had never planned to speak to Yasmin again, until I saw her in Norwich. I made Emma ask around from time to time, and fill me in on what she was up to. I heard that they went to London together, as a couple. They were together for years. Then they split up. I don't know what happened. I was pleased when I heard, but not ecstatic, as I had expected. At least if they had been the loves of each other's lives, the betrayal would have been inevitable. It would have meant something. I would not have had my heart broken casually.

*   *   *

I start packing my backpack. I am ignoring Yasmin. Whenever I think of Ivan, I want to tear her hair out. She is fussing around, as if she is the only person who has ever left the country.

'You should make sure you get a money belt,' she tells me, nosing through my wardrobe. 'Bloody hell, you have the weirdest collection of clothes I've ever seen in my life. Are you taking this?' She holds up a pink satin bra.

I look at it. 'No. Yas, those are work clothes. I don't wear them for fun.'

'Right. Now, you haven't called your parents yet, have you? You need to tell them you're going. Do you want me to look Emma up when I get home, tell her what's going on?'

'If you like.'

'Give me her number, then. No, you're all right, I'll just copy it off this letter. Emma Austin. That is seriously odd. Emma Wilson and Jeremy Austin. You're going to miss the baby being born, aren't you? Tell you what, do your parents have email or anything? I can send them an email for you, let them know where you are.'

I shrug. 'If you want. I don't know what reply you'll get. Remember, the last my mum and dad heard of you was when you and Ivan got together.' I look at her, and see her looking back at me, surprised. 'You might not be the golden girl with them any more.'

'Maggie,' she says. 'I'm so sorry about that.' She kneels on the floor next to me. 'You're still upset about it, aren't you? Mags, I was a bitch. I was eighteen, but Christ, that's not an excuse. Look, Ivan and I split up a long, long time ago.'

I look away from her. 'That's fine. It's all fine. Water under the bridge.'

'Sure?'

'Sure.'

She puts an arm around my shoulder. I shake it off.

'Come on,' I say. 'We'd better get to the bus stop, if we're catching that train.'

I look at Yasmin. I can't decipher the expression on her face. If I didn't know her better – if I didn't know she was a self-ish bitch – I think I might wonder whether she was worried about me.

chapter nine

Libby – Havana

When Libby wakes up, she knows where she is instantly. She is more tired than she was even as a new mother, but she's not going back to sleep. It is light outside. Charlie whimpers in his travel cot. She struggles to shake away the heavy head of someone woken from a deep sleep long before they were ready. This is Havana. The air is hot with sweat. She is lying, naked and disgusting, on top of a green nylon sheet. The sheet is slippery and wet. David is grunting at her side. She can't touch him. They are both too hot. They've kicked off the top sheet in the night. Charlie has slept in a vest and nappy, with no covers.

Some light is coming through the wooden slats at the windows. It must be morning.

Libby props herself up on her elbows, and looks at David's watch on the table next to her. Quarter to seven. That's not a bad time to start the day. In fact, it's a good time to get Charlie's routine going, on Cuban time.

The baby is making little coughing noises. He is shifting around, and Libby knows he will break into a wail within the next few minutes. On the street outside the window, a heavy vehicle rumbles by. The windows shake.

How can she stay in bed when they are in Cuba? She is consumed with curiosity, with excitement. Even though she didn't want to come here, now that they have arrived, she wants to see where they are. The flight came in late last night, and neither she nor David was able to pay any attention to their surroundings. They found this flat through a friend of a colleague of David's who came to study here two years ago, and got him to help them book it. Libby had pictured it as exquisite. She thought there would be elegant doors on to a balcony, and that she would step outside and see the city spread before her. It would look, she had decided, a little like Florence. Havana would have turrets and balconies. She imagined herself, for some reason, as a Merchant-Ivory heroine. In her daydreams, she would mysteriously acquire a wardrobe of starched white nightdresses the moment she arrived, and she would recline on her large balcony, next to an orange tree in a terracotta pot, and observe everything.

Naturally, the reality is different. They staggered in at midnight to breeze-block walls and brown formica. Their landlord, Luis, was effusive in his greetings, but although Charlie had barely napped in the preceding twenty-four hours, he screamed furiously when they lowered him into his cot. Within minutes of Charlie's wailing commencing, another baby began to cry. Libby and David were amazed. The other baby sounded as if it was in the next room. They'd had no idea the soundproofing was so bad. A third infant joined in. Libby had pictured all the babies in Havana waking up, one by one. Everybody was awake, now. The city was echoing to the sound of high-pitched wails; and it was all Charlie's fault.

As soon as he dozed off, at half past one, Libby and David had stripped off their sweaty clothes and fallen on top of their lumpy double bed.

He has slept for five hours. Today she will make him stick to his routine, on Cuban time. This means that they must get up. Libby is possessed by excitement, and is suddenly convinced that she mustn't wake David. She wants to check out their surroundings first, by herself. Then she will report back to him. She will show him how adventurous she can be, and he will be proud of her. She's always enjoyed doing things first. She loves to feel she knows more than her companion, wherever she is. Her competitiveness, which has recently only applied to babies and developmental milestones, returns with a vengeance.

She gets up as quietly as she can, and picks Charlie up. Their bedroom is large – Charlie's cot is at the other end of it – and David barely stirs as she tiptoes out and closes the door gently behind her. Their suitcase is open in the open-plan living and dining room. She takes a clean pair of knickers and bra, and a large, forgiving cotton skirt and blouse, and gets dressed as best she can without putting the baby down. Then she sits on the stained brown sofa and breastfeeds him.

This flat displays a strange mixture of styles. She wonders whether these are the surroundings in which all Cubans live. All the floors are hard stone, and most of the walls aren't plastered. The decor has a definite Soviet flavour. There are a few plastic flowers gathering dust in jam jars, but otherwise, everything is functional. It is a far cry from her beautifully designed flat in Hove. No stripped floorboards here; no salvaged fireplace, no agonising over the exact shade of eggshell for the walls. This place is robust. There is something appealing about its earthiness.

There is also an element of beauty, Libby decides, as she squeezes her nipple to encourage Charlie to carry on sucking. From the sofa, she can see into the kitchen, which she didn't even look at last night. It is lined, from floor to ceiling, with rectangular white tiles. The window is high above the big white sink, and the sunlight falls on to the terracotta floor. She stares at her new kitchen for a while. It reminds her of the subtitled films that David sometimes gets out on video.

Charlie pulls his head away from her, and burps happily. They look at each other and smile. His curls are stuck to his head where he's been leaning against her breast. He is hot. Charlie was born in October. He has never been hot before.

Libby dresses him in a new vest, and slathers him with sun cream, to his dismay. She straps him into the baby backpack, runs her fingers through her hair, which is so damp that it feels as though it's full of styling gel, and picks up a key from the top of the dusty brown television. Then she opens the glass door, closes it as quietly as she can, and descends the stairs to the street. With a deep breath, she opens the front door.

'This is Havana,' she tells Charlie. 'We live here, now.'

There are holes in the pavement. Libby concentrates on avoiding them. She sees no one. Doors are closed, windows shuttered. The building opposite the flat looks like a warehouse. Everything seems tatty. There is no hint of colonial splendour, not here, not on San Miguel Street. She wonders why she had assumed that the city would be bustling at quarter past seven. On the occasions when she goes out early in Brighton, she savours the fact that no one is about. But Havana is hot, and in hot places, people are supposed to make the most of the cool times, and take a siesta over lunch. Perhaps it is not, after all, going to get that hot. Maybe the sticky night into which they arrived was an exception, or an illusion. The temperature is just right. Everything feels strange.

Libby walks down to the main road – Infanta – and tries to get her bearings. The baby backpack is digging into her shoulders, and she feels conspicuous and vulnerable. She knows she's not far from the sea, but she doesn't know where to find it. The university is somewhere around here. She wonders whether she's in danger. She is clearly a foreigner, and obviously lost. Charlie tugs on her hair, and she almost turns back to the flat. She would like to wake David, and try the outside world again later. The air is still. She can hear distant traffic, but nothing is happening in her particular corner of Havana. The city smells of old food, and dust, and the sun.

A car passes at top speed and rounds the corner without braking at all. The young man at the wheel takes no notice of her. She turns left, randomly, planning to go round the block and creep back into the flat.

They walk beneath a concrete colonnade. Libby's flip-flops make a brash noise on the concrete pavement. She uses her toes to try to keep them closer to her feet, to dull the sound, but it hurts her calf muscles and makes her feel more conspicuous than ever. A lone window is open, and as she passes, she notices that it's a drinks shop. A woman behind the counter calls out.

'Oh, que lindo!' she shouts, delighted. Libby realises it would be rude to indulge her instinct and ignore the woman. She walks to the window, and the woman leans across the counter and tries to reach Charlie with a knobbly brown finger. Libby leans over awkwardly to allow the woman to stroke him. Charlie doesn't make a sound, but when Libby looks round at him, she can tell from the shape of his cheek that he's smiling. The woman, who is older and thinner than Libby, addresses them both with a stream of Spanish.

It hadn't occurred to Libby until this moment that she is going to have to learn the language, too.

'Inglese?' she hazards, smiling apologetically.

'Ingles?' asks the woman, and resumes her monologue. She points to Charlie, and asks questions about him. Libby is mortified. She has come to this country, under sufferance admittedly, without any more than the haziest idea of how to say the most basic words.

'Five months,' Libby says, holding up five fingers.

'Cinque meses?' asks the woman. 'Si? Grande.'

They smile at each other. Libby nods, and decides there is nothing in the world she would like more than something to drink. She points to a glass, and raises her eyebrows.

The woman nods, delighted. After some bustling, Libby finds herself holding a yogurt drink. She drains it. It tastes of bananas and pineapple, and she hadn't realised that this was exactly what she was craving. She smiles her appreciation, and wonders how much to pay. A sign on the shutter reads: 'Refresco $1'. The drink was certainly refreshing, so that's probably what it means. She locates a dollar bill from her money belt, and leaves it on the counter. The woman looks amazed, and thanks her several times.

Libby finds the courage to utter the word 'Supermarket?' in her version of a Spanish accent, on a rising cadence. The woman points in the direction she was walking, but waggles her finger and shakes her head. From nowhere, a word pops up from holidays in Barcelona.

'Abierto?' Libby asks.

'No,' the woman says, and holds up eight fingers. Libby nods to thank her, and decides to continue around the block. She will go shopping at eight.

More and more people are out on the street. One moment it was deserted, and suddenly it is full. The sun is stronger on Libby's face, and she hopes it won't be too hot for Charlie. People are walking purposefully. Children walk in one direction, wearing uniforms. Adults mill around one section of the pavement, on a corner. Libby has to smile and push to get through the crowd. As she passes, a bus pulls up and, rather than piling on, they step on one at a time. There wasn't even a queue. She glances through the window of the bus. People are crammed aboard. She shudders at how hot and airless it must be. As she looks, she catches the eye of a middle-aged woman, who is pushed up against the window. The woman smiles at her and mouths a few words. Libby looks away, shyly. She walks past a big hotel, and sees tourists coming out and getting on to a shiny coach. Hotel Vedado. This is the area in which they now live: Vedado. Already, she feels a thrill of superiority. These people are on holiday. She, Libby, is living here.

'Hola,' says a young man sitting on the wall outside the hotel.

Libby looks at him. He is wearing a faded mauve T-shirt, and he is smiling. 'Hola,' she replies uncertainly.

'Taxi?' he asks, nodding encouragingly.

'No thanks,' she tells him, and walks on purposefully. She looks at her reflection in a parked car. Charlie's head has fallen forwards: he is asleep on her back, like a baby koala.

On the corner, she sees that she has reached a big road. She looks up and down it. Suddenly, now, there is a lot of traffic. Battered old cars, mopeds, and buses pass by. When she looks to the right, her heart leaps. She sees the sea.

But she can't reach it, because she can't cross the roads. There doesn't seem to be a crossing anywhere, and she's not taking her chances in the four lanes of traffic, not with Charlie on her back. She turns back, and down a random street. Everywhere she goes, people stop to admire her son. Nobody hassles her. It seems that a baby is an effective deterrent to potential suitors. The sun rises in the sky. The air begins to smell of old fruit and fumes and dust. She walks through back streets, away from the sea. She passes crumbling mansions. People sit out on balconies, and on doorsteps, to watch the world go by. They point Charlie out to each other, and ask about him in Spanish. After a while, she stops at an imposing set of steps. In the middle of them is a statue with the words 'Alma Mater' on its base. This, Libby decides, must be the university. This is where David will be studying.

Little boys walk alongside her until something diverts them. Children play baseball in the squares and the quiet back streets. She passes a beggar: a proud-looking middle-aged man in a tatty pinstriped suit, who has a hat out in front of him. She puts a dollar into it, self-consciously. The roads become busier. There are piles of rubble on the pavements at intervals, which can only have fallen from buildings. Libby is nervous crossing roads. The straps begin to tug on her back, and she is hungry. She can feel the sweat along her hairline. Looking at the watch of a passer-by, she realises they have been out for almost an hour.

On the way to the supermarket, Libby accidentally finds herself on their own road, outside the brown front door. The street is suddenly busy. A puddle of brown water by the kerb smells bitter and foul. An old woman smiles from the doorstep next door.

'Que lindo!' she says, looking at Charlie.

'Thanks,' Libby replies, forcing a smile. The woman will know what that means.

David is dressed. He is sitting at the table flicking through the guide book. Libby glows with new confidence, and with sweat. She can suddenly smell herself.

'Hey!' she says, happily, and swings Charlie down from her back. He is still asleep. She stands the backpack, carefully, on the floor before looking up at David. His face, she realises, is tight with anger. 'What's wrong?' she adds.

'Where the fuck have you been?' he demands. 'I was so worried. I wake up and you're not there. My baby isn't there. You've just gone. You pull that stunt in Brighton and it's one thing. You pull it here, and . . . I had no idea! We're in a strange city, a strange country, and you just bugger off. Anything could have happened.'

'But you knew I'd got up with him. I told you I was taking him out.' She is lying, but doing it convincingly. 'It's not my fault if you went back to sleep and forgot. I was trying to do something nice for you,' she says, emphatically. 'Letting you sleep in. I thought I'd do some shopping, get us some breakfast, but the shop doesn't open till eight, and I came back here when I was meant to be going there, by mistake. I was pretty much lost. We've been walking around for ages. David, it's absolutely amazing out there, it really is. You should see how much people love Charlie! It is all so, so foreign. But I like it. I think it's going to be fine. Honestly.' She is radiant. David watches her, and begins to relent. He had expected Libby to cower indoors, terrified of everything she didn't understand, and crying for the loss of Brighton. He never imagined his wife acting like this.

'Are you serious?' he asks. 'You like it?'

'It's a bit early to say, but still. Would you be so shocked?'

David puts his arms around her. 'Of course I'd be shocked! I've been terrified that you'd gone to the airport. I mean, look at this place. If I were to sit down and design an apartment that is, in every way, unacceptable for Libs, this would be it. There isn't a bath, the shower is a cold trickle, and we have no toaster, kettle, or normal oven, let alone a microwave. Just four rather crappy gas rings, and no matches. No copies of *Heat* magazine available, without a doubt, and no food in the shops, probably. And yet you appear to have had a wonderful outing. Did you take a lover or something? Wouldn't you rather be crammed into the Thameslink on your way to Blackfriars?'

'Not today, no. We agreed not to talk about that. It would make my head explode. And there was a taxi driver who gave me rather a charming smile, but we haven't actually consummated the relationship, as yet.'

He grins. At that moment, someone knocks on the door. Not on the front door that leads to the stairs, but on an internal door, in the kitchen. Libby vaguely remembers Luis disappearing that way, last night.

'Hola!' calls a voice. 'Hola, David?'

'Hola, Luis!' shouts David, pleased with his grasp of Spanish.

Luis opens the door, and bounds into the kitchen. Libby peers through the door. Beyond it is a little roof terrace, with a caged bird on it.

'Bienvenido!' he exclaims, and moves to kiss Libby on each cheek. She has to tear her eyes away from the terrace. She wonders if they're allowed to use it. Luis shakes David's hand warmly, then points at Charlie, who is still slumped, asleep, in the backpack. As Luis laughs, Charlie opens his eyes and succumbs to an enormous yawn. His face crumples, and Libby picks him up before the screaming begins.

'Hola, Sharlie,' says Luis, in a special baby voice. Charlie blinks, and smiles. 'Oye, oye,' Luis continues, and speaks to him in a stream of Spanish. Libby wishes she understood. She hands him over. He reaches immediately for Luis's glasses.

Luis has smile lines so strong that his face looks as if the creases have been ironed in. He's probably about thirty-five. He is tall and broad, and wears a cotton shirt untucked over light trousers. Everything about him seems foreign.

He shakes his finger, laughing, at Charlie. 'No, no, no, no, no,' he admonishes, and unpeels five little fingers from his specs.

Charlie giggles, and grabs them again. Luis returns him to Libby and says something she doesn't understand, but which she takes to mean that Charlie is a beautiful baby. She thanks him, in English, because she imagines that he understands 'thank you' as well as he would her rendition of *muchas gracias*. She resolves to make David go through each day's Spanish lesson with her, every evening.

David is oddly able to hold a mime conversation with Luis. The two of them understand each other fairly well, despite the almost total lack of a common language. Soon they are sitting on the stained brown sofa together, copying their passport details into Luis's book. Libby takes Charlie into the bedroom and they sit on the bed, together, and look down on to the street.

The sun is beating down, whitewashing everything. There are strong black shadows. Libby thinks, momentarily, of Brighton's shades of grey. In Havana, everything contrasts with the thing next to it. Things are bright or white or black. On the other side of the road, a man is meticulously polishing a metallic-pink Cadillac. His brow is furrowed in concentration, his skin leathery. Further along, a group of young men are lounging on a ledge, drinking from beer bottles that have been stripped of their labels. Two of them jump up, and seem to be arguing. The others watch and begin pointing as the discussion becomes more animated. For a moment Libby thinks they are going to come to blows, but then they laugh, and sit down. Girls slink down the street, their pert bodies encased in pink lycra. The eyes of the young men follow them. An old man with a huge grey moustache is sitting on a doorstep, staring out. His walking stick leans against the doorway.

Libby feels suddenly self-conscious, confronted by such an unfamiliar scene. She knows how foreign she is, here. She finds it hard to believe that she's spent all the morning, so far, walking around. She steps back from the window, even though no one's looking up. She tries to see herself, David and Charlie through Cuban eyes. A fat blondish woman, a man, and a fair baby. They are aliens. For the next six months, they are going to be horribly and inescapably conspicuous. Intruders. Capitalist intruders, at that. We have used our economic freedom to come here, she thinks suddenly. No one I can see from this window has one hundredth the privileges that we have taken for granted. We must appreciate our luck.

There is a burst of laughter from the other room. Somehow, David and Luis have managed to share a joke.

In the next flat, a baby cries. On the other side, a woman shrieks, 'Myleene!' This is Cuba. Having resisted it so vehemently, Libby finds she cannot wait to become a part of it.

chapter ten

Maggie

Dear Bob,

By the time this letter arrives, you will have noticed that I didn't come to work this evening. This is to let you know that I won't be coming tomorrow, either, or ever. When you read this, I will be in the Caribbean.

I thought it was only polite to let you know.

Yours,

Maggie

My legs are trembling as I hitch my bag up my shoulders, and step down from the coach. The ground beneath my feet is wet. It seems to be shifting. The rain is falling steadily and my hair is soon covered in tiny droplets. I don't care. I am scared. I am exhilarated.

I am leaving. This time tomorrow I will be in Cuba. I arrive on Sunday night, and on Monday morning I will be at the university, enrolling myself on David's Spanish course. He will have to speak to me, then. I am well on the way to becoming a family friend.

I have left Yasmin behind. Now that she's gone, I am convinced that she came back into my life, briefly, for a reason. She was there to encourage me to follow Libby and David to Cuba. She did not, naturally, know anything about them. But she helped me out, and

I hope I will never see her again. Yasmin is the only person who knows I've gone. I'm going to phone Emma, and Mum and Dad, with my Visa card, from Madrid.

I went to work last night, and I'm never going again. Whatever happens in Cuba, at least I am no longer a Vixen.

I check in, hoping the airline woman doesn't notice my ticket flapping in my shaking hand when I hold it out to her. My bag is half the allotted weight. I couldn't find much to pack. I left my flat exactly as it was, and gave Yasmin the keys. Half of that building is empty, now. I wouldn't be surprised if Yasmin moved in.

'Did you pack your bag yourself?' the woman asks, bored. 'Are you carrying anything for anyone else? Has your bag been with you since you packed it?' I provide all the expected answers, and try not to look guilty. She doesn't give me a second glance. I was half expecting to be told I couldn't possibly go to Cuba on my own, that I wasn't the kind of woman who was permitted to do anything impulsive or interesting. I thought I might be sent packing, back to the lap-dancing clubs of Brighton. Instead I proceed through passport control entirely smoothly.

I am too hyped to concentrate on anything, so I walk round and round the departure lounge. It smells slightly stale. I locate the loos and splash water on to my face. I am white, with purple half-moons under my eyes. I am painfully thin. I have no idea how much I weigh, but it's not much. I hold my wrist up and examine it. The bone juts out. My fingers are knobbly. My hair is tied back in a bushy ponytail. My cheeks are hollow. I look horrible. Perhaps I should have worn make-up after all.

I'll look better when I've got a Caribbean tan.

I am going to the Caribbean. I stare myself in the eye, and say it quietly. 'I am going to live in Cuba,' I say. The girl in the mirror looks baffled.

I am in the departure lounge. I think this means I am no longer officially in Great Britain. I am certainly not in Cuba yet. I'm in between. In between being a lap dancer and a student.

I can't wait to study again. I never appreciated it properly at the time, because I was too busy trying to fill the gap Ivan and Yasmin had left in my life. This time, I will pay attention, to every minute of every lesson. It will be a luxury. I will be the best Spanish speaker in the class. I will help David out, because he'll be concentrating on making Libby happy, since he forced her to go. I will make vocabulary lists and memorise them every day. My shaming job has bought this for me.

As I step out of the toilets, a man barges straight into me. He doesn't look up, let alone apologise.

'That's fine,' I say, loudly. 'Don't mind me.'

He looks over his shoulder. He is a respectable looking man, with silver hair. He's holding a briefcase, and wearing a good-quality coat.

'Oh, piss off,' he says.

For a moment, I want to run after him and take his head in a lock, and punch him repeatedly. I don't do it. I walk on.

I sniff loudly. This is not a good time to catch a cold. I am wearing a pair of black jeans that skulk around my hips, and a washed-out red T-shirt under Yasmin's denim jacket. She threw it at me when she saw the contents of my wardrobe.

'Please!' she said dismissively when I demurred. 'Just give it back when you've got something half decent to wear. I can't let you travel in this.' She was holding up my overcoat. When I saw it through her eyes, I realised the buttons were hanging off and the fabric was threadbare. It used to belong to Mark. I never gave much thought to my non-working wardrobe. I just wanted things that made me invisible.

The denim jacket swamps me, but it makes me feel a little bit funky. I try to hold my head up like Libby, to stride like Yasmin, to tilt my chin like Emma. None of those three women has any idea that the things they do naturally are the focus of my envy. Particularly not Libby. I try to look like the kind of person who flies to Havana on her own.

I walk manically around, checking the indicator boards every few minutes for my gate number. I look at toys in a tiny branch of Hamleys, and shake my head and smile when a twelve-year-old assistant asks whether I need any help. In Smith's I buy a couple of books and cram them into my rucksack. I glide up an escalator and decide to while away the time over a coffee, with one of my new books. Then change my mind and make the barman decant it into a takeaway cup. I continue walking round obsessively, unable to keep still. People mill around me. An elderly couple look up as I pass, and smile. They seem slightly lost here, too. I stop for a moment, and consider the seat next to them.

'You look excited, dear,' says the old woman as I pause beside them.

I look at her, and then wildly cast my gaze around the room.

'I am,' I say, forcing a smile.

'I suppose you're going somewhere wonderful?' She has her hands clasped on her lap, and although she looks ancient from a distance, close up I realise she's only about sixty. She's the same age as my mother. Mum looks older than she is, as well.

'There's a man involved, no doubt,' suggests her husband, laughing.

'Something like that,' I confess. 'I'm going to Cuba.'

They exchange delighted glances. 'Cuba, my dear?' she says. 'Well, you have the time of your life.'

'And you?' I ask, politely.

'Oh, we're off to Australia, to visit our daughter. We have five grandchildren out there. One of them we've never met. Little Annie-Rose. Five weeks old tomorrow.'

I wish them well, and wander on. The last thing I want to be doing is admiring someone's baby photos.

All the other travellers have purposeful expressions. Some are in suits, some are in holiday attire, and a group of lads are dressed in football shirts. Or rugby shirts, I'm not sure which. I am delighted to see a gang of men without having to fear that they'll see me naked later. Mothers shove dummies into their children's mouths and bribe them with sweets to keep quiet. The place buzzes with transience, with potential. People here are setting off towards places I have probably not even heard of. I wonder how many, if any, are going to Cuba.

The journey passes uneventfully. As we take off, I am briefly breathless at the realisation that I have left everything behind. I have left my job. I have left Brighton, and Yasmin. I have left it all. I am free.

Then the fear sets in. It's a long flight, with a couple of hours' break in Madrid, and I exercise mind control to stop myself going wild with terror.

'I'm in Madrid,' I tell Emma, when we stop.

'You what?' she asks.

'I'm not staying long.'

'Good!'

'Because my next flight leaves in an hour. I'm off to Cuba, Ems. I'm going to be away for months.'

She doesn't say anything. Yasmin clearly hasn't called her, yet. Emma is upset that I'll be away when her baby's born. I feel bad, for a moment. Then I stop. I have to follow my instincts. Emma wouldn't want me to carry on stripping, just so I can see her baby.

'Mum?' The next call is better.

'Darling? How are you? Wait, I'll call you back. Are you at home?'

'No, Mum. I'm in Madrid.'

'Oh, how utterly gorgeous! What are you doing there?'

'Changing planes. The next one goes to Havana.'

'Maggie! I am so pleased you're doing something so exciting! Well done, darling, and have a marvellous time.'

She sounds brave but I know she's worried. 'I'll be fine,' I tell her, uncertainly.

'I know you will. What did Amex say?'

I have to think for a moment. 'Oh,' I tell her, casually, 'they were fine. It's kind of a sabbatical.' Inspiration strikes. 'I'm doing a Spanish course,' I explain. 'They wanted me to learn Spanish, so I can perhaps work in their Madrid office.'

On the second plane, I blank myself out. Maggie is not here. The girl who has temporarily taken her place drinks more than is advisable, and gets a headache. She eats all the food without complaint, and rebuffs an attempt at conversation from her neighbour. Maggie retreats inside herself, and she thinks of nothing at all. I stare at a film, but could not recount even the basic premise of the plot as the closing credits roll. I read the in-flight magazine, but words are just shapes on a page. I look, but see nothing. I imagine that I'm going to Australia to visit Annie-Rose. I think about the rude man, but can't even get worked up about him. I am completely numb.

I'm going to see David and Libby. It seems impossible that they are already there. They are waiting for our friendship to begin. They just don't know it yet. I convince myself that David and Libby do not even exist, that I am suffering from an almighty delusion.

The hours pass, and a voice comes over the tannoy to announce the imminent descent into Havana. It speaks in Spanish, first, but when I hear the city's name I know what they're saying, and I fold up my tray table obediently. I find my shoes, and look around, noticing my fellow passengers for the first time. The plane is packed with young Europeans holding guidebooks. I am not, it seems, doing anything exceptional, after all. Across the aisle, a young man with cropped hair like Mark's is reading a small blue Spanish phrase book. For a second my heart leaps as I try to force this man into Mark's body, but I know all along that it isn't him, that if my former boyfriend was sitting next to me, I would have noticed, and so would he. He feels me staring at him, and looks round with a smile. I flush what must be a deep crimson, and look away. When I look back, he has turned back to his book. He had a nice face. I should have let him speak to me.

I knew it was going to be hot. I knew it, and yet I hadn't prepared myself. I didn't allow myself to imagine the end of this journey. I descend the steps on to the tarmac, jostling with the other passengers, and wonder what to do with Yasmin's jacket. I won't need it, for all the time I'm here. I wish I wasn't wearing it now. It is my sole fashionable item, and it is redundant. I am already beginning to sweat.

Most people are chattering in Spanish. I am foreign, now. Havana airport is small, and my sense of panic grows as I realise that, within minutes, I will be out of it, and into a huge, unknown city. An immigration official scrutinises my passport, welcomes me to Cuba and wishes me a good stay in his country. Unseen baggage handlers deliver my suitcase to the carousel. Customs officers wave me through. I look at the crowd of people gathered at arrivals, and scan the name boards as if there was any chance whatsoever of anybody being here to meet me. I am not trying to fool myself that David and Libby might be here – I strongly doubt they are in Cuba at all – but, rather, am trying to look self-assured and not lost. I hesitate, to buy myself time.

'Taxi?' asks a middle-aged man with a greying moustache.

I look at him. He looks all right. 'Taxi,' I confirm, with a little smile.

I keep my nose to the window all the way. Everything is foreign, from the trees to the rickety cars. My accommodation, chosen at random from the guidebook, is a *casa particular*. I will be staying at someone's house, because it's cheaper than a hotel. Yasmin selected one for me, on the grounds that it was billed as having a 'stunning view', and was run by a woman. It is in the middle of Old Havana. The journey from the airport takes me along wide roads with relatively little traffic. Painted billboards give what I imagine to be improving messages about saving water, and the fact that children are the future. Then we edge into town. Soon, I am gazing out of the taxi at a scene that looks as if it hasn't ever changed. The buildings are crumbling in a charming, Caribbean manner. Creepers grow up them. The street is narrow. Children are playing, and older people are gossiping, or doing nothing. The taxi edges along, honking its horn. The inside of the car is stiflingly hot. I have the window closed in case anyone reaches in to steal my bag. The denim coat is rolled up next to me. I peer nervously at everything we pass.

The driver, who has attempted to talk a couple of times before realising the extent of my lack of Spanish, stops entirely, and indicates a doorway with a flourish. He stops the meter on $25, and I pay him from the money belt I bought especially for the trip. He retrieves my backpack from the boot, and drives off with a cheerful wave.

I stand out horribly. People are watching me. I need to get in before I am robbed. I hitch my pack on to both shoulders, and march through the doorway, looking neither right, left, nor up. I hear a few calls of 'Hola!' but resolutely ignore them. The hallway smells of stale urine, and has a concrete floor. This is not the Cuba I imagined, but I suppose it is the way one ought to imagine a communist society. A juddery lift takes me to the fourth floor. I locate an apartment with a notice reading 'Elena – Rentahouse!' and bang on the door. I haven't booked. If she doesn't have a place for me, I will cry. I need my own little room. I need to sit somewhere for a couple of hours and shut it all out. I need a shower. I need to go home. I wish I was in Norwich. I might even prefer to be in Brighton.

An hour later, I am leaning on my windowsill, staring at the city. Elena – large, welcoming, and without a word of English – has overwhelmed me with concern for my happiness. She fussed around me, gave me coffee and fruit, offered an omelette. She showed me into her best room, which has everything I need. The double bed is covered in a fluffy red eiderdown. The walls are pale pink, and are hung with watercolours of dogs sitting amongst flowers. There are drawers and hangers for my clothes. I share a bathroom with whoever stays in the other bedroom, which is currently unoccupied. This room already feels like my home.

Yasmin was right to pick this place out for me on the grounds of its view. Darkness is falling, and lights are beginning to go on. I can sit on my bed, and see Havana spread out before me. It is a strange mass of imposing rubble. Elena pointed out the landmarks to me. 'Capitolio,' she said, gesturing towards a smaller version of Washington's Capitol. 'Hotel Sevilla. Estacion de ferrocarriles.' I let it all wash over me. What interests me are the flat roofs, with people hanging out washing on them. I watched two young men practising some form of martial art, until ten minutes ago. A girl, or perhaps a tiny woman, is dancing, now. She is twirling and jumping above the city. I am exhilarated just watching her. I can dance, too.

I slump down, supporting my head on the windowsill with my hands. I have, it seems, arrived in Cuba. Tomorrow I must find the university, and meet my friends, officially, for the first time.

chapter eleven

Libby

Libby lies on top of the slippery sheet, and looks up and back at the window. Whoever wrote the book that told David it was going to be twenty-seven degrees was lying. Every single day, the sun pours through the wooden window slats on to their bed, and every day, she looks at the sunshine and feels happy. Then she sighs as she remembers what it means. Today is Monday. It is the first day of David's university career. Her first day back as a housewife, a stay-at-home mother. She had hoped for clouds and drizzle today. Naturally, it is sunnier than yesterday.

She and David get up. David looks terrified.

'How about if you went, for me?' he suggests, as he tries to decide what to wear. 'You know you'd enjoy it more than me. I'd be happy enough hanging out here with the lad.'

'I know. But no one would employ me to run a Madrid office.'

'They might.'

'Do you reckon?'

Libby watches David padding around in his underpants, and feels nervous on his behalf. She looks at the shape of his legs, at his brown hair flopping over his face. She feels, suddenly, that he is her child, too. Sometimes she adores being maternal. The rest of the time she wants someone to mother her, to father her.

'You look lovely,' she tells him. He looks at her and laughs.

'You think so?' He twirls round. 'Shall I go like this?'

'You'll stun them. You know what kind of people do language courses? People who want sex, is who.' She is overcome with jealousy. 'You watch out, husband. All right?'

David chuckles. 'You're very paranoid this morning.'

'Someone has to keep an eye on you. You have no idea how irresistible you are, to the opposite sex.'

David looks at her and shakes his head. 'What are you going to make me wear, then? How about this?' He takes Libby's long Monsoon dress and holds it up against himself. Depressingly, it would actually fit him. 'That should keep the screaming hordes at bay.'

Libby thinks about it. She wants David to look good, but not to look as if he's available. She knows her husband too well. He is naïve about women. Because it would never occur to him to be unfaithful to her, he feels free to flirt meaninglessly. He has no idea how attractive he is; no clue that he embodies the Western woman's ideal man. He could get himself into trouble. Libby pictures a classroom full of skinny girls in their late teens sucking meaningfully on the end of their pencils and gazing at her husband with huge sincere eyes.

'Wear what you like,' she tells him. 'Wear your wedding ring. Just you remember to tell everyone you're married, with a son.'

She dreads David leaving the flat. He will, she knows, be gone all morning.

'If it was just a little bit cooler,' she says wistfully, as she mashes her son's morning banana, 'Charlie and I would have such a wonderful time. We could get him a buggy and I could push him all over Havana. I'd lose weight, he'd get to meet half his fan club, and we wouldn't be stuck in this fucking flat all morning. Hon, when you're at uni, I am going to be bored out of my tiny mind.' She pulls her hair in absent-minded frustration. 'Today. This is the day when you go to uni and I begin to fester. For months on end. I thought it was bad in Brighton.'

'You're losing weight anyway,' David tells her, while pouring them each a bowl of cereal which, though called P'tit Bonjours, seems to be a clone of Rice Krispies. He knows it's going to be difficult. After pushing so hard for this trip, he is now the one secretly wondering why they are here. Libby is getting into the swing of it. She can talk to anyone. David is awkward. He sees the boys who hang out on their street, and he doesn't know how to conduct himself. Is it patronising if he says 'hola'? Are they laughing at his clothes and his pallor? Do they hate him because his country is allied with America, the cause of all their problems? Or are they curious? Perhaps when he feels more settled, when he speaks some serviceable Spanish, he will try to strike up a conversation. The worst that can happen is that they'll laugh at him, or steal his wallet.

Two weeks ago, David reflects, he was a management consultant. He wasn't the most successful one in London, as is evidenced by the fact that he was deemed disposable enough to be here in Havana, on a Monday morning, rather than enduring the morning commute. He has lived within the confines of a respectable job since he left university, nearly ten years ago.

'What do you do?' people would say.

'I'm a management consultant,' he would reply, and nobody from outside his professional world would know how to respond.

This morning, he is going back to the classroom. He will be a student again. The very idea scares him rigid. But at least people know what it means when you tell them you're a student.

'Are you okay, then?' asks Libby, trying to look cheerful as she hands him Charlie for a goodbye kiss.

'Course, I'm fine,' says the head of the household, firmly.

Libby is wishing she could go instead. David is wishing she could go instead. They each know what the other is thinking, and decide not to mention it again, because it is impossible.

'Got your satchel?' says his wife. 'Pencil case? Bring friends back for tea, if you like.'

David frowns. 'You're taking the piss.'

'Mmm. Only a little bit. You really do have to bring some people home with you. Girls, boys, men, women, from any country in the world. I'll communicate in mime if I have to. You are my link to the world outside this flat. You have to get me a social life. Even if it does involve girls who adore you. I'll sort them out. It is your marital duty. It's essential for your wife's sanity.'

When the glass door slams behind her husband, Libby sits down on the brown sofa, and sighs. There is noise all around her. Something is crashing around in the alley at the back of the flat. There's banging from the warehouse opposite. She hears raised voices from somewhere in an adjoining building. She listens to a neighbour bellowing '*Myleene!*' and wonders how the name is spelt.

'It's very noisy,' she tells Charlie, who is podgy and pink clad in just his nappy. She wonders how many people can hear her speaking. 'But lonely, too.' She feels self-conscious, and talks quietly.

Charlie doesn't say anything, but he looks as if he understands.

'Let's do some sitting practice,' she decides. She arranges him into a sitting position on a blanket on the floor, and lets go. He holds the pose for several seconds before toppling over and lying on his back, looking up at her reproachfully.

Libby thinks tender thoughts of David all morning. She knows he is anxious about his classes, and tries to imagine him getting to grips with basic Spanish grammar. She can't wait until he comes back, and tells her all about it. She can't wait to learn what he's learnt. She checks the time frequently.

She wanders around the flat, looking for anything that might entertain her or her son. What, she wonders, will it be like for Charlie to grow up in a conventional family? She often asks David, trying to absorb some essence of what it is to be secure and wanted. She can listen to his baffled replies to her questions, but she cannot understand what he says. Her own childhood was, she suddenly realises, miserable. She has never confronted the misery head-on before. Here, lonely in a strange place, with a child of her own, she abruptly sees herself differently.

'Of course it wasn't my fault,' she tells Charlie, no longer caring who hears her. 'I was a child.' Nothing she or David did could ever be Charlie's fault, and yet she has always held herself responsible for her father's behaviour. She remembers herself at the age of five: small, blonde and eager to please. One day her father left. He didn't tell her he was going: he just vanished. She has no recollection of her mother's reaction. She was too caught up in her own confusion to think about her mother. She recalls her mum telling her that Daddy had gone away. After a while, when his letters stopped, Libby thought he had died. That was what she used to tell people. Her mother heard her say it to one of her friends, one day, and was horrified.

'He didn't die,' she said forcefully. 'He left, that was all. He didn't want to live with us any more.' This had been news to Libby.

He sent her a birthday card on her sixth birthday. It didn't say much, but she still has it.

'Dear little Liberty,' it said. 'With best wishes for a happy birthday. Missing you, my sweet girl. Love from Daddy.' There was no address on it, so she couldn't write back. Then she got a Christmas card, and after that there was nothing.

He was never replaced, either. One afternoon she went home with a girl from her class, Helen, and discovered that some people had stepfathers. Helen's stepdad, Alan, was kind and friendly. He was just like a real dad. Alan made them drinks and gave them biscuits, and asked if they wanted him to listen to the cricket on the radio instead of watching the telly. Libby went home that afternoon and requested a new dad.

'I wish,' was all her mother said.

Although there was a succession of possible replacements, none of them stayed around very long, and Petra made sure none of them got close enough to Libby for her to mind when they weren't there any more. Nobody came close to acceptability. Libby was always pleased when they went. From as early as she can remember, she struggled with jealousy. She hated it when her mother brought a new man in. Whenever she was left with a babysitter, she would dread waking up in the morning and finding a stranger in her mother's bed. She stopped padding into her mother's room in the mornings, and climbing into her warm bed, just in case. The men always gave her exactly the same look – initial distaste, followed by feigned pleasure at meeting her – and she hated them. Her mother has never had any taste in men. Libby is glad her mother never married any of them. It was just the two of them, for as long as she can remember.

She is determined that Charlie will never have to experience what she went through. She picks him up and cuddles him. The back of his hair is sweaty. He is soft and hot.

On impulse, she knocks on the kitchen door, wondering whether Luis will be able to hear it across his roof terrace. She waits, and knocks again. After a few minutes, she hears footsteps approaching, and someone unlocks the heavy wooden door.

'Hola, Luis,' she says, smiling. Charlie quivers with excitement, and beams. Luis is holding a baby, completely naturally, as if he does it every day. Libby had no idea he was a father. It is a dark-haired, placid-looking child, a little smaller than Charlie. Charlie immediately reaches out and takes the baby's hand. Luis and Libby look at each other and laugh.

'Gracia,' Luis says, indicating the child. 'Me, sister, baby.'

'Si? In apartment, you? Habito, con you?'

'Si si, aqui.' He indicates his own flat.

'You et sister, habito aqui?'

'Y sister marido.'

Luis makes a lovely uncle. Libby bends down to talk to the child. 'Hola, Gracia,' she says. 'Aqui, Charlie. Charlie, say *hola*.'

Charlie is entranced by the child. He reaches out for her hair. Gracia smiles back at him. Libby offers Luis a cup of coffee, and is slightly relieved when he says he has to go. She's not sure where it is he's going, but it seems important. She believes that, as he's going, he says his sister will come to see her. She hopes she will.

'Got a girlfriend, darling,' she tells Charlie when the door is shut and locked. 'Well done, mister. Charlie and Gracia. We approve.'

Libby makes herself some coffee, and daydreams about waking up to the sound of light rain, washing away all the dust and soaking the washing that hangs from balconies. She feels confident that she'd be able to walk around Havana all day, finding new places, little bars and cafés, and talking to everyone who wanted to look at Charlie. She'd probably learn Spanish quicker than David, that way. The funny thing is, before she was a mother, she would have been terrified at the idea of talking to strangers.

She used to be uptight. She never bothered to talk to anyone unless she judged them worthy of her attention. This restricted her social intercourse to anyone better dressed than her, and anybody with an interesting job. She sat on the train to Blackfriars every morning, reading her book or her newspaper, and she made eye contact with no one. At work she ignored the work-experience people and most of the secretarial staff. She wouldn't have dreamed of talking to anyone she didn't know, of chatting to another woman at the coffee stall on the station, or of seeking out someone new to the office, to befriend and encourage them. When she got pregnant she closed herself off more than ever. Her priority was suddenly to get through the day. She was exhausted, and sick, and was apt to snap at people, and to fall asleep at her desk.

Then her bump became visible, and strange women thought they had the right to march up and ask about her womb.

It affronted her for the rest of her pregnancy. It started at twenty-five weeks, when a woman suddenly sidled up to her on the platform and asked her, out of the blue, when it was due. 'October,' she said briskly, and looked in the other direction.

'I've got a seven-month-old,' the woman confided. Libby wanted to push her away. She did not care. If she'd encouraged the woman at all, she would have been talking about labour and breastfeeding.

These conversations made her sick. A week before her due date, she was at the shops in George Street, in Hove, when an old woman fell into step beside her.

'That's a girl you're having there, is it?' she asked, smiling.

Libby glared. 'I don't know.' She couldn't shake the woman off, because she couldn't walk any faster.

'Oh, it's a girl,' said the woman. 'A pretty little girl with fair hair.'

'Right.'

'You're carrying it like a girl, you see.'

Libby turned to her. 'That's because I *am* a girl,' she snapped, and walked into the Sussex Stationers, where she was disgusted to find herself crying. She hated people interfering like that. She hated the fact that this woman had been looking at her body. It was none of her business.

Everything changed after Charlie was born. Without noticing what had happened, she immediately became the kind of woman who walks up to other mothers in Boots or Mothercare, and asks how old their baby is, whether it has a routine and how it sleeps at night. Sometimes she swapped numbers with women she met in this way, and met up with them another day for coffee and baby talk. She has even been known to strike up conversations with pregnant women, but has been careful only to do that if they make eye contact with her first, or if they look at Charlie.

She tries to imagine the old Libby in Cuba. It would not have worked. The woman she used to be would have taken one look at the flat and booked a suite at one of the smart hotels. She would have stalked around noticing the dirt on everything, and she would have rebuffed all attempts at conversation on the grounds that anyone who tried to speak to her must have wanted her money. For the first time, she considers that motherhood might not have marked the end of her life as an independent human being. Rather than making her a conspicuous failure, she wonders whether it could, in fact, have made her nicer.

She knows, however, that it is also making her want her father. Other people's parents get divorced; but she is the only person she knows who has been abandoned completely by one of them. She has always wanted her dad to track her down, but she now sees that he is not going to do it. She doesn't want to look for him. She wants him to look for her. Hot tears rise to her eyes. She mustn't be weak. But he owes it to her.

Libby lies Charlie on a folded blanket, where he rolls onto his front, pauses, and then carries on over, to his back. He has never executed a full roll before, and she applauds him enthusiastically. 'Yay!' she calls. 'Charlie! Go Charlie!' She wonders how many neighbours can hear her.

While he has his morning nap, Libby writes a few postcards. She does one for her mother, reassuring her that they are a lot more than fine, then one for Natalie and one to Jen. After that she is at a loss. She won't be sending one to her father. David can do his own family's cards. She might do a few to the old colleagues who came to their leaving party. That was the first time she's seen them since Charlie was born. There was an impeccably tasteful bouquet of pale blue tulips straight after the birth, and then silence.

Her mind goes back to Natalie and her vile husband. She wishes she knew the scarlet woman, the uninvited guest at her own party. That tall skinny Barbie woman was definitely no friend of theirs. She is not a neighbour. She came from nowhere, had sex with Graham, and disappeared to nowhere. Libby feels personally responsible for what happened, and she isn't even there to comfort her friend. Natalie was devastated when she spoke to her before they left. She was in pieces. She felt humiliated, and didn't know what to do. Natalie should be here, with her.

She takes another postcard, a view of the Capitolio by night, and addresses it to Nat, as well.

'Another thought, following on from the other card,' she writes, as small as she can. 'Come out here! Book a flight on Graham's credit card, bring Alfie. We'll find you somewhere to stay. All my preconceptions of Cuba as shitty scary place were wrong. It is superb. You'll love it too. You know you deserve a break. Would love to have you – can explore together. Take your mind off all bad things. Believe me, you will feel a million times better. What's stopping you? Much love, Lib xxx PS Please come and play, Alfie mate, love Charlie x'

'Myleene!' shouts the neighbour. For once there is a faint answer.

'Si?' calls Myleene.

Libby adds the postcard to the pile. She doesn't care if Graham reads it.

By the time she hears the downstairs door bang, she is ready to climb the walls. David's class finished at half past twelve, and from midday onwards she has checked her watch twice a minute. Four more days like this until the weekend.

She picks Charlie up from the sofa, and stands at the top of the stairs.

'You're home!' she yells, and listens as her voice echoes down the stone stairway. 'Save me from certain madness!'

'Hi, honey!' calls David, and she is overwhelmed with relief at his familiar voice. She hears his footsteps on the concrete stairs. 'I've brought a friend back, just like you said.'

'You didn't! Well done.' She stands back, suddenly self-conscious, and waits for them to come up.

David arrives at the top of the stairs, and gives her a big kiss. She kisses him back, trying to look over his shoulder at his fellow student. She sees a girl, a tiny wiry little thing with masses of wild hair. Typical of David to have befriended one of the little girls who come to Cuba to be swept off their feet. David has no sense for nuances at all, and Libby loves him for it.

'Hi,' she says, giving the baby to David and holding out her hand. 'Nice to meet you. I'm Libby.'

She looks expectantly at the girl, and frowns, puzzled. This girl isn't eighteen. She is an adult; and Libby knows her from Brighton.

'Hello,' says the woman, with a quick, nervous smile. 'I'm Maggie.'

'Lib,' says David, triumphantly, 'Maggie's on the beginners' course with me. Guess where she's from.'

Libby looks at her. 'Hove. I recognise you. Do you live on our street? You live downstairs, don't you?'

David looks disappointed. 'How did you know that?' he asks. 'I didn't. Don't you think it's the funniest coincidence?'

Libby has seen Maggie coming and going, probably said a cursory hello in passing. She remembers that sometimes, when she's awake with Charlie, she hears doors banging in the middle of the night. Maggie clearly has a social life. She is also extremely thin. She looks like she's on drugs. Her body could be astounding, like the Cuban women's bodies, but she's dressed in droopy backpackers' clothing, and her hair is a wild mess. Libby itches to give her a makeover. She is, nonetheless, intimidated by her. She is skinny, after all, and single, and she has had the courage to leave everything behind and come here on her own. Libby feels she'd better keep an eye on her.

'What are you doing here, though?' she asks, confused. 'How come you came, too?'

Maggie smiles brightly. 'Looks like it's one of those bizarre things, doesn't it? I mean, it's like David and I were saying. I don't even know you two. Our paths haven't ever crossed in Brighton, have they, but here we are, in Havana. I've always wanted to travel, and to speak Spanish. I mean, it's the best language in the world, isn't it, after English. For talking to the most people. Apart from Mandarin or something I expect but that wouldn't be so practical. And it sounds like you guys have had the same kind of idea.'

'Mmm,' Libby agrees. She sees that Maggie is extraordinarily nervous. 'I'd always wanted to travel, too. So what brought you to the Universidad de la Habana?' She hopes Maggie realises she's being ironic in calling it by its Spanish name.

'Oh, Cuba sounded so inviting. I was fascinated by it – as a communist state ninety miles off the coast of Florida. And I wanted to come before Castro died.'

David nods emphatically. 'Us too.'

Libby is still confused. 'I guess it's a very popular way to get to know a country – doing a language course? And I suppose Havana is an obvious place to come. How unbelievably unlikely. But welcome. David, did you bring lunch?'

He nods. 'Pizzas all round. For the adults.'

Libby smiles at Maggie. 'Carrot purée for the younger generation. Could make an interesting pizza topping, if you'd like some.'

Maggie smiles and strokes Charlie's hair. Libby notices her hand shaking, and wonders if drugs are to blame. 'No thanks,' Maggie says. 'I wouldn't like to deprive this young man.'

Libby looks at Maggie as they sit down, and notices Maggie quickly looking away. Libby cannot absorb the fact that their downstairs neighbour is doing David's course. It must be coincidence: there is no other explanation. 'I don't know where to start,' she says. 'How was the morning's lesson?'

Maggie is slightly too animated. 'You know, it was great. I was a bit scared because I don't speak any language except GCSE French, which I've kept up because my parents live there, but they really do start you from scratch. We had to do a test to see how good we were.'

'Or how crap,' adds David, 'as the case may be,' and they both laugh.

'One of the questions,' Maggie explains, 'was writing a hundred and fifty words about ourselves, in Spanish. It was all I could do to work out what they were asking.'

'I used the dictionary to write down some words roughly approximating "I cannot do this. No parlo espagnol",' David says. 'Then I remember, too late, that parlo isn't a word. It's hablo. What a dick. And the room was full of these intimidating, clever types, scribbling away. You know, serious people, with little round glasses.'

'We were obviously as bad as each other,' says Maggie, nibbling on the edge of her pizza. 'How old is Charlie? He's gorgeous.'

'Five and a half months,' Libby tells her.

'And it's okay bringing him out here? How was the flight? I was thinking when I was on the plane, how difficult it would be travelling with children.'

'I think the flight was like labour,' says Libby lightly. 'One of those things you forget as soon as it's over. I could quite easily sit here now and tell you the flight was fine, and labour wasn't that bad either. But no, it was tough. Everyone gave us a wide berth. I've never felt, when I've got on a plane before, that everyone is looking at me and sending me "don't sit next to me" signals. But we got here, and we've all adapted to the time difference. The climate's a different matter.' She tails off, disliking her whiny voice. Libby wants to tell Maggie that she is more than a wife and mother, but she would feel boastful abruptly informing her that 'I am a highly competent solicitor'. Maggie must look on her as a dull housewife. She probably used to see her hauling the pushchair up the front steps at home and pitied her dreary life.

It is definitely time for a change of subject.

'So,' Libby says brightly, 'why now? What have you left in Brighton?'

Maggie smiles tightly. 'I've never travelled like this, alone, before,' she says slowly. She appears to Libby to be choosing her words carefully. 'I wanted to get away from my life back there. I'd split up with someone, and my job was boring, and I felt I needed to shake myself up a bit. It was a bit of a leap in the dark, to be honest. I had to do something or I'd have gone mad. You know when – well, you probably don't – but when you suddenly feel you have to run away?'

'And has it worked?'

Maggie smiles. There is a lot lurking, unsaid, behind that smile. 'I think Havana's a brilliant city,' she says blankly. 'It's, well, it's great. There's so much going on. I have this amazing view from my bedroom window, and I love watching it all. I'm very aware of safety as a single woman, and I've only been here a day so I haven't got much to go on, yet. David said you've been here since Thursday?'

Libby is disconcerted by the way Maggie is staring at her.

'Wednesday night,' she says. 'I didn't really know what to expect, but it is so much more fabulous than I imagined. I love it. I love it apart from the fact that we have to stay indoors all bloody day long, because of the sun. When we do go out, it's gorgeous. People are so wonderful to Charlie. I really don't think you need to be paranoid about safety, you know.'

'That's good.' Maggie has been looking into Libby's eyes for ages. Libby is slightly unnerved. Maggie seems to realise, and looks away. 'Hey,' she says, 'this flat is all right, isn't it?'

David grins. 'It's not exactly up to the standards of Sixth Avenue, Hove, but yes, I think we'll be fine here. It's a little odd to be sharing a bedroom with the lad again.' He turns to Libby. 'Maggie's living in a *casa particular*, in the old town.'

Maggie nods. 'Like I said, the view's the selling point. The landlady's great, too, but it's a bit expensive. And far from the uni. I might move.'

Libby is pleased to note that Maggie doesn't fancy David much. She has hardly looked at him. She seems extremely intense. The only facet of her that threatens Libby is her body. She can't take her eyes off those upper arms. They actually go in, between her shoulder and her elbow. Her legs are obviously matchsticks beneath those horrible baggy trousers. Her cheekbones cast black shadows across her face. She has no fat on her body. She has every reason to be supremely confident, and yet she looks terrified. She doesn't know that she is gorgeous. The Western world must have ten women like Libby, struggling to shed the dough from their thighs, to every Maggie. If she was taller, she could be a model.

Libby pushes half her pizza across the table to David, even though she's starving.

'I can't eat anything in this heat,' she mutters weakly, and takes Charlie on to her lap. 'Come on, darling, let's get your carrots out.'

Maggie looks up. 'Does he always have carrots?'

'Today he's having carrot purée for lunch, and carrot purée for dinner.'

'Whereas yesterday,' says David, 'he had carrot purée.'

'And the day before,' Libby continues, 'it was carrot purée. He has a fairly wide vegetable repertoire at home, but of all the things he eats, we can only find carrots here. I might try green beans tomorrow, but they look a bit stringy.'

As she walks to the kitchen, she feels Maggie watching her. Libby turns round, catches her eye, and smiles. Maggie grins back, with genuine warmth. 'It's nice that there's another woman here,' Libby tells her, impulsively. This is no time to be fussy about who she's friends with. She needs to break down Maggie's defensiveness. 'I was hoping there'd be someone for me to talk to. Luis next door lives with his sister, I have just discovered, and he's friendly enough and I'm sure she will be too, but really, it's fantastic to be able to speak English.'

Maggie smiles, and looks down at the table. 'Mmm,' she says. 'Me too. I've been so scared I wouldn't meet anyone, that I'd be all on my own . . .'

She tails off, as Luis bangs loudly on the kitchen door.

'Hola!' David and Libby shout in unison.

Luis exudes energy. He shakes David's hand, strokes Charlie's cheek, and kisses Libby. David introduces Maggie, who also gets a kiss. Then Luis starts trying to tell them something.

After much miming, Maggie realises what he's saying.

'They're going to fumigate your flat!' she says, smiling shyly. 'I read in my book about this. It's compulsory – I think you can be arrested if you don't let them in. It's the public-health people or whatever. They fumigate everywhere, regularly. That's why they've got no malaria and hardly any dengue fever.'

Luis is grinning at her. 'Foo-mee-gate,' he says, pronouncing the English syllables carefully.

'Mañana?' Maggie asks him.

'No, no. No mañana. Jueves.'

Use of the dictionary reveals this to mean Thursday. Luis is so pleased to have conveyed his message that he kisses Maggie firmly on each cheek.

'Linda cosa,' he says fondly. They can't wait for him to leave so they can look this up, too.

'Pretty thing!' David exclaims triumphantly. 'Maggie, I think we have found you a boyfriend.'

Libby looks at Maggie. Her cheeks are pink, and she is looking from David to Charlie to Libby with a small smile. She is one of those opaque people. She guards herself fiercely. Libby hopes she'll be able to get to know her. She decides to view Maggie as a challenge.

chapter twelve

Maggie – a week later

Dear Libby,

I wish you knew how glad I am that I came here, to meet you. I can look you in the eye and call you my friend. This is the joy of being so far from home. I wanted this so much when we were in Brighton. Now I have it.

Ever since I first heard your voice in Brighton, I wanted your life. You're happily married, you have a brain, you have a career and a beautiful baby. When you and David speak to me, I feel fuzzy and happy. I know I have done the right thing.

You inspire me to get my act together. I'll never go back to that club. I'll try again for a proper job. I might even train as a lawyer.

You will never know that I am here because you are here. You won't know that I used to follow your lives from my dingy basement. Those weekends when I'd listen to you, the nights when I woke with Charlie – it all seems so long ago. I had to cross the world before I got to speak to you. Things are evened out now.

I haven't been this happy in years.

With much love,

Maggie

Obviously I'm not going to send it. She'd think I was weird, and I'd probably never see any of them again. I tuck it between the pages of my diary. Nobody's likely to see my diary except possibly Elena, when she cleans the room, and she wouldn't understand it. There is, I tell myself, no harm in keeping a record of these feelings. I smooth it down. It reads rather oddly, when I look it over, and it is definitely not suitable for anyone else's eyes. In a funny way, though, I think it sums everything up quite neatly.

I look out of my window, again. The view is hypnotic. Every time I look, I see something new. Today, a band is playing on one of the roofs below me. It is a full, Buena Vista-style Cuban band. There is a trumpet, trombone, guitar, double bass, a drummer and a singer. I lean out to try to listen, and hear the music, faintly, above the noise of the city. The air is dusty, and although it's only eight o'clock in the morning, it's too hot for me already. I didn't pack any sunblock (for which I would blame Yasmin, if I could be bothered to think about her), and I haven't yet found anywhere to buy some. I'm pink, which doesn't help my confidence.

I didn't expect Cuba to be like this. I can't think what I did expect. I didn't really think about the physical environment. All I wanted from Cuba was the friendship of David and Libby, and now I seem to have it. I try to pin down my preconceptions. If I did have any, they were all true. There are immaculate old Chevys on the roads. The architecture is Spanish colonial style, and most of the buildings seem to be falling down. It's friendly. It seems to suffer economically. And, I now see, there really is music in the most unlikely places.

All these ideas, I realise, came from David and Libby. None of them were my own.

Yet, for all the excitement, I don't feel safe. Quite possibly, I was in more danger when I climbed gratefully into my taxi outside Vixenz at 2.30 every morning. But I knew Brighton. I knew England.

I have no idea what to expect here. I love being in classes and sitting next to David, and getting full marks for my homework. I love meeting up with the family after classes – going to the flat at lunchtime, or meeting them in the late afternoon, with Charlie. The rest of the time things feel strange. My life, here, is almost too exciting.

I pick up my bag and check I've got everything. Pens, course book, notebook. Money, student card, passport. I grab a hairband and tie up my hair. I don't have to check the mirror to know that I look ridiculous. The heat has made my hair completely wild. I crave straight hair, like Libby's. Emma and I were both landed with Dad's dreaded frizz. It was all right for him, having it short. Perhaps, like Dad, like Emma, I will have it all cut off.

As I leave the flat, I call goodbye to Elena. Elena is keeping me grounded, when I'm not with David and Lib. I am beginning to appreciate the way she mothers me. She is always exclaiming that I'm too thin, and she tries to fatten me up with buttery omelettes for breakfast. I wouldn't mind filling out a bit. Sometimes she's so kind to me that I want to cry, and I have to look away and push my fingers into my palm, to stop myself. I know she's only looking after me because it's her job, because I'm paying her twenty dollars a night. All the same, I have never been fussed over like this by anyone.

She is chatting to her neighbour along the corridor. 'Adios!' I call, as I head for the lift. She comes running over, exclaiming over something, and pointing to her beaming friend. I'm surprised at the amount of Spanish I understand. When I recognise a word, I repeat it. 'Casa,' I say. 'Amiga. Si.' I have no idea which house she's telling me about, or whose friend, but I imagine I'm hearing the neighbourhood gossip. I smile at everyone, to show that I may be stupid, but that I am, at least, amiable with it.

When the clunking lift arrives, Elena kisses me firmly on both cheeks and pushes me inside. Three boys of about eight are standing in a row, staring up at me. I've seen them before, riding up and down for fun. This morning, though, they are neat and tidy in school uniforms.

I look away, embarrassed by their unashamed interest.

'Buenas dias,' says one, and the others giggle and look away. The one who spoke has tightly curled hair, and a cheeky smile.

I wonder whether to say hello back. I look at the floor. All three of them are staring at me. I hate this. I hate being as conspicuous as I am, here.

'Hola,' I mutter.

Immediately they besiege me with questions. I recognise a few words, but don't want to get drawn into a discussion.

'No entiendo,' I tell them firmly, and stand by the lift door, looking out, until we reach the ground floor. Even as I do it, I regret my coldness. I am not good with children.

The doors open, and they all stand back politely, letting me out first. I clutch my bag as I walk to the top of the street, my head down, and struggle with a contradictory mass of feelings. I'm delighted that I'm not in Brighton, that Vixenz is a distant memory. I am happy to be welcomed by Elena as her own daughter. I am fairly sure she called me that last night. I am ecstatic that I met Lib and Charlie on my very first day at the university, and that their neighbour told David he thinks I'm pretty. I am not in the least bit interested in that neighbour, but Libby and David loved his interest in me (which was only relief that someone had understood him), and that is what makes me happy.

But I am also struggling. I fear for my security, walking down a crowded street in a foreign city that I barely know, all on my own. Anything could happen, here. When I am on my own, I am walking a tightrope over the Niagara Falls. I could slip and lose myself at any moment. If I vanished, no one would know where to look. I am not sure about my sanity. I don't feel grounded, any more. I have no cosy routine. However miserable I was in Brighton, I did at least have a job of sorts, a flat. To the casual, uninformed outsider, I was doing fine.

Cuban Heels

Here, I am alone. I am whoever I want to be. I can escape everything except for my own thoughts, and they scare me. More and more, I find myself remembering Grace. When that happens, it seems that the only people who can save me are David and Libby. I sense that they will offer me true friendship. Grace might have turned out like Lib. They have the same silky hair. Libby could fill that hole. When I am near her, I sense that I could be complete, that everything could go right again. That is why I must do everything in my power to strengthen our friendship.

The street is heaving with activity. Children like my lift boys are pouring into the school up the road, their uniforms immaculate. Adults are, variously, sauntering or hurrying. Some sit on their doorsteps and watch everything else go by. I see a blonde head in the crowd in front of me, and my heart leaps for a moment, but the people part, and it turns out to be a nondescript woman in her forties, who looks German or Swiss. I pass a couple of policemen, sitting on a low wall. I always expect someone to try to rob me, but no one appears particularly interested. The heat oppresses me. I showered an hour ago, but I can smell the fragrance of my deodorant, coupled with my own sweat. I'm not good with heat, and I urgently need new clothes.

I keep my head down, and walk quickly through the bustle. I turn left up Brasil, and dodge cars in both directions to get across the busy main road by the Capitolio. I find the Capitolio the strangest of Havana's buildings. It looks exactly like Washington's Capitol, and yet it's in the centre of a crazy, chaotic city which seems to represent Satan in Washington.

I pass some smart hotels and watch the well-dressed tourists emerging into the sunny Cuban morning. Touts and taxi drivers approach them, and are waved away. I envy the tourists. They look as if they have a direction. When I reach Neptuno, the street which stretches all the way to the university, I hail a cab. I shouldn't be paying two dollars each way to get to and from classes every day, but I don't know what else to do. The buses scare me. Some of them are *camellos* – massive juggernauts, with dips in the middle like camels, packed with people. You see faces pressed awkwardly against the glass. I wouldn't have the nerve to get on one. My purse would vanish, if I did. I would disappear into someone's armpit. I can't walk, because it would take me at least forty-five minutes, and I would arrive shiny and panting. I don't feel happy, walking. I feel vulnerable. I have the money for taxis. There is no harm in my spending it. I love to see Havana from the back of a cab; like watching it from my window, it makes me feel safe.

The classroom is dusty and old-fashioned. It has a high ceiling and ancient wooden desks. The sun shines through the narrow windows and lights the dust. I unpack my books and my pens, and sit with a straight back, waiting for David to arrive. I love it. I adore every moment of these classes. Being at university again is a treat. Sometimes I feel myself slipping back to a simpler time, and then I know that I'm losing a little of my edge. That scares me. I need my edge. I wouldn't get by without it.

The Australian girls try to engage me in conversation about Europe again, and I exchange banalities while watching the door. David has turned out to be surprisingly nice. From the way he spoke to his wife in Brighton, I'd expected him to be less funny than he is. My researches had led me to expect a humourless wanker. In my mind he was bossy and difficult. Libby must rub him up the wrong way, because in real life, he is absolutely charming. He is better looking than I thought he was in Brighton, as well.

Meeting him was ludicrously easy. Negotiating the bureaucracy of the university was the difficult part. As soon as I was in that room, and discovered that he was, indeed, in there with me, I knew I was home and dry. I surreptitiously took a seat next to him for the test, pretty much wrote the same as he did, and the rest has been easy.

On the first day, I was terrified that David would introduce himself to the class before me. I practised feigned surprise. Luckily, in the

event, my turn came before his. I said, carefully: 'Soy de Brighton.'
David immediately leapt in. 'Really?' he said. 'Brighton in Sussex?'

Michelle, one of the Australians, added, 'Yeah, I went there –
Brighton rocks!'

'Actually,' I said casually, 'I live in Hove, not Brighton, but pretty
close to the border.'

'Which road?' David asked, eagerly.

'Espagnol!' barked the teacher.

'Sixth Avenue,' I said, and turned to Michelle. 'When were you
there?' I asked her, as if I could care less.

'But we live on Sixth Avenue!' David exclaimed. 'What a small
world!'

'No!' I said, laughing. 'No way. I'm at number seventeen. How
about you?'

I was brilliant. I should go into the theatre.

Coming face to face with Libby for the first time has been one
of the best moments of my life. It was still stressful. She was a
little bit suspicious of me at first. I saw it in her face. She isn't as
gullible as her husband. After a while, she began to rationalise the
coincidence, and now she seems to have forgotten it.

I replay my three encounters with her – so far – over and over
again. The first time, I babbled. I was scared. I was living my dream.
I had to pretend to be Yasmin to get through it.

I can't stop thinking about her. Sometimes I stop for a while,
but then I feel adrift, ungrounded, and scared. That is when Grace
comes back. I make myself think about Libby again until I feel
better. She always looks at me. She looks me up and down and
I wonder if she guesses that I am a loser.

David comes through the door, and I wave and smile. He takes
the desk next to me, as usual. I think it irritates some of the
other students that we always sit next to each other, and chat
in English. I don't give a fuck what they think. I love it. He is

125

my friend. And if anyone were to ask him, he would say the same about me.

He smiles. 'All right?' he says. He is wearing a blue T-shirt and a pair of long shorts. His legs are honey-coloured, and covered in light, soft hairs. I want to stroke them.

'Great,' I tell him, with a grin. *Now that you are here*, I want to add. 'You?'

'Mmmm. The lad's sleeping's not quite back on track.' He yawns and stretches. 'Had us up three times in the night, the little sod.'

'So who gets up? You or Libby?'

'Mmm. Strictly speaking, I'd have to say Lib does. But I *wake* up, you know? I don't exactly get a full night's sleep.'

I give him a sympathetic smile. 'You poor things,' I tell him. I am about to offer to babysit one afternoon or evening, when our teacher, Melinda, sweeps into the room. She glares at us.

'Espagnol!' she barks, and we look down, meekly.

I am by far the best student in the class. This is my secret. I'm scared of letting anyone see how good I am at the language, because I don't want to be moved up into 'beginners plus'. But I always know the answer, I always get my homework right, and I usually help David out by whispering words to him. The other students are a mixture of nationalities: Australian, Japanese, Turkish, Canadian, Norwegian. Everyone speaks English but some of them don't want to, on principle.

'How's Lib finding it?' I whisper to David, angling for another invitation. 'Doesn't she get lonely, with you out half the day?'

'No, she's fine,' he assures me briskly. I bet she's not. He never notices how she's feeling. I don't think it occurs to him that she could be unhappy. I am missing my easy insight into their lives. Now I have to earn my confidences, and that is annoying.

Perhaps his glasses make him appear more studious than anyone else, but David is the only member of this class who looks fit to be studying at Fidel Castro's alma mater. He tips his chair back and chews his nails. If he wasn't already taken by the woman I admire most in the world, I would be quite interested in David. I haven't thought about a man in that way since Mark. In fact, since Ivan. I never felt very strongly about Mark.

This must be progress. I must remember to make an effort to apply these feelings to Luis, next time I see him.

When class finishes, I leave the room with David, hoping to trot along back with him, for lunch. I love being in their flat. Even though it's pretty grim inside, it is their own, and it's full of their clutter. I tried to memorise every single detail. Charlie's toys were piled on a blanket in the middle of the floor. Libby uses lots of Clarins products. When I get back, I'll buy some of them. Mine are just Boots No. 7.

'What are you doing this afternoon?' David says, casually, as we stroll out into the sunshine. The university is surrounded by huge trees with big leaves. The grand stone staircase is dappled with shade. Other students – real students – are milling around, clutching piles of books to their chests. Lara, one of the Australians, catches us up. I will her away. Mentally, I put a hand to her chest and give her a shove.

'Thought I'd walk back along the Malecon,' I say, randomly. 'Maybe grab something to eat on the way, or raid Elena's fridge when I get home.'

'Who's Elena?' demands Lara.

'My landlady. I'm staying in a *casa particular*. What are you guys doing with the rest of the day?' My question is addressed firmly to David, but Lara purposefully misunderstands.

'We're off to explore,' she says, and I look at her properly for the first time. She is tall and broad, with the unmistakable wardrobe of the international traveller. Her blue cotton trousers are teamed with a white T-shirt bearing the legend 'London', over a picture of a red bus. Her hair is short and messy. I don't want to be her friend.

'Oh yeah?' asks David. 'Where are you going?'

'Well,' she begins, 'we thought we'd make a start with the Plaza de la Revolucion, you know, go up that tower, have a bird's-eye view. Then make our way down to Habana Vieja, have a mosey around, you know? From there, who knows? You're both welcome. The more the merrier.'

'Cheers, but we're stuck indoors with the baby. My wife is going out this afternoon to do some emailing, so I'm afraid I'm not going to be able to play.'

Both of them look at me.

'I'm going back to my place,' I say firmly, but, because I want David to like me, I decide to be magnanimous. 'Why don't you and Michelle pop by when you're in the old town?' I say to Lara. 'Here, I'll write down the address. You can meet my landlady and we could go for an ice cream or something.' I turn to David. 'If Libby's coming down my way, she's more than welcome to pop in, too.'

David looks thoughtful. 'She won't be down in town this afternoon. She'll be in the ETECSA up the road. And unbeknownst to her, Charlie and I will be at the Hotel Habana Libre doing some secret emailing of our own. I'm planning a surprise for her. Don't say anything. But, you know, we were thinking about heading your way with Charlie later. Do you want to maybe join us for an early dinner? We were going to try one of those restaurants in the guidebook, the ones where you're at someone's house.'

Lara folds my piece of paper, and pockets it. '*Paladares*, that's what you mean. Cheers, mate, but we can only afford the peso places. We'll drop by later, Mags.'

David turns down San Miguel, his street, with a cheerful wave. 'I'll maybe see you this evening, then,' I tell him.

'The place is called Julia, something like that. It's in your neck of the woods, anyway. About half-six-ish?'

'Sure!' I tell him, thrilled. I put my hands in my pockets, and head for the sea.

By the time I open the door to Elena's flat, I feel confident and happy. I have determined that my short-term project will be the updating of my wardrobe. Nobody should look as drab as I do, in Havana. I need tight T-shirts, and a couple of short skirts. The walk home has made me feel dowdy, next to all the local women. I should have brought my lap-dancing clothes. A Union Jack sequinned bikini would go down a storm, here. I need sandals. Libby has some beautiful beaded flip-flops, but I'm sure she didn't get them in Havana. I remember that, back in Brighton, she mentioned the lovely sandals in Accessorize. I should have followed her lead, and gone there. My feet get horribly sweaty in trainers.

I am exhilarated from the brisk exercise. There really is no need for me to get all those cabs. If I walked to university, I would see a thousand aspects of Cuban life, every day. I strode home along the promenade, dodging the pot holes in the pavement. I passed lots of tourists, admittedly, but also Cuban joggers, groups of young men who called out in Spanish to ask whether I was German, and a couple of slinky wet children. They were taking turns to jump from the sea wall into the Atlantic, expertly avoiding the rocks. Watching them made me want to join in. I know they would have been horrified had I stripped down to my underwear and thrown myself into the sea. I watched the horizon, knowing that America wasn't far beyond it.

On the other side of the road, the buildings took my breath away. They were crumbling before my eyes, but they were beautiful. I want to live in one. A Spanish colonial mansion, with a balcony with a creeper. I would sit out on it every morning, with a Cuba Libre, and I would look down at the traffic – the battered Lada taxis, the shiny fifties Chevrolets. I would stare at the sea, and speak to my neighbours in Spanish, and no one in Europe would ever hear from me again. I would fill the time until I died.

Elena is lying on the sofa, the fan pointed directly at her head, watching a Brazilian soap opera on her huge television. She is chewing a strand of her artificially blonde hair, and is tense with excitement. She barely acknowledges my return. I like blonde hair on Latin women. It looks so fake that it's positively classy.

When the action shifts to a cellar, where a woman is tied to a chair, Elena looks up briefly, smiles, calls me 'chica' and asks me something. I don't catch it, so I smile and nod, and motion her not to bother getting up. She levers herself to a sitting position, and points to my bedroom door. Elena wears lycra, and she is extremely generously proportioned. It looks good on her. I wouldn't even lap dance in the hotpants she's wearing. I would look like an embarrassed twelve-year-old at the school disco.

'Amiga,' she says, pointing to my room. 'Chica.'

I open the door, ready to throw down my bag and collapse on the bed. But someone is already there. A woman is lying down, gazing, away from me, out of the window. She has long, silky blonde hair.

I shiver. It is her. It has all been a mistake.

'Hello?' I say, uncertainly. 'Hola?'

She turns around. Of course it isn't Grace. I feel myself trembling and clasp my hands together.

'*Yasmin?*' I ask. The very last person I want to see.

She hoists herself upright and swings round to face me.

'Hey, bird,' she says, with a wide smile. 'Surprise!'

Yasmin is wearing a tiny white dress. Her legs stretch out towards me. Immediately, I feel small and ugly. I put my bag down and walk towards her. I do not need her here. She will ruin everything.

'Yas?' I ask, not even bothering with a fake smile. 'What are you doing here?'

She shrugs, and plays with her hair. 'I was jealous,' she says, looking up winsomely. 'Norwich was doing my head in. I borrowed the money from my folks. Knew where to find you.' I frown. 'Hey,' she adds. 'Bad sunburn. Have some of my factor thirty. Your landlady is a dude. I don't understand a word she says, and vice versa, but she's done me a deal on the other room. I've moved in! We're neighbours.'

I sit heavily on the bed next to her. 'Great,' I say, listlessly.

chapter thirteen

Libby – later that day

When she is in Old Havana, and the day's glare is fading, and the people are bustling around her, Libby is so happy that she wants to sing. After a week of lonely mornings, she is developing the ability to live in the present. When she's alone in the flat, she cannot believe that David will ever come home. And while she and David are out with Charlie in the backpack, she forgets about her boring day at once. She doesn't care that she's going to do it again tomorrow, and Wednesday, Thursday and Friday. For now, she is out. She is strolling around this beautiful city, with her two gorgeous boys, and she is, she realises, extraordinarily happy.

The three of them are ambling along a pedestrian street called O'Reilly, which seems to be at the centre of Tourist Havana. Libby can't help feeling a little patronising towards the other Westerners. These people are on holiday. She, on the other hand, *lives* here. 'We live in Havana,' she says, under her breath. On balance, perhaps she will expand her postcard list, after all. 'We're living in Cuba for a while, with our baby.' You don't get much more stylish than that. 'Our flat is a half-hour walk away from the tourist areas,' she adds. She will buy more postcards today. The walk has actually taken forty minutes, and she is knackered. She can feel the weight falling off her. Suddenly, it seems so easy. Simply move to a country with an

American trade embargo, and watch the pounds melt away! She'll say that in her next batch of emails.

She is troubled by an email from Natalie this afternoon. Nat has made Graham move out, and she sounds as if she's barely coping. Libby thinks it wouldn't take much more pressure on her part for Nat to book herself a ticket to Havana. She wrote as persuasive a reply as she could manage, and wonders what else she could do.

The light of the early evening is soft and golden. David looks wonderful in long shorts and a big blue T-shirt. Summer suits him. He has good legs. His feet look fine in sandals. As soon as the first rays hit him, he turns a warm golden brown, the colour of his hair. Libby wishes their son had inherited his father's colouring, rather than hers. She catches herself thinking that the next baby might be luckier. She has never been able to contemplate the idea of a second baby, before now. She wishes, however, that she could feel happier within herself first. She cannot stop thinking about her father at the moment. When she gets the chance, she's going to ask David whether she should try to contact him. Being proud and waiting is clearly not going to get her anywhere.

Charlie is strapped to David's back, white with sunblock and waving his arms in excitement. He has become a highly accomplished flirt. He scans the people that crowd this small street, settles his gaze on a likely candidate, and grins charmingly. If they fail to respond, he lets out a loud crow of excitement, and smiles again. Everybody seems to love him. The streets reverberate with the words, 'Oh, que lindo!' In Brighton, Charlie was a normal baby. Everything he did, he did according to the textbook. Here, he has transformed himself into the most sociable child on the planet. He is a joy. He is hilarious.

Two young women point Charlie out across the street. 'Mira,' they say, 'que lindo!' They rush to him, and are rewarded with a giggle. As they stroke his hair, he gets so excited that he waves all four limbs simultaneously. David and Libby exchange glances, and laugh.

'Your son,' she says, pretending to be embarrassed.

'I demand a DNA test,' replies David, trying to hide his delight.

The people who pass by range from obvious foreigners to the men, women and children who live in the cramped apartments round here. Everyone seems happy, Libby decides cheerfully. She realises that this is an enormous and patronising generalisation. But there are no homeless people begging. No one seems destitute. Few people are fat, except for the tourists, but, equally everyone seems to have at least the bare minimum for survival. The girls, as ever, strut beautifully, dressed minimally.

A young man walks beside David and grins broadly.

'Hola, amigo,' he says. 'Hello, my friend. Your country?'

David smiles testily. He hates these encounters. 'England,' he says, without slackening his pace.

'Oh, England! Very good country. You want cigars?'

'No cigars, thanks.'

'Restaurant?'

'No thanks.'

'I take you to bar where Hemingway drinks? Very friendly for baby!'

Libby leans across David. 'No thanks. It's very kind of you, but the baby's tired and we need to go. Thanks.'

The man shrugs. 'Okay. Have a good evening.'

'Thanks.'

David looks at Libby. 'Bugger. Every single time, you get rid of them and I don't. How do you do it?'

'You just have to be nice. Don't think of them as the enemy. They're just blokes trying to make a living.'

David frowns. 'But I *know* that. And I still don't know how to talk to them.'

Libby nudges him. 'Hey, this is funny, isn't it? Me being good at something?'

David stares at her. 'What do you mean?'

'You know. I've been so crap since Charlie was born. Fat and tired and bored. I've been shocking. And you dragged me here and I'm feeling like a new person.'

'But, Lib,' says David, 'you're good at everything.' He takes her hand, and they swing their arms as they walk. 'I mean it.'

This trip has changed something in her. It is no longer something she must endure before she is allowed to go back to the law. In fact, she sometimes notices that she is feeling like herself again. She hasn't felt like this since somewhere around the middle of her pregnancy, and even then it was different.

David stops abruptly in front of a restaurant.

'This is the one,' he says. 'You know, the one I read out from the book. It's the place we're meeting Mags. I should have asked Luis along too, shouldn't I? They might have been able to go on for a drink somewhere afterwards.'

Libby looks at it. 'La Julia. It looks nice. We'll get Luis out another time, if you really are determined. Maggie doesn't seem that keen, and Luis might have a wife tucked away somewhere, for all we know. That baby could be his.'

'Are you saying he could be the father of his sister's baby? That sounds a little harsh.'

Libby hits him. 'I am not saying that, and you know it.'

They both smile at the young man standing on the pavement with a menu, who is motioning them in. The restaurant is a *paladar*, a private enterprise, forbidden by law from seating more than twelve patrons so it doesn't compete with state-owned restaurants. It is decorated in the familiar Cuban style, with paper sheets over a heavy tablecloth, a tiled floor, and a fine Madonna on the bar. They are, as usual, the only patrons. Charlie's bedtime prevents them from eating out late. During Libby's early twenties, she would have scoffed at the idea that she could ever become the sort of person who would sit down to dinner at half past six. Now she thinks nothing of eating as fast as she can, taking a taxi home, and playing cards for the rest of the evening before going to bed at ten.

A young man materialises at the table. 'Dos cervezas, por favor,' David tells him, seriously.

'Wow,' Libby teases. 'You really do speak fluent Spanish! Good thing you're at the university or we'd never have managed to place *that* order.' She takes Charlie out of the backpack, and hands him a board book to eat. They order pork with all the trimmings, and sit back to watch the street. An old woman comes out of the kitchen to admire the baby. Libby has already learned the necessary Spanish phrases, thanks to Luis.

'Ahhhhh,' says the woman, 'que lindo! Niño o niña?'

'Niño,' Libby tells her confidently. 'Cinque meses.'

'Aahhh? Grande!' She reaches out for him, and wanders away with him in her arms, addressing him in a soothing stream of baby talk. Libby looks triumphantly at her husband.

'And I'm not even learning Spanish,' she tells him.

'You're wonderful,' he replies, and squeezes her leg. 'Look, Lib, there's something I was planning as a surprise for you. Can I tell you?'

'My *father*?' Libby is astonished. 'But I just decided that I'd find him myself.'

David laughs. 'Then let me give you his email address, his postal address, and his phone number.'

'And you got these how?' She knows she should be pleased, but she is finding this disconcerting, instead.

'From your mum. She hears from him from time to time.'

Libby looks at the table. She struggles not to let her disappointment show. 'He keeps in touch with her and not me?'

'Because she told him to leave you alone, I think. She thinks she's been protecting you.'

'Typical.'

'He lives in Australia.'

'I knew that.'

'He wants to see you.'

'Well he's got a funny fucking way of showing it.'

She cannot look at David. She doesn't know what she thinks, but it does not feel good.

Two women walk into the restaurant, and Libby and David both look up, relieved to have a distraction. Maggie walks over to their table, and she is not alone. Libby places the other woman, the blonde one, in seconds.

'Hi, Mags,' says David, happily. 'Sorry, we went ahead without you. You know how it is.' He turns to the other woman, who is tall and blonde, and looks amused. 'Hi,' he says. 'Hola.'

'That's fine,' says Maggie. 'Truly, it is absolutely fine. I'm late. Hey, guys, you'll never guess what.' She pauses, and seems to Libby to be forcing a smile. 'This is an old school friend of mine, Yasmin. She's just arrived in Havana. She's the one I was telling you about, who came back from India. Yasi, this is Libby, and David. Where's Charlie?'

They all look round.

'They've taken him away,' Libby explains, taking care not to look at Yasmin. David looks worried.

'They won't be giving him things to eat, will they?'

'No. Don't stress. Enjoy it.'

Libby turns her gaze to Yasmin, hoping their eyes won't meet until she decides how to handle the situation. This is the very last person she wanted to see. She has no doubt that it is her. Yasmin is wearing a tiny sundress. She is intimidatingly pretty, and sexy in a very obvious way. She is the Barbie woman.

'Pleased to meet you, Yasmin,' says David, standing up.

Libby interrupts. 'Yasmin, you've spent time at Maggie's flat lately, haven't you?' Yasmin looks back placidly, and nods.

'Yep,' she confirms. 'Not long before Mags came away. I stayed for a few days. Then she came to Cuba and I went back to Norwich.'

'That doesn't seem fair,' says David, and Libby glares at him. She notes that, despite his protestations in Brighton that she wasn't his type, he doesn't seem able to take his eyes off her.

'Too right,' says Yasmin with a big fake smile. 'I kept thinking of all the fun I could be having, so in the end I just kind of said fuck it, and borrowed some money from my folks. So here I am. Not planning to join in the studying spree, though, I have to say.'

'Has Mags told you about her boyfriend?' asks David, grinning. 'Aka our next-door neighbour and landlord?'

Maggie goes a little pink. 'He is *not* my boyfriend,' she says firmly. She seems genuinely upset. 'Luis is a lovely man,' she adds, 'but he is not and never will be my boyfriend.'

Yasmin pokes her. 'Funnily enough, she didn't mention lovely Luis. Is he handsome?'

Libby is not going to answer. Maggie clearly isn't going to, either. After a pause, David nods.

'Well then,' continues the woman they have been speculating about for weeks, 'you should have a fling with him. Think about it, hon. For the rest of your life, you'll be able to drop the phrase "my Cuban lover" into your conversation. Go on. A good shag will do you the world of good.'

Libby glares, unable to restrain herself any longer. 'You'd know all about that, wouldn't you, Yasmin?'

David frowns in surprise and embarrassment. Maggie looks from Libby to Yasmin, confused. Yasmin doesn't look in the least bit surprised.

'Sorry, Maggie, but Yasmin knows exactly what I'm talking about,' Libby continues. 'I'm talking about my best friend's husband. I'm talking about a party David and I had before we came here. I recognised you as soon as I saw you. David should have recognised you too, but he seems to have been distracted. Christ knows where you were, Maggie. You'd obviously let her off her leash. Yasmin, you disappeared upstairs with Graham. Or didn't you bother to ask his name? He turned up later covered in lipstick, yes? Pants inside out? Classy. Very classy. They've split up because of it, and Natalie's devastated, as you'd expect.'

Maggie opens her mouth to speak, then looks at Yasmin, and

closes it again. Libby sees realisation and recognition dawning on David.

Yasmin looks down at the table and smiles to herself. Then she meets Libby's gaze. 'Tell your friend I'm sorry it's got that heavy,' she says, casually. 'They should lighten up. It's only sex.'

'Yasmin McLeod!' Maggie is not given to outbursts, but this seems to have shocked her. 'Is that true?'

Yasmin grins at her and winks. 'You know me!'

'You were watching telly when I left, and you were asleep when I got back.' She pauses. 'But I did notice that you'd tried on lots of my make-up.'

'That's the one,' says Yasmin. 'Your make-up's fab.' She addresses Libby. 'You wouldn't expect Mags to have good make-up, would you, but it is seriously fabulous. And, Mags, my darling, I don't do eleven o'clock bedtime. You wouldn't take me to the *office* with you. I could hear the party.' She shrugs. 'It sounded like fun.'

Maggie looks from Libby to David, stricken. 'I am so sorry, Lib,' she says. 'I had no idea. I didn't even know there was a party. Goodness. Christ. This is awkward.'

At this, David jerks into action. 'It needn't be,' he says, firmly. 'Water under the bridge. Yes, Natalie has had a terrible time and that is unfortunate. But there's nothing to be done about it now. Come on, girls. We're in Havana. We're thousands of miles from the scene of the crime. And, Mags, what were Amex thinking of, making you go to the office at eleven p.m. on a Friday? No wonder you couldn't wait to leave.'

Libby doesn't let Maggie answer. She doesn't give a toss why Maggie had to work late. 'David,' she says sternly, 'Natalie is my best mate. We didn't invite this woman to our party. She slept with Nat's husband. Does the word loyalty not mean anything to you? She has behaved despicably.'

Yasmin hits the table. 'Enough!' she says, leaning back and ordering four beers in sign language. She looks Libby in the eye, and addresses all her words to her alone. 'Fine, okay? Hello, Libby, nice to meet you. Lovely flat you've got in Hove. I knew it was you as soon as Maggie said she'd met her neighbours.' She props her elbows on the table and rests her chin on her hand. This is Yasmin's contrite look. 'Okay,' she continues softly, 'I went to your party without being invited. Sorry about that. It's actually a compliment to you – it was a good party. I'm very discerning. So. I met a reasonable-looking bloke there and had my evil way with him. Possibly you have a moral objection to me fornicating in your bathroom. If so, apologies, but these things happen when you have parties. At least we didn't do it in the baby's room.' The beers arrive and she pauses while the waiter pours them and they all thank him effusively. 'We did actually consider it. And funnily enough, he didn't tell me he was married,' she continues, still staring at Libby. 'He was on his own when I met him. And I didn't exactly rape him. If I'd known his wife was at the party I would have thought twice. I thought it was just a case of two horny people entertaining each other for a half-hour or so. You might not love me, but I think it would be a little bit unfair to hold me fully responsible for your friend's marital problems. I would say it's pretty much her husband's fault.'

Her cheeks are flushed. Libby can see that men would find her attractive, since she has all the traditional attributes, but there is a hardness to her face that is repellent. She may have the blondeness, the height, the breasts, but by the time she's forty she'll look as odious as she really is.

'And if it wasn't you,' Libby suggests caustically, 'it would have been someone else?' They stare at each other.

'You can take the piss all you like, but yes, it definitely would have been, and I'm sure it has been many times in the past, and I'm sure it will be again. Look, I'm sorry I came here, I realise I must be the last person you want to see, but I came because of Maggie. Not to make your lives difficult.'

David is looking at his wife. He doesn't have to say anything: she can feel him pressurising her to be gracious. She doesn't even have to look at him to know his expression.

'OK,' she says, sullenly. 'Since you're Maggie's friend, and Maggie's our friend, we'll pretend it never happened.' She looks at her husband, who smiles fondly.

'Of course we will,' he says, and squeezes Libby's hand. 'So, Yasmin, when did you get to Cuba? And where are you staying?'

'She's staying at my place,' says Maggie, looking sideways at her friend. Libby wonders how naive Maggie actually is. With her prissy little job at American Express, her expat parents with their retirement home in the south of France, and her one long relationship since university, Libby suspects Maggie hasn't seen much of life. She has been sheltered from reality. 'I was thinking of looking for somewhere nearer the uni,' Maggie continues, 'near you guys. I'm sick of paying so much money. But Elena's so sweet, I don't think I could leave, now. She asked me this morning if I would teach English to some of the kids in the building. I don't really want to, but how can I say no?'

Yasmin perks up. 'Brilliant. We can teach them swear words. Once in India these guys wanted to learn some English from me and my mate, so we told them that the slang way of saying thank you was to say "bite me".'

Libby is grateful that the proprietor returns to the room with Charlie, so she doesn't have to comment. Instead, she looks at her baby's cheerful face, and notices the way it brightens still further when he sees her. He reaches for her, and she puts down her fork and lets him throw himself into her arms.

'Muchas gracias,' Libby tells the kind woman. The woman tousles Charlie's hair, smiles broadly, and returns to the kitchen.

'Hey,' says Yasmin. 'Nice baby.'

'When were you in India, Yasmin?' asks David. 'I went when I left school. Seems like a million years ago. I remember being so sick I felt I'd turned inside out.'

'We don't have to see Yasmin,' Libby whispers to Charlie, while

David and Yasmin try to outdo each other with tales of tropical illnesses. 'She's not our friend. Nat's our friend.' And suddenly, she realises she's going to have to tell Natalie not to book a flight out here, after all.

chapter fourteen

Maggie

Dear *Auntie* Mags,

I hope this email reaches you. We have to share this news with you: at half past two this morning, three days before her due date, Madeleine Grace Austin was born, weighing in at a robust 8lb 4oz.. The labour was tough for all of us, but mainly for your brave sister. She did a heroic job under horrible circumstances. We ended up with an emergency Caesarean because Maddy's heart rate was dropping and labour wasn't progressing. Pretty scary at the time, I can tell you, but the outcome was happy and now we are all getting to know each other. Maddy has no hair whatsoever (so she might not take after the Wilsons in that department), but she is the most gorgeous girl in the world (picture attached so you can agree with us). She's already beautiful, and she's only, as I write, fifteen hours old.

Emma is a superb woman. Maggie, I was so proud of her. I know she'd love to hear from you, even if just an emailed message I could print out and take into her in the Norfolk and Norwich. She misses having you around. My family have been in to see the new addition, and your parents are on their way across the Channel as I write.

We will keep you updated with progress reports. Emma and Maddy will be in hospital for about four days because of the operation. Hope all is going well for you in Cuba and that you'll be back nice and soon to meet your niece.

Hugs from all three of us,

Jeremy x

Five days later

Dear Mags,

As we haven't heard from you I'm guessing that internet access is limited, but we're hoping that you'll receive these messages soon. If we had a number for you, we'd have called you many times by now, and sod the expense. If you do have a number, let us have it and we will phone you.

Emma and Maddy came home this morning. It is amazing to have them in the house. They are my girls. I can't tell you what it feels like. I have turned into an emotional old sod, as anyone around me will confirm. Emma's feeling much better. None of us had realised before quite how much a Caesarean is major surgery, and recovery is going to take ages. It's a neat scar – a little smile. My job is to stop her trying to do anything. Maddy is growing before our eyes. She's quite wonderful. I'm sure she understands more than she lets on. She smiles at us, and it's definitely real smiling, not wind. This, of course, means that she's highly precocious. She's been sleeping okay on the ward – waking up fairly often, though, and we're hoping she'll be more settled now she's home.

Ems will write to you when she has a minute. She's breast-feeding every moment of the day right now, so she might be typing one-handed.

Call us!

Love, J, E & M xxx

Two days later

maggie!

can't wait to hear from you, big sister. so much to share. jeremy says email's not up to much in cuba but every day we check it and we know that one day soon we'll hear from you.

life has gone completely mad. it's wild. all of us here are completely in love with our gorgeous maddy. she's the most amazing baby. i have a daughter! can you believe it? i'm actually typing this with her on my breast. she says hello to her auntie.

we're knackered, but the funny thing is, it doesn't matter. maddy hasn't got her days and nights sorted out yet so jeremy and i have been watching an awful lot of late-night movies on tv. it's great. mum & dad are going to stick around for another week or so. they've been so brilliant. i get to sleep in the day, and by magic the washing-up is done, and miraculous meals appear on the table. i could definitely get used to this. we've had tons of visitors, and presents, and flowers. maddy is going to be so loved.

jez goes back to work the day after mum & dad leave. i know that that's when it's really going to hit home. for now it is like the most wonderful amazing holiday ever.

come back soon mags! we can't wait to see you.

masses & masses of love,

emma and madeleine xxxxxxxxxxxxxxxxx

I hold my head in my hands. I had forgotten how close we were to Emma's due date. I have disgraced myself. I haven't bothered to check my emails for weeks, because it didn't occur to me that I could have any. I never have emails. I only went to ETECSA because I wanted to get away from Yasmin.

Fuck. Stupid fucking idiot girl. I scroll back to the photo of the baby and try to make myself feel like a fond auntie. I scrutinise the red face and the scrunched-up eyes, and try to marry that with her parents' descriptions of the most beautiful girl in the world, ever. I suppose the world would be a worse place if every parent didn't think like that.

I can barely move. I want to write a reply, and to leave, but I can't. I am rooted to the chair by sadness. I stare at that baby's fat cheeks, and try to stop myself wishing she wasn't there. Then I close down the internet connection.

I pay for my time on the computer, and buy two $20 phone cards. At the payphone, I take a deep breath, and call Norwich.

It takes ages to connect, but finally I hear the comforting sound of a British telephone ringing. Emma answers almost straight away.

'Hello?' she says, cheerily. I listen for wails in the background, but there are none. I take a deep breath, and steel myself to be cheerful, and happy, and apologetic.

'Ems!' I exclaim. 'It's me! I'm so sorry it's been so long! The email was down all over Cuba.'

'Maggie! Oh, Maggie, it's you! We've been worried about you.'

'Me? I'm fine. What about you? Tell me about my niece.'

She sighs. 'We're still on a bit of a high. She's perfect. She's asleep right now, actually, but I'm going to have to wake her up soon to try to get her to sleep tonight. She's breastfeeding really well now but it took about a week. Learning to breastfeed has been one of the hardest things I've ever done.' From the tone of her voice, I can tell that she's starting to cry. 'It's amazing, Mags. It's just so fantastic. It's the weirdest thing.' She pauses, and sniffs. 'And I'm so bloody emotional all the time. I wish you were here.'

'I wish I was, too,' I tell her, pulling my trousers tighter around my waist and retying them. Emma will never guess that I am lying. I don't want to be anywhere but here. 'Am I really crap, or what? Are Mum and Dad still there?'

'Yes, they're going on Monday. They've been great. I really feel like it's brought us all so close together, as a family. All that's missing is you.'

And Grace, I think. I don't say it.

'I'll be back within a few weeks,' I tell her. I'm trying to sound like a reassuring older sister. I want to drop the phone and run away. 'I never even sent you those monitors, did I?'

'Don't worry about that, hon. Jeremy's mum got us some the other day. We don't need them at night – she sleeps in our bed – but we do during the day. Normally she naps in the living room in her Moses basket but sometimes we put her upstairs. That's the only time we need to listen in.'

'Oh God, and I bought them months ago. I'm so sorry.'

'Look, forget about the monitors, you silly thing. They don't matter a bit. Family's what matters. Just come home. Do you want me to go and fetch Mum?'

I think about it for a moment. I'd love to hear her voice. On the other hand, I couldn't bear it. I don't feel strong enough to explain myself to my mother.

'I'm running out of money here, Ems, and I can't take incoming calls. Look, I'll ring again soon. The photos are stunning. Well done. I can't wait to meet her. Bye!'

I press the catch down and hope it sounds like my money running out. Then I hang up. I only used one of the phonecards, and I still have seven dollars left on it.

I walk through Vedado for twenty minutes. I walk faster and faster, turning randomly right and left down whichever streets catch my eye. I walk along main roads and dodge traffic, feeling the rush of air as cars and lorries nearly hit me. The sun is hotter than ever, and I am sweating. I have nearly run out of deodorant. I ignore everyone. Most people ignore me, too. Some men try to talk, and when I walk past a hotel, they offer me taxis, and when I pass restaurants, they invite me in for lunch. I walk on. When I look up, I see Grace everywhere, even though everybody here is dark.

So I don't look up. I only see the pavement in front of me. I dodge holes when I spot them in time. I don't care about anything else. I can only think about putting one foot in front of the other.

I pass a man in a pinstriped suit, begging outside the church. He has one leg. He is always there, sitting in the same place. He seems to be the only beggar in Havana. I wonder what disasters befell him. I don't care.

I try to shut Emma out of my brain. I can't cope with my birth family any more. This is logical. I don't know why I didn't think of it sooner. David and Libby are my new family. I picture Libby's face. She is kind. She is good. She cares about people. She doesn't know about Grace. I can't be a part of my old family, now. Any contact with them hurts me. I need to start again.

After a while, I am tired, and I have a headache, so I sit down on a plastic chair. Then I look around, and see that my chair is one of many on the pavement. There is a hole in the wall serving drinks. I could make my headache better by drinking some water. On the other hand, I could also make it worse by having a beer.

Everyone else here is Cuban and everyone is drinking beer from plastic cups.

Yasmin will never find me here. Emma won't find me and nor will Mum. I am hiding from a week-old baby.

The man behind the tiny counter calls out, asking me what I want.

'Cerveza,' I call back, and he smiles, and brings one over. I doubt they serve anything else. To my astonishment, he asks for six pesos. That means the beer costs twenty pence. I haven't been to a peso bar before, and now I have stumbled upon one. I can't think of anything else to do. I'll have to stay here all afternoon and get drunk.

I suddenly realise that people are looking at me. I catch a couple of eyes. They are smiling, but people are talking about me. They are friendly, I remind myself. These people are friendly. These ones are not the problem. I keep my head down, and avoid eye contact.

If Yasmin wasn't here, I would be able to get on with my new life. I could be whoever I wanted to be. Instead, she's forcing me to carry on being Maggie.

I hate her. Everyone likes her because she's pretty, but I hate her. Libby hates her too. Libby has good judgement.

I hate the way she followed me here. I hate the fact that she knows me, and knows my secrets. She knows everything about me.

I have to ostracise myself from my family. Emma clearly sees her baby as some sort of healing panacea for the Wilsons. I feel sick at the idea. It's cloying, sentimental. That's what Emma's all about, though – sentiment. I bet she believes her little daughter to be some sort of reincarnation of Grace. That's why they're so excited that she hasn't got any hair. Grace was a bald baby. The whole idea is twisted and sick. I don't want to go back.

I am friendly with Libby, now, but not friendly enough. It is obvious to me that her friendship is the only thing that can save me from the abyss. She will stop me falling off the edge. I come closer to it every day. Only Libby can help. I wonder what she'd say if I told her.

She would think I was obsessed, because she doesn't understand. It's not obsession, though. I think about her as much as I possibly can because I have to. She, and only she, has the power to block the rest of them out.

I wave to the waiter for another beer. I can't believe it's so cheap.

As he brings it over, a young man comes and sits at my table. He doesn't ask if it's okay; just pulls out a chair and plops himself down.

'Hola,' he says. I recognise him. I've seen him around the university.

'Hola,' I reply, and look away.

'Ingles?' he asks.

'Si,' I tell him. I send out powerful go-away vibes, but he ignores them.

'I see you at Habana University,' he says. I look up, and catch his eye for a second. He is a couple of years younger than I am, and he looks like a proper student, with his round glasses and their tortoiseshell rims. He looks studious, and, in a purely objective sense, I note that he is good-looking. Not that I care.

'I'm learning Spanish,' I tell him.

'I think it's very good for foreigners to come here and learn Spanish,' he says, with a smile. 'Tell me, what do you think of my country?'

'I love it,' I say automatically. 'The people are so friendly. I love the way of life. It really is so different from Europe and America.' I wish he would piss off. I need to be on my own.

He looks excited. 'You have been to America?'

'Only once.'

'To Florida?'

'No, to New York. With my boyfriend. Well, my boyfriend at the time. We went for a week.'

'It was good?'

I think about it. Mark and I got on pretty well at that point, and I adored New York. 'It was good,' I confirm, 'but Cuba is better.'

He sniffs. 'For foreigners, maybe.'

I chuckle mirthlessly. 'And America is Utopia, is it?' He starts to speak, and I stop him. 'You know,' I say, 'there are poor people in America, and in Britain and all the other developed countries. Lots of poverty. Many people don't have homes, and sleep on the streets. You mustn't idealise it.' I realise that I sound prim and preachy. 'Don't you like socialism?' I add.

He laughs. 'Sure, I like socialism. But life in Cuba has become ridiculous. Do you see that? I mean, over there.' He gestures towards a supermarket. 'The girl that takes your bag. You know? She is a friend of mine. You go there? You give her five cents, American?' I nod, and look pointedly at my watch. I haven't actually been there, but I've been to other supermarkets, and I've tipped the woman who looks after the bags, because she's always had a saucer of American change on the counter.

149

'She have more money than a doctor,' he finishes triumphantly.

'Not really.' I am slightly interested in this fact, but I still wish he'd leave me alone.

'Really. Because she have dollars. Doctor have twenty-five dollars per month.'

'That is bizarre.'

He nods. 'Yes.'

'The dual economy isn't a good thing, then?'

He leans forward on his elbows. 'It was necessary,' he tells me. 'I see that Castro have to do it. So many people have money sent from Miami, from families, and it was illegal to spend it. This doesn't make sense. But for a socialist society, it makes many problems.'

I am looking at him. I search within myself for a tiny bit of normal human feeling. I try not to think about myself, but to concentrate on this young man. I recognise the fact that he is interesting and intelligent. I know I should learn as much as I can about Cuban society from him. But I can't get her out of my head. Grace, Grace, Grace.

'So do you think Cuba's going to become capitalist?' I ask, with an effort.

'When Castro die. I think there will be big problems. Many big problems.'

Elena and I have never discussed politics, beyond the fact that she is taxed to high heaven for having visitors. I pretended to myself and to David and Libby that I was coming here to see what it was like living under communism, while Castro was still alive, but I haven't given it a moment's thought. I can't find it within myself to care. I make an effort.

'Do you like Castro?' I ask, wondering whether I'm even allowed to ask questions like that.

'Yes,' says my new friend, decisively. 'I think he is a brave man, and good. We have very good hospitals and doctors. Rations are almost enough for everyone. But I do not like living in Cuba. There is no choice, not enough food. There is no possibility. In your country, everyone has the possibility.'

'What do you do?'

'I teach at the university.' He laughs. 'Perhaps I take a job at the supermarket? It would be better for me.'

I hold out my hand to him, formally. 'I'm Maggie,' I tell him.

'Like Maggie Thatcher? I am Raul.'

I think on my feet. 'Like Raul Castro?' I ask, tentatively. I am almost sure this is Fidel's brother's name.

'Yes!' He is impressed. We both laugh.

I know the way this encounter should continue. I know what Yasmin would do if she was here, and suddenly I wish that she was. She would take him off my hands. Raul is a nice enough random man. He's charming and handsome. I imagine he would like us to go to dinner together, and then perhaps to a party. The trouble is, I can't hang around him any longer. If I let myself think about other things, I end up with a head full of Grace. I can't bear it. I have to get away.

'Raul,' I say, abruptly, 'I have to go now.'

'But will you meet me later, for a beer? I know a good peso restaurant. No tourists go there.'

'I'm busy tonight,' I tell him.

'Tomorrow? My friend has a party tomorrow. Near to the university.'

I smile sympathetically. 'It's been lovely to meet you,' I tell him. 'Goodbye.' And I turn and stalk off. I will never see him again. I don't make friends with men on the street. It's just not me. I don't look back. I try to leave Grace with him, sitting at the table, messing with his head, not mine, for a change.

'Emma had a girl,' I tell Yasmin briskly. 'And I chatted to a lovely interesting good-looking man in a bar, about the contradictions inherent within Cuban society.' I take my shoes off and sit on the edge of my bed. Yasmin was in my room again. I wish she'd go somewhere else.

'Lovely,' she says. 'When was it born?'

'You can't call it *it* when you know the sex.'

'She, then. And name?'

'Born about ten days ago now. I hadn't checked my emails.'

'They didn't phone?'

I shake my head. 'I haven't given them Elena's number.'

'Why the fuck not, you dozy cow?'

'Because I came here to escape. And she's called Madeleine. Madeleine Grace.'

'Grace?'

'Madeleine.'

Yasmin sits next to me, and puts on a sympathetic face. 'Mags,' she says, seriously, 'tell me if I'm way out of line here, but I can kind of see that you're cut up about Grace right now. Emma having a baby girl was bound to stir things up for you. If you want to talk about everything that happened, you know, I think it would do you good. I'm always here for you.'

I turn to her. 'You're right,' I say sharply. 'You're way out of line.'

I stand up and leave the room. The only place I can go to be alone is the bathroom, so I lock the door, sit on the floor, and put my head in my hands. I am faltering. I can't falter. I curl up into a ball, and force myself to think of Libby.

chapter fifteen

Libby

As she gets ready to go out, Libby is delighted to discover that the trousers that were so tight that her thighs almost split the seams are now loose and elegant. She decides to put on some lipstick, and sits on the bed to look at her face in the mirror. This mirror – patchy, and covered with Charlie's fingerprints – is nonetheless absurdly flattering. She wonders whether she can buy it from Luis and take it with her when they leave. She'd have to wrap it up and carry it as hand luggage.

Libby and David are going to drink cocktails at the Hotel Nacional, and she is excited. She will not think about the letter she has drafted to her father. She will not feel guilty about Natalie. She will stop comparing herself to the lissom girls of Havana. Tonight, she will force herself to relax. As she twists the lipstick, she thinks of something.

'Yasmin's going to come too, isn't she?' she calls to David. Maggie is on her way over to babysit, but Libby is suddenly certain that Yasmin will tag along, purely to annoy her. She pictures Yasmin and Graham together. Yasmin is right: the fault is largely his. She hates to picture them having sudden, urgent sex in her bathroom. Her heart aches for Natalie, and she tries to push those feelings aside.

'What?' he asks. David is holding Charlie with one arm, and

clearing away his dinner with the other. He pretends not to hear, because he, too, considers it likely that Yasmin will be in their flat for the evening.

Libby appears in the kitchen doorway. 'Yasmin,' she says. 'Do you reckon Maggie'll bring her?' Libby has managed to avoid Yasmin since that evening in Old Havana. She has, however, emailed Nat to tell her that she's here. She did not relish that. Natalie hasn't written back yet.

'If she does turn up, you mustn't get stressed,' David says gently. Charlie holds his arms out for his mother, and she takes him. 'I know how you feel about her, but it's not for us to judge, not now. You know she feels terrible about what she did.'

'She's evil!'

'She is not evil!' David rinses his hands, and puts his arms around them both. 'You silly thing. She's thoughtless and silly and she's a bit of a strumpet, but she's not evil. She can be quite amusing, actually.'

Libby pulls back and stares at him. 'When have you seen her?'

David shifts his weight from one leg to the other. 'She's come to meet Maggie after uni a couple of times,' he says casually. Libby tries to work out whether David's pretending that this is nothing, or whether he really believes it.

'Why didn't you say anything?'

'Because I knew you'd take it as meaningful, that I've seen her and you haven't. And, Lib, it just isn't meaningful, not at all. So it was easiest not to upset you.'

Libby looks at him. 'Well, in future you can bloody tell me if she shows up sniffing around. You know what she's like. Everything she does is calculated, and if she's out to seduce you, I want to know about it. Given her track record. Is that fair?'

David sighs. 'Sorry. Yes, of course. By the way, you look gorgeous.'

Libby winks at him. 'I know. I'm just going to feed this boy, then can you put him to bed while I get my hair sorted? I can't do a thing with it, without a hairdryer. It's going to have to go up.' Libby is secretly wondering whether there's anywhere in Havana where she can get it cut and coloured. She feels ready to go back to blonde, and she might lose the length, just to see if it suits her. At the moment she is obsessed with the idea of a short sharp bob. She suspects that one of the posh hotels could probably help.

'Yasmin!' says David, standing at the top of the stairs and exuding insincerity. 'How lovely to see you.'

'You too, my darling,' replies Yasmin. She kisses him on each cheek. Libby hears the smacking kisses from the bedroom, where she is hunting, in the dark, for their passports. David thinks they might need ID at the hotel bar. Charlie is stirring, and she is desperate not to disturb him. She picks up her latest letter to her father, and tips it towards the light coming in around the window slats to read the first lines: 'Dear Mr Betts, You might or might not remember me.' That is definitely too cutting. She puts the letter and a pen into her handbag.

'Hi there, Mags,' David continues, with real warmth in his voice. 'Done your homework?'

'Yeah, right!' says Maggie, with a little laugh. 'I was hoping to copy yours.' Libby smiles. She knows that Maggie wipes the floor with David when it comes to speaking Spanish. She does his homework for him every day. It is sweet of her to pretend otherwise.

'Likewise. Why don't you do it tonight, and I'll copy it when we get home?'

'Oh, cheers.'

'You won't be able to copy it later,' says Yasmin, smoothly. 'You'll be too drunk.'

Libby hears David laugh. 'Bring it on!'

She finds the passports, sneaks a look at Charlie's photo, taken when he was two weeks old, and puts his back into the top drawer. She breathes deeply in anticipation of the vile woman. David is wrong. She *can* judge. She thinks again about Natalie's face, the last time she saw her; and she resolves to speak only to Maggie.

'There's a possibility we might get a call on Luis's phone,' David is telling Maggie as Libby comes out of the bedroom. He is speaking quietly and warily. She wonders what he could possibly be talking about.

'Hi!' she says quietly, and closes the bedroom door behind her. She kisses Maggie on each cheek. 'What call? No one rings us here. Ignore him, Maggie, and thanks for coming over. You can't appreciate how much it means to us to be able to go out by ourselves for once. All those things you take for granted before you have kids. Make the most of it, hey?'

Maggie smiles. She's looking healthier, lately. Her face has filled out, and she's dressing better. She's showing off her figure, now. She's loosening up. Libby suspects she's never worn a revealing garment in her life, before now.

'Not a problem. Any time. Honestly, Libby, that's what friends are for. I really mean it. I'll babysit every night if you like.'

'Cheers. Just every once in a while would be fabulous. Help yourself to anything in the fridge.'

'Thanks.'

David splutters. 'Don't thank her until you've had a look. What's in there, Lib? A few spongy carrots, half a bottle of boiled water, and a splash of UHT milk.'

Libby opens it. 'And a can of beer. A baby bottle. And some stringy green beans. Mags, you can cook yourself up a feast.'

Yasmin plants herself firmly next to Libby.

'Evening, Lib,' she says, loudly. 'I came too. For your information. You don't seem to have noticed.' She tosses her hair and looks challengingly at Libby.

'Oh, I noticed. Look, we'll be off now. Mags, if he cries, leave him for a few minutes, then give him a cuddle, and if he's really upset, he can have some water. I put some ready in his bottle in the fridge. You know where to find us if you really need us.'

'Sure,' says Maggie, and Yasmin adds, 'No problem.'

Libby decides to give Maggie a goodbye hug, just to prove her point. 'Thanks,' she says quietly. 'You're a really good mate, you know.' She doesn't feel particularly matey with Maggie, but out here, she's the best friend, and the most reliable person, she's got. At home she wouldn't give her the time of day, as is proven by the fact that she didn't. But next to Yasmin, Maggie is a rock. There is, she thinks, a lot to be said for predictability.

'Luis said he'd pop over and see you,' David adds as they leave. Libby looks back and sees Maggie blushing.

Libby had no idea that Cuba could do posh quite this well. She knew it had a reputation, in the twenties and thirties, for stylish decadence, but her experience in Havana has in no way prepared her for the Hotel Nacional. Habana Vieja, where the tourists congregate, is beautiful, with its warm flagstone pavements, and restored colonial architecture, but it is full of shrieking children and old people. Humanity is everywhere. This hotel radiates exclusivity. It is huge. The grass at the front is manicured. The doorman smiles warmly, and the guests are a world away from anyone else they have seen here. As they walk into the lobby, suddenly feeling like homeless people in London attempting to gatecrash the Buckingham Palace garden party, a woman strides out, dressed entirely in Versace. Libby recognises it by the garishness.

'Do you know how much her outfit would have cost?' she whispers to David.

He smiles and shakes his head. 'Enough to feed Centro Habana for a week?'

She squeezes his hand. 'At least.'

They are intimidated by the shiny floors and the high ceiling of the lobby. The hotel smells of polish and perfume. For a while, they pretend to be engrossed in the pictures of famous guests from the past. They pick their preferred drinking companions.

'Winston Churchill,' Libby suggests.

'Frank Sinatra,' David replies.

They walk through to the outside bar. Libby looks at the sofas ranged around the cloistered courtyard, and thinks that it is perfect. The night is still and warm, and from this vantage point, they can see the lights along the Malecon twinkling in the darkness. A small band is playing for the drinkers. The lawns roll away into the night.

'You realise,' says David, following Libby's gaze, 'that this is the first time since we've been here that we've been out in the dark. Cuba by night, with my beautiful wife. One of those times you remember for ever.'

'You know what this is like?' Libby asks him. 'Apart from the fact that we're in Havana, this is like the way we used to live, in London.'

'In what way? Do you want a mojito?'

'I'll have three. Impeccable service. Opulent surroundings that are serviced by armies of cleaners who we never see. Lighting perfectly designed for maximum flattery. Paying over the odds for a cocktail and barely even noticing.'

David signals to the waiter. 'Dos mojitos, por favor,' he says confidently.

'Two mojitos, sir?' asks the waiter, smiling. 'Of course. One moment please.'

As he walks away, David and Libby look at each other and laugh. 'It's like bloody Paris,' she says. She tries to put on a French accent. '*I detect from your accent that you are a native English speaker. Therefore I will answer you in English, just to make you feel small.*'

'I don't think he said it to make me feel small,' David concedes, 'although he did unwittingly have that effect. But you're right. It's design that makes this place different from all the places we go with Charlie. I mean, in the bars, and in the *paladares*, and in Chinatown, you know that the person who serves your food is closely related to the person who's cooking it, and that they all double up as cleaners, and that the strip lighting is there because it was there when they bought the joint, or because they knew someone who could get the fixtures on the black market.'

'And don't you just love all that?' Libby is suddenly so happy she can barely sit still. She kisses David impulsively on the lips, and puts an arm around his shoulder, stroking the hairs on the back of his neck. 'I mean, isn't it wonderful? I really, truly thought I was going to detest living here. I fully expected it to be the hardest experience of my life. I was preparing to count down the days until we could go home. But it's great! And everything, you know, all those things that are niggling at the moment, they're going to be fine.' She takes out a piece of paper and a pen, and starts writing swiftly.

David looks at his wife, and wonders how she has managed to surprise him after all this time. 'I'm so happy that you love it, darling,' he says. 'I don't feel so bad about forcing you to come, now. Do you still want to go back to work when we get home?'

Libby looks up. 'I think so. I feel that I can do anything now. Before we came, I was really down. Depressed, I guess. Not postnatal depression or anything official like that, but I did seriously feel like a failure. I thought I was a crap mother. Now I realise I was just crap at being a mother in Brighton. Because here, even when you're out learning Spanish with Maggie, I feel fine. How about this? "I know that we lost touch some time ago, but I also know that you would like to know what's been happening to me."'

The waiter arrives with the drinks. Libby admires them. Whatever they taste like – and she hasn't yet had a mojito, as she's been concerned for her breast milk – they look the part. She can imagine Frank Sinatra sitting at this table, a cluster of glasses in front of him, empty but for the sprig of wilted mint. The bottoms of their glasses are filled with crushed mint stems, and the liquid is clear and viscous. She takes a sip, and beams at David.

He is frowning at her. 'Are you serious?' he says, concerned.

'Serious about what? Did that sound terrible? I thought it was okay.'

'About having depression? Were you unhappy all that time? I

know you said you were when you wanted to go back to work, but I thought you were just adopting an extreme bargaining position.'

Libby is piqued. 'You thought I was lying to make you let me go back to work?'

'*Let* you?'

She is cross. 'Yes. Let me. That's the way we've always been, isn't it? I do what you want me to do. I'm not complaining about it – I've bought into it, too.'

David puts his mojito on the low table. 'I thought the decisions we took were joint decisions.'

Libby looks at the starry sky, and laughs. 'In what sense were they joint decisions? Coming out here, it turns out, has been a fabulous idea. But it sure as hell wasn't my idea. Ditto moving to Brighton, getting married, having Charlie, me giving up work rather than taking maternity leave. All of them, except the last one, have been positive moves and all of them have been great. But they all came from you. You even decided I needed to get in touch with my father again. You did that for me. You were going to contact him without telling me. All those things I just said, I wouldn't have chosen any of them at the time.'

David is astonished. 'Lib? How can you say that? We decided we wanted all those things. Apart from your dad, and I thought you'd be pleased. Are you saying I pressured you into having *Charlie*?'

'Charlie is fabulous. I wouldn't change anything about him for the world and I would happily throw myself in front of a car, just for his entertainment. But when you brought up the subject of having a baby, it took me a while to get used to the idea. That's not such a surprise, is it?'

David frowns. 'Lib, you're looking at it all wrong. Think back to how you were when I met you. You were totally screwy. I mean, mad. Christ. You were fixated on your social life. You drank too much, stayed out too late, and you were working yourself into an imminent grave. Literally. Your skin was covered in eczema, you'd wheeze just walking down the street, and it was only a matter of time before you were going to drunkenly tuck into a bowl of peanuts. I encouraged you to change, and I did it because I could see your potential. I loved you. I thought I was helping.'

Libby frowns at him. 'I was nowhere near that bad. I was a young, skinny, successful girl about town, and you wanted me to settle. In the end I did. You were right, it was time for me to move on. And you were right, it's time for me to write this bloody letter.'

'Lib! You were losing the plot. You *were*. If you ask me, you were working through all these feelings you had about your father rejecting you. You're still working through them, and you're absolutely right that you need to write that letter. You were a daddy's girl without a daddy. You should thank me for getting you on track, not blame me for controlling you.'

'I never said you controlled me. I have never said that ever ever ever. And my father is a minor part of all this. I'm not a daddy's girl – that is pure crap. How can I be? I've managed without him fine all these years. I knew what my options were with you. You made them plain. I could have you, and leave London, and have babies; or I could have left you, stayed in the city, and dedicated myself to my career. There wasn't much to compromise on there, and I chose you. It wasn't difficult.'

Libby is surprised to see David looking angry. In their three years together, she has rarely seen him like this. It doesn't suit him. His is a face made for serenity. Screwed up like this it looks monstrous.

'Darling,' she tells him again, 'it's a compliment.'

'It's not, because you led me to believe that you were of the same mind as I was. I thought we both loved Brighton.'

'I do love it.'

'And that we both wanted a baby.'

'I did. It just took me longer to think about it. Because for you, starting a family had always been of paramount importance. It was always your main ambition. I'd often thought I might never have children. I thought I'd be terrible at it. So it was an adjustment for me to make, and it wasn't an adjustment for you.'

161

'I thought you were happy to stay home with him.'

'When I was pregnant and working, of course I could think of nothing more inviting than staying at home all day long, lolling on the sofa. It sounded great. But when it came down to it, I was bored out of my brain. There was literally nothing to do. I sat and watched telly with the baby on my breast. I changed his nappy, I put him down for naps, and I waited for you to come home. And even though we spend lots of time waiting for you to come home here, somehow it's completely different.'

The night is warm and breezy. Libby is confused. She'd always assumed David was sympathetic to her.

'But you could go out!' he says forcefully. 'You had Natalie and Jenny, and as far as I could tell, you were always at various coffee establishments. Weren't you?'

Libby tries not to cry. She shrugs and blinks. 'Coffee didn't really fill the gap. I've been terribly miserable,' she says, looking down at her drink, then looks up with a smile. 'I'm okay now, though. Working things out.'

The band arrives at their table. Libby sees five faces beaming at her, and forces herself to smile back. All the musicians are dressed in tuxedoes.

'Buena sera!' says the double-bass player. They wait for a request. Neither David nor Libby has been aware of the music as anything other than background noise. David motions to Libby to ask for a tune, and her mind goes completely blank. She doesn't know any Cuban music. Or rather, she can only think of one song.

'"Guantanamera"?' she asks, tentatively. She sees the musicians exchanging glances.

David laughs. 'They just played that!' he says quietly. Then he addresses them, with the only other Cuban music he can think of. 'How about something from *Buena Vista Social Club*?'

They all nod impassively, and break into 'Dos Gardenias'. Libby watches them playing, and imagines their minds drifting. She decides that the double-bass player is thinking about women, judging by the secretive smile on his face. The trumpeter, she thinks, is planning a risky escape to Florida. Maybe she should tell him that the grass is not necessarily greener. He would never believe her.

David speaks loudly to be heard above the music.

'Libby?' he says, tapping her knee. 'Have you really, truly hated it?'

Libby considers this. She feels it is imperative that she is honest. She has never felt confident enough, since Charlie was born, to tell David the unvarnished truth.

'I couldn't regret a moment spent with Charlie. He's just amazing, isn't he?' David nods fondly. 'But apart from that, I've actually felt that my world has fallen apart. I lost my sense of myself. From the moment I went to university, I was a lawyer. That was who I was. Libby the lawyer. Suddenly I wasn't any more. I was a mother, instead. I can't say I found it easy. In fact, yes, I pretty much did hate it. But that is in the past, now. I'm happy, now. And we'll get my dad sorted out, won't we, and we'll all be fine for ever.'

Libby looks at her husband. She feels a stab of relief. Now she has, at last, been honest with him. She's told him how she felt, and now she's happy anyway. Everything will be fine. He will sympathise, and they will share more secrets. They will write the letter.

David is looking at her accusingly.

'Why didn't you tell me how you were feeling?' he demands. 'Christ! I feel like a fool! A bloody dickhead! You never told me. I thought, *since* you didn't tell me, that you were as immersed in the domestic bliss as I was. Forgive me for feeling that I'd never been happier. Forgive me for believing you when you said that you hadn't, either.'

'Oh, excuse me,' Libby says, astonished. 'You were not immersed in domestic fucking bliss, David. There's no such thing. You were a management consultant. You went to work at the crack of dawn and came home at seven if I was lucky. Weekends were playtime, and I was there too so you didn't even scratch the surface of what it's really like. You have no idea what it's like when you spend all day, every day, doing the same things over and over again. Changing nappies. Putting the baby down for a nap. Getting him up again. Feeding him. Changing another nappy. Discovering that there's no such thing as popping out to buy the paper any more, that it takes twenty minutes to get through the door. I'm a lawyer. I know lots of things. I was successful at what I did, and I'm crap at being a housewife.'

The band suddenly reach the end of the song, and Libby hopes she and David haven't been too rude. These men have been playing just for them, and they have argued throughout. She reaches for some money, but David beats her to it and hands the singer a five-dollar bill. This is far too generous, but probably not unknown at the Nacional.

The man pockets it and grins widely. The bass player gives Libby the thumbs-up, and they all move on to the next table, where a young white couple in matching tie-dyed trousers are clearly having a rare treat.

Libby sits back, and looks out at Havana by night. It is very different from, say, London by night. There are fewer cars, and the electricity is erratic. All she can see is a sprinkling of orange lights. There is a huge black hole where the sea laps the city. Libby remembers when she and David first arrived in Brighton. They had cocktails at the Grand Hotel one night, to celebrate their arrival in the town. As they stumbled down the front steps after three Sea Breezes, Libby watched the cars speeding along the seafront. Beyond them there was darkness. Libby was consumed by an urge to stand on the edge of the sea. She took David's hand and ran across, dodging both lanes of traffic. They climbed over an ornamental hedge, walked down to the beach, and stood with their backs to the lights, and the noise, and the people, and looked out towards France.

David put his arm around her waist. The salty wind blew her hair across her face.

'We live at the edge of England,' he said. 'This is where it stops. There's nothing out there.'

'There's France,' Libby reminded him.

'Exactly. To your left, Eastbourne. To your right, Portsmouth. Straight ahead, Dieppe.'

Libby loves cities that are lapped by the sea. She loves the way they can expand on one side, but not on the other. She loves the immovable boundary.

She looks at David. He is staring in the other direction, at the door that leads back into the hotel. An elderly couple emerges from it. The man wears a white suit with blue shirt and pale tie, and the woman is expensively clad in what looks to Libby like Chanel. She tries to imagine them out on the Havana streets, and fails. They must spend all their time sheltering here, in the hotel.

Neither of them wants to say anything. As the silence grows more and more pointed, Libby decides that she will not break it. David will speak first. However long he waits, she can hold out for longer. She's practised at this. When she was a teenager, and her relationship with her mother was suddenly transformed, on both sides, from 'she's my best friend' to 'she's a moody cow', Libby used to retreat into silence. It drove her mother mad, and it worked every time.

It works on David, too.

'Right-o,' he says eventually. 'Shall we talk about it?'

'Mmm.'

'It's good to have things out in the open. I can't say I understand, Lib, I really can't. Sometimes women really are from Mars, I think.'

'Women are from *Venus*, you stupid twat.'

'Are men from Mars?'

'You should bloody know. Of course they are. Mars is the planet of war. Venus is the planet of love.'

David frowns. 'Well, that is *really* sexist.'

'Oh yeah? How many wars can you name that have been started by women?'

'The Falklands? And as the ruler of the Empire, I'm sure Victoria put her name to one or two, as well. And Elizabeth the First. No doubt.'

'And every other war ever fought has been fought by men, with men, for men. But we've strayed into a different argument here.'

'Okay. Forget women. I realise that having a baby involves a big adjustment. And it's a far bigger adjustment for the mother than the father. But why in God's name did you not tell me? That's what makes me angry. The notion of your suffering in silence. I'm looking back now to the first few months of Charlie's life, I'm thinking it was all a pretence. Was everything a show? I used to love coming home from work. I'd practically skip down the road. You'd be there, waiting, and you'd look so happy, and you'd pour us a drink and tell me all these tiny things that had happened. Charlie looked at his hands. Charlie took a toy from me. Charlie nearly rolled over.' He stares at Libby. 'Was that real? And did Golda Meir start any wars? Israel's always fighting.'

'I don't think she actively started them. But she was around during the Yom Kippur war. You see, these incidents are totally the exception. The thing was, I didn't want to upset you. You thought I was fabulous, and I knew I wasn't. I knew I wasn't cut out to be a wonderful mother. I could barely struggle through the days. Sometimes I didn't get dressed until I saw you coming down the road. I didn't want to fail you. When I met you, I really thought I was special. You moulded me into someone normal, and then I found I couldn't even be that.'

David is putting his glass down, and considering ordering more mojitos. His hand freezes midway to the table.

'I did *what?*'

Libby wants to retract the word 'normal', but she feels it's too late, now. 'You heard,' she tells him, instead.

'Is that really the way you see it?'

Libby doesn't know how to reply.

'You think you were special and then I made you normal? You

were a silly, self-obsessed little girl who thought she was better than everyone else because her mother had always told her beauty was the most important thing. You pranced around wanting to be daddy's little girl, but you never saw your dad, so you demanded adoration and indulgence off everyone you met. It was sick. And you didn't care about your long-term health. You lived like there was no tomorrow. Christ, Lib! And now I've found your father for you as the final piece of the jigsaw. How many times do I have to tell you? I saved you.'

'You saved me? What was I, a kitten up a tree? I did have a mind of my own, you know. I chose you. You didn't rescue me. And I would far rather have contacted my dad by myself.'

David picks up his glass, looks at crushed mint, and slams it back down. 'You would never have done it. And actually, I believe I did save you. You needed to leave London. You had to get away from that job and those hours. Your friends weren't helping. You needed to focus on something other than yourself. That was why a baby was such a good idea. You're so much healthier since you've been with me. You're a better weight. You don't have work pressure. You walk by the sea every day. I've created an existence for you where you don't have to worry about anything at all. And now you tell me you've been hating it?'

'You stupid bastard! Do you really think I'm not grateful enough to you for marrying me? Do you? The only thing I've had to worry about is dying of boredom.'

'I had no idea you saw our life like that.'

'Well, you do now.'

'Fine.'

'Fine.'

'Fine.'

Libby sneaks a glance at him. His hair is falling on to his cheekbone, as ever, but he doesn't look handsome any more. He is no longer the ideal husband. He is a conniving control freak. He is a sexist bastard. He thought she was under his thumb. He thought he was the boss. His eyes are glinting with rage, although she knows he will not let it rip. He will keep it buttoned up and will fume silently.

Libby would like to have a blazing row and make up, as long as she could convince him in the process that he has looked at their relationship in a pompous, proprietorial and entirely inappropriate way, apparently for ever. David, however, does not do blazing rows. She might be able to force him to shout back if she started yelling at him, but that would be exhausting, and there is nowhere to do it. They can't do more than exchange poisonous whispers in this illustrious setting. At home, she would be constrained by the knowledge that Myleene's family, Luis and his household, the old woman who sits on the steps and the man who polishes his Cadillac, among others, would be listening. They might not understand the words, but they would understand enough. She has no intention of casting herself, for them, as a weird, shrieking foreigner.

Libby bites her lip and stops herself speaking. David is going to talk first. However much the tension hangs in the air, she is not going to break the silence. He will see how strong she can be. She looks up. The moon is almost full. She stares at it, and at the stars. She clenches her nails into her palm, and tries to remain calm. They are thousands of miles from home, and she doesn't know what she wants. She is married to a supercilious git who has treated her as a project. David thinks he's better than her, cleverer than she is. She wonders if she should leave him.

Libby runs through some scenarios. She could take Charlie back to England. She could move into a flat like Elena's with him, and leave David to knock around that big apartment on his own. If she did that, David would sleep with Yasmin. Natalie and Libby would have to set up a support group. Women Cuckolded by Yasmin McLeod Anonymous. She imagines that adverts and a website would yield up other potential members.

Libby feels a stab of loneliness. The people she considered

friends at work have turned out to be nothing of the sort: they are friendly when she sees them, but that rarely happens. Anna is nice, but she would be bewildered if Libby came running to her in desperation. Her older friends are scattered around the world, and those friendships have been neglected. She couldn't call any of them in tears, to talk about her marriage. Only Natalie and Jenny are day-to-day friends. A year ago she didn't know them. If the email place was open right now, she would go and write to Natalie. She decides to do it tomorrow afternoon.

In the meantime, she wishes she could confide in Maggie – an unlikely confidante, but the best available. Maggie knows nothing about the fights they had before they came here. She would be amazed. But she is David's friend before she's Libby's. She and David study together. If Maggie knew about this, things would be awkward for everyone.

'You may as well know,' David says, cross at having, once again, been the first to speak. 'I've been emailing your father. He comes across as perfectly nice. He asked me if he could contact you, so I gave him our address and Luis's phone number and your email. You don't really need to finish your little master-piece.'

'Great. Thanks. Nice to know I can't be trusted to write the most important letter of my life. Far better that you take control and do it for me. I'd much rather you spoke to my father before I did. Cheers.'

'Sorry. Are you going to divorce me, or what?' He is looking at her, half smiling. This is David's way of offering a truce. He wants to make it all into a joke.

'Oh, don't be so facetious. You've just told me that I'm your puppet, that you've been pulling my strings all this time. I wouldn't mind some time away from you, to be honest – if you think I could survive for five minutes in the big wide world on my own – but that's not exactly practical. For now, we'd better have another drink. I can't tell you what I do want, but I know what I don't want, and that is to go home and chat inanely to Yasmin and Maggie.'

David sighs and motions to the waiter. 'Two more mojitos,' he calls. 'And make them strong.'

chapter sixteen

Maggie

'Today,' Yasmin says bossily, 'we are going to *do* Havana.'

I glare at her, over my omelette. She has been here three weeks, she slept with my friend's friend's husband, and she is trying to control me. Every day she tells me what we're going to do. She thinks I can't manage on my own. I hate it.

'What do you mean?' I demand, rudely. 'I've lived here for four weeks. I don't need to *do* anything.'

'Don't you buggery, madam,' she says, with a cheeky smile. 'We're going out, to see the city the way the locals see it. We, my dear, are going to start living.'

'Don't want to.'

'Don't want to live? Maggie, please!' Yasmin giggles. She never takes me seriously.

'I don't have to do what you want.' I turn away from her and shovel some food into my mouth, wondering what I could possibly say that would make her leave me alone. I'm supposed to be reinventing myself. The last thing I want is to find myself living on top of someone I've known since I was eight. She knows everything about me. If Libby didn't justifiably hate her, I would worry about what she was telling them. I wish she would go away.

I look around Elena's living room. I see, in retrospect, that I was happy here, when I used to eat my breakfast on my own at the table in the corner. I loved the tapestry of the black horse on the wall, and all the retro-style furniture. I loved watching the neighbours passing the open door. The egg woman comes around every week. I was entranced by the idea of an egg woman, selling them from house to house. I loved the fact that Elena and I were each beginning to understand what the other was saying. Then Yasmin came along and muscled in on it all. She laughs at the decor. She giggles with my landlady. She's used me to do all the groundwork for her, and now she's trying to boss me about.

'Oooh,' she says, mockingly. 'Someone got out of bed the wrong side, Miss Grumpy.'

'Fuck off, Yasmin,' I say. Elena hears me, and calls through from the kitchen.

'No good,' she admonishes.

'Desculpe.'

'So,' says Yasmin, stroking my arm. She smiles a smile that probably works on men. I wish she wasn't so pretty. 'Why don't you want to come out on the town with me? I met these guys yesterday, they spoke brilliant English, and they said there's a party at this bar in the vedado. We can go along, do some dancing. No other tourists there. They said it'll be wicked.'

I laugh, in spite of myself. 'I bet they didn't. Did they actually say "It will be wicked"?'

'They practically did. They would've if they'd known how to. Come on. You can practise your Spanish. We'll get you a Cuban boyfriend yet.'

My heart sinks at the inevitability of it. I know she's going to win. I know I am going to have to go out and be sociable, and stand around on my own while Yasmin deals with her admirers. 'Yasmin!' I say. 'I do not want a boyfriend. I don't care what nationality, I just don't want one. My experience of men has been nothing but grim. You know what happened to my one nice boyfriend. He ran off with my best friend. See, even the nice ones are fuckwits.' I look nervously towards the kitchen, but Elena didn't pick it up this time. I wait for Yasmin to defend Ivan. I want to ask her how long they stayed together in London, and why they broke up. I am longing to know everything that happened, but she always blocks the subject.

'You are no fun,' she says, reaching for the coffee pot and topping up both our cups. 'Lighten up, hey? So don't have a boyfriend. Carry on being resident spinster. At least you can speak Spanish. Come on, you can do the talking for both of us. Be my interpreter. Do you know lots of rude words?'

I consider this. I like the fact that I have a skill that Yasmin entirely lacks. For once, she needs me.

'Only if you'll lend me something to wear.'

I have bought a few clothes, recently. They are better than my hiding-away outfits. I have some bright T-shirts, and a short skirt and a pair of shorts. They are hardly the shiny hotpants that Cuban women wear with such panache, but they are better. Yasmin's clothes, however, are in a different league. It could, of course, be the way she wears them.

Yasmin dresses me in a tight pink T-shirt with 'Angel' written subtly across the breasts, and one of her tiny skirts. The skirt barely stays on my hips, and I change into my best knickers, in case it falls to the floor entirely.

She stands back and considers me, her arms folded across her chest. Yasmin's tanned legs are muscular. I am extremely well aware that mine are white and bony.

'What are we going to do with your hair?' she demands. 'Did you bring any of those demon styling products with you?'

I laugh. 'Some bog-standard gel. Nothing that would do anything other than glue it down.'

'Would you let me cut it?'

I scrape it defensively into a ponytail. 'Are you mad?' I ask her. 'You? Cutting my hair? What with? Nail scissors?'

She sniggers. 'Elena's got some kitchen scissors. I saw her dissecting a chicken with them, yesterday.' She goes to the doorway. 'Elena?' she calls.

'Very tempting. Cheers.'

'Si?' calls Elena.

'Niente,' replies Yasmin, imagining herself to be speaking Spanish.

I decide to wear some lipstick to go with my outfit, and sit down in front of my mirror to apply it. As I work, rather expertly, I watch Yasmin idling around the room behind me. She picks things up, looks at them, and puts them down again. She scrutinises my paperback, and asks if she can read it after me. She picks up my course book, and skims it for a few minutes, before throwing it down with a sigh. Then I see her stretching for my diary.

'Don't read that,' I say briskly.

She looks surprised. 'I didn't know you were spying on me.' She sounds aggrieved.

'I'm not spying. I'm looking in the mirror.' I turn to face her. 'My room, Yasmin. My mirror. My stuff.'

'So what's this? Your diary?'

'Doesn't matter what it is. It's mine. How do I look?'

She snaps into action, and assesses me with her head on one side.

'Like a different girl. Like a babe. If we could just get the hair sorted, you'd be a stunner. Shame my clothes are so frigging humungous on you.'

'Do you think Libby might want to come out with us tonight?' I ask as casually as I can. I put away my lipstick and busy myself with my make-up bag as I say it. Yasmin is not fooled.

She laughs. 'You know, you were exactly like this when you fancied a boy at school. You remember those discos we used to go to, well you'd always be, like, "Hmmm, I don't really mind, but do you think it would be okay if we checked whether Ivan was going to be there?" And you thought you were being really subtle about it.' She looks at her nails. 'Not that we really need to go there. But what is it with Libby?'

I throw a pillow at her. 'I was not like that! It was different for you. If you liked someone you could just saunter over and have them. As we both found out.'

'You know, Ivan was years ago for both of us. We need to get over it.' For a moment, there is an awkward pause. Then Yasmin sits on the bed. 'Mags,' she says, 'you say you don't want a boyfriend. You go on about Libby twenty-four-seven. You're not a lezza, are you?'

I look at her, and realise that she is serious.

'No,' I tell her. 'I am not gay.'

'Because it would be fine.' She throws my hair gel in the air, and catches it. 'You could tell me, you know.'

'Of course it would be fine. But I'm not. I happen to feel sorry for Libby being stuck in that flat with that baby all day long. That's all.'

'Fine. We'll go there now and see if we can tempt her along for a night of hot lesbian action.'

I am astonished by the difference, as I walk down the street. Men look at me, pointedly talk about me, and walk alongside me. This happens whenever I go out with Yasmin, but it's never been aimed at me before. I have been offered her leftovers, but now I am attracting attention in my own right. I rather enjoy it. I like chatting to them in Spanish, and watching Yasmin trying to work out what I'm saying. It makes me feel I have gained the upper hand. I must hide my diary, though. If Yasmin read it everything would be ruined.

I made friends with Yasmin on our first day at school, when we were eight. Mum and Dad compromised their principles and sent me to the private girls' school in town, rather than the local primary. I was delighted. I wore my green uniform with pride. Years passed before I realised that it marked me out, conspicuously, to the outside world as 'posh', rather than clever; that it was a curse rather than a blessing.

I remember walking through the wooden front door with its stained-glass windows, holding Mum's hand, on the first day. I had read girls' school stories back-to-back for the past two years, and all of a sudden I was living the dream. The hallway was mosaic-tiled, and smelt of polish. We located my classroom, and I stood on the threshold, my green blazer buttoned up, my hair forced into plaits, and looked at a large room full of old-fashioned desks, with hinged lids. It was not unlike our classroom at Havana University. The room was populated with little girls exactly like me. There were pegs in one corner, and through the window I could see a large lawn with a climbing frame. I dropped Mum's hand, and smiled up at her. She looked down at me tenderly.

'I'll be all right here, Mummy,' I remember saying.

We were allocated seats in the order in which we arrived. Yasmin came through the door after me, so we sat together at the very back. As soon as I saw her, I thought she looked like fun. She was tall, and she had hair as blonde as Grace's. She was swiftly the most popular girl in the class, and she took me along with her. Without Yasmin, I would have been on the sidelines. We have always known that – it has always hung in the air between us – and we have never mentioned it.

I must be fair to Yasmin. She proved her true worth after Grace went, and I will always be grateful for her instinctive reaction. That is why I will talk to her now, even after what she and Ivan did to me. Her mother used to bring her to our house, and we sat in my room and talked, or we would go out and play. She let me set the agenda, then. I never thought I'd see her again after she stole Ivan, let alone stroll through the streets of Havana wearing her clothes. Yasmin is my past personified. I cannot shake her off.

I walk into the flat, shyly. I know I look different and I hope they say it suits me. I hope they think to mention it.

'Wow,' says David. 'Maggie, you've got legs! If I was a single man, I'd . . .'

He tails off, grinning at his wife, who smiles generously.

'No, he's right,' she says. 'I'll have what you're having. That's Yasmin's get-up, right? Hence, you look like a swamped waif in it?'

I nod. 'Of course. Not really my style.'

Yasmin bursts out, 'Not your style? Who are you kidding? What about your work clothes?'

Lib looks confused. 'At Amex?'

I frown. 'No,' I say hastily. 'My work clothes were really, really dull. Yasmin's joking, aren't you, Yas?'

She rolls her eyes. 'No one understands a joke round here. Yes, Maggie, you used to wear grey suits and prissy little blouses every day, right?'

'Right.'

Charlie's sitting on the floor sucking a plastic brick. I kneel down with him. At least it's always easy to change the subject with a baby around. I watch the fat of my leg squeezing out as I kneel. I am definitely putting on weight.

'Charlie boy,' I say. He turns to look at me, with his clear blue eyes, and giggles. 'Hello, Charlie. How are you doing?'

David adopts his baby voice, which has, it seems, taken on a Cuban accent lately. 'I am doing so fine, thank you, Maggie. So kind you are to ask.'

'What's this?' asks Lib. 'Our son's turned into Yoda?'

'I tell you what,' says David, suddenly. 'I know someone who'll want to see the new sexy Maggie.' He walks to the kitchen, and hammers on the interconnecting door. 'Hola!' he shouts. 'Luis?'

While everyone is looking towards the door, I notice an envelope on the table, addressed in Libby's handwriting, to a man in Australia. Curious, I slip it into my bag. I will read it later and replace it. I miss the baby monitor. If I had something like that here, I wouldn't need to do this.

After a while, the door opens, and Luis puts his head around it. 'Hola,' he says cheerfully, taking in everyone. 'Oy-ey, Charlie. Buenas dias!' He picks him up expertly, and kisses him, before handing him back to me. 'Maggie! Que linda! Libby, buenas.'

I consider Luis. David is constantly trying to get me interested in him, and now that I look at him, he is good-looking. He is certainly charming, and attentive. I would have to make an effort, but I might be able to find him interesting. A relationship with Luis would be an effective way of spending much more time with this family.

And he's told David that he thinks I'm pretty. Men have not beaten down doors for the pleasure of gazing upon my fair form; not outside Vixenz, anyway. I may not want a boyfriend, but I am in no position to brush aside interest. I know that David is an awful lot more attractive than Luis, but he is off limits. I will give Luis a go, I decide. I will invite him out with us tonight, and drink as much rum as I can, and see what happens. I will experiment with sex, and see if, for once, it might make me happy. It would be a distraction. I might be ready for it, at last.

'Luis, this is Yasmin,' says David. Yasmin looks him up and down, and takes his hand with her most radiant smile. He leans forward and kisses her on the cheek. She simpers slightly. He laughs. He is standing closer to her than he did to me.

'Encantado,' he says. Yasmin doesn't understand, but I do. *Enchanted*.

'Luis,' she says loudly. 'Yo y Maggie. Tonight. Questa noce. Nous sortons in Havana, si? Con toi?'

David translates. Luis points to himself. 'Yo?' he asks. 'Si?' He beams and bows his head towards Yasmin. 'Muchas gracias.'

To Yasmin's apparent astonishment, I try to bow out of the evening. I invite myself, repeatedly, to spend the time with Libby and David, to go out with them for an early dinner and to relax on their sofa with a beer and a game of cards. None of them will hear of it.

'I didn't get you dressed up like this so you could play snakes and bloody ladders all night,' says Yasmin. She puts one hand on her hip and looks at me challengingly. She looks like a model when she stands like that.

'Go on, Maggie,' says David. 'A night out will do you the

world of good. God knows we'd like one. Make the most of it.'

'So you two go,' I say grumpily, knowing I am defeated. 'I'll babysit.'

'No,' says Lib. 'You deserve it. And you'll enjoy it when you get in the mood. Have a couple of drinks. Speak some Spanish.'

Luis has disappeared back to his own flat. No one is on my side.

'Fine,' I say, in the end. 'But I'm not staying out late. I've got uni in the morning.'

'Oooh,' says Yasmin. 'Last of the party queens.'

It is Ivan all over again.

We sit outside a large colonial house on a leafy street in the middle of Vedado. Yasmin and Luis manage to sit on a step together, their thighs touching, while I perch on a chair opposite them. The garden is heaving with people. A band is warming up. The sun is close to the horizon, and the sky is a gentle pink. Yasmin waves to the men she saw earlier, and they come to chat, then disappear into the crowd.

I look at her. She knows that Luis is jokingly referred to as 'Maggie's boyfriend'. I never told her I was planning to give it a go. She doesn't realise quite what she is doing to me, this time. It is not the same as it was with Ivan. It is still painful. I watch Luis's open face, and see that he is transfixed by her. This is not surprising. She has managed to get a gentle tan, which has turned her skin golden. Her hair is blonder than ever, and she is slimmer even than before, but she retains her curves. I was mad to think that any man would like me, once he'd set eyes on Yasmin. Luis seems to be captivated by the terrible mixture of English, French, Italian and Latin that Yasmin uses in the place of Spanish. From time to time, one of them looks to me for a translation. After a while, I get bored, and leave. They hardly even notice.

'See you, then,' I say, quietly. 'Adios.'

I fight my way through sweaty bodies, and buy another plastic cup of beer to get me home. I walk up the wide road, lined on either side with huge old houses. I sip my beer as I go, and wonder what I will do now. On the main road, I hail a cab.

It is a hot night, as usual, but the taxi's window doesn't open. I look at my reflection as we speed down the Malecon. I am superimposed over the dark sea. I am ethereal, barely there. I am nothing. I read the letter Libby wrote to her father. Her hurt jumps out from the page at me. I didn't know she hardly knew him. I replace it carefully in the envelope and decide to post it for her, in the morning.

I listen out for Yasmin, all night. She doesn't come home.

chapter seventeen

Libby

Libby doesn't mind the fact that she waited forty minutes to get on to the computer. She appreciates the odd hour to herself. She chatted mindlessly to the guy who is now trying to read her emails over her shoulder. She noticed people looking at her, and seeing a single woman. It was a small thing, but she liked it. She is making an effort to consider herself in different ways, at the moment. She cannot be defined by labels. She is not just *a lawyer*, or *a mother*, and most certainly not *a wife*. She is Libby. She is all three, and she is also her own person. She is considering herself out of David's context, and wonders to what extent she has submitted to his will. She is itching to spend some time without him. At the moment, her daydreams involve her, Charlie and Maggie (because she needs another adult for sanity) renting a big Cadillac and whirling around the island.

Today, she has demanded the entire afternoon off. Unfortunately, Yasmin heard of this arrangement, and announced that she would come too. David said Libby had to give her a chance, so she is meeting her in half an hour. With any luck, Yasmin will forget to turn up, or else she will be so late that Libby will be justified in not waiting. She will give her fifteen minutes, and that is all.

The American is still waiting for a computer. She hopes his

eyesight isn't perfect. It would need to be excellent for him to read her emails at that distance. She hears his chair shifting. He's shunted it a little closer to her back.

Libby finishes her letter to Natalie, and reads it through before she clicks send. She refuses to write exclusively in lower case, or to use text-ish phrases like 'CU l8r'. She won't even let an 'adn' or a 'teh' slip through. She knows she is unhip, and she doesn't care. It is the lawyer in her.

Dear Natalie, *she has written.*

How are you, my dear? I'm sorry I haven't written for a while – internet access is slow and unreliable. I've just received your last email. I wish I was there to give you a hug. More than that, I wish you were here, but I know that since the trollop is among us, you won't be crossing the Atlantic any time soon. That was such a brilliant idea of mine, too, until She showed up and spoilt it.

Have you allowed Graham home yet? I know you said you couldn't use access to Alfie as a weapon, but I actually think you can. Make Graham realise the consequences of his actions, because that's the only thing that's going to stop him in his tracks next time. Sorry to be so blunt, hon, but it's true.

David and I are also fighting (pause for a deep breath). No one else has noticed, as far as I know. We keep it to ourselves, which probably isn't healthy. A while ago we went for a posh drink, and during the course of an idle chat, he finally accepted just how frustrating I found early motherhood, and I discovered that he thinks he 'rescued' me from a life of irresponsibility. He has also taken it upon himself to bring my absent father back into my life (long story). I am considering the whole of the relationship in the light of the things he said that night. I'm furious. How dare he tell me I can't function without him?

The worst thing is, we can't clear the air. David refuses to argue, and the tension hangs there and is never addressed. I am ignoring it as best I can, and to be honest, I am craving some time away from him. I wrote my dad a letter, which has vanished, no doubt posted for me by my all-controlling husband. I wasn't even going to send it – I was about to redraft but it seems that option has been removed. I swear, one day soon I'm going to pick up Charlie and a spare pair of knickers and walk down to the end of the street and get on a bus. However, this afternoon we are leaving for two nights at the beach. Maggie's coming too, and we've booked an apartment/hotel. It's only 15 km from the city, but everyone says it's fabulous. I'll try to shake him off as much as I can. It should be a little cooler there.

There is a bloke behind me, called STAN, waiting for this computer, and I'm sure he's READING over my shoulder. If he is, PLEASE STOP. Being an American in Cuba isn't that cool – this guy seems to think he has made an enormous courageous political statement by coming here ('veee-a Canada!'), when I know he just wanted a cheap holiday in the sun and one over on his mates.

Cuba, incidentally, is wonderful. I am full of admiration for Castro. We love the weekly paper, printed in English as well as Spanish, especially for people like us. The paper (you will love this) is called *Granma*. That's the name of the boat that Fidel and Che and co. used when they sailed from Mexico and launched the revolution. They bought it off a North American – so it really does mean Grandma. I find this endlessly poignant and endearing. And it must be one of the only government newspapers in the world that can slag off the US on the front page every single issue.

God, Nat, I wish I could talk to you. Maggie's nice enough, but she won't divulge anything about herself, so everything is one-sided. Actually, you might know people who know her from Amex – Maggie Wilson, small and skinny with long curly hair, worked in HR I believe. Any inside info appreciated. I am so desperately in need of a friend. I am half tempted to come home early, with Charlie. Things I miss include: English weather (crazy but true), good food, and shopping. Things I will be sorry to leave include: baby-adoration, general friendliness, and slimming with no effort whatsoever. What would I give to be able to weigh myself, now.

Take care,

Lib xxx

Libby considers writing an email to her mother, but decides she is too angry with her to bother. Her mum deliberately kept her father away from her for years. Like David, she doesn't trust me, Libby thinks, to make my own decisions. She wonders what her father will be like. All she can remember is a tall man, with a red face.

She turns swiftly to the American, and catches him looking quickly away from her screen.

'All yours,' she says cheerfully. Stan is big and rugged-looking, with red hair, and he is from Colorado.

'Hey,' he says, holding out a massive hand. Red hairs sprout from his fingers. 'Maybe I'll see you again some time.' He smiles in what he imagines to be a sincere and direct manner. He would be wounded if he knew how creepy Libby, and most other women, found him.

'Maybe.' Libby wonders whether he's flirting with her. She swings her hips as she walks away. As she pays for her time on the computer, she glances back to check whether he's still watching her. He is logging into Hotmail. She tells herself she's glad. The last thing she needs is a stalker. She looks instead at the pregnant woman behind the counter.

'Dos,' says the woman, in a bored manner.

'Niño?' Libby says, pointing at the bump and wishing, once again, that she was the one learning Spanish. She hands over two dollars.

The woman shakes her head. She is pretty; dark and rosy. 'Niña. Daughter.'

'Quando?'

'Dos meses. Junio o Julio.'

Libby points to herself. 'Niño, seis meses. A la casa.'

They grin at each other. 'Good luck,' Libby says, as she leaves.

'Thank you.'

She steps out of the air-conditioned room, and into the mid-day heat.

When five minutes stretch to ten, and ten stretch to another bottle of water, Libby decides, with great relief, that Yasmin is not coming. The old Libby would have put her foot down and refused to meet her anyway, but Cuban Libby was too tired, and too intrigued by the prospect of an afternoon away from the baby and the flat, to be fussy about who was accompanying her. She gulps down the water and decides to brave the heat and walk along the Malecon, alone, into the old town. She wants to go to the touristy market by the cathedral square. The beads and sequins are falling off her flip-flops, which were made for light evenings outside seaside bars in Europe, not for pounding the uneven streets of Havana.

She puts her hat on, and looks round for the waiter. As she attempts to catch his eye, Yasmin enters her peripheral vision, as she strolls around the corner, deep in conversation with a young man. Libby sees her look around, and smile brilliantly when their eyes meet. Reluctantly, she halts her quest for the bill.

'Hi, Yasmin,' she says, flatly. Yasmin is wearing a cotton dress that reaches halfway down her thighs. Libby tries not to look at her legs. She knows they are slender and long, and tanned to just the right degree. Yasmin always makes her feel inadequate.

'Hey, Lib! Ready to hit the town?' Yasmin sits down, stretches out her legs in front of her, and looks up at her friend, who is tall and slim, dressed only in a pair of purple shorts.

'Adios, amigo,' she tells him with a wave.

He smiles charmingly at Libby.

'But I meet your friend?' he suggests, with a wink.

'Oh, sure. Pedro, Libby. Libby, Pedro. There, you've met her. See you!'

'Later, okay? Ten o'clock, right?'

'D'accord. Okay, vamos, vamos.' She yawns. 'Sorry about that.'

'That's okay,' Libby tells her. 'He's rather handsome.'

'You think? You think I really should date him? I would have considered it, you know. But I'm actually holding out for someone right now.' Yasmin blushes. Naturally, she turns a delicate shade of pink. Libby always goes deep purple.

'Holding out for someone? What, someone in Cuba?'

'Mmmm. Oh, sod it, I'll tell you. Your sexy neighbour. He's kind of occupying my thoughts.'

'Luis?'

'Mmmm.'

'But he likes Maggie.'

'Maggie doesn't like him. But, going back to that last guy, Pedro or whatever, I have to agree to dates to make them go away. It's harmless. And we'll be at the seaside tonight, won't we, so I couldn't go if I wanted to. At least this one claims he wants me to teach him English. A couple of points for imagination. The others mainly want to be my "guide around town". I'm like, hello? I don't need one thank you.' She grins. 'They all want sex, I do realise that, and right now I don't. Novel, I grant you. Not with them, anyway.'

'How many dates have you broken?'

'Oh, hundreds. How are you for a drink? Do you mind if I grab a water before we go? Actually, I'd kill for a Coke. Do you think they have them? And what are Coca Cola doing in Cuba anyway? I always wonder how they swung that.'

'They must have a way of getting round the embargo,' Libby agrees. 'It's made in Mexico, it says that on the cans. It's probably made under licence and imported from there. I wouldn't touch the stuff, myself. It seems all wrong.'

Yasmin looks at Libby and smiles a strained smile. 'All wrong?' she echoes. 'Pourquoi, if I fancy a particular beverage, is it *all wrong* for me to have it?' Yasmin looks bored, rather than aggrieved, and Libby can't be bothered to fight. She puts up a token argument.

'We're in Cuba. I know you can get Coke everywhere, but I wouldn't say that's entirely a good thing. Specially not seeing how this place is suffering from America's economic policy towards it. But that's just my point of view. I'm not exactly in a position to stop anyone else drinking it, so please, go ahead.' Yasmin looks at her and rolls her eyes to the sky.

'That is so righteous,' she complains. 'Now I can't have one. You make me feel like an airhead.'

'You look like an airhead.'

'I know! So let me order a bloody water and we can talk about shopping. Let me live up to my image. Anything worth having, do you reckon?'

'There must be something. I need shoes. That market's always heaving with tourists. Shall we walk into town?'

'Lib, you crack me up. "Into town," she says, just as if we were talking about Covent Garden, or Brighton. In Norwich we always used to say, "Are you going into town?" I don't really think walking's the greatest idea your lawyerly mind has ever come up with. We'll get a cab.'

Libby sighs. The shopping had better be good.

In the taxi, Libby makes an effort to get on with Yasmin. She is increasingly aware that she needs to be self-sufficient. She cannot rely on David to run her social life. She needs friends and she can't afford to be fussy about where they come from.

She tries to analyse exactly why she has always bristled at the sight of Yasmin. The sound of her voice makes Libby's skin crawl. Even without the issue of Natalie and Graham, she knows she wouldn't feel comfortable in her presence. Yasmin is loud and brash, but Libby could still like someone with those attributes.

It is, she realises suddenly, David. Libby has always been the most attractive woman she knows. She has never felt vulnerable like this before. Yasmin is prettier than she is, she doesn't have a child, and she is a proven temptress. David takes people at face value. Their marriage is at a point where Libby suspects either of them would be vulnerable to outside comfort. She knows that, were she lucky enough to have an admirer, she would also be determined to say no. David, however, could be seduced. He would be devastated afterwards, but Yasmin could reel him in. Libby is certain of it.

'Yasmin?' she says, tentatively. Yasmin is staring out of the window, at the low wall of the Malecon, and the choppy waters of the Atlantic beyond it. She doesn't look round.

'What?'

'I need to ask you something.'

Yasmin carries on staring through the window. 'Go ahead.'

'Um. Do you have any plans to seduce my husband?'

She looks around, frowning. 'Do I *what*?' Libby is silent. 'You seriously think I'm going to try to shag your husband, under your nose? Of course I'm not, you silly cow.'

'Promise?'

Yasmin sighs and holds her head in her hands.

'Yes!' she says. 'Promise! Libby, I am not like you think. I know that you hate me, but I am not that person. I know that impulsive sexual encounters have got me into trouble in the past, but I'm not the evil tart, really I'm not. If I'd been a bloke and turned up at your party and seduced Natalie, you'd have been all excited and girlie about it. What happened was extremely unfortunate, and I am actually very sorry and I feel worse about it than you would ever believe. I don't make a habit of shagging people's husbands. I do have moral standards.'

The taxi swerves across the road to avoid a pot hole. Yasmin grabs Libby's arm, and Libby hangs on to the back of the driver's seat.

'You really, really promise?' she asks, when the terror subsides. 'About David, I mean?'

'Why the sudden paranoia?'

Libby laughs. 'It's not sudden, that's for sure. I've been worrying about you and David from the day I saw you in the *paladar*. And right now, David and I are, well, you must have noticed.'

Yasmin flashes her wide smile. 'Trouble in paradise?' she says, raising an eyebrow.

'Something like that. A rough patch. A rough patch and then some. I'm concerned that David could easily be tempted right now by someone like you.'

'You're wrong. David would never be tempted by anyone like me. He's far too earnest. He would prefer Maggie, without a doubt.'

'But I've seen him looking at you. Plus, he didn't tell me when you turned up to meet him and Maggie after classes.'

'I was strictly meeting Maggie, I can't help it if David's there too. He rushed straight off to send some email anyway. And as for the looking at me, it's window-shopping. Means nothing. They all do it.'

The driver looks over his shoulder. He seems to take Yasmin in for the first time, and drives on and on staring back at her. Then he looks ahead, slams on the brakes, and announces: 'Catedral.'

'Tell me something,' Libby says, as the taxi drives off. A little boy waves at her from across the street, and she waves back. The sun is hitting her head so hard that it is already starting to throb. 'What's the longest relationship you've ever had?'

There are a few cafés with tables spilling across the pavement. Libby heads towards the alleyway that leads to the cathedral square, walking slowly to let Yasmin catch up.

Yasmin laughs. 'This is where you expect me to say two weeks, right?'

A couple of Cuban men pass them. 'Chicas,' says one, appreciatively. Looking at her companion, Libby can see why. She is stunning. Her dress leaves little to the imagination, and her body appears to be perfect. Libby begins to enjoy the glamour by association.

Yasmin bats the men away, and strides on. Libby walks quickly beside her. The early-afternoon sun is shining on the old flagstones, polished from hundreds of years of footsteps. The cathedral is squat in the middle, with a different-sized tower at each side. The façade is intricately carved, and Libby is secretly relieved to note, as she is each time she comes here, that the gate has been firmly padlocked. This, in particular, is not the moment for some improving sightseeing. They divert their course to avoid a group of tourists wearing wristbands from an all-inclusive resort. A Cuban man dressed impeccably in a cream linen suit walks slowly by, with a walking stick.

'Three years, actually,' says Yasmin, as they fall into step together. 'I know, you wouldn't expect it. We were the "it" couple. There's always one at university. It was Ivan and Yasmin, Yasmin and Ivan. King and Queen of the University of London. Everyone wanted to be us. We were the centre of the universe. We got engaged. We had mucho sex. We loved each other. It was a charmed life, if you believe in such a thing. I should have known it couldn't last.'

'So what happened?' Libby's mind is racing ahead. By the time they reach the top of the square, she is picturing Yasmin's true love, Ivan, tragically mown down in a freak accident, and Yasmin at his funeral, glamorous in black, vowing never to love another man as long as she lives. Either that, or she had an affair with his best friend.

She shrugs. 'He left me.'

'Why?'

'Why not? I don't know. It wasn't me, it was him. We were too young for that sort of commitment. He thought we both needed some space. All the usual crap. I guess he just went off me. Shit happens.'

She is trying to be brave. 'And you've never got over it,' Libby tells her.

'I have!'

'Not really.'

'It's easy for you to stand there, all married, and say that. Mrs Ooh-we're-going-through-a-bit-of-a-rough-patch-poor-old-me.Part of me would give anything for a rough patch. I *am* over Ivan, okay? I hadn't given him a moment's thought for years, until Maggie started mentioning him, oh so subtly. We split up six years ago. Last I heard he had a fiancée. I'd have to be a bit of a sad case, wouldn't I?'

'But you've never met anyone else.'

'Au contraire.'

'You know what I mean.'

'I don't really go in for relationships.'

Libby touches Yasmin's arm. She doesn't flinch, but she doesn't respond, either.

'You know the worst thing?' Yasmin asks after a minute.

'What?'

'I stole him from Maggie. He was making her happy. She was really coming out of herself. I stole him because I could. I thought it was worth losing my best friend over, because I decided we were going to be together for ever. Which, given that we were eighteen at the start, was never especially likely.'

Libby frowns. 'You stole him from Maggie? Seriously?'

Yasmin spins round.

'I knew they were bloody following us. Leave us alone, you twats. We are not interested!'

The men smile, shrug, and wander off.

By four o'clock, Yasmin and Libby are on their second beer. They are sitting in a cheap and cheerful outdoor bar, which seems to be assembled around a cluster of old cannons. They have purchased three posters of Che Guevara, four Che T-shirts, a mobile of an aeroplane made from a water bottle, a necklace each, and two pairs of leather sandals. The urge to shop has been satisfied.

'So tell me how you came to steal Maggie's boyfriend,' says Libby. 'I just can't imagine . . .'

Yasmin laughs. 'You can't imagine Maggie and me with the same man? Mags hasn't always been as screwy as she is now. And she's very pretty underneath it all.'

'I can't imagine Maggie with a boyfriend, full stop.' Libby stops, realising that, finally, she is with someone who might be able to explain something of what goes on inside Maggie's head. 'What is it with her, Yasmin? Why is she so guarded? She can't still be upset because you stole Ivan?'

Yasmin shrugs. 'No, not exactly, but I do feel terrible about it. She was coming out of herself with him. It happened at a crucial time. Me nicking her bloke probably set her on the course that's made her how she is now. I didn't realise till I caught up with her this year what kind of a state she was in. Before that I'd always thought she must have pulled herself out of it. I expected her to be sorted, but she's not. She's *so* not. That's why I make it my business to look out for her. That's why I'm here. I came to look out for Maggie. When I told my parents that's what I was going to do, they were like, great, Yas, go for it, you have to.' Yasmin sighs, glad at last to be talking to someone.

'Yasmin!' says Libby with a frown. 'That is so patronising. Maggie's twenty-eight. She seems pretty capable.'

'It goes back a lot further than you realise, Lib . . .' Yasmin lights a cigarette, and considers her words carefully. 'It's not that she's not strong. But she's damaged. I've known her a long time. Sure, I fucked her over when we were eighteen. But that's not the reason she's fucked up.' Yasmin inhales deeply and blows the smoke out of her nose.

Libby is interested. 'So what is, then? She doesn't seem that bad. I mean, slightly off kilter, but there's nothing abnormal about her. What makes you say she's damaged?'

Yasmin sighs. 'I shouldn't go into it. Maggie would absolutely kill me if she knew. But fuck it. I have no idea what to do about her, and I'd really appreciate your input. I don't know how to handle her. I'm really feeling on my own over this. I mean, I'm emailing her parents, and they are absolutely great, but they're in France. She has no idea about that, by the way. She won't talk to them, and they're so worried about her.'

'Her parents?'

'Lib, has Maggie said anything to you or to David about her sister?'

'Of course. She's just had a baby, Maddy. What about her?'

'Not Emma. Her other sister. Grace.'

Libby tries to recall Maggie mentioning another sister. 'No,' she says, 'I don't think so. Why?'

'You would know if she had. Grace died, when Maggie and I were nine. That is why Mags is the way she is. She hasn't come anywhere close to getting over it. I had to tell someone and I always wanted it to be you, but I was stymied by the fact that you hated me.'

Libby is horrified. She hadn't connected Maggie's demeanour to tragedy, although it makes immediate and perfect sense. 'What happened?' she says. She imagines a little girl being hit by a car, or dying of leukaemia, and she shudders.

'She was murdered,' says Yasmin, as she stubs out her cigarette on the metal table. 'By a paedophile.'

chapter eighteen

Maggie – the same afternoon

Dear Mum & Dad, Sorry that this is just a postcard, so very brief. Do you like the picture of Havana? And would you believe that the view from my bedroom window is actually better than this? Life here is wonderful. I am loving it and the Spanish is really going well. So pleased to hear about Emma and Maddy, and sorry not to have been there. Hope you had a fantastic visit and that you like being grandparents. See you soon! Much love, M xxx

After classes, I go back to the flat with David. As soon as we arrive, Libby goes out. She throws Charlie at us and picks up her bag and leaves. 'Bye, Mags,' she says, and ignores David. He has to call her back to kiss him goodbye. If I was in a marriage like theirs, I would never be thoughtless. I would count my blessings every single day. I would kiss David all the time. The trouble is, I know I will never have what she takes for granted.

David puts the pizzas on to a plate. 'You don't mind sharing a plate, Mags?' he says. 'Bloody washing-up! We've had a dishwasher for years. I'd totally forgotten how boring it is, when you have to stand there and rub every single thing clean with your own hands.' He looks at me and pouts. 'Do I sound spoilt and ungrateful?'

'No,' I tell him. 'When I lived in Brighton I sometimes wouldn't eat just because I knew I wouldn't get around to washing up for weeks. Or else I'd eat a piece of bread straight off the table because brushing the crumbs away was easier.' I sit Charlie on my lap. I'm wearing a short skirt, and Charlie's leg sticks to my bare thigh. I'm feeling confident, dressed like this. I like my body far better with this extra weight.

I feel perfectly comfortable chatting with David. We are a unit in class. Libby is the one I want for a friend. Because I've never been particularly interested in David, I relax much more when I'm with him. I don't have to worry what he thinks of me.

On top of that, I am far better than he is at Spanish. I do our homework every day, and he copies it. He barely tries any more. I love that. He relies on me, completely.

I realise that I am sitting where Libby normally sits, and that I have Libby's son on my knee. Libby's husband puts two glasses of water on the table. This afternoon, I am living Libby's life. And it's Friday, and I'm going to be spending all weekend with Libby and her family. I'm going to be at the beach with them. I'm part of the family. This is why I came to Cuba. This is what I wanted.

'Mags?' says David. He sounds hesitant, and I look up at him, concerned. 'What?' I ask, stuffing a bit of pizza into my mouth. I love the fact that I don't have to stress about paying David back for it. Normally I feel awkward about things like this, but this pizza cost sixpence, so I will happily accept it.

'When you were going out with Mark?'

'Mmmm?'

'Did you ever have, you know, rough times?'

I laugh. 'Of course we did. We split up, didn't we?' Then I stop and think about it. I remember evenings when we sat in silence watching whatever was on the television, when we wouldn't speak to each other for four hours. Mark would say, 'Curry?' and I'd nod. He would order what we always had, and it would be delivered to the door. I would get the plates out, and we would dish it up between us. We did not need to say a word. This did not necessarily mean we were fighting. We just didn't have anything left to say to one another.

'Actually, I don't think we did,' I tell David. 'We couldn't be bothered with arguments. We just stuck together out of habit. It was a crap relationship. He's a wanker. Are you and Libby having problems? Because if you are, you shouldn't use me and Mark as role models.'

David sits down next to me. 'You must have noticed,' he says. 'Christ, it's better already, just acknowledging it. We seem to have got way off track somewhere along the line. It's been over a week, now.'

'I'd noticed you were a bit subdued. But you've argued before, haven't you? You wanted to come here and she didn't, and you sorted that out just fine. What's up now?' I am thrilled. For a moment, I've got my inside view on their life again. I need to get David to tell me everything. He will be as good as the baby monitor.

'Did Lib tell you about that? Yes, it was pretty bad there for a while, but it's different now. Then I knew we were fighting about a particular issue, and we resolved it, and that was fine. Problem over. It's different this time.'

'What's up now?'

'Hard to describe. I feel that my wife has just thrown everything I thought I knew about our relationship back in my face. I shouldn't be saying this *devant l'enfant*, of course.'

'Surely you should be making the most of being able to talk in front of him while he can't understand?'

'Yeah, let's say that. She thinks I'm bossy and that I belittle her. And she thinks she was this great person when she met me and then I brought her down. I thought the opposite had happened. I truly thought I'd helped her. You know, I tracked down her father for her, and she's even thrown that back in my face?'

'Of course you helped her. You got her to move to Brighton and have Charlie. Both of them are good things, surely?'

David smiles. 'You'd have thought, wouldn't you?' I smile back at him, and for the first time in years I feel a genuine warmth flooding over me. David is my true friend. We get on. My relationship with David is two-sided. He likes me as much as I like him.

'What's Libby's father like?' I ask, with keen interest.

'I'm so glad you asked! She knows I've spoken to him, but she hasn't asked. He seems really nice. He's married to a woman in Australia, and he's got two kids. So Libby actually has a sister and a brother she doesn't even know about. Sammi and Zack. I haven't told her. With the way things are at the moment, I think she needs to find these things out for herself.'

Libby has a sister. This news stabs me through the stomach, and I instruct myself not to take it personally. Other people have sisters. I have one myself, and besides, Libby's is only a half-sister. Libby's long-lost Australian sibling has no impact on my life: none at all.

'David,' I say, and I am aware as I say it that I have not spoken like this to anyone for a long time. In fact, I have not engaged properly with anyone since Ivan. 'You mustn't let this make you feel bad about yourself. I can see that you're a fabulous husband, and Libby knows that really. She's never going to leave you. She knows that she's got a life most people would kill for. You're a great person. Not many men would do what you've done for Lib. God knows, you have no idea what bastards there are out there. Look at yourself. You're handsome, funny, and lovely. You adore your son. Libby would be absolutely crazy if she jeopardised your marriage.'

David rubs my arm. I love the feel of his hand on my bare skin.

'Mags,' he says fondly. 'You're a pal, you really are. Where would I be without you? I'd be hanging out with scary Lara and the rest of them. Yasmin. I don't think I'd be getting very far with the Spanish, either. You're one of a kind, and I value you enormously. You do know that?'

'Thanks.' I can't meet his eyes. 'It's been a long time since anyone's said anything like that to me, actually,' I tell the top of

Charlie's head. 'I didn't have many friends in Brighton. None, really. Just the odd work acquaintance, and then Yasmin when she came to stay. I decided that the Brighton experiment had failed, and that I needed to try my luck somewhere new.'

Libby has a sister. Grace flashes into my head. I see her clearly. She is running across the common and laughing. She's dressed as she was that last day, in the clothes that were to take on a deeper significance. I feel sick. I open my mouth to tell David about her. Then I close it.

'Only to encounter the sniffy neighbours who were among the Brighton residents who didn't bother to speak to you,' he says, laughing.

'I never thought you and Libby were sniffy,' I say, truthfully. There is no point telling him about my sister. He would keep his distance from me, if he knew. He wouldn't know how to handle me. 'I saw you around – rather, I saw Libby around with the pushchair – and I just thought, they've got a baby, they've got a different life from mine, nothing in common. You know.'

'I still can't get over the coincidence of us all being out here together. When I think about it it makes my head explode.'

I smile as openly as I can. 'Me, too. Just when I thought it was safe to reinvent myself! And not only that, but my former best friend follows me here! I think God is telling me that I can run but I certainly can't hide.'

David finishes his pizza and takes Charlie from my lap. His hand brushes my arm, and I wonder whether he did it on purpose. 'I think he's letting you know that you've got people to look out for you.'

I snort. 'That would be a first,' I tell him. Grace would be looking out for me, if she was here. I make an effort to hold myself together.

David laughs. 'Don't be ridiculous! You had Mark, however much you think he's a wanker now. You can't have thought that for the full six years. And what about your family? Your parents in France, sister in Norwich, now a new baby niece?'

I want to tell him. I am desperate to tell him, but if I did it would ruin everything. I breathe deeply, blink, and look him steadily in the eye.

'You're right,' I say, and get my homework out to close the subject.

Charlie goes for his afternoon nap, right on schedule. The two of us sit on the sofa and I attempt to explain the subjunctive to David. It turns out he is entirely unable to grasp the concept.

'It's like, say I said to you, I should be grateful if you would get me a drink.'

'You want a drink?'

'No, it's an example. Or, say, I hope you will be my friend when we go home.'

'I hope you mean that one.'

'I actually meant it about the drink, too. Beer, if possible. But let's get this sorted first. The subjunctive is used when things aren't definite. Things like would, should, could, things that might not happen. We don't really have a subjunctive form in English.'

'We're far too matter-of-fact, aren't we?'

'Must be. I hope you can come with me. Espero que puedas venir con me. Puedas. The subjunctive form of poder. You've just got to learn them, but I don't think you actually need to use them much, in day-to-day conversation.'

I look at David. He is looking at me, with a look I have never seen before. 'Maggie,' he says, slowly, 'I shouldn't say this. But what the hell. Could I use the subjunctive to say "Would it be all right if I kissed you?"'

I look at him. He can't really want to kiss me. He's got Libby.

'Te podria dar un beso?' I tell him.

He repeats it. We look at each other in silence. I think, again, of his wife. I have always longed for her life.

I am nervous. I lean towards him. David reaches down, and our lips meet.

199

I shift myself closer to him, and he takes me in his arms. I never thought of doing this before, but now, it seems that this is why I came here. It was David I wanted all along, not Libby. David and I are two of a kind. We should be together. Libby is needlessly neurotic and makes David miserable. I would never do that. I appreciate happiness. And, for this moment, I am happy.

I prolong the kiss. The feeling of being wanted, touched, appreciated is almost more than I can bear. David's hand rests on my waist. His other hand cups my chin. He wants to be with me. He is married to Libby, but he wants to be with me.

Then he pulls away. He looks at me and smiles. It is not a straightforward smile. He pulls my head towards himself, so it rests on his shoulder.

'Wow,' he says. 'Maggie. I don't know what to say. Christ.'

'It's all right,' I tell him. I panic as I see our friendship disintegrating in a frenzy of guilt. I must not scare him away. The worst outcome would be for David to feel so ashamed of himself that he tells Libby. Neither of them would ever speak to me after that. Even if he never kisses me again, this has to be our secret. I realise that I must pull myself together and take charge.

'I've never done anything like that before.' He sounds dazed. 'Bloody hell. I don't know what came over me. Sorry.'

I squeeze his hand. 'It's all right,' I say, again. 'It really is. There's nothing to be sorry for. You and Libby have been having a rough time. All marriages have them. You needed reassurance or something. You needed some physical comfort. It's all right. I know I should have stopped it, but I was caught up in it too.' I push his chin up, so he's looking at me. 'David,' I tell him firmly, 'this is me. I'm your friend. I'm not going to tell anyone what just happened, all right? I'm on your side. And I'm not going to go crazy either, boil your rabbit, whatever. Trust me.'

He picks up my hand and plays with my fingers. 'Of course I trust you,' he says, straightening and bending my index finger. 'The trouble is, I seem to like you rather too much.'

I smile. I am handling this surprisingly well.

'Don't be silly,' I tell him. 'We kissed. It was a one-off. No one will ever know. You have a wife a couple of miles away and a son asleep in the next room. This is never going to go anywhere. You and me are going to stay friends and we'll always know that there could have been something between us in different circumstances. And that is going to have to be enough. I don't want you flaking out on me, David. Am I making sense?'

David looks me in the eyes, and smiles. 'Christ,' he says, 'you're wonderful when you're bossy. I didn't know you had it in you. Thank, Mags.'

I wink at him, and pick up my grammar book. We will do that again. I am certain of it.

chapter nineteen

Libby – later that day

They stroll along the sands late in the afternoon, marvelling aloud at the fact that they are no longer in Havana. It is silly, Libby thinks, how beautiful this is. This is what everyone imagines when you say you're going to the Caribbean. The sand is white and fine. Clear water washes the shore. A little way out, there is a line in the sea, and beyond that, the water is turquoise and opaque. Tourists and Cubans lie on the sand. Security guards with radios police the beach, and the only people who try to talk to Libby are interested, as ever, in Charlie.

The act of breathing this air makes Libby feel healthy. She knows that David is right about her never taking her health seriously. She has always assumed that massive asthma attacks, and huge allergic reactions, happen to other people. Her allergies, she has told herself and anyone who was asking, are minor. In fact, she never mentions them, because she dislikes the fact that they make her feel vulnerable. When she tells someone that she has eczema, asthma, a peanut allergy and various other ailments, she feels like a failure. She has used her inhaler, discreetly, on the streets of Havana, but she's never let Maggie or Yasmin see her doing it. It is odd that a city with so relatively few cars can nevertheless be polluted enough to make her wheeze. The warm wind picks up strands of hair and blows them across her face. She takes a deep breath of tropical air. Everything here feels clean. A few groups of people are walking along the sand, and most of the sunbathers have gone in.

Their apartment is right next to the beach. It is sparsely furnished, but large, and perfect for their purposes. The staff have been delightful. Libby doesn't care about any of it. She cannot stop thinking about Maggie and Grace. She wonders why she thought the state of her marriage meant anything at all. She and David have no problems, at all. They love each other; they are faithful to each other; and they have a beautiful son. They are unspeakably lucky.

'She was abducted,' she whispered to David, soon after they arrived. She had tried not to tell him, but she couldn't hold it in. She had to whisper, because Maggie had shut herself away in the room she's sharing with Yasmin. Yasmin was out at the shop. The coast was as clear as it was going to get. Libby felt that, even before he knew about Maggie, David was making an effort to be nicer to her. She's glad that their problems seem to be blowing over. She resolves to be the best wife in the world, from now on.

She watched his face as she told him. He didn't know how to react.

'Really?' he said, looking away from her. 'Maggie's sister?'

'Really. Maggie's sister.'

David was silent for a while. 'You know,' he said quietly, 'in the first week of the course, we all had to talk about our families. I remember thinking it was funny that Maggie said she had two sisters, and then changed her mind and said she had one. I even said to her, make your mind up. I thought she was getting her Spanish numbers confused.'

Libby took his hand. 'You mustn't tell her that we know. I'm going to try to get her to tell me, of her own accord. Yasmin says we have to tread carefully. And she said Mags really likes us, the three of us, so we have to look out for her. Poor Yasmin. She only came here

203

to look after Mags. I don't mind admitting, I judged her too soon. I thought she was going to seduce you.'

Libby looked at David and smiled at her own folly. David smiled back, thinly.

Libby slips her sandals off, and walks barefoot. She decides to hang back, to make Maggie walk slowly with her, and to strike up a conversation which will, she hopes, lead to confidences. Yasmin catches her eye, and shakes her head, an almost imperceptible movement. Libby smiles reassuringly at her. Yasmin shrugs.

'Hey, Charlie,' she says, cheerfully. 'What do you make of this, then, mate?' She falls into step beside David, and speeds up his pace.

Libby doesn't speak to Maggie for a while. She watches her. She sees that Yasmin is right: an extremely pretty woman lurks beneath that defensive façade. She will get to know the real Maggie. She will bring her out of herself. She will help her to get over what happened to her sister. Even in her head, Libby cannot articulate the words. 'What happened' is as close as she can get.

She knows that, until now, she has taken Maggie for granted. She has almost ignored her. When they met, she judged her unworthy of her friendship. She based her assessment on Maggie's troubled manner and her lack of personal grooming. Rather than being concerned, Libby was dismissive. Maggie was no threat. It occurs to her that she is not, after all, very perceptive about people. Or very nice.

'I've missed fresh air,' she says conversationally. 'For a small city, Havana's very polluted.'

'Mmm,' says Maggie. 'Yes, I know. It's funny, isn't it? I always love the smell of the sea. I know it's different here from in Brighton, but both are still wonderful.'

Libby watches David and Yasmin chatting, while Charlie, in his backpack, pats his father excitedly on the shoulder. Perhaps she's stupid, but she trusts Yasmin now.

'I totally agree. Maggie, can I ask you something?'

Maggie looks at her, half smiling. 'Sure,' she says. 'What?'

'Why did you come here?'

She folds her arms across the front of her T-shirt and looks away.

'What do you mean?'

'I mean, were you running away from something? What made you come to Cuba?'

Maggie looks at the sea, and then at a Cuban family sitting on the sand.

'Did I ever tell you about Mark?' she asks, eventually.

'Your ex-boyfriend?'

'We were together for six years,' she says tonelessly. 'Then we split up, and I moved to Brighton to make a fresh start, but it turned out that Brighton wasn't far enough away. It takes time, you know, to get over those things. So when I bumped into Yasmin again, she inspired me to go travelling.' Maggie is looking straight ahead. Yasmin is right. She will not talk about Grace willingly. Libby cannot believe that she never suspected that Maggie was hiding something big in her past. It seems obvious, now. She gives it another shot.

'Were you and Yasmin close at school?' she asks. 'I try to imagine you as little girls, sometimes, but I just can't. You're so different from each other.'

Maggie keeps her arms folded. 'You mean, Yasi's tall and fun and outgoing and gorgeous, and I'm practically invisible.'

'I don't mean anything of the sort, Mags. I mean, she's very brash and she's not everyone's cup of tea. Christ, she slept with Natalie's husband! I've only recently felt able to give her the time of day. What I meant was, you're a really nice girl, and obviously quite deep, but you wouldn't do anything to hurt anyone. If anything, you're a little bit too accommodating. I imagine you don't stand up for yourself enough. You need to set your sights on something and go for it, like Yasmin does.'

Maggie is looking at her, and Libby can't read her expression. 'You reckon?'

'Course I reckon. You're a good person, Mags. You're lovely. You choose something you want from your life, and you go for it, okay? That job at American Express, for instance, it doesn't seem like your sort of thing at all.'

She laughs. 'You're right. Okay then, I will. And I have no intention of going back to my job, that is absolutely definite.'

They walk a bit further. Libby watches Yasmin pointing out a group of blokes to David. She is undoubtedly telling him which ones she fancies. They take no notice of her, and Libby realises that's because Yasmin, David and Charlie look like a family. The young men notice Maggie and Libby, and smile at them. Charlie is waving at a woman walking alone along the shore, and Libby watches her smiling, as she waves back.

'Bet you can't wait to see your sister's baby,' she says, making one last attempt.

'Maddy? No, I can't. I feel bad that I'm away. I know Emma would have loved me to have rushed straight to Norwich. Mum and Dad are probably quite upset too, but they all say they understand. I used a whole twenty-dollar phonecard the other day, talking to them all. Everyone's deliriously happy. Babies seem to do that to people. Well, you must know.' Maggie is saying all the right things, but she is speaking mechanically.

'It's different for different people,' Libby confides. 'We were over the moon when Charlie was born, but I came down to earth pretty bumpily soon afterwards. As you know, I'm a partner in a law firm, or I was, but looking after a baby is by a long way the hardest thing I've ever done. I'm sure your sister will be fine, though.'

'Yeah, Emma's always fine. She's Mrs Domesticated. It's all she's ever wanted.'

'Well, that's good, then.'

Maggie looks at Libby. 'What about you?' she asks. 'Aren't you curious to meet your sister? And your brother? It must be weird to know that they're there, in Australia, but you don't know them.' She smiles a private smile.

Libby laughs. 'What are you talking about, Mags? I haven't got any brothers or sisters.' She winces as she says it, wishing she had phrased it better. 'I'm an only child' would have been more tactful.

'Oh,' says Maggie. She blushes. 'Sorry, you're right. I'm getting confused.'

Libby sees that Maggie is backtracking and tries to work out what she knows. 'My father does live in Australia, though. Maggie, what has David said?'

'About your dad's other children. Sorry, I didn't know you didn't know. I really am sorry. David shouldn't have told me but I suppose it slipped out. I was pleased for you, that's all.'

Libby looks at Maggie and her heart breaks for her. She is torn between wanting to look after her, and wanting to kill David.

'My dad has children in Australia?' she asks, wanting to be sure.

'A boy and a girl. God, I feel awful.'

Libby smiles and touches her on the shoulder. 'It's all right. It's not your fault. It's entirely David's fault. I'll have it out with him later. Really? Do you know their names?'

She regrets asking immediately. Maggie must be devastated that Libby has a new sister. This is the last conversation she'll want to have.

'Sammi and Zack. I'm so sorry you have to hear it from me.'

They reach a wooden shack on the beach, with a thatched roof. David and Yasmin have found a table, taken Charlie out of his rucksack, and ordered four beers.

Libby glares meaningfully at David, who pretends not to notice. Then she smiles sympathetically at Maggie, and sits down. She has given it a go, but Yasmin was right. She is not telling anyone anything.

chapter twenty

Maggie – that night

I'm surprised I didn't see it in Libby's face straight away. I would have done, normally. Kissing someone's husband seems to warp your perceptions a little. I avoided her eyes all the way there. When we arrived, I hid in my room because I couldn't bear to watch them snuggling around each other. David was acting so awkwardly that I was sure Libby was about to guess what we had done, and that, I thought, would have brought my world crashing down.

I didn't look at Libby properly until we were walking along the beach. Before that I thought it was me that was making things feel odd. It didn't occur to me that it could have been her; that everything might have been ruined for ever.

But it is. My life in Cuba is finished, and it is all because of Yasmin. I hate her. I was doing fine. I had been close to a man for the first time since Mark booted me out. Admittedly, the circumstances were not ideal, but I was feeling good about it. I am a friend of the family. I'm good at Spanish. I loved living at Elena's, until Yasmin butted in there. My life in Cuba was infinitely better than it used to be in Brighton, or even in Edinburgh. Five weeks ago, I used to strip for a living. I used to go home at half past two, to a cold damp flat and spy on my neighbours through a monitor. I had moved on. Now I may as well go back.

I can never be friends with Libby, now. She would never have found out about me and David, and I would have enjoyed the fact that the two of us had a secret. That would not have affected Libby and me. But as soon as I saw the pity in her eyes, I knew that she and I were finished. We will never be on equal terms, now. Even if she never mentions it to me, it will always be there, hanging in the air between us. She feels sorry for me. Nothing I say or do will change that. That's why I told her about her family. It was a small malicious act that achieved nothing.

Yasmin has probably told her about my job, as well. I imagine Libby on the phone to Natalie. 'You'll never guess what? *Her little sister was murdered!* Yes, I know. Terrible! And she was working as a lap dancer in Brighton, told everyone she was at American Express. Well, you can understand, can't you? I'm going to suggest she sees a counsellor.' She will gossip about me. It's a great story. Grace makes a great story.

The stupid thing is, the moment that Libby started wanting to be my friend is the exact moment at which I stopped wanting anything to do with her. She wasn't really bothered about me, one way or the other, before. Now she wants to get to know me. When we walked along that stupid sandy beach this afternoon, she kept trying to strike up a deep conversation. It was so transparent that I almost laughed in her face. She wanted me to tell her. She is longing to know the details. She wants me to know that she knows, but Yasmin has made her promise not to mention it. So she will continually leave openings for me to tell her. I can't bear it. I'm glad I had a fact to retaliate with, but I have played that card, now.

I am hiding in the bedroom again. Yasmin comes in here over my dead body. I am not sticking around. I'll find a cab and make it take me back to Elena's in the morning.

Libby wants to be close to me, but I don't like her any more. I don't want her friendship, now. It is tainted. Yasmin, my supposed friend, has taken away everything that was holding me together. She has done that once before. I should not be surprised.

Emily Barr

When she called out to me in Norwich library, I should have got up and left. I should have marched off to Mothercare and told my sister and brother-in-law to buy a cot bed, whatever that is, and some neutral yellow blankets. Yasmin destroyed me when she stole my boyfriend. I was not duty-bound to pick up our friendship.

And now she has betrayed me again, and I hate her for it. She knows I don't talk about what happened to my sister, and she knows that nothing on earth would have made me tell David and Libby. She knows that my policy is to ignore the past and get on with life. She might, perhaps, think I haven't done a marvellous job on that front, but that is just her opinion. It does not give her the right to go out and gossip about me. Besides, I would have done a better job if she had let me keep Ivan for a little while longer.

I am filled with impotent rage. I introduced Yasmin to Libby. And before she'd even met her, she slept with Libby's friend's husband. And then she came traipsing out here, after me. And she knew how much Libby's friendship meant to me. And she went ahead and ruined it anyway.

Before this happened, I was just another human being to Libby. That is what I wanted. That is why I came here. My ambition was to be Libby's friend. I was going to have to work for that friendship. Now I can have it on a plate, but I can't bear to be in a room with her. If she carries on hinting, I might have to tell her about David and me. It's the only thing that would make her leave me alone.

I left David and Charlie before Libby came home. It seemed tactful. I was buzzing with excitement. For once, my brain was full of happy memories. I was plotting to do it again. I would set up an innocent scenario, and David would be unable to resist me. I knew it would happen. I didn't want to tempt him to leave his family or anything like that. I just wanted to have a secret, to have a reason to feel attractive. I loved having something to smile about.

I was happy when I got back to Elena's, and sat on my bed and wrote my diary for an hour. Then Yasmin came home, laden down

210

with shopping. She wandered into my room without knocking. I was lying on my bed savouring the memory of the kiss. I have it for ever now, in my head.

There was a breeze from the open window. I kept looking at the view and marvelling at the way my life had changed. The days when I used to live in a damp basement and lick my lips for a living were long gone. I was feeling more positive than I had for years.

'Here you are,' Yasmin said, grinning and throwing a T-shirt at me. 'Got it for you at the market. Thought it would suit you.'

I held it up. It was a skinny-fitting red one, with Che Guevara on the front.

'This is fab,' I told her, feeling a wave of affection. 'Thanks, Yas. How much was it? I'll give you the money.'

She pretended to slap my face. 'Don't be ridiculous, girlfriend. It's a present, yeah? Don't look gift horses in the mouth, right?'

I pulled my baggy top off, and put it on.

'Maggie,' said Yas, watching me, 'I still can't get over you. Being a lap dancer, I mean. It's so not like you. I could think of loads of people from school who could have ended up selling themselves, but Margaret Wilson?'

I shrugged. 'The money was good. I wouldn't do it again. You won't tell Libby or David, will you? No one knows about it, apart from you.'

'Lips,' she said, pointing to her mouth, 'sealed. Trust me.'

I kick my bag. It skids into the door with a bang. I can hear them all talking in the living room. I shouldn't have come here. Libby must have told David about Grace by now. He must be regretting our kiss. I can hear them arguing outside my room, in hushed, poisonous voices. This is good, I suppose.

I hate Yasmin so much that if she walked through the door right now I'd fly at her and tear her hair out. I wouldn't care that I was being unimaginative. I would do all those bitchy girlie things that I've always scorned. I would scratch her eyes. I would rip her clothes. Then I would fight like a man. I'd punch her in the face and I'd knee her in the groin. I'd throw her across the room and when she was down, I'd kick her.

Trust me, she said. I thought I could. I did trust her. I didn't even ask her not to mention Grace. I knew she wouldn't, because I knew that, in spite of everything, she was my friend. She is a bitch. The worst thing is, I know exactly why she did it. I've known all along that she's wanted to be friends with Libby, too. The surefire way of achieving that is by the judicious use of information. Yasmin had to tell Libby something that would immediately make Yasmin's promiscuity look trivial. Something Libby wanted to hear; something that would amaze her and affect her whole day. Perhaps I should have been wary, but it never occurred to me that Yasmin was capable of using my sister for her own petty advancement.

She was there when it happened. Yasmin knew Grace.

There is a tap on the door.

'Maggie?' calls Libby, softly. Her voice is like caramel. I will have to be very, very strong. Otherwise I could end up hating Libby, too.

I sit on the bed and pick up a book.

'Mmmm?' I reply.

She opens the door and stands just inside the doorway. Her hair has grown since she's been here. It is tangled with salty water, but she still looks lovely.

'Are you okay?' she asks, looking at me sincerely. I make eye contact and abruptly look away, because I can't bear to see the pity. I look at her Che Guevara T-shirt, the cotton trousers that hang loosely from her hips. I gaze at the chipped pink nail varnish on her toes.

'I'm fine,' I say casually, and pretend to be interested in my book.

'Sure?'

I look at her and force a smile. 'Sure.'

'Right. You can come out and join us if you like. We were just talking about nipping to the bar across the road. David says he'll stay here to babysit. We'll bring him back some food. I don't know if you're interested . . . ?' She tails off and looks at me. She is trying to hide the argument she and her husband are having, but I am not fooled.

'No, that's okay. I'm a bit tired tonight. I might just grab a beer and find a film to watch on satellite. Make the most of having the telly.' I think about it. 'Tell you what,' I add, 'David can go with you. I know you've got stuff to talk about. I'll babysit.'

I don't want to be with anyone, now. Not even him. I would have to tell him why I told Libby about her siblings, and I haven't thought of an excuse, yet.

She hesitates. 'I could stay behind with you if you liked? Or David? You look like you could do with some company.'

I sigh. 'No, you go.' I am making a supreme effort to be polite. I form the words in my head. *I kissed your husband today*. She would be astonished. 'I'll be fine. I need some time to myself.'

She smiles. Her eyes are different. 'Fair enough. We'll clear off out of your way. Bring Charlie over if he wakes. Take care.'

Yasmin and I got a taxi to the beach, picking them up on the way. At first, everyone was involved in fitting David and Lib's vast quantities of luggage into the car, and it never occurred to me that anything might be wrong. Charlie travels with a folding cot, a bag of vegetables, a hand-held blender, a hundred nappies, sunblock, and Christ only knows what else. I remember looking at my own little satchel containing bikini, towel and clean knickers, and feeling a rare stab of satisfaction.

I sat in the middle of the back seat. Lib was on one side of me, with Charlie on her lap, and Yas was on the other. David made a hurried beeline for the front. I think he would have felt a little uncomfortable with me on one side and his wife on the other. I tried to picture Libby's sister, Sammi. She must be blonde, since she's Australian.

I like Charlie – he's sweet, and not as much trouble as I thought he would be, after hearing the way she banged on about motherhood in Brighton – but he is pretty boring. He spent the whole journey fiddling with my hair, and I had to let him even though it was irritating. He kept tugging on it. Lib would say, 'Don't do that, Charlie,' but she knows as well as I do that he doesn't understand words. I had to say, 'It's fine,' and I suppose it was. I was too busy fantasising about David to care. She didn't talk to me much. She just looked out of the window.

We checked into this apartment, and I still hadn't realised. In fact, I was busy anticipating how much I would enjoy the weekend. It was only when we reached the beach that it clicked into place. Libby hung back deliberately. I could tell that she didn't want us to walk with David and Yas, and I was pleased. I've loved the times when I've had her to myself. The sea was crashing around and I was preoccupied with the unexpected joy of it, for a moment. I watched the massive waves pushing people underwater, and saw them emerge laughing and spluttering, rubbing their eyes. It was the perfect temperature for a swim, and I briefly contemplated going back for my bikini. The sky was pale blue, and the wind was blowing straight into my face.

I looked to Lib to share the delight involved in walking along a Caribbean beach in March. And I saw her expression. I was ready to talk about the warm wind and the sand that was making my ankles itch, and all she was interested in was murder. She didn't need to speak. You poor, poor thing, said her eyes. I'm sure if you spoke to me about it, she implied, wordlessly, then you would feel better. People have said that, occasionally, and I have hated them for it. They want the details, first hand. It is about gossip, not about sympathy.

To be fair to her, she didn't say it aloud. She didn't tell me that Yasmin had told her. I should have come straight out and said it: 'Yasmin told you about my sister.' I wonder whether she would have bothered to deny it.

I stared straight ahead, at some children throwing an inflatable ball. A security guard walked past us, his radio crackling. I didn't respond to anything she said, and in the end she gave up. People always do. We walked in silence, looking at the people on the beach, wondering what secrets they were hiding. Some things are best left undisturbed.

The door slams after them. The apartment is silent. I go into the living room. I take a Cristal from the fridge and open a jumbo bag of crisps. I am sick of starving myself. I can't have histrionics every time someone finds out about my sister. I feel hopeless and angry, but that's not unusual. I have become more than used to disappointment.

There's an old episode of *Friends* on one of the American channels. I used to watch *Friends* on Friday night, before I went to work. As soon as it finished, I would get up and scurry off to strip. Chandler is trapped in a bank lobby with a famously sexy woman. Hilarious consequences ensue. I've seen it before, and that's fine. I don't want to concentrate.

I thought it was going to be different with these people, and now it's not. David has become a real friend. He is more than a friend. I forget, most of the time, that I'm only learning Spanish because he is. It feels like we're in it together, as equals. We laugh together. We do our work together. I am better than he is. He is special to me. That is all shot to pieces, now. The three of them are talking about me, at this very moment. They are worrying about me. Fretting. Looking back on my quirks, and reassessing them in the light of the new information. David will never touch me again. My invisible repellent shield has been redeployed.

This afternoon, David and I were two travellers who met in Havana. We brought no history with us. We lived in the present. Nothing can ever be normal when people know you've got a dead sister. They always want to protect you. It's too late. I am the last person who needs protection, now. The damage has been done, and nothing else will ever hurt me.

I take a huge gulp of beer, and feel the tears overflowing. These tears are not for Grace. They are for myself, for my past, for my future, for the fact that both of them were destroyed on the day I walked away from Clare's dad.

By the time they come back from the restaurant, I am in bed. It is only half past nine, but I feign sleep and lie awake, listening to them clattering about. I hear them getting beers out of the fridge, and finishing off the bag of crisps. Libby is obsessing about Charlie's mundane life.

'I really should have bathed him tonight,' she moans. 'It's part of his routine. He's confused enough already. But he was so tired!'

I want to jump out of bed and shout at her. Even though she knows about Grace, she is still preoccupied with boring trivia. She has no idea how lucky she is. She should be savouring every moment with her baby. She doesn't know what pain is. Somebody should teach her.

I hate Libby.

chapter twenty-one

Libby

Havana stifles her, but Libby hums as she whiles the morning away. 'Bouncy, bouncy, bom bom bom,' she sings loudly, jigging Charlie up and down as she does it. She is unable to stop singing that song, which was played constantly around the pool at the hotel. The flat is getting Libby down, and her head is still full of Maggie. She is no longer shocked by what happened to little Grace, but she is obsessed with knowing details. Yasmin just said it was one of the neighbours, and that Maggie felt responsible because he'd acted strangely towards her the day before. Libby hadn't liked to demand to know everything, but now she can't wait to be alone again with Yasmin, so that she can ask more. She doesn't even care about her new family, now. They are halfway around the world, and they might as well not exist. Her father can come to her when he is ready.

'Bouncy, bouncy bom bom bom,' she repeats. She hears one of the neighbours whistling along with her. Charlie squirms in her arms, desperate to get on to the floor. The flat smells wonderful. Libby hadn't noticed it until they walked in last night. It smells of warm air and clean laundry, of babies and dust and Cuba. It is her little piece of Havana. She feels secure, here.

Libby tries to recall the smell of their maisonette in Hove. It must smell of carpets. Salty air. Baby products. Shower gel. She closes her eyes and pictures the local branch of Waitrose. The shelves are fully stocked with everything you could possibly want to pass your lips. If a recipe calls for halloumi cheese or fresh coriander, for grated ginger or marinated scallops, she always knows she can find them on the shelves of Waitrose. It is impossible to imagine that level of choice in Havana. When she goes to the supermarket here, she is embarrassed, because she is invariably buying several times more goods than anybody else. She buys a little at a time, for this reason, but she is still the only person who emerges with two well-filled carrier bags. The bulk of what she buys is bottled water.

There is a knock at the interconnecting door. Libby hitches Charlie up on to her hip. She is happy at the prospect of company. She hopes it's Yasmin. She knows that Yasmin spent last night with Luis.

'Hola?' she shouts. 'Luis? Yasmin?'

'Hola, Libby?' says a female voice, hesitantly.

'Maria?' she asks. She hasn't seen much of Maria, since, unlike her brother, she does not hang around the flat on the off chance that Yasmin might drop by.

'Si.'

Maria opens the door. It locks on the landlord's side, which aggrieved Libby at first, as she felt she was being shut in like a dangerous animal. She can see, however, that, with new tenants every couple of months, they need that security. It is not a personal insult.

'Hola!' Libby says, again, as Maria walks shyly into the kitchen, her daughter on her hip. The two women kiss each other on both cheeks. Libby's vocabulary is extremely limited, and she tries to convey everything she means with wide smiles. 'Hola, Gracia!' She holds Charlie next to the Cuban baby, with her mass of dark hair. Charlie makes an approving sound, and lunges for her face. Libby holds him back, and he grabs her hand instead. The women laugh, and Maria strokes his blond hair and says, hesitantly, 'Boyfriend.'

'Charlie, you have a Cuban girlfriend, you classy boy,' Libby tells him, unsure whether Maria understands much English.

'What does it mean, "classy"?' she asks.

'It means, oh, cool. Um, hip, glamorous.' She is picking the very worst words. In the end she opts for something simple. 'Good.'

'Is good,' Maria agrees. She points to Charlie. 'Does he sit?'

'He sits! Yes. Only for two weeks. Does Gracia sit?'

She shakes her head, sadly. 'No, not sit. I try, but no.'

'But Gracia is five months? And Charlie, six months. Seis meses. It's normal.'

Maria nods, and Libby berates herself for her use of pidgin English. Maria's English is infinitely better than Libby's Spanish. She shouldn't be patronising her like this, but the fact is, Libby is embarrassed. She is in Maria's country, and she's forcing her to dig up her English because she can't communicate.

Maria has extremely long hair, and large violet eyes. She is slim, and wears a pair of purple shorts and a green vest. Libby knows she would look horrible in those clothes. Even with her new weight loss, she would look lumpy and lardy. Needless to say, Maria doesn't.

'Coffee?' Libby asks, and Maria nods enthusiastically, and reaches a slender arm for Charlie. She balances a child on each hip, looking as though she has done it many times before.

'How old are you?' she asks abruptly, as Libby fills the percolator.

Libby looks at her, and laughs at the babies. 'Older than you are, that's for sure. Thirty. Treinta.' She adds the Spanish word not because she suspects Maria doesn't know her English numbers, but to let her know that she knows a little of her language.

'No! Treinta? I think, maybe twenty-five!'

Libby shrugs. She doesn't believe her. 'Thanks. How old are you?'

'Me, twenty-one.'

'I thought you were twenty-five, too. In England, twenty-one is very young to have a baby. In Cuba, it's normal?'

Maria smiles, a dazzling smile. 'In Cuba, everything is normal. I, young. My sister, twenty-nine, no baby. My sister is divorced. Now she meets new man. Very good man. She wants baby. Twenty-one, normal. Thirty, also normal.'

Libby takes Charlie from her arms. He protests, and lunges back towards Maria and Gracia. Gracia is the very opposite of Libby's active baby. She is the most contented creature Libby has ever seen. She sits sturdily on her mother's hip, and looks around impassively.

'Vaccination?' Libby asks, pointing to the prominent TB jab scar on Gracia's upper arm.

'Yes. TB. Charlie?'

'He had that, just because we were coming to Cuba. Otherwise, we have it at eleven years old.'

'Eleven years? In Cuba, at birth.'

They grin at each other, and Libby gives Charlie back to Maria while she pours the coffee. They manage to chat for an hour about the marvels of Cuba's health service, and about various aspects of motherhood, and the fact that Luis likes Yasmin 'very very much'.

'He likes Maggie, too,' Libby manages to say, loyally.

Maria shakes her head. 'No, I think not.'

Libby is still distracted by thoughts of Maggie. She looks at her son, at Maria's daughter.

'Babies are so precious,' she says. Maria nods. 'You don't realise at the time how much you are putting yourself on the line when you have a child. You're leaving yourself open to heartbreak. If anything ever happened to Charlie it would completely destroy me. The parents who get through it must be very strong.' She glances at Maria, and sees that she hasn't completely followed. 'Sorry,' she adds.

'A baby changes your life,' says Maria, solemnly, as she prepares to go home and cook lunch for her brother and husband.

'Yes!' Libby says. She wants to offer her a beer before she goes, but she doesn't want to appear to be a bad mother who drinks in the morning. 'Before I had Charlie, I was a lawyer.'

Maria puts her cup down, and laughs. 'Me also! I was at university, to be a lawyer.'

They look at each other, grinning broadly. 'Why did you leave?' Libby asks.

'I got married but we thought, no babies for maybe five years. Then baby comes.' She shrugs.

'Will you go back?'

'Some day, I hope.' She smiles. 'Some day, maybe we go to Florida. My mother and father, my other brother. Not Luis. They are all in Florida. They send money, so I was at university. I will be lawyer in America.'

'You think life in America is better?' Libby is curious about this.

'Oh yes, so much better. Really. Much food, much work.'

'But no rations, no help from the state. No socialism.'

Maria nods happily. 'No socialism,' she confirms.

Charlie is demanding a breastfeed, so Libby sits down and lifts her T-shirt. 'Very good for a baby,' Maria says approvingly, and leaves with a little wave. 'You come see me tomorrow,' she calls as she shuts the door.

When David comes home, twenty minutes later, Libby is in a happier mood than she has been since that conversation with Yasmin. She hears the door slam, and rushes to meet him on the stairs. She has not forgiven him, but she embraces him.

'Maria came over,' she gabbles, and follows him as he puts his bag down, gets himself a glass of water, and sits down. 'She's a lawyer too. She's lovely. I'm going to see her tomorrow. I think I'll get her to teach me Spanish while we're here. Her English is great. Her and Luis, their parents live in America! They send them money.' She places Charlie on David's lap, and Charlie immediately grabs his glasses.

David looks at her, and laughs. 'Glad to hear it.'

'What, that they send them money? I did wonder how Luis came to have a digital video camera. I thought our five hundred dollars per month wouldn't really cover it.'

'Not that. Glad to hear all of it. Glad to hear you sounding happy. Am I to take it that I'm out of the doghouse?'

Libby smiles. 'For now, yes. I can't bring myself to care. You were only trying to help, though fuck knows, it was the last thing poor Maggie needed to hear. But, David. There's something so special about finding I've got things in common with a Cuban woman. When we came here, I would never have imagined it. I can talk to her just the same way I talk to Jenny and Natalie.'

'Lib, that really is great. Get her and José and Luis round for dinner one night, if you like.'

'What, for pasta à la casa, with warmed tinned tomatoes and rubbery cheese on top? Would Luis bring Yasmin as his escort?'

David stretches out. 'No. I don't care. Not Yasmin. She and Maggie are doing my head in. Sulking at each other for reasons I have no interest in at all.'

'Hey, that's not fair.'

'What, on Maggie? I'm sure the last thing she wants is to be treated with kid gloves because of something that happened umpteen years ago. Maggie can look after herself. I think she's pretty tough.' David looks at Libby, and sees the sadness return. 'Come here,' he says. Libby sits next to him, and they both hug their son. 'Sometimes children die,' he says. 'You've always known that. The fact that it happened to Maggie's sister doesn't mean anything's ever going to happen to Charlie. Okay?'

Libby looks up at him, and feels grateful. 'You're right,' she says. 'Thank you for reminding me.'

David and Libby are in love again. He told her that he wanted her to find out about her family herself. He had, he said, told Maggie in confidence, because he couldn't keep it in any longer. If he had known about Maggie's lost sister, of course he wouldn't have mentioned it. They agree that Maggie must have told her because she was upset. They don't mind. As soon as they started talking properly, they couldn't remember why the argument had been so important. Maggie's history has trivialised it so much that Libby cannot believe they were taking a silly argument so seriously. She realised that she adores David, that he has indeed saved her, that she would do anything for him. She has discovered that she is the happiest person she has ever met. Their relationship needed to be challenged, she has decided. Otherwise they would never have cleared away the misconceptions.

'Remember our wedding day?' she says, as they slump on the sofa during Charlie's afternoon nap. David tousles her hair.

'Um, yes, I think so.'

'I'd never fit into that dress, now.'

'You would! Lib, have you looked at yourself? You're as thin as you ever were. Thin, slim, skinny, whatever you like to call it. There's nothing of you. That dress would be baggy on you. In fact, I'm going to fatten you up when we get home.'

She hits his arm. 'Don't you dare.'

'I will,' he says dreamily. 'Fish and chips. Crème brulée. Garlic mushrooms. Scones with clotted cream and jam. Just you wait.'

Her wedding dress is boxed up, in her mother's attic. There is no room for it in their flat. She hadn't been planning on a traditional dress, but the moment she tried it on, she couldn't look at anything else. The stiff bodice exposed all of her collarbone, shoulders, arms. It nipped her waist in, and then the skirt exploded in a half-circle of net and silk. She felt like a fairy, a princess, Grace Kelly, and Marilyn Monroe. If she hadn't loved David before, she would have loved him for giving her a chance to wear that dress. It practically accessorised itself: a diamond necklace, discreet earrings, a tiara and her hair down her back.

'I adored that dress.'

'I remember. I used to worry that you loved it more than me.'

She looks him in the eye. 'It was a close thing. Just don't ask me

to choose between you. Did you really? You must have thought I
was a little shallow.'

'Jesus, I thought you were hilarious. You remember when I
proposed?'

'Derr.' They were having a picnic in Regent's Park. Libby had
resigned herself to the fact that, as all her friends and her mother
warned her, David wasn't the sort of man who would rush into
anything. She was fully expecting to have to sit out two long years
of a normal relationship before she got a ring on her finger. It was
a sunny day. David was wearing a pair of jeans and a sweatshirt.
She had been unable to take her eyes off him. She was besotted.
When he knelt down in front of her, she thought he was tying his
shoelace.

'We agreed then that we'd have a simple civil ceremony in
London without any fuss, and just our closest friends and family
there.'

'It seemed only sensible. And anyway, we *did* have a civil
ceremony!'

David pulls her on to his lap. 'In a castle in Scotland! With two
hundred guests, you dressed like Glinda the good witch, me in a
morning suit, five thousand doves released to symbolise something
or other, a sit-down seven-course meal, and the most expensive
string quartet in the northern hemisphere.'

'It was two hundred doves, and they symbolised peace and
happiness, as far as I can remember. And it was a four-course
meal.' Libby remembers the one aspect of her wedding day that
made her sad. 'All that was missing was my errant parent. That,
and Charlie's birth, have been the only times I've properly missed
him. Do you think it would be wise for me to see him, ever? I'm
sure he'll be a disappointment.'

'Only you can decide that, my love. He doesn't deserve you, but
I think he's weak, rather than malicious. We had a superb wedding.
We've got a brilliant baby. Who needs your dad?'

'How far would the money we spent getting married go in Cuba?'

David shudders. 'I can't bear to think about it. Our wedding must literally have cost more money than most Cubans see in their lifetimes.'

'Can we renew our vows when we go back to the beach next week?'

'No.'

The buzzer rings.

chapter twenty-two

Maggie – two hours earlier

Emma will always appreciate Madeleine Grace. I know she will, because I would, too. She will appreciate her, and she will live her life in terror of her dying. She will have to force herself to let Madeleine out of her sight. She will constantly imagine her daughter's death. Libby lives in terror of Charlie getting a little snuffle, or having his dinner ten minutes late. I think if something happened to scare Libby, it would do her the world of good. I have come up with a plan for her. I am doing it because I still like her, in spite of everything.

I walk around the market stalls three times before I get the courage together to buy anything. I haven't done much vegetable shopping here. I've stopped at the stall opposite the university with David, and have helped him point to carrots – he can never pronounce their name, *zanahorias* – and ask their prices, but I've never bought anything. Elena cooks for me, or I eat out. Elena's kitchen is perpetually stocked with fresh fruit and vegetables. I have treated the markets as a picturesque aspect of lively crumbling Havana, put there for the delectation of privileged passers-by such as myself.

I'm not privileged. Not one native Cuban would swap places with me, if they knew the way I am. They might think it's good to be a

Westerner, but as soon as they felt the pit of my stomach, which has felt, for as long as I can remember, as if it's been kicked by a horse, they would rush back to their overcrowded apartments and their ration books. Nobody would want my money, if it came with my misery, my dread.

I point to some carrots. Then I change my mind. Charlie eats carrots all the time, and the last thing Lib will find appetising is anything with *zanahorias* in it. I try some green beans, instead, and tomatoes. Then garlic and onion. I want this to be interesting, so I proceed to the nearest supermarket, and buy some tomato sauce, dusty-looking herbs, and a jar of chilli. That should cover the taste. Lib thinks Cuban food is bland. She's said so often enough.

I wander around the upstairs of the supermarket, avoiding all eye contact. I see Raul passing at the other end of an aisle, and duck out of his way. When I look up, he is watching me. He doesn't say a word, and walks on.

At the far end of the room, where I never go, I see some shoes for sale. One pair catches my attention. They are teetering stilettos, with large pink flowers on the front. The heels are thin and clear. I hate them, but I try them on anyway, and, since they fit me, I buy them. I don't know why, but I feel that I need a little extra height. They look cheap and tacky on their own, but on my feet they are irresistible.

With my basic provisions and my shoes swinging in bags from my wrists, I set off along Obispo to purchase my star ingredient.

I surprise myself by enjoying the cooking process. Elena watches me for a while with some amusement. I'm glad that my Spanish is now good enough for us to communicate properly.

'Why are you cooking?' she demands again, hands on hips.

'Because I want to!' I tell her, laughing.

She squeezes my midriff, which is visible between my tight Che T-shirt and a pair of denim shorts I picked up in the department store last week. 'You're getting fat,' she tells me, with pleasure. 'My

227

other guests, they always lose weight in Cuba. In Europe, they eat hamburgers and chocolate every day. Like Yasmin. They come here and we have no food, and they eat fruit and go home skinny, like Cuban girls. But little Maggie comes to me with no flesh at all.' She pinches my cheek. 'And now she is fat. We'll call you La Gorda. What are you cooking?'

I gesture to the pile of vegetables waiting to be chopped. 'Vegetable sauce,' I say. 'Just because I like it. Anyway, you're fat, too.'

Elena nods. 'I know. It's good to be fat. And spaghetti?'

I nod. 'And spaghetti. You want some?'

She shakes her head. 'No, thanks. I'm going to the hospital.'

'How is she?' Elena's neighbour was rushed to hospital at the weekend, with a kidney infection. The entire building seems to have rallied to her aid.

She puts her head on one side. 'Mmm. Better, I hope.'

I hold up a spoonful of sauce for her to taste. 'I hope so too. Tell her to get better soon, from me. And from Yasmin.'

Elena pulls her golden hair up. Her roots are pitch black. Her skin is honey brown and saggy. She is triumphantly voluptuous. I will miss her, when I go. I think I will be going soon.

'Wait a minute,' I tell her, and run into my bedroom and put my new shoes on. When she sees me attempting to stand upright in them, my landlady laughs until she cries. She kisses me firmly on each cheek, wipes away a tear, and breezes out of the door. I stand by the kitchen window, chopping a mound of garlic, and for a while I wonder if I could stay, after all. I could not, of course, continue to pay twenty dollars a night to Elena, and she couldn't charge me any less because of her taxes. I would have to have an income of one kind or another, to stay in Cuba, and I'm not allowed to work here. I could probably stay for a year on what's in my bank account at home. I couldn't get a visa for a year unless I enrolled on some other course at the university, or unless I left Cuba every two months. Going to a different Caribbean island six times a year wouldn't be the worst way to live my life. I think I would be all right. Yasmin and David and Libby would go home, and I would be glad to see the back of all of them. They will be leaving soon. They don't know it, but I do. Libby will be running for the sanctuary of Brighton before long; if she is lucky.

I chop the garlic with vigour. The juice finds a tiny cut in my finger, and stings. I cut it smaller and smaller and smaller, and finally I squash it into a pulp with the side of the knife. The breeze from the window picks up, and gusts through the room, slamming the front door. I love the smell of this flat. It smells of old bedspreads, of ripe fruit, and of Elena's heady perfume. This place is my sanctuary, as long as Yasmin is out of it.

Yasmin is rarely in. She seems to think I don't know that she's with Luis. I don't mind that she's going out with him – I never felt anything for him in the first place. But it still irritates me. She did that to me ten years ago, and if I ever did meet anyone I loved, she would do it to me again. I need to lose Yasmin from my life. I drop the garlic into the hot oil. It sizzles and spits. I consider the dynamics of our little group, for a moment. I came here to make friends with Lib and David. David became a real friend. Libby didn't. Yasmin came here because I was here, and because she was bored. She didn't like to think of dull little Maggie having all the fun, and turned up to take it from me. Now Yasmin and Lib have become best friends, and David and I share our Spanish classes and the memory of a furtive encounter. Yas and Lib have bonded over my sister. I grab an onion and cut it savagely. I hate them both, with their stupid yellow hair. I hate the way they swan around being friends, sharing my secret. I've seen them at it. I watched them at the beach. They have used me to obtain each other's friendship. Most people manage to make friends by talking about books and films and hair products. These two prefer to use someone else's tragedy.

I shiver in the breeze. For a second, I see him standing in the bushes, watching us. I close my eyes and stand perfectly still. It has been years since he last came into my head. We are playing, the three of us, and he is watching, spying. Wanting us. I could have stopped him. I was the only one who knew.

With a shake of my head, I pull myself together. It's over, now. It was over long ago, and nothing I do will ever bring her back. I throw the onions into the pot, and carry on with my cooking. At least I am doing something about it. For once, I am not going to be passive.

I smile as I walk up their street. I am wearing my new shoes, and I love the extra height they give me. The world looks better from up here. Although walking is a struggle, I feel more confident. If only I'd realised that I just needed three more inches to bring me into the human race. It was simpler than I ever suspected.

Walking on Havana's pavements isn't easy, but I am getting the hang of it. I am making an effort not to walk awkwardly, with my bottom stuck out and my knees bent. I am trying to strut, to take the pot holes in my stride. I haven't fallen over, so far. Men look at me. Denim shorts and heels are an excellent combination. I know this look would have gone down well at Vixenz. But the context is different. I choose to look sexy, now. No one is paying me.

On the corner of San Miguel and Infanta, a pool of water has been stagnating for weeks. I have watched its progress. It is now light brown, with a rainbow film on top. It smells foul. The stench hits me several yards away. It is evil. As soon as I see it, I know I'm going to slip as I pass, and fall in it. I step out into the road.

A lorry comes around the corner without braking. I hear its horn blaring, loud and long. Someone grabs my hand and pulls me out of the way. I feel my feet leaving the ground. I am yanked to the side of the road, and two hands steady my shoulders.

One of the young men who sit on the ledge is looking at me and laughing.

'What were you doing?' he asks. His face is wide and open. His teeth gleam at me.

Cuban Heels

I smile at him. I'm shaking. I point to the stinky pool. 'I didn't want to fall in the water,' I explain. 'It smells so bad.'

He laughs, and turns to tell his friends. While they discuss my stupidity, my vanity, my all-round foreignness, I check my bag. Elena lent me a tupperware-style container with a secure lid, and thankfully it has done its job. I have to deliver it.

'Would you like a drink?' asks my saviour. I look at him, at his four friends. I have passed them almost every day that I've lived here, on my way to and from the university, and I've never acknowledged their existence. I remember my manners.

'Thank you,' I tell him. 'I have to go over there' – I gesture at the brown front door – 'to see my friends for a minute. Then I'll come back and buy you all a beer, okay? Don't go away.'

'They beam. 'Okay.'

David buzzes me in with a cheery 'Hello, Mags.' I take the stairs two at a time. I have to do my duty, and leave as soon as possible. I'm only doing this because I like Libby and David. I'm giving them an opportunity to get their problems into perspective.

I stand on the threshold. David kisses me on the cheek, as casually as he can. I am as tall as he is. He steps back.

'What's different?' he asks with forced jollity. 'What the fuck have you got on your feet? Have you gone mad? Lib, come and look at Maggie.'

'Don't bother,' I say quickly. 'Look, I'm not stopping, I've actually got a date with five young men. One of them just saved me from going under the wheels of the most enormous lorry. Anyway. I was coming over here because Elena and I cooked a load of veg and we made a rather stunning sauce, if I say so myself. It all needed eating, you see, or it would have gone off in her fridge. And there's far too much for the two of us, or the three if Yasmin ever shows up. She's not here, is she?' I look around. I have to stop babbling. Lib and David are looking at me, slightly confused. 'So, what I meant to say is, here you are, some fabulous spicy sauce. Have it with pasta. Save

231

you having to worry about food tonight. My way of apologising for setting the cat amongst the pigeons, the other day.'

I turn to go.

'Maggie, are you sure?' Lib is being all sugary again. She reaches out and touches my arm.

'Course I'm sure. It's nothing.'

'What was that about someone saving you from a lorry?'

'Oh, I walked out in the road because of that puddle on the corner, and someone nearly ran me over.' I shrug. 'Happens a lot, doesn't it? It would help if they put a couple of pedestrian crossings somewhere in Havana. I'm beginning to think I'm on borrowed time with all the rushing between speeding cars.'

David sighs. 'Join the club. It's a death trap out there.'

I notice Lib frowning at him. She is transparent. She wants him to spare my feelings. He uttered the word 'death' and she's scared it's going to upset me. The sooner she learns that lesson, the better.

'But I was saved by a dashing young man, and now I've promised to buy him and all his mates a beer. We'll be in the peso bar. See you tomorrow.'

Lib looks concerned. 'You take care,' she says. 'David'll come down to the bar in a bit to check you're all right, if you like. And those shoes! They are the most ridiculous things I've ever seen. You look pornographic.'

'Aren't they amazing? I'm getting better at walking in them. Would you believe, they came from the supermarket? And you don't need to check on me. I can look after myself. Truly, Lib, nice thought but I'm fine. Enjoy your evening.'

She smiles. 'Well, thanks for this. Come back for lunch after Spanish tomorrow, if you like. Oh, by the way, I wouldn't wait for Yasmin tonight. We saw her earlier. She went out.'

'With Luis?'

They both look embarrassed. I leave.

chapter twenty-three

Libby

'I wish she'd tell us about her sister,' Libby whispers to Charlie. He is just about to go to bed, and she is giving him his last feed. She adores breastfeeding him. She feels that he is still a part of her. Libby is beginning to feel slightly affronted by Maggie. She puts on such a brave façade all the time that Libby feels she can't get to know her. She is brittle and defensive. Libby wants to help her, but she is beginning to realise that Maggie doesn't want any help. 'She thinks she can manage on her own,' Libby adds, 'but she can't.'

She looks down at Charlie's squidgy cheeks. He has a beautiful little snub nose. Libby loves him naked. He rarely wears more than a nappy, here. When she thinks of him wrapped up in Brighton last winter, it seems like a different baby. There, he was a young Englishman. Here, he is, as Luis often says, a Cubanito. His skin is so smooth. Nothing in the world is quite that soft. His fingernails are tiny. When he breastfeeds, he concentrates on it to the exclusion of everything else. She is not sure whether she is meant to love him quite this much. Does Maria love Gracia like this, for instance? Logically, she supposes she must do, but she cannot imagine it. This bond is unique to her and Charlie.

*　　*　　*

When she emerges from the bedroom, David is boiling water for the pasta.

'Why the hell did Maggie traipse all the way over here with our dinner?' she demands. 'I mean, it's very nice of her, but she doesn't owe us anything. And what was she on about, with those guys? She looks like a stripper in those shoes. I'm worried about her, David.'

David shrugs. He doesn't look up from the pan. 'I don't know,' he says. 'She's our friend? She brought us dinner because she knew we needed some time alone together?'

Libby smiles. 'You've told her, haven't you? I know you, husband of mine. You've confided in her about our small marital troubles, as well as everything else. I know you have. And you know what? I don't mind. I told Yasmin.'

'You told Yasmin, you cheeky woman? As you would be the first to agree, Yasmin is a far worse choice of confidante than Maggie.' David's voice is slightly strained. He is trying hard to be normal.

'Oh, Yasi's all right.' Libby opens the fridge. 'David! We haven't got any beers. How did that happen? Shall I nip down and get some?'

David puts down the battered wooden spoon. 'No, sweetheart. You stay here. I'll go. Can't have my wife traipsing around Havana by night. Not with evil puddles apparently on every street corner, waiting to push you into the road. Plus that place is closed as often as it's open and I don't want you wandering off down the back streets in search of beer.'

'You sexist pig. Havana is far safer than Brighton.'

'And I'd prefer to go to the offy myself in Brighton, too.'

'Very overprotective.'

'Because I love you. So you stir these two. The sauce is heating nicely, and the spaghetti'll be ready in five minutes or so. I had a taste. It was strangely delicious. More flavour in there than in everything else we've eaten in Cuba, put together. We should have got Maggie and Elena to cook our wedding feast. It would have been cheaper.'

'Wedding breakfast,' Libby corrects him, as he disappears through the door. 'It's called a wedding *breakfast*.'

'But it was in the afternoon!' he calls, as he disappears down the stairs.

Libby stirs both pans, mixing pieces of sauce into the spaghetti water as she transfers their sole wooden spoon from one to the other. As she stirs, she realises that life is better than it has ever been. She is a long way from London, from her mother and from her old job. She is far from Brighton, scene of her postnatal misery. Her son is sleeping peacefully with a milky beard dried on to his chin. Her father, stepmother, and half-brother and sister are in Australia, and she might or might not bring them into her life, Charlie's life. Her husband, who has loved her all along, who would never cheat on her, least of all with Yasmin, is her friend again. She has loved him all along, too, and now she is excited again. Her stomach turns over at the very thought of him. She and David will last for ever. She can go back to work if she wants to. She can stay at home with Charlie if she doesn't. She is living in Havana for a while, and making friends as she does so. She can talk to any other mother in the world. She is immensely privileged. She is only just beginning to realise exactly how lucky, and blessed, she is.

She is still upset about Maggie and her sister, but she is beginning to consider the possibility that there is nothing she can do, unless Maggie wants her help.

Libby extracts a strand of spaghetti, and tastes it. It is cooked perfectly, so she turns off the gas. She slurps a generous amount of sauce from the spoon, to judge its temperature. It is spicy. Those chillis are masking something sinister.

She knows at once. Her throat tightens and she throws the spoon down. Her throat is swelling up. Her chest is heavy. This hasn't happened to her for years. She runs, panicking, into the bathroom and tries to locate her epi-pen. It is not there. It was there last week. She runs back to the living room and searches for it, throwing cushions around and kicking Charlie's toys across the floor. All the time, her head is ringing. She is gasping for breath. It has never been this serious before. It must have been packed with peanuts. Maggie knows about Libby and nuts. Doesn't she? But she doesn't. She can't. Libby has made a point of hiding her allergies.

The epi-pen is in the middle of a pile of junk, next to the fan, on the sideboard. Libby grabs it and injects herself. Immediately, she begins to breathe again.

She is alive.

She puts her hands to her head. Tears are pouring down her cheeks. She had a huge anaphylactic reaction. She knows she nearly died. David was right. She should take her allergies seriously. Nothing like this has happened for years. But it has happened. It's happened in the past and she has brushed it aside each time. This is her closest shave yet.

She can't calm down. Maggie didn't do this on purpose. In her head, Maggie and her sister and Libby are all tangled up. People die. They die all the time. She needs David.

Acting on an instinct, Libby goes into Charlie's room and takes him out of bed. She does it gently so that he might stay asleep. With her baby on her shoulder, she picks up her keys and walks out of the flat. She knows she ought to lie down after a reaction like this. She should really go to hospital, to be sure. She knows she'll be all right now, because of the adrenaline, but sometimes people can have delayed reactions. She is shaking so violently that she has to grip the rail with one hand to make her descent of the stairs. She just needs her husband. Tears course down her cheeks. She needs him to hold her, to look after her. He will take care of everything. He has only gone down the road to buy the beers. They will meet in the doorway, and she will tell him what happened. Then he will take charge.

He is not on the street. Libby looks up and down the road, but she can't see him. She walks gingerly down to Infanta, holding tight to her nearly naked Charlie with both hands. She is trembling all over. She takes care to avoid the stagnant puddle.

David isn't at the drinks stall. The stall is there, and it's open, and there is nobody queuing. David isn't there. All he needed to do was to come here, buy four cans of Cristal, and go back to the flat. He should have been home in time to inject her.

She remembers that Maggie was going to the peso bar. It is just down the road.

As she walks she repeats her mantra. Maggie didn't know. Maggie didn't know. It was a mistake, an accident. It's my own fault, she reminds herself, for being so weak. Maggie didn't know. It is not her fault.

She rounds the corner to the bar. Maggie is sitting at a table with five young men. And one slightly older one. David is sitting on a plastic chair, sipping a beer and laughing. When Libby sees him, she nearly drops Charlie. She doesn't understand.

Maggie sees her before he does. 'Libby!' she says, quietly. She looks surprised.

David spins around. He stands up and walks towards her. She edges, backwards, away from him.

'Come back, Lib!' he calls. Libby pauses to give Charlie to a woman at a nearby table. She doesn't know what she's going to do, but she needs Charlie to be safe. Cuban women know how to look after babies.

'Lib?' says David, frowning. 'What are you doing?'

She turns and runs. She's not going home. She doesn't want to be anywhere else. She runs out into the road, just as a car is speeding towards her with its lights off. She sees it coming and increases her pace. It clips her ankle, and she is sent, sprawling, across the bumpy tarmac.

chapter twenty-four

Maggie

I feel nothing. I strut through the tatty streets of Centro Habana, my bag swinging from my shoulder, and I feel empty. I pass a bread shop, where a crowd of people are clutching their ration cards and surging forwards. They take no notice of me. A couple of young men sitting on a step shout suggestions to me. I ignore them. Even when I concentrate hard and try to dredge up some emotion, I can barely find anything. The sun is shining, as it shines every day. These streets are washed out, white, with black shadows. They are always like that. Nothing has changed. I thought I would be happy. Libby's pain was supposed to cancel my own. Nothing is different. Nothing has changed. Libby has been forced, by me, to contemplate a misfortune of her own. I am a little bit sorry that she was hit by the car, and quite glad that she wasn't seriously injured. I have no intention of visiting her in hospital.

I have every intention of spending as much time as possible with David, while she's away. I'm glad she saw us together, even with the other men there. I knew from the way she looked at David that she was thumped in the face by his infidelity. It must have been horrible for her, to have eaten peanuts, and then to be faced with that. She doesn't even know that he's kissed me. She just saw the more abstract infidelity inherent in hotfooting it to the bar after me, to have some fun, when he was supposed to be buying her a beer. He was besotted with me last night. I saw it in his face.

None of this matters. Libby is all right, and so are David and Charlie. If anything had happened to Charlie, then I would have been truly remorseful. But it didn't. I knew it wouldn't, because I engineered everything. It was me. I took action. I did this thing.

I did my thing, in the same way Clare's dad did his.

I shake my head, and try to think of something else. I walk through the middle of a children's baseball game, and duck as the ball flies towards me. The little boys and girls giggle, and shout to me in Spanish. I should understand what they are saying, but I don't, and so I smile, because they clearly mean no harm, and kick the ball in their direction. As I walk off I turn and look at them again, at the happy boys and girls, who do not, yet, know what the world is like. Cuba is no different from anywhere else. All the debates about different types of societies are meaningless. People will always harm other people. I stop to give the children a wave. A little girl waves back. The others are engrossed in the game.

The heat has become stifling. I am wearing a floppy crocheted hat that Yasmin produced from her suitcase the other day. I still have a headache. I walk down a street and turn left, randomly. I'm good on my heels, now. I know I am heading in the approximate direction of David, and I am sick of the route I always take.

This street is smelly. I walk past a group of overflowing bins. A woman carries two handfuls of rubbish towards them, and opens the lid of one. The stench hits me at a distance. This is the whole neighbourhood's rubbish, and it must go back at least a week. She forces the rubbish down with her hand, and adds her contribution. That is one thing I will not miss about Cuba, when I have to leave.

Brighton may have a disastrously privatised rubbish collection service, but at least the place smells all right. This heat amplifies the pungency. I have never known anything smell as vile as certain pockets of the streets of Havana. I have never been anywhere this extreme.

Brighton. Sometimes I catch myself thinking about life beyond Havana. I seem to be assuming that I'll go back to Sixth Avenue, but I can't think beyond that. I cannot go there, of course. I have shown Libby, now, what it is to be hurt. She might have learned a small lesson. She knows that the fact that someone is familiar, a friend, does not mean they are necessarily benign. She has, I hope, learned not to interfere with me. I can't live below that family again. I couldn't listen to their lives. What a stupid waste of time that would be. Occasionally, I envisage David and me as a unit, but I can't rely on that happening. We would be good together, but I have to assume that we will never test that assumption.

I know that I'm not going back to stripping. The very idea of it fills my body with fear and dread. I almost admire myself for the fact that I did it and survived, without going completely mad. I would like to go back to university properly, to do a masters.

I pass two young men, who smile, and ask, in Spanish, which country I am from. They make me think of Raul. I was mean and rude to him. Next time I see him, I will stop and talk, and I'll accept any invitation he proffers. I'll go for another drink with the men from San Miguel. I need to do things – any things – to keep myself going. Today, more than ever before, my instincts are telling me not to stop, not to look down.

Both these men are dark, and one is noticeably better-looking than the other. I pretend not to understand them. When I look at random men like those two, I can't believe how I used to earn my living. I used to take all my clothes off, for people I didn't know at all. For men I knew less well than these strangers, who have at least spoken to me. When I sat in the peso bar last night, I was the object of attention, and probably lust, from all the men on my table. Five men and me. I enjoyed it, but only because I had every intention of keeping my clothes on. I was waiting for David, and he came.

Men look at me differently, when I dress like this. I'd rather be invisible. I suddenly realise what the look means. The men at the bar, last night. The men in Vixenz. These two men on this street, right now.

They all look at me in exactly the same way as Clare's dad.

I spin around. Activity is everything. I must keep busy.

'I am English,' I tell them, in Spanish.

'Yes?' asks the ugly one, coming back towards me. 'I don't know anything about England. Would you help me learn English?'

'Do you have a husband?' asks the other.

I smile as prettily as I can. 'No,' I say, making eye contact with each of them in turn, before settling my gaze on the handsome one. I address my next remark exclusively to him.

'Would you like,' I ask listlessly, 'to have sex with me?'

I lie on my back, on my pink bedspread, and I try not to cry. I didn't ask his name. He never asked mine. Of course he accepted my proposition. He wasn't rough. He was a perfectly normal young man who couldn't believe his luck. He pushed himself inside me, his face tense with concentration, and I bit my lip and looked away from him, at the ceiling, and tried to force Clare's dad out of my head. He's dead now, I told myself. He is as good as dead. He might even really be dead. He is nothing. As my random lover came to a climax, I tried to be somewhere else. I couldn't think of anything but that man. The grief pulsed through me. I shut my eyes tight and wondered how I could carry on living.

I could hear Fidel Castro's voice on Elena's television in the next room. The ugly friend was waiting politely. I prayed Elena wouldn't come back before they left.

'I think we might get married,' my lover suggested, as I wiped myself with a tissue and put my bra back on. I hadn't mentioned condoms, and nor, naturally, had he. This gives me a concrete worry, which is good. I wore my shoes throughout the experience. That made me feel cheaper than anything.

'We can't,' I told him. I desperately wanted him to leave, yet I could not bear the idea of being alone.

He tried again. It was not the romantic proposal of every young girl's dream.

'We don't have to live together or have children,' he explained. 'Just for my passport, okay? How long can British people stay in America? Do you need a visa?'

'Three months,' I told him. 'You don't need a visa for that. But I'm not marrying you. Not even to give you a passport. Sorry, but I don't really know you.'

He looked hurt, but he did not make the obvious riposte. Eventually he left, picking his friend up on the way out. I heard him filling him in, in a bitter voice. Now I find myself in tatters. I hadn't had sex since Mark kicked me out. Now I have. I wish it had been David. He is the only one who looks at me like Ivan used to look at me. He is the only one who doesn't remind me of Clare's dad.

I try to look back on it and to force myself to enjoy, retrospectively, the feeling of being touched and desired. I can't do it. I hated it. I loathed every single moment. It did me no good. It did harm: it cancelled out the warmth of David's kiss. I am cheap. I feel exactly like I used to feel at Vixenz. I have, once again, exposed my body to a stranger. This time it wasn't even for money. I don't know why I did it.

chapter twenty-five

Libby – the same morning

Libby curls up in bed. The room is full of other patients, but her curtains are closed firmly around her. She doesn't want to see anybody else. She doesn't want them to see her, to wonder what is wrong, why she is crying.

She wants Charlie. He is the only one she can trust. David lied to her, and went for a drink with Maggie. However much she tries to explain it away, this fact will not leave her head.

Her husband told her a lie. He went out to buy some drinks to go with their dinner, and he slipped away to meet Maggie and the boys from the ledge. While she was struggling to survive, he was laughing and buying everyone a drink. He didn't tell her where he was going. She never expected that of David, and now she is wondering when and where he has done that before. When has he innocently gone for a drink with a friend, and met a woman for a clandestine encounter? She will never trust him again.

She pulls a strand of hair into her mouth, and chews it. Everything is different. It is all wrong. Maggie gave her that sauce, and it was full of peanuts. It makes no sense. She is sure that she has never said anything to her about the nut allergy. But if it was an innocent mistake, why were the nuts disguised so heavily? It must have been a mistake. Otherwise, Maggie would have wanted to hurt her. To kill her.

She landed on the tarmac with a thud. Her hands and knees were stinging like a child's in the playground. She knew at once that she was not seriously hurt, but she could not find the energy to get up. A crowd had gathered around her, and she looked up at the concerned faces. All she wanted was Charlie. She wanted to be far away from David, with Charlie. The woman stood on the edge of the crowd, with Charlie in her arms. Libby managed to smile at her, slightly.

They took her to hospital in somebody's car. She lay in the back, her leg propped delicately along the leather seat. David sat in the front. She looked out of the window, at the black Havana night and the blurry lights flashing past. The hospital was on the Malecon. She remembered finding it, soon after they arrived here. She thought they might need it. David kept trying to talk to her, but she didn't even listen to the words.

Libby is lonely here. She needs her baby, and her mummy. She would like to see Yasmin. David can go to hell, as can Maggie. All the time she's spent trying to help Maggie has been thrown back into her face. Her mother is on a flight out here at this very moment. Last night was the first night she has ever been separated from Charlie. She didn't sleep. She thought about him all night long, and missed him, and wondered how much he was missing her, if at all. David will have bought him some formula milk by now. Charlie has never had it before.

Libby is going home this afternoon. Her ankle is mildly sprained. Her cuts are superficial and barely even sting. The bruises look worse than they feel. The only reason they kept her in was because of the anaphylactic episode. She knows she's fine. She wants to go right now.

Libby has never been particularly tearful, except at certain points in her pregnancy and during the first few weeks of motherhood. Now, though, she can't stop crying. All she wants to do is to lie here and let the tears fall down her cheeks. She nearly died. She doesn't know why it happened. Yesterday she was desperately keen to help Maggie, to be the best friend she has ever had. Today she is scared of her. Although she can't piece it together, she knows that something is very wrong. Maggie is doing strange things. She is on the edge. Libby knows she will work it all out, sooner or later.

The curtains part.

'Hey,' says a familiar voice. Libby wipes her eyes and smiles weakly. She watches Yasmin's bright smile turn to concern, and at once she is in Yasmin's arms. They feel strong, and she allows herself to relax a little. In a second, she is sobbing. Through all the time she was depressed in Brighton, she would not have dreamed of sobbing in anyone's arms.

'What was he doing with her?' Libby manages to ask Yasmin. 'Why did Maggie bring me that food? Why did David run off to meet her, in secret? No wonder he wouldn't let me go for the beers.'

Yasmin strokes her hair, gently. 'I don't know what's been going on, honey,' she says softly. 'Maggie didn't know, did she? She told me she had no idea that you couldn't eat nuts. She said she just bought all the nice things she could find at the market. She didn't even know that ground nuts and peanuts were the same thing. That's what she said.'

Libby looks up at Yasmin. She notices that her face is tired and strained. 'Do you believe her?'

Yasmin strokes Libby's hair. 'Lib, Maggie's screwed up. We both know that. But she's not evil. She wouldn't hurt you on purpose. God, the way she goes on about you, you are her absolute role model. She worships you. Has done from the moment she met you. She's gutted about what happened.'

Libby frowns. 'Really? That can't be right, Yas. I thought she didn't like me.'

Yasmin snorts. 'You're wrong. She loves you. She wants to *be* you. It's been Libby this, Libby that, can we ask Libby to come, shall I go and see Libby. I seriously asked her once if she had any lesbian tendencies.'

Libby wipes her nose on the back of her hand. 'Yas, you have to be exaggerating.'

'I'm not. I swear.'

'Bloody hell.' Libby looks back on the weeks that she has known Maggie, and tries to reassess them. She cannot see Maggie worshipping her. Nothing fits together. 'What was she doing with David?' she asks, suddenly. 'What was David doing with her?'

Yasmin takes her hand.

'Obviously we went through it a million times last night. David says the stall was closed and he remembered that Maggie'd said she was at the peso bar, so he thought he'd pick some up there, and check she was all right on her rather crazy date with all the random men while he was at it. He was just concerned for her, like we all are, because she's been getting screwier lately.'

'But the stall was open.'

'Maybe it only just opened.'

'Must have done.' Libby sniffs, rubs her eyes, and leans back on her pillow. Now that she is almost well, she is beginning to wonder whether she might enjoy herself, just a little bit. She has been a mother for the past six months. All her energies have been devoted to looking after someone else. For a week or two, she deserves to be looked after, herself. She will join her son in his little world of dependency. Their every need will be catered for by David and her mother.

'How's Charlie?' she asks abruptly.

'Charlie's fine.' Yasmin smiles. 'He's gorgeous. It must be horrid for you being shut away here, but he really is all right. Maria's been over with Gracia. I've been round. David's fine with him, and your mum'll be here soon. We've emailed your dad, too.'

'We'd better get the next flight home, hadn't we?'

'I think you had.'

'What about you, Yasi? What are you going to do? Will you stay around for Maggie's sake?'

Yasmin smiles and becomes more animated. 'I'm running out of money, to be honest,' she says. 'But I'm not ready for Norwich. Luis is very persuasive. He's got it into his head that I have to move in with him. Now, I don't think it's strictly allowed. And I'm not sure I want to get that serious, yeah? So I might take some time out, get an English teaching gig somewhere. I don't think I'm allowed to work in Cuba though, plus there's no spare money for private tuition. I'm thinking Mexico, that kind of direction. But I can't go anywhere until I'm sure that Mags is all right. Or else I'll take her with me.'

Libby smiles wanly. 'Sounds like hard work. Have you written to her parents? Can they take her off your hands?'

'Mmm. Sent them an email this morning.'

'How is she, today?'

'God knows. I'm the enemy right now. She's closed up more than ever. You know Mags.'

'Actually,' says Libby, 'I don't think I do.'

chapter twenty-six

Maggie – later that day

Dear Maggie,

I hope you don't mind me emailing you. I don't know whether you remember me from Norwich. What am I saying? I'm sure you remember me. We went out together for several months, back in 1992. I'm afraid I didn't treat you very well and I have always felt guilty about you and hoped that you did find someone more honourable and that you are happy and so on. When I saw your name on Friends Reunited I felt that I had to get back in touch, largely to apologise. So: sorry.

As you doubtless know, Yasmin and I split up after a couple of years. I don't know what she's up to these days but the last I heard she was travelling. I'm getting married in June, and Mel and I are discovering that weddings take over your life. We'll be glad when it's done and rings are safely on fingers. How about you? Any husband or kiddies on the scene?

Where are you living? If you're in or near London (we live in Putney and I work in IT in the City), drop us a line, and if you wanted we could maybe catch up and resolve a situation which has been niggling me for ten years. I hope this doesn't sound presumptuous. If you want to ignore me, or to tell me to fuck off, I will understand.

But I have thought of you with affection, over the years, and I would like you to be able to think well of me, too, now that I have grown up a little.

With best wishes,

Ivan

I stand on the threshold, behind the glass door, and look at the scene. Ivan's email is printed out in my pocket. I see David walking around the flat, picking things up and putting them away. He takes Charlie's toys, one by one, to the sideboard, and piles them up. His face is blank and I can feel his tension, from here. Charlie is running around in his walker. He, at least, seems to be happy. He doesn't miss his mother, after all.

When Charlie sees me, he grins and waves his arms, and charges towards the door. I bend down and tap on the glass with my fingertips, and he reaches out for me. David looks round, notices me, and comes to open the door. His face is puffy, and he looks as if he's been up all night, rearranging things. His tanned face looks different with the shadow of a beard. He is wearing his long cream shorts and an old T-shirt, which has been bleached by the Cuban sun. He looks at me without much love, but I know in the instant that our eyes meet that I love him. I love him more than Ivan. David could be my salvation.

I pat Charlie's soft head, and offer David a kiss on the cheek. He turns away, but I don't think he means to be rude. He picks up a bag, and seems to force a smile.

'Mags,' he says. 'I knew you'd show up.'

I am still sore from my nameless lover's enthusiastic efforts. I feel as if I have been unfaithful to David. He never needs to know. I only stopped off at the internet place to put some distance between David and the Cuban. The last person I expected to enter the equation was Ivan. I don't care about him any more, I have discovered. I will ignore him utterly.

'Thanks for coming,' he adds. 'I'll get off to the hospital, then.'

'Hey,' I tell him lovingly. 'You look terrible, David. Why don't you let me make you a coffee, first?' I reach up to stroke his cheek, but he pushes my hand away.

'No, I've had some,' he says. 'I've made up some formula milk, which he'll have before his nap. It just needs heating in hot water. There's a pan just boiled on the ring. I left the lid on.'

I had half forgotten that, last night, I promised to look after Charlie while David went to visit his wife. He should be taking him – Libby will be furious when she realises that he's come alone – but it is not in my interests to point that out. I look at my watch. It is half past two. I haven't had any lunch. I open my mouth to ask whether there is any of my pasta sauce left, then think better of it.

'Okay,' I tell him meekly.

'I'm sure I won't be gone too long,' he adds, smiling weakly. 'Lib'll be needing her rest. If I'm not back by half five, there's some vegetable mush in the fridge that you can give him. Then he has a bath – the baby bath's up on the wardrobe – and some milk, and you know how to put him down for the night, don't you? Just stick him down awake and don't worry if he rolls over. But I'll be back long before then. He'll have a nap in half an hour or so. Leave him a few minutes if he cries – he'll get himself off to sleep. While he's in the walker, you have to leave all these chairs in the doorways to stop him falling down the steps.'

'David,' I say as firmly as I can, remembering that he liked it when I was bossy. 'Charlie and I will be absolutely fine. Don't worry about us, for God's sake. Just concentrate on Lib. Tell her to get better soon, and tell her again that I am so, so sorry for what happened. You know, she'll need to make sure she gets a new epi-pen while she's at the hospital.'

David turns and smiles. 'You're absolutely right, my dear. Thanks. And thanks for all of this. We know it was an accident. It was my fault really. Certainly in my wife's eyes. I just feel like the biggest bastard that ever lived.'

'Well you're not. You're fantastic. Now go and sort it all out with your beautiful wife.'

He is halfway through the door when he turns back. 'Here are Lib's keys, in case you need them,' he says. 'She'll be home tomorrow morning, and her mother's coming on today's flight, so we won't have to lean on you like this again.'

'Well I'll stay till Libby's mum gets here, so you can meet her at the airport. She'll be worried about her daughter and the last thing she's going to be thinking about is finding a cab. Stay as long as you need, and give Libby my love. And Yasmin's.'

'Yas is with her now, actually. Thanks, you're a star.'

I push him through the door, taking care only to touch the small of his back. 'Lean on me all you like. Go on, off.'

The keys hang heavily in my pocket.

I sit back while Charlie runs around the flat. I look idly through their things, but nothing is particularly interesting. My pasta sauce seems to have vanished, which is irritating, and I find myself a stale bread roll and a lump of rubbery cheese for lunch. I drink some water straight from the tap. Libby would never do that, but Elena and the neighbours do, and I don't see much wrong with them. Apart from the neighbour with the kidney infection.

I hold Charlie close while I give him his bottle of milk. He doesn't seem to notice the difference between this and breast milk. He doesn't complain that I am feeding him, rather than Libby. He doesn't need his mummy at all. I sniff the top of his head. It is warm and sweet. I cuddle him. I could be a good stepmother to him; though really I know it will never happen. If David and I got together, that would constitute my happy ending, and I have never envisaged myself with one of those.

He rolls over and goes to sleep as soon as I put him in the travel cot. While he sleeps, I lie on the sofa and wonder whether I am evil. I hurt this baby's mother on purpose, and she really could have died. No one has suggested that I did it deliberately yet, but I know that they will. Libby is probably putting the possibility to David at this very moment. She will forgive me because of Grace, but she will no longer want to be my bestest confidante. She knows I did it. I know that she knows. That is why I can't go back to Brighton; so I may as well stay in Cuba.

I look around the sparsely furnished flat and see an envelope almost hidden by a book. I pick it up. If either of them has been writing letters, I want to know what they have said.

The letter is addressed to Libby, care of Luis. The postmark is Australian. It is unopened, but it takes me just a couple of minutes to steam the glue away. The letter is written with an expensive fountain pen, in looped blue handwriting.

Dear Liberty, *it says.*

'Thank you for writing to me. I can't tell you enough how much it means. I have been asking your mother for your contact details for years, and David emailed me months ago to talk about re-establishing contact. Your mother feels, quite understandably, that you are better off without me but David has suggested that you might, if not welcome, then tolerate the chance for us to get to know each other.

Thanks to your husband, I know about my grandson. I would love to see a photograph of him, or, who knows? to meet him one day. But let me go back further. I need to start with a sizeable apology (and I fear that no apology could ever be large enough). I left your mother, not you, and it was unforgivable of me to lose contact with my baby girl. I missed you so much, and felt so sure that I had handled the situation so badly, that in the end I thought I should just walk away for everyone's sake. You know, I was thirty when I left: very certainly old enough to know better. Now twenty-five years have passed, and you are thirty, and by all accounts making a far better job of family life than your mother and I ever did. I have always missed you terribly. This, I know, is a feeble thing to say.

You ask about my life. I have been living in Australia for over twenty years. I am married to an Australian woman, Marly, and we have two children. Sammi, your half-sister, is seventeen, and Zachary, your half-brother, is fifteen. We live close to Sydney, in a town called Windsor.

I realise that this is difficult for you, and I can see from your letter that you are angry with me. I hope you will find it in your heart to allow me back into your life. I have written countless emails to you, but they have remained unsent. Email seemed ultimately too transient, and I didn't want you to think I wasn't taking you seriously. I have your landlord's telephone number in Cuba and have almost dialled many times, but I didn't want to put you on the spot with a surprise. Then your letter came. Thank you.

My contact details are all above. I will pray to hear from you again.

With all best wishes, and love,

Alec, your father

I can barely finish reading, I am so enraged. Libby is rubbing my face in it now. This is the proof that she has a spare sister. A new one, who is seventeen. People like me long for sisters, and they never appear. Libby has got one she doesn't even know. I crumple the letter and put it in my bag. Then I take it out and carefully copy down the address into my Spanish book. I will tear it up and send him back the pieces. That should keep him away for a while.

I have hurt his precious daughter. I want to write to this man and tell him all about it. Your daughter is a fake, I will tell him. She was supposed to be like a sister to me, but she changed. She hurt me with her sickly sympathy. I hurt her back, because I heard her saying through a baby monitor that she was allergic to peanuts, and now nothing has changed. I am supposed to feel better, but I don't. You, Alec, think David is so great, but if he's the wonderful son-in-law you are imagining, why did he sneak off to see me? He was besotted with me last night. That much was plain. Libby saw him with me and now she will never let him be my friend again. I am on borrowed time.

I would like to talk to her, at some point, to make sure that she knows that she and Yasmin were poisonous. They gossiped about me and Grace. That is why she is in hospital, now. I need to be sure that she has made that connection. But I can't stick around for a moment after I do.

The trouble is, I haven't hurt her enough. She had a reaction to my sauce, and she cured it with an injection. She was grazed by a car, but she doesn't seem to be suffering. I know she wants to meet her father, and I will postpone that moment, but that means nothing.

Everyone feels sorry for her. Treacherous Yasmin sits by her bed telling her how mad I am. David dumps the baby on me and rushes off to proclaim his eternal love for her. Her mother flies halfway round the world to look after her. Her father miraculously reappears.

I stand up and pace around. I wish I could harm Charlie – not badly, just enough to make her realise what it's like – but I couldn't. The very idea of hurting a baby makes me sick.

I used to want everything Libby had. Now I don't. I just want her to have my life, instead. I want her to realise.

I know that David likes me. I never asked him to come to the peso bar. He came to see me of his own accord. If I played it right, I could steal him away from her. I could move into their flat upstairs, in Brighton. Libby could go to Devon to be near her mother. I could be a good stepmother. We might even have another child, a daughter. A cousin for Maddy, a sister for Charlie, someone who would love me. Another niece for Grace.

I try so hard not to think about her, not to say her name. Every moment of every day, I try to forget her. She is always there. She won't go away. She has never left. I never consciously revisit the day it happened, but I can't forget it. I can push it from my mind, but its shape is still there. It is a black hole of a day, and it pulls in everything around it. The day she left, and the day they found her and the dead time in between. They will always be there. Grace is part of me, and I am a part of her. When he did that to her, he destroyed me, too.

I pull myself together. I must keep control. I must keep control. Somewhere, I know that the only reason I think about Libby is because she's not Grace. She is not Grace, but she is close to the person Grace might have become. I can't face that, though. I'm not ready for it. I tear the letter from Libby's dad into tiny pieces, and put it back into the envelope. I stick it back down and cross out the address. Then I write Alec's address and put it away. I'll put stamps on it later.

I take Ivan's email out of my pocket again and busy myself trying to read between the lines.

Someone knocks on the kitchen door.

'Hola?' I say, dully. I might see if Luis wants me. Yasmin stole him from me. I could steal him back for a quick fuck. It would be exactly what Yasmin deserved. Sex has lost all meaning. It is an act that occupies my body and mind. I hate it, and that is why I will carry on doing it. I still feel tender from the last time.

'Hola?' calls a voice, uncertainly. The door is unlocked, and a woman comes through it. She has waist-length light brown hair, and a baby sitting on her hip. She seems anxious, and I rearrange my features to give me an appropriate demeanour.

'Are you Luis's sister?' I ask, in Spanish.

'Yes!' she says. 'You speak Spanish! I am Maria. Are you Maggie?'

'Yes. I'm looking after the baby.'

'That's good. Is he sleeping?'

'Yes. David's at the hospital. Would you like a coffee?'

She looks anxious, not wanting to trouble me. 'I'm making one,' I reassure her, and she nods.

While I make it, I try to think of things to say.

'Your Spanish is very good,' she tells me, hesitantly.

'Thank you. I study at the university with David, but I'm quite bad, really.'

'No you're not.'

'Would you like me to say anything to Libby for you?'

'Tell her we are so sad that she's hurt. That we hope she gets better very soon.'

'I feel very bad about Libby,' I tell her, smiling wanly as I share this fake confidence. 'I didn't know she couldn't eat nuts.'

Maria touches my arm. 'It's not your fault. We feel bad because Havana is our city, and there are so many bad drivers.'

I turn and hand her a cup of sweet black coffee. Elena has always been horrified that I drink it with milk and without sugar. It seems reasonable to suppose that Maria is the same. She sips and smiles.

'Very good coffee,' she says.

I look at her baby, who is sitting happily on her hip and playing with a strand of her mother's hair. She has shiny black eyes like buttons, and chubby cheeks. She looks like a baby in a cartoon. She's much cuter than Charlie. I feel disloyal saying it, but she's prettier than Maddy, too.

'What's your baby's name?' I ask, stroking her cheek. 'She's lovely.'

'It's Gracia. In English, Grace,' says Maria, turning to put her coffee on the sideboard.

It strikes me like a physical blow. I lean on the edge of the sink to steady myself. I take a deep breath, force myself to focus, and I look at the child closely.

Grace is wearing a disposable nappy fastened with a big nappy pin, and a pair of lacy socks. I stare at her, and her face breaks into a huge grin. She knows me, too.

'She's beautiful,' I say quietly, in English.

'Beautiful, si,' Maria agrees.

Cuban Heels

I can't take my eyes off baby Grace. I hold my arms out, and Maria passes her to me. She comes without complaint. She is a substantial weight. I feel her soft skin, stroke her thick black hair, and smell her baby smell. She smells different from Charlie. She smells of Cuba. Charlie smells of Johnson's products. I go through to the living room, and sit on the sofa, with the baby on my lap. She looks around expectantly. I hand her one of Charlie's rattles. She takes it and puts it into her mouth.

'Grace,' I whisper. 'Baby Grace. Last time you were blonde. But black hair suits you.'

She is happy with me. She knows. She reaches for my hair, and tugs it. Grace used to do that. I can't pick up my coffee, because Maria would see that I am shaking. I can only think of this baby. I can't believe I was distracted by thoughts of David and Libby and Charlie, and Ivan. This is my sister. She has come back to us. I need her as much as she needs me. She has come back to save me.

'How long have you been in Havana?' Maria is asking politely.

I barely look up. 'Nearly a month,' I tell her. 'I love it here.'

'That's good.'

I know I should think of something else to say. 'My sister had a baby two weeks ago,' I announce, since my mind is suddenly fixed on my family. My family is complete again. 'I'll show you a picture.' I sit Grace on my hip, and go to the table to find my bag. I take out my printout of the photo of Emma and Maddy, in the hospital. Emma has enormous black bags under her eyes, and a radiant smile. Her hair looks thick with sweat, and she's wearing a huge T-shirt. Cradled in her arms is a tiny pink baby. Madeleine is shrivelled and ugly. I may be her aunt, and thus obliged to call her beautiful, but it's the truth. She has nothing on Grace. I can't wait to take Grace back to my parents. They will be so happy to see her again. I know they will recognise her, like I did.

I hand the photo to Maria. 'This is my sister, Emma,' I tell her, 'and this is baby Maddy.'

'Mad-dy,' she says slowly. 'I haven't heard that name.'

'Really it's Madeleine.'

'Ahhh. Beautiful baby. And your sister is very pretty.'

I hear Charlie whimpering from the other room. Shut the fuck up, I think. Keep out of it. He builds up to a cry, and I notice Maria looking anxiously towards the bedroom door. Reluctantly, I hand Grace back to her mother, and go to fetch him.

He is confused to see me, and takes a while to stop crying. I hold him close and jiggle him around the room.

'Poor Charlie,' I say. 'None of this is your fault.'

He sniffs heavily and rubs his teary face on my shoulder. I walk around the bedroom, rocking him, and take the opportunity to look in the drawers.

I flick through their documents with my free hand, and pick out Charlie's passport. I tuck it into my waistband. It might, I think, be useful.

chapter twenty-seven

Libby – that afternoon

Tears pour down Libby's cheeks. She doesn't know what's wrong with her. There is no reason for her to be like this. She's not ill. She's going home from hospital in the morning. Her mum's on the way, for God's sake. She can't crack up.

But she can't stop herself. Ever since Yasmin left, she's been finding it harder and harder to stifle her sobs. She manages to smile when the nurses come round. They are always concerned for her, but she can't explain. She couldn't explain even if she did speak Spanish. She smiles through her tears when she remembers why they came to Cuba. The excellent health service. It is truly living up to its reputation.

'I want to go home,' she whispers. 'I want my baby. I want my mummy.'

She has loved Havana, but Brighton is her home. She needs to go back. She needs Natalie and Jenny. She needs windy walks on the seafront and tea and cakes in cafés. It doesn't matter if they make her fat. She can't believe she ever cared about that. She needs her own life.

But she wasn't happy then. She can't stop herself. She gulps back the sobs, but they keep coming, all the same. She wasn't happy in Brighton. She was happy in Havana. She thinks she was. Perhaps she has never been happy.

When David arrives, an hour later than he promised, he finds his wife lying on her side, her face stained with tears and snot soaking straight from her nose into the pillow. She is a mess. She looks up eagerly when he comes into her cubicle, stares at him for a moment, and then looks away.

'Where's Charlie?' she says, in a dull voice.

'Darling?' He kneels next to her and strokes her hair back from her face. 'What's wrong, darling? Why are you crying? Everything's all right. You're going to be fine. You *are* fine.'

'So where the hell is my son?'

'I left him at home. It's his nap.'

Libby is overcome with frustration and anger. 'Who is with him? Or did you leave him on his own? For fuck's sake, David! David! He is my baby! Did it not occur to you that I'm missing him like I'd miss my right arm? That I've been waiting for you to bring him to see me all day and all night? That I've been counting down the minutes? I've never been away from him before.'

David sits on the chair beside her bed. Libby refuses to look at him, but she's glad to see, from the corner of her eye, that he is dishevelled and unhappy. 'I'm sorry, darling,' he tells her wearily. 'I didn't think. I just thought he'd need a nap. I thought we could have a chat now and I'd bring him in later. Christ, I didn't even know babies were allowed in hospitals.'

'Babies are born in bloody hospitals.'

'I'll go back for him if you like.'

'He's with Maggie, isn't he?'

'Here. I brought you some bananas. There weren't any grapes. And some bottles of water. I *had* to leave her in charge. There wasn't anyone else around.'

'Maria could have had him. Maggie's the one that did this.'

David bites his lip and reaches out to stroke Libby's hair. 'Maggie didn't do it on purpose, darling. Why on earth would she? Maggie wouldn't hurt a fly. It was an accident.'

Libby turns away from him. She doesn't know whether Maggie

did it on purpose, or not. She suspects she did. But she doesn't want David taking her side, and she definitely doesn't want Maggie looking after her son.

'Go away,' she says suddenly.

David forces a smile. 'You don't mean that, sweetheart.'

'I do! I mean it. I don't want you here. Go away.'

'Lib! I'm sorry I left Charlie with her. I'm sorry I went and had a beer with her. I didn't plan to. It was just a spur-of-the-moment thing, to make sure she was all right.'

'And she was.'

'Yes.'

'Fuck off, David.'

'I'm not leaving you. You're in a hospital in bloody Cuba. And you don't even speak the language.'

'Nor do you. I don't need you. I'm only here in case I have a belated peanut reaction, which I won't. I'm coming home tomorrow. And Mum'll be here this evening, won't she? So I'll be fine. I don't want you here. I want you with Charlie. I mean that.'

'I'm not leaving.'

Libby hauls herself to a sitting position. 'Go.'

'No.'

They glare at each other for a while. Then Libby lies down and turns her back on him. 'David,' she says, addressing the curtain, 'you have left my baby with a woman I don't trust. A woman who I sincerely believe is capable of harming anyone. A woman who seems to have strange issues to do with me. Get him back.'

David opens his mouth to reply, then closes it. He stands up, and starts to speak again. He stops before any words have come out. Then he lifts his hand in a futile wave that his wife can't see, and slips through the curtain.

Libby lies on her side and stares into space for the rest of the day. She waits for David to come back with Charlie, but he doesn't. She knows she has done nothing wrong, and she didn't expect David

261

to exploit the fact that she is immobile. She is powerless to go and fetch her son.

As she lies in the small, clean bed, Libby decides not to think about her marriage. She doesn't care about it. She cares about Charlie, and he is several miles away. She feels vulnerable. She has no control over what happens to her son. She nearly died. She has a condition which means this will happen from time to time. Her mortality is closer than other people's. She thinks of Grace, of Maggie, and wonders exactly how messed up Maggie is. She wants to cut her out of their lives, but she thinks that everyone – from her ex-boyfriend to Yasmin as a teenager – has been pushed by Maggie so hard that, eventually, they have walked away from her. It's probably what she wants, because it allows her to carry on drifting through life without dealing with anything. Maggie needs help. No one can force help upon her. Libby thinks, on balance, that she had better give up. One day, Maggie will sort herself out. She and David owe her nothing.

chapter twenty-eight

Maggie – the next morning

I am ready to go. I have a small rucksack on my back. It looks innocuous; it is the sort of bag that might hold a *Rough Guide*, a pair of sunglasses and a bottle of water. Instead, this one contains Charlie's passport, two bottles of formula milk (properly sterilised), a tupperware pot full of mashed carrot and malanga, another containing pulverised banana, a couple of nappies and a pack of baby wipes. I wander into David and Libby's room and look at Charlie's clothes. I will need a selection for the journey. I help myself to three vests, two babygros, a cardigan (tucked away at the back of the drawer, and clearly unworn for months), a sunhat, and a pair of denim dungarees. That should cover all eventualities. I cram the clothes into the bag. Now I just need the baby. I must gently extricate my sister from her well-meaning, yet clueless, guardians.

Everything that I have taken will be missed. It might be missed soon. I need to leave without delay.

I have dressed myself in a way that will attract as little attention as possible. My baggy cotton trousers are tight around the waist, now. They sat on my hips when I arrived. I must be the only person who comes to Cuba and gets fat. I am wearing a black T-shirt, and I've plaited my hair back, because this is the only way to tame it.

It doesn't look wild, in a plait. No one notices me. I look like a classical musician.

I am ready to leave. I don't have long. David, Charlie and Libby's mother will be home soon, and I do not want to see them, at all.

I knock on the door that leads to Luis's flat. While I wait for the answer, I close my eyes and try to be calm. Do not ruin everything, I tell myself, by making Maria suspicious. I breathe deeply. This is normal. She is expecting me. Grace is on her way.

When she opens the door, it takes all my self-control to keep myself from bursting into trembling tears. Maria stands in front of me, with her 'daughter' on her hip. Grace looks at me and smiles. I smile back as naturally as I can. Adrenaline is coursing through me. I know, without the flicker of a doubt, that I am doing the right thing. This is a test and I am going to pass it.

'Okay?' I ask, remembering to smile at Maria as well.

'Okay,' she agrees, and hands me her baby. 'Are you sure this is all right? It's very kind of you. I'm going to do some studying.'

'Of course! It's fine. Gracia is a beautiful girl. I love spending time with babies, so far from my niece. When shall we come back?'

Maria considers. 'She needs her dinner at eight o'clock. So, any time before then.'

I look at my watch. It's five to four. I have four hours before anyone will realise. Four and a half, or even five, before they start to suspect that I haven't just been held up. The flight is at ten. I need to be in the departure lounge as early as I can.

'No problem,' I tell her in English, and she kisses me firmly on each cheek. 'Thanks,' she says, also in English. 'Foreign lady is very kind!'

We laugh. Maria kisses Grace goodbye, says something in Cuban baby language, and closes the door.

I stand firmly for a moment, in the tiled kitchen, and hold my baby close. I have her. She is mine, returned to me. I breathe her in. She whimpers a little. I run my fingertips lightly over her soft skin. Grace is back. She is a different Grace, but I know her spirit has survived. My loss is lessened.

I must not fall apart. What is happening is momentous. She is my baby and my sister. She and I belong together. Grace is back. I never gave a thought to reincarnation before, but she is here. Grace has been reborn as a Cuban girl, and all my adventures with the baby monitor and the Spanish lessons happened for a reason. They were all part of Fate's grand plan to bring me back to my sister. Now I have to take her away with me, because no one else would understand. I have found her in time. I do not, yet, have an overall plan. I think I have to take things one step at a time. I'll take her to see Mum and Dad. Then I will devote my life to the nurturing of this little girl. This time she will be safe.

Holding her in my arms, I walk straight out of the flat, and stand on the corner of Infanta to hail a cab. The sun is uncompromising. It is bleaching the colour out of everything, again. It beats on my head and my baby's, and I fumble in my bag to find Charlie's hat. I slip it over her head. She doesn't complain. Charlie might have complained, but Grace understands.

She settles on to my hip, and I scan the traffic. People pass us, and many of them stop to admire her. I consider telling them that my husband is Cuban, but just in time, I remember that they might know Grace, and so I tell them the truth. I am looking after her. Raul passes by, on the other side of the road. He looks at me and raises his hand, but continues walking.

Over the road, I watch a man begging outside the church. I pass him almost every day. He has one leg. I have never given him so much as a peso. He always wears the same tatty old suit. I should give him something. Now that I am complete, I can see the world around me clearly. Cuba is heaven, to me, right now. I watch two girls running around their mother, and jumping up like dogs. Cuba has rescued my life, restored my loss. I owe the people of Cuba all I have.

'Maggie?' David sounds guarded, and curious. 'What are you doing with Gracia?'

I look around. David is looking at me. He is not a threat. He will believe whatever I tell him. I haven't met Libby's mother before, but I see hostility in her eyes as soon as David says my name. Libby has told her about me. Libby's mother is, precisely, an older version of Libby. She has very short hair, which looks surprisingly good, and she's wearing flapping layers of cotton, which are ridiculous.

'I'm babysitting,' I say, ignoring the mother and addressing my answer solely to David. 'I've had some practice with Charlie, and Maria wanted to do some studying, so I said I'd take Gracia out. We're going to Habana Vieja, to visit Elena. She's expecting us!'

Libby's mother looks at me without a glimmer of a smile.

'Quite the Mary Poppins,' she says. I decipher her gaze at once. She thinks I poisoned her daughter on purpose, and so she distrusts me, but she also knows about Grace, so she doesn't dare be nasty to me. That suits me fine. She reaches out a bony finger to stroke Grace's cheek. I pull my sister away.

No one says anything for a few minutes, and a cab pulls up beside me.

'Right, then,' I say brightly. 'See you later. I'm bringing her back by eight.'

'Bye,' says David.

'Aguacate,' I tell the driver, and hand him Elena's card. We speed off. I don't look back.

I ask the cabbie to wait, although I could very easily find another one. While he clogs up the narrow street, and the children and adults mill around him, I jiggle Grace impatiently and wait for the lift. The bloody thing always takes too long. Elena was visiting her daughter and grandson today. I know she won't be back till six, because she never is, but all the same, I'm scared. Yasmin wasn't with David. That means she might be home, too. I cross my fingers and will her to be off having sex with Luis, or, failing that, to be at the internet café relaying her latest adventures to her friends. Or even to be at the hospital, telling Libby any remaining secrets of mine that she can remember. Yasmin spends very little time sprawled on her bed reading, but it would be just my luck if this was one of those times.

The front door is locked.

'You see?' I whisper into my little sister's hair. 'It *is* Fate, just like we said.'

I pack in no time. Most of my stuff stays behind. I don't want to clear right out of my room, or they'll know. These clothes I've been wearing are a pile of crap anyway, and most of them are Yasmin's. I pack a couple of pairs of knickers, my toothbrush and my money belt. It contains my passport, money, credit card and our tickets to Paris. I bought new tickets for us both, yesterday, from Air France. My bank account is still stuffed with stripping money. We all came out here with Iberia, because it was slightly cheaper. I am throwing the return half of that ticket away. No one will think to look for us on Air France.

I prop Grace up on my pillow, and talk to her as I get ready.

'There's so much for me to tell you,' I say, looking into her wise eyes with a smile. 'I know you understand.' I put the money belt on, and transfer Charlie's passport into it. 'I was with this guy called Mark for six years, but it didn't work out. I'm glad, now. We lived in Scotland. You never went to Scotland. I'll take you there when you're older. Then I moved to Brighton. Well, that was a low point, I don't mind telling you. We won't be going back there.'

I look at her little face. She says, 'Ra, ra, ra.' She is my sister. I recognise her soul.

'We'll have a chat, later,' I say, seriously. 'There are a few unpleasant things to get out of the way.' This will be the unavoidable discussion of what happened to her. 'Not now, though.'

I pick the bag up and walk out of the door. I don't look back. I will miss Cuba. I have been so happy here. Coming here was the best thing I ever did. It has, it turns out, been my salvation.

*   *   *

267

Because she's wearing his sunhat, vest and shorts, everyone assumes Grace is Charlie. I am not afraid when I go through immigration control. I just hand the officer our passports, and wait. The woman behind the counter looks bored. She doesn't ask why my baby and I have different surnames. She doesn't even see Grace's black button eyes, because, most obligingly, she has fallen asleep, with her head leaning trustingly on my shoulder. We are in this together.

I find an inconspicuous seat in the corner of the departure lounge, and try to settle in. I am elated. I will not relax until we are on the plane, but I have almost managed it. I have legally left Cuba, and brought my baby with me. I divide the journey ahead of us into stages. Once we are on the plane, and in the air, no one can do anything to us. When we land, we just have to get off the plane and slip away. No one at French immigration is going to be checking the passports of EU citizens.

Suddenly there is a commotion. The people around us are calling out. I snatch Grace up and hold her close. All around us, travellers are jumping to their feet and climbing on chairs. Tanned, happy couples, men in suits, a group of lads who are just out of university: all of them, all except me, are suddenly jostling with each other. No one seems to know what they are trying to see. They are animated, pushing and shoving and trying to get to the front of the scrum to see what is happening. I sit motionless, holding Grace, and not daring to look. I imagine a team of police, come to arrest me.

They wouldn't understand. Until she can talk, I won't be able to prove anything. Grace turns her head from side to side, on my shoulder, and wakes up. I see her lip trembling. I wonder whether I should get her bottle out.

As I hold her on my lap, Grace gulps down the cold milk. While she sucks with all her concentration on the bottle, I dare to look around. I see everyone else from the departure lounge clustered together in the far corner of the room. They are holding cameras above their heads and flashes are going off every couple of seconds. I breathe out. It must be a famous person. You would have to be astonishingly famous to get this sort of treatment. You would have to be an icon. Relieved that it doesn't seem to be the Havana police force on my case – I look at my watch and decide that we have definitely been missed by now – I crane around to see who it could possibly be. There is a sudden cheer from the crowd, and people begin to move. I take the bottle out of Grace's mouth, and stand up, and position myself next to the glass partition. Then people are sweeping towards us. On the other side of the glass, an entourage is moving down the corridor. There is a glass wall between us, but even from a distance there is no mistaking the fact that Fidel Castro is heading our way.

I gape. This is a sign. I am overwhelmed by the fact that the revolutionary leader is feet away from me. He is wearing his green military uniform, and his beard is long and grizzled. As he passes, with his security guys, he looks at Grace, and his face lights up with a smile. He slows his pace and raises his hand, and he waves to her and to me. I lift my hand, and Grace reaches out and pats the glass. Before I realise what is happening, the man at Castro's side, who is holding a large camera, turns and takes our photograph. He beams at Grace, and she gurgles back at him.

On the plane, I try to calm myself down. It doesn't matter that we have been caught on film. We are on hundreds of security cameras, anyway. Everyone will find out from the passenger list that we have flown to Paris, before long. It will be ages before anyone even sees Fidel's official photographer's shot, and by then it will be useless. It will tell no one anything. The whole episode is, nonetheless, unsettling.

The air is stale in here. The plane smells of hot, grumpy people. It is nearly full. No one takes much notice of us. I am sure, when they see us, they briefly hope that we won't be sitting next to them. Nobody thinks there is anything weird going on. We have an aisle seat, next to an elderly German man. He offers to put my bag in the overhead locker, but I tell him I need it with me, and shove it under the seat in front. This bag contains everything we have, everything we need.

I am shaking as I change Grace into a babygro for the night flight. She fights me, and begins to whimper. I have to force her arms in, and I do the poppers up all wrong. By the time I finish, she is wailing, and I have to stand in the aisle and rock her against my shoulder. I love her weight in my arms. She is solid, substantial. She is my life.

The German man looks at us, and smiles thinly.

'She'll be asleep in a minute,' I tell him, although I have no idea about her sleeping patterns. They will be shot to pieces, anyway, with this disruption. I should have said 'he', since she is travelling as Charlie. The man smiles more genuinely, and turns to his book.

'It's okay, my darling,' I whisper into her ear. 'You're with Maggie now. Your big sister. Much bigger than you, this time. I'm taking care of you. You're going to be fine.'

She nuzzles into me, and calms down. I sit her on my lap. As the plane takes off, I feed her the rest of the milk in the bottle, to make sure her ears don't hurt. Libby told me she'd fed Charlie for take-off, and that it had worked. It works for Grace, as well. She drinks her milk lazily, and gradually falls asleep in my arms. I hold her tight, and stay awake all night.

Now she is back, her disappearance cannot hold the same horror. The day she was taken has been coming back to me, intermittently, for months. I have always pushed it away, but now I can do that no longer. I can't stop it happening. I have to open myself up to the memories that I have blanked out for the past nineteen years.

We were playing, like children used to play, on the common land around the village. Grace and Emma and I went there all the time. We took a long skipping rope, or elastics. That particular summer, we were all obsessed with elastics. Two of us would stand opposite each other, the elastic around our ankles, and the third would jump around and on to it. We would chant as we did so. 'England, Ireland, Scotland, Wales, inside, outside, donkeys' tails.' There were other rhymes, but that is the only one I remember. Grace was the best at elastics. I was second best. Emma was too young to be much good, and she always tripped over and grazed her knee or her elbow, and cried. So we made her stand at the end, most of the time, while we took turns to jump around.

The sun was shining, that day, and a brisk wind was blowing shreds of cloud across the sky. I am surprised that I can remember it so clearly, now, after all the years of trying to forget. Grace was wearing blue cotton shorts and a white Aertex shirt. She had Green Flash plimsolls on her feet, with her white socks pulled up. Her pale hair was in a ponytail. She had a cheap little plastic bracelet on her wrist. That was how Grace was. She was sporty, and girlish. I wore a red T-shirt and grey shorts. Emma was in her yellow dress. There weren't many people around. The common was big, and we used it as an extension of our garden.

Grace and Emma didn't notice him, watching us through the trees. I did. I had seen him several times, that week. The day before, he had found me on my own, on the patch of land next to our driveway. He'd walked quickly over to me.

I had looked up at him. He was quite short, for a man, with light brown hair and a jutting lower jaw which made his speech a little bit strange.

'Hi, Maggie! Come for a walk with me,' he'd said. 'I'll show you a secret hiding place.'

We were always after secret hiding places, but I didn't like the idea of going anywhere with him. He wasn't a stranger, but all the same, I didn't want to go. He was looking at me intensely.

'No thanks,' I said.

'Why not?'

'I don't need any more hiding places.'

'But this is a really good one. Even Clare hasn't seen it.' He patted me on the shoulder.

I don't know if I would have gone, if Mum hadn't come out of the house, and called me in for lunch. I might have, because he was an adult, because he was Clare's dad. Then it would have been me who had died. Grace would have been spared. I could have saved her, and if I had known, I would have done. Mum saw me standing, talking to him, and wandered over.

'Lunchtime, Mags,' she said. 'Hi, Andrew, how are things?'

'Fine, thanks. I was just asking Maggie if she wanted to come over and see Clare later on.'

'I've got ballet,' I said abruptly.

'Maybe another day,' Mum said, with a smile, and we went in.

He wasn't your classic paedophile. He was Clare's dad, and Clare had been our friend when we went to the village school. She was quiet, but nice, and we had all been to her house many times. Mum and Dad weren't particularly friendly with her parents, but they said hello to them in the road, and stopped for a cup of tea when they went to collect us.

The man had a wife and a daughter. He was a family man. There was nothing unusual about him, nothing at all.

I had never taken much notice of him, before. After he told me about the hiding place, I was a bit scared. I thought it was silly to be scared, so I didn't tell anyone, but I looked out for him all the time, because I didn't want to go anywhere with him.

I saw him watching us through the trees, and I knew we had to go home. I took a couple of steps forward, slackening the elastic in the middle of Grace's leaping. She looked up, frowning.

'Maggie!' she said. 'That was a really good one!'

'Well, we've got to go home now,' I told her, and put my arm around Emma. I could see Clare's dad, still in the trees, still watching us. He saw me looking at him, but he didn't look away.

'Why?' demanded Grace. 'It's not time to go home. We're allowed to stay out till half past two.'

'I'm the oldest and I say we have to go. Come on, Em.'

Emma walked with me happily. She always did what we told her to do.

'You're being horrible,' Grace called out, as Emma and I walked away. 'I'm telling Mum.'

She bounded importantly ahead of us. When Emma and I went through the back door to the kitchen, blinking to adjust our eyes to the darkness, Mum was standing with Grace, looking tired.

'You didn't need to stop the game, Maggie,' she told me, without interest.

I looked around the kitchen, knowing I couldn't tell them the real reason. Mum was making biscuits.

'I was bored,' I said. 'When are the biscuits going to be ready?'

'At teatime. Emma, you can help me finish them off, if you like.'

Emma nodded. 'Can I use the star cutter?'

'I'm going to my room,' I said, and took the stairs two at a time, without looking back at Grace.

She went out on her bike to visit her friend Amy. We sat in the house and waited for six days, and then they found her body.

The wheels touch the runway. I hold her close, and try, frantically, to believe everything that I thought I knew. I make a big effort to breathe. I can only take short, shallow breaths. The inside of the plane is the same as it was when we got on. Then, I was certain that I had done the right thing. I look down at the baby in my arms, and my mouth fills with bile. This girl has no connection with my sister, none at all, beyond a name. This is an innocent stranger, a little dark baby. She is not a part of me. Grace is dead.

I cannot look after this girl. She is a Cuban child. Her name is Gracia. I have kidnapped her. Panic rises in my throat. I will never be able to forget the days and nights we spent waiting for news of Grace. At first, everyone told Emma and me that she would be fine, that she had run away from home for fun. They stopped saying that after a few days. Clare's dad came round, with her mum, a couple of times to offer support. He helped search for her. I knew it was him, from the moment she was late home for supper. After a few days, I told Mum. That was when they found her.

I have done exactly what he did. I have inflicted that empty waiting time on another family. I have snatched a child. I have stolen someone's little girl. I have done the worst thing in the whole world. I am evil, deranged, foul, despicable. I am a criminal. I was entrusted with her well-being, and I abducted her. Maria – lovely, friendly, happy Maria – is going through what my mother went through, right now.

The baby and I are in France. A strong sense of dread takes hold of me. I cannot possibly return her, now. I will go to prison. I thought I was bringing my sister back to our parents, to make them happy again, but I wasn't doing anything of the sort. I was cracking up.

chapter twenty-nine

Libby

Libby expects to be picked up by David, and she is delighted when her mother and Charlie get out of the taxi, instead. She is alone, in a wheelchair, in the hospital lobby, waiting for them. Doctors and nurses say hello when they pass her, even though she doesn't know most of them. Her ankle is firmly bandaged, and the bruises are more spectacular now that they are fading. Her whole body is a tender symphony of blue, purple, black and yellow. They are all booked on the Iberia flight, the day after tomorrow. She has never been as pleased to see her mother as she was yesterday. She wants her by her side, for ever.

'Sweetie!' says Petra, giving her a kiss. 'Look at you. My word.'

'Hi, Mum,' says Libby, looking at her mother, and seeing only Charlie. She doesn't notice Petra's lack of zest this morning. She doesn't notice her anxiety. She is only interested in her son. She has been away from him for three nights, and now she is coming home. He waves his arms in excitement and lunges towards her with a grin. She catches him, and sits him on her lap. She has always assumed she would hate to be in a wheelchair. She thought the conspicuousness and the awkwardness would be intolerable. It would, she imagined, be like a buggy, with all the associated difficulties with doors and steps, but worse. In fact, she likes it. She

275

has thoroughly enjoyed being wheeled along corridors, and seeing the inside of the hospital tower block from a sitting position. Charlie keeps twisting round to look at her face. When he is satisfied that it really is his mother, he turns his attention to the group of staff and visitors who have gathered to admire him.

Libby smiles at them. 'Adios,' she says, 'y gracias.'

Charlie sits on her lap all the way. It only takes five minutes to get back to their street. Her heart lifts when she sees the brown front door and the group of young men sitting opposite. She turns to her mother.

'Mum!' she says, happily. 'I'm so glad you came instead of David. Thank you. And that you brought Charlie.' She leans down and smells his hair. She will never let him out of her arms again. 'Before we get out, tell me, is David sulking with me?'

She smiles expectantly at her mother. She is exhausted, but they are home. This is the beginning of the end.

Her mother pays the taxi driver with crisp dollar bills. Libby opens the back door and waits inside for David to come and help her inside. She thought he might at least be waiting for her.

'Liberty,' her mother says nervously. 'Darling, something's happened. We didn't tell you last night because there was no point upsetting you. We thought it would all be over by now, but it's not.'

She presses the buzzer. 'We're back,' she says tersely, into the intercom.

'What?' Libby demands. 'Something's happened to David?'

'Nothing's happened to David. It's Maggie. I'm afraid she snatched a baby.'

Libby thinks of Charlie. He is the baby. She looks at him in her arms. She cannot imagine what her mother is talking about.

'What baby?' she asks. 'Charlie's fine.'

'No, it was Gracia. Maria's baby. She offered to look after her yesterday. Now, Maria said she'd met Maggie before, in your flat, looking after your beautiful son. Your seedy and depressing flat,

276

I might add, but that is an altogether more trivial matter. So she thought Maggie was part of the family, and handed her daughter over. She was grateful for the chance to do some studying, I think. But they never came back. Charlie's passport and some of his things are missing.'

Libby is confused. 'No. Maggie wouldn't do that. She's mad, but she's not that mad.' She realises that Maggie could be capable of anything. She doesn't know her at all. 'Christ Almighty. If she stole Gracia, it means she did poison me on purpose. Are the police looking for her?'

David opens the front door and comes over to the cab. Petra acknowledges him with a nod, and carries on speaking. 'Yasmin, it would seem, has taken control,' she says. 'Personally I was entirely against any of us becoming involved. Maggie seems to me to be a wicked little bitch, and prison is the only place for her. But Yasmin seems to feel some vestige of personal responsibility for her. She managed to persuade Maria and José and Luis not to go to the police until later today.'

David takes up the story. 'Welcome home, hey?' he says glumly, and kisses her. 'Maggie was on last night's flight to Paris. So was Charlie, according to the passenger list. Yasmin's called Maggie's parents in France. They're on their way to Paris now, to meet the plane. As long as they can make her listen to reason, her dad's going to be on the next flight back here, with the baby, and her mother's going to take her home and get her sorted out.'

'Get her locked up,' says Petra, 'one would hope. And the key thrown away. She tried to kill my daughter, and then two days later she took a defenceless child.'

Petra takes Charlie, and David lifts his wife. She winces, but manages not to complain.

'Fuck me,' says Libby. It is beginning to sink in. 'It could just as easily have been Charlie. Nothing Yasmin said would have stopped me calling the police.'

'I know,' says Petra. 'Maria is out of her mind with worry, and personally I would have got the gendarmerie to greet her in Paris with handcuffs and an armoured van – I would have made sure she was sectioned the moment the wheels hit the tarmac – but Yasmin seems terribly concerned with Maggie's mental health. Unduly concerned. She hurt you, darling.'

'Maria and José were just glad when Yasmin got her name and Charlie's from Air France,' says David. Libby feels strange in his arms. She is glad she's lost weight. He is panting as he goes upstairs, all the same. 'They knew where their daughter was going,' he continues. 'They knew she was safe, on a plane, in a confined space. Yasmin got them worried that if she was confronted, Maggie might harm their baby.'

Petra turns and looks at her. 'What have you got yourself into, Liberty! Who on earth is this Maggie girl?'

Libby shakes her head.

Maria, José, Luis and Yasmin are sitting on the sofa. Maria's head is resting on her husband's shoulder. Luis is staring into space. Yasmin is sitting at his side. On the table in front of them is Luis's telephone, which he has brought in from his flat, and plugged in. It is the focus of the tension. Nobody is speaking, and the phone is not ringing.

Libby joins the waiting. She sits on a chair with her foot up on another chair, and she watches the phone. She talks quietly to Yasmin and smiles sympathetically at Maria. She breastfeeds Charlie, and is quietly pleased to note that her milk is still there. When she notices Maria watching her, she wishes she had fed him in the bedroom. She wonders whether Maggie stole their supply of formula milk. She hopes so.

After a while, Libby can only think of Grace. She pictures Maggie's family going through this waiting, the agony of a missing daughter, for day after day. Yasmin said it was six days before the body was discovered. Six days of waiting for the phone to ring. Briefly, Libby wonders how her father could have intentionally walked away from his only child. He lost her on purpose.

Maria is pale and haggard. From time to time, since Charlie was born, Libby has forced herself to imagine losing him. She has been scared to realise that, now, another life is far more important than her own. In Maria's face, she sees her own worst nightmare. Maria looks bereft. She stares alternately at Charlie and the telephone. Maria must wish Maggie had taken Charlie, instead.

Their eyes meet. 'I thought Maggie was good,' Maria says.

'I know,' Libby tells her. 'So did we.' She doesn't know what else to say. Yasmin makes everyone coffee.

'How you doing?' she asks Libby quietly when she sits back down.

'Oh, I guess I was feeling all right,' she remembers. 'Yas, surely we should be calling the police?'

Yasmin looks at her watch, although she knows exactly what time it is. 'The plane will be landing in the next twenty minutes. Her parents called an hour ago to say they're there – they're at arrivals. If she won't listen to reason, or give the baby back, then they swear they're handing her over straight away. It's all going to kick in. I'm sure you think we should have called them as soon as we realised. You mum certainly does. She went apeshit. I'm just worried about Mags. If she's arrested, I don't know what she'll do.'

Libby puts her hand on Yasmin's arm.

'Yas?' she says. 'Are you mad? Maggie has snatched a baby. The baby is what matters. Frankly, I don't give a fuck what happens to Maggie now. She's dangerous. She *should* be locked up. For her own good, as well as everyone else's. I felt sorry for her, sure, but other people lose their sisters without going loopy. She should have dealt with it by now. She's mad. Literally, mad. She gave me those nuts on purpose. Everyone in this room knows that. I don't know what I did to upset her, but obviously for some reason she wanted to hurt me, and I was lucky she didn't kill me. It wasn't for want of trying. And now she's done this. She's lost a sister, so she steals someone's baby?'

'Libby, Maggie will completely break down when they confront her. I read her diary last night. I just wish I'd done it before. It was eye-opening. I'll tell you a few things sometime.' Libby notices David's eyes going to Yasmin, but she doesn't think anything of it. 'This breakdown has been coming for ages.'

'Surely she won't hurt Gracia?' Libby stops, realising the significance of the baby's name. 'Is that why she took her? Because she's called Grace?'

'Without a doubt. She's horribly fucked up. Yeah? I could tell you a lot about Maggie, and I will, when this is all sorted. I just think her mum and dad are the people she'll need. They're good people. Strong people.'

The phone rings. Yasmin snatches it up.

'Hello?' she says breathlessly. Everyone leans forward. 'Michael! Is she there?'

chapter thirty

Maggie

Gracia is let into France, as Charlie, without a murmur. I wish they'd stopped us. I almost handed her to the stern immigration man. I can't keep this up. I want to sit down and let everyone else deal with me.

I am trying to concentrate on the next step, as I walk through customs. A train into Paris. A taxi to the Gare de Lyon. A train to Avignon. I have to care for this creature all the way. I step into the airport, and look wildly at the crowd. I am searching for the police; but I see my parents.

I stumble towards them, suddenly unable to feel anything, unable to cope with anything, ever again. My mother runs to me and holds me, and I push Gracia into her arms. I cannot believe I thought I was doing them a favour by dragging this child across the ocean. As soon as the baby's weight is out of my arms, my legs give way. Black patches appear over everything. My head begins to echo. I sink to the floor and close my eyes.

They take me to a table in the café, and prop me into a sitting position. It feels ridiculous. I am an uncooperative toddler. I seem unable to do anything for myself. I force myself to keep my eyes open, to focus on my parents.

I can only see Mum. 'What about the police?' I ask her.

She strokes my hair. 'Don't worry about them, sweetheart,' she tells me gently. 'This has nothing to do with the police. Yasmin persuaded the parents not to go to them. You've got Yasmin to thank for a lot, Maggie.'

'Yasmin?' I cannot attach the name to a person.

'Never mind. Now, you and I are going to go home. And we're going to get you some help, darling. Will that be all right?'

I look at her. Her hair is a little longer than it used to be, and it is completely silver. Her face is wise and open. She is my mother. She is my rock. She will look after me.

'Help,' I say. 'Help sounds good. Where's Dad?' I look around the airport. There are thousands of people here, all making noise, all ignoring us.

'He's over there,' Mum says, and touches my arm and points. Dad is standing at a payphone, with Gracia on his hip. Gracia is grabbing the phone and laughing. Dad is smiling too, but his demeanour is not happy.

'She probably needs a new nappy,' I tell Mum. 'There's a couple in here.' I point to the bag at my feet. 'I brought all the baby stuff.'

'Shall we have a coffee? I'll go and order them. You stay here, Margaret. Don't move.' I smile at the very idea of moving. I watch her at the counter, smiling briskly and handing over euros with nonchalance. Then I turn to Dad and Gracia. My heart is breaking. She is the wrong Grace. She is not our Grace; not Grace Wilson. Grace Wilson is dead.

Dad replaces the receiver and moves to the Air France desk, where he joins a queue. My parents are coping with me, with everything I have done, because they are my parents. I am the one breaking down; and they are the capable ones. My world is topsy-turvy. I try to imagine the logistics of everything that has to happen now. Yasmin stopped them calling the police. I stole a baby. They should have called the police. I ought to be in a French cell by now. That is where I belong. I poisoned somebody. I ripped up a letter, but I never posted it. Then I took a baby. I realise that I am mad.

A white coffee appears before me with a clatter.

'Drink up!' says Mum with a forced smile. 'Maggie, you really do look terrible, darling. Did you sleep at all on that flight?'

I try to smile back at her. 'Oh,' is all I can bring myself to say.

She strokes my arm. 'Darling,' she says. 'Will you be all right until we get home? Then I'll put you to bed and you don't have to do anything at all until you want to.'

I nod. 'Am I mad?'

'No, you're not mad. You just need to deal with a few things, don't you?'

'On the plane, I remembered it all.'

When I look at her, there are tears in her pale blue eyes.

'Sorry,' I add.

'You mustn't be sorry,' she says firmly, and puts an arm around my shoulders, pulling me in close to her. 'Maggie, sweet thing, we've been waiting for you to talk to us about what happened to Grace for the past nineteen years. At first we thought you were doing fabulously well, but you were only nine. Do you remember, darling? You fielded the phone calls and made supper for you and Emma. We shouldn't have let you take it all on, of course, but we weren't strong enough to stop you. You were so young, and it was too terrible for you to understand. Everyone said it would catch up with you in your teens. It didn't. When you were with Ivan, we thought it was going to happen then, but it ended, didn't it? Then you went to uni and we were expecting something to happen, but it didn't. Now you're twenty-eight. Maggie, your father and I have been longing for this breakdown, in a perverse way. It's hard, but it's high time you faced up to it. I'm just glad we've got you in time.'

'But Grace . . .' I remember the moment Dad put the phone down and turned to us all, and said, 'They've found a body.' I can remember it all, now. 'I can't bear it. I used to see her everywhere in Cuba.'

Mum strokes my hand. 'I've often felt that I can't bear it, you know. I still do. I always will. Life will never be like it used to be.

It has lost its colour for ever. But, darling, we have to bear it. Dad and I had to deal with it because of you and Emma. It's the worst thing that can happen, isn't it? To lose a child . . . But, Mags, we've lost you, too. We lost two of our girls. All your cheerful letters and cards from Brighton, as if we wouldn't realise. Em said when she last saw you you were thin as a rake, and she and Jeremy thought you were on drugs. Then you ran off to Cuba, before the baby was born. That wasn't coincidental, was it? We've been frantic with worry. I dreaded getting a call from Havana.'

I look at her. I never imagined that I wasn't convincing them that I was fine and happy. 'Really?' I ask, and take a slurp of the strong, hot coffee.

'You have no idea. We knew there was nothing we could do, short of going to Havana ourselves and escorting you home, and you were too old for us to do that. Yasmin's been keeping us up to date by email. She's a wonderful girl, Maggie. She's been the best friend you could ever ask for.'

I drain my coffee. I need another. 'But I don't like Yasmin,' I say.

'Yes you do. You do now.'

'Suppose. And then you did get the call.'

Mum and I both look across to Dad and Gracia. Dad is signing a credit-card slip, and Gracia is struggling in his arms. 'Maggie, that poor child. I'm not going to ask you why you did it. I know it's complex. But she belongs in Cuba. You do know that, don't you? She's not Grace.'

I nod. I don't speak.

'Her poor mother,' Mum adds.

I remember that I have done to Maria and José the same thing that Clare's dad did to us. I have stolen their daughter. I try to imagine them, in their corner of Vedado, sitting, tense, waiting for the phone to ring. Not eating or drinking. I can remember it too clearly. I know that they were imagining their daughter suffering where they could not reach her. All because I wanted to bring Grace back to my parents. I cannot bear it.

*　　*　　*

Dad takes Gracia, still masquerading as Charlie, back to Havana. They fly out on the same plane we arrived on. Mum and I travel by TGV to Avignon, collect the Citroën from the car park, and drive for an hour to reach the house. We don't talk much on the journey. I can't think of anything to say. The train and the car are not the right setting for the talking I want to do. Mum falls asleep on the train, and I look at her properly. She looks her age – sixty – and she seems to be comfortable with it. Her face is creased, and even in sleep she looks anxious, but it is worry for me and for Gracia. She is not weighed down by Grace's murder in the same way that I am. She has absorbed it. She is scarred by it and she will never really be happy again, but she has some kind of a life, all the same. I have always assumed my parents to be nervous wrecks, destroyed by what happened to Grace, and utterly unable to take any more grief. I felt I could not lean on them, even slightly. All that time, they have needed me to lean on them, to prove to them that they are still parents.

The house is in a hamlet on a hill. No one else is around. The sun is shining in a pale blue sky, and I can see a field of crimson poppies several miles away. A cool breeze is blowing. The air smells of herbs, and fresh vegetation. It is completely different from Havana, and I am glad. I don't want to go back there. It will never hold anything but troubled memories for me.

I wish I had said goodbye to Elena. When I think of Libby and David, I find it impossible to engage with the idea of them. The girl who threw herself into their life was someone completely alien to me. I don't have the mental energy for those pursuits. I will never go back to the flat in Brighton, and I don't want to see Libby or David or Charlie ever again. I thought Libby was perfect, but she is perfectly normal. I made myself believe David was the ideal man, but although he is kind and loving, he kissed me, so he is clearly flawed as a partner. They were random people. I could have fixated on anybody. I remember the letter from Libby's father in my pocket, and take it out and throw it down the hill.

I take a deep breath of crisp spring air. I turn to look at the house. It is an old stone farmhouse, with a blue front door and blue shutters. This house, I decide, is the nearest thing I have to a home. I take another breath of fresh air, and follow my mother indoors.

The stone floor is shiny and worn. Mum leads me into the sitting room, and I pace around, surprised at the changes. I pick up new ornaments, look at pictures, and examine books.

'You've got loads of new things,' I tell her. 'Even the sofa's different. I haven't been for ages, have I?'

'Three years.'

'Really! Have I not been here for three years?'

'And even then, you came with Mark for the weekend. We didn't get to chat with you much.'

I remember that. Mark wasn't interested in my family, any more than he was interested in anything. France, to him, meant vineyards and wine tasting. That was all he wanted to do here.

'Sorry.' I stand next to the mantelpiece, and look at the photos. The whitewashed walls are decorated with framed pictures of the three of us: me, Emma, and Grace. I pick up a shot of Grace shortly before she died. She is grinning at the camera with her face screwed up. Her hair is loose and messy. I look at her closely. I haven't seen Grace for ages. I have missed her.

'Can I have this in my room?' I ask Mum, turning to her and forcing myself to stay strong.

'Of course. There are lots more. Take whatever you want.' She is forcing herself, too. I see it in her eyes.

I see a photo of Emma's graduation. There isn't one of mine, because I didn't bother to go. I imagine Grace's graduation photo. She would still have had long blonde hair, and she would have got a first. A first in history, maybe, or in politics.

Above the fireplace, I notice a set of prints still in their folder. I pick them up, and leaf through the shots of Emma, Jeremy and the baby. Emma looks happy. Even with a scrunched-up little bundle in her arms, she is radiant. Jeremy is still wearing that horrible cardigan. And little Maddy stares at the camera. I hold a picture which must be more recent than the others. She looks bigger here, smoother, and positively pretty. In fact, my niece is beautiful.

I realise that Mum is standing next to me.

'What do you think?' she asks.

'She's amazing.' I stare at the baby, Emma's baby. 'I can't believe Emma made her. I haven't sent a card. I haven't bought her anything. I never even gave them those baby monitors. Bloody hell, Mum. Those are where this all began.'

I suddenly realise that I am going to tell my mother everything.

Mum puts an arm around my waist.

'I'm sure they are. Have a bath, then we'll have some supper and some wine, and you can tell me all about it.'

chapter thirty-one

Libby – the same day

Libby and David sit in a bar in Old Havana. This is the last drink they will have in Cuba. Libby's foot is up on a chair. It's throbbing, and she cannot move it without wincing. Getting here was a complex operation, but she doesn't mind. She is feeling bruised but relieved.

'Lib,' says David, 'what do we do next? I'm unemployed for ten more months.'

Libby tries to be brisk. 'We'll go back to Brighton. My leg will mend. I will be super-vigilant about nuts, and will carry my epi-pen with me at all times. And I think we should put the flat on the market. I know you haven't got much of a salary at the moment but if I went back to work we'd be able to increase the mortgage and get a house.'

Libby looks at him. She is trying to be brave. She doesn't want him to know how weak she feels, how battered she is by everything that's happened.

David strokes her hand.

'Because of Maggie?'

'If that woman moves back into our basement . . .'

'She won't. She won't be going anywhere for a while, I'm sure.' He sips his beer, and looks at Libby, wondering when and if he should tell her about what he did with Maggie. 'But we could certainly do with a house, couldn't we? Okay, you're right. We'll get the flat valued.'

'You always liked Maggie, didn't you?'

David hesitates. 'I didn't realise,' he says, looking around the square. 'I was completely taken in by the way she seemed. She always gave the impression of being pretty straightforward. And she was much better than me at Spanish, and she let me copy her homework . . .' David tails off.

'How is your Spanish these days?' asks Libby. 'You hardly said anything to Luis or Maria or José, and they were in the flat for hours. In fact, I haven't heard you speak Spanish properly for weeks.'

'That's because I'm crap. Bollocks to running some Madrid office. I am not a linguist. We're staying in Brighton, if that's all right with you.'

Libby looks around the Cathedral Square. She can feel the warm evening sun on the back of her neck, on her shoulders, and on the leg that rests on the chair. She watches an old woman moving between tourists, offering to tell their fortunes. She sips her cold beer, and slips off her flip-flop and feels the smooth flagstone under her foot.

'We'll stay in Brighton for a bit,' she concedes. 'But when Charlie's old enough to take it all in, I wouldn't mind having some more adventures. Cuba has been fabulous, in spite of everything.'

'How about Australia?' says David, tentatively.

Libby smiles thinly. 'That depends. When we get home, we'd better see what Alec Betts has to say for himself.'

'There was a letter. At the flat. I forgot all about it.'

'Plenty of time. I'm not honestly expecting much from him.'

They smile, and sit in silence for a while, watching the tourists and children, the touts and the ordinary people, going about their business. Libby is more excited than she will let on. I have a father. Libby turns the phrase over and over in her head. She has been wondering whether Sammi and Zachary know about her, whether their father took any photographs of her with him when he left. Many people are sitting around the colonnaded perimeter of the square, enjoying the perfect spring evening. Libby considers going into one of the souvenir shops in the streets nearby, to buy things for Natalie and Jenny. Then she remembers about her crutches, and decides it would be too much trouble.

After a while, Petra and Yasmin walk across the square, with Charlie in the backpack on Yasmin's back. Libby thinks that they look like the mother and daughter. Both are walking with a relaxed, long gait, and laughing. They are carrying several thin carrier bags crammed with souvenirs. They are deep in conversation.

'Here we go,' says David. He drains his beer. 'Better get the cocktails in.'

'But you should never have stayed with him for a *moment* after he did that!' Yasmin is laughing as they reach the table. 'Christ's sake, Petra, where was your self-respect?'

'My dear girl, I had his bags packed by the time he got in. I gave his best clothes to the charity shop, and he went and bought them all back. He implored me to give him a chance, but I didn't. Leopards and spots, you know.'

Libby holds her head in her hands. 'Please, Mother,' she says, '*please* tell me you're not talking about my father. Not today. This is the very last thing I want to hear. Please.'

'Well, exactly,' says Petra, 'I had a daughter to consider. He may have been her father, but the last thing Liberty needed was constant disruption of *that* sort.'

Yasmin nods, and hands the backpack, with Charlie inside, to David. 'Quite right. Good girl. So you were a single mum? Did Libby see him at weekends?'

'Shut up! Both of you!' cries Libby.

'He showed his true colours soon enough. The second that he realised I was serious, and he wasn't darkening the door again, he buggered off to Australia. Neither of us has heard a peep from him since, have we?'

'You are entirely out of date, Mother,' says Libby, smiling. 'You interfering old battleaxe. I know it all. Apparently I have a letter from him.'

'And is this welcome?' asks Petra, nervously.

'Yes,' says Libby. She is surprised at how grounded the very existence of the letter is making her feel. She cannot even dredge up any anger, at the moment. She just wants to meet her daddy.

'Well then, that's fine.'

Yasmin squeezes Libby's shoulder. 'I'm so happy for you, Lib,' she says.

Libby looks up. 'Thank you,' she says with a smile. She is happiest of all for Charlie. A part of her had always hoped that, even if she was easily abandoned, no grandparent could live without his grandson. It feels to her as if Charlie has brought the family back together.

Petra smiles up at the waiter. 'Hello,' she says loudly. 'Four mojitos to begin with, thank you, darling boy.'

Libby catches David's eye, and they both smile. David places Charlie on her lap, and they start to laugh. Delighted, Charlie joins in. He twists round to look at his mother, and reaches for her nose.

'Mother!' says Libby, when she manages to calm down. 'Have you told Yasmin everything about my childhood?' She turns to Yasmin. 'How embarrassed should I be?'

'I like the way you pretended to have a sprained ankle to get out of sports day,' says Yasmin. 'And then it changed legs.'

'I was ten years old! Mum!'

Petra laughs. 'My darling, Yasmin is a shining star. She is my new best friend. We chatted. I'm not going to censor myself on any account. And besides, it's so wonderful to see you laughing.'

Libby straightens her face. 'I was not.'

'You were, and it's the best sight I've seen for years. And what about Havana? Is it, or is it not, the most divine place you've seen in your life?'

291

'Petra's been getting to know the locals,' says Yasmin.

'This girl really is the ideal companion,' says Petra. 'All the young men flock around us, and I get to bask in the reflected glory. Of course they think I'm her mother, and, let's face it, I might as well be.'

David is the only one who notices the waiter putting the drinks on the table, and he smiles his thanks.

'Guys,' he interrupts, raising his glass, 'I'd like to propose a toast. To the three of you. Yasmin for managing the baby abduction situation so calmly, and ensuring a happy outcome, and for being a good friend to us all despite the rocky start. Petra, my dear mother-in-law, for dropping everything to rush to her daughter's side. And to Libby for being the best wife and mother in the whole of the Americas, and in fact, in the world. I know I've made your life difficult, but I love you more than ever. So thank you, and sorry.' He gives her a kiss, and they all clink glasses.

'I know you probably don't want to hear this,' Yasmin says, when they have all taken a sip, 'but I was just saying to Petra, I'm going to stay out here another few weeks, and then fly back too. I'm not going to carry on bumming around. I'm going to France to see Maggie for a while, check that she's getting her head together. When I spoke to her mum about the Gracia situation, she invited me. Then I think I'll try to get my act together. Try and find some kind of career.'

Libby smiles. 'Yasmin! I don't believe it. A responsible job?'

'So, what are you going to be when you grow up?' asks David.

Yasmin looks around and shrugs. 'Don't know. I'll find something. A spy, maybe, or a pilot. Engine driver. Fireman. Something'll turn up.'

chapter thirty-two

Maggie

dear ivan,

thank you for getting in touch with me. I know it has taken me a while, but I'm happy to reply to you. and I accept your apology. it will amaze you to learn that I am not only in touch with yasmin, but that I've recently realised that she is the best friend I've ever had. if I can forgive her, it stands to reason that I also forgive you. I'm genuinely pleased that you're getting married and it's good to hear you sounding so happy. I won't be able to meet up because I'm living in france at the moment (my folks moved out here years ago), but if I do ever find myself back in the south-east – I lived in brighton until earlier this year – I will look you up.

it has been a strange time. yasmin and I spent a couple of months in cuba recently, and while we were there I had what I suppose you would call a breakdown. it was, I realise, because I'd never dealt with what happened to grace. now I am staying with my parents, trying to get to grips with it all. it's a long process, but I am feeling positive.

I have to say that I don't think this would have happened if you and I had stayed together longer, because you were so good, so caring, so amazing at bringing me out of myself, that I think I would have sorted my head out much earlier on. however, this is a big burden to place on you, and it's not your fault, not at all. we were teenagers, and teenagers are irresponsible.

so in response to your question, there is definitely no man in my life, and there are also no babies, apart from my little niece, madeleine grace, who was born six weeks ago, and who is a little angel.

take care, and consider yourself absolved.

your friend,

maggie x

I spend at least an hour every day on the internet. Making my peace with Ivan feels right. I force myself not to contemplate what could have been. We were too young then, and now Ivan is with Mel, and I do not need to be with anyone. I can't become dependent on anybody. I need to stand alone, with the support of my family. When I am not emailing, I walk in the lanes, between fields, up hills and through hamlets. I stare at birds in the sky, at bees in the flowers, and I try to work out who I am, and why. I am regularly shocked by a memory of Havana. I behaved appallingly. I am astonished at the things I did. I hope Elena remembers me fondly, at least. Nobody else will. I hope she makes good use of all the things I left in my bedroom. She can throw away those hideous shoes, for a start.

Several weeks pass before I am able to tell my parents everything. I cannot bear to look my father in the eye and tell him that his eldest child was a stripper, so I wait until he is out one evening, pour two large glasses of red wine, and sit down next to my mother. She looks at me, and turns the television off.

'Do you really understand the news in French?' I ask, putting off the moment when I have to tell her.

She smiles. 'Yes, darling. We've been here for years now, haven't we? And lots of our friends are French, as you know. Plus we've been going to conversation classes from the word go. It's funny, isn't it, the language was the thing that worried me most about moving here, but it hasn't been a problem at all.'

'Like me and Spanish. We must be good at languages, in our family.'

'You're right.'

I pull my legs up and cross them. I do not want to do this, but I will never get anywhere if I don't. 'Mum,' I say, 'can I tell you some things?'

I watch her as I speak. I try to judge the impact my story is having on her. She is clearly shocked. Shocked that I stripped and gyrated for a living. Shocked that I spied on my neighbours and followed them across the world. She is most shocked of all, I think, by the fact that she had nothing more than the vaguest idea of what I was up to. I think she would have preferred it to have been drugs, after all.

'Darling,' she keeps saying, 'why didn't you tell us? We would have rescued you in a second.'

'I didn't want to worry you,' I keep mumbling. I pull my legs up to my chest, and feel sick. I can't bear to be weaker than my parents. It is a harsh equation, but losing a child is worse than losing a sibling. They have had more to cope with than I have, and they have come through it. I have barely existed since I was nine. I look back at the past ten years. I tried to live as an adult, but I failed. While Mark and I were together, I could just about stumble from day to day. Then everything went downhill. I failed to find a job in human resources, so I decided that lap dancing was a valid alternative. I became obsessed with my neighbours, to the extent that I followed them across the world. I poisoned someone because she felt sorry for me. Then I stole a baby. Nobody could call that coping.

'I thought you couldn't take it,' I tell her. 'I mean, all that bullshit about working at American Express, that was entirely for you, for you and Dad and Emma, so you wouldn't have to worry about me.

I used to ache with how much I wanted my mummy. But because of Grace, I felt I didn't have the right . . .' I tail off.

'Margaret Wilson,' she says, putting an arm around my shoulders, 'did I really give you that impression? Maggie, look at me. Losing Grace was beyond anything. You, more than anyone, know that. You never get over the loss of a child, and it will always be the first thing I think about in the morning, the last thing at night, and I will always miss her physically. I will always go back to that day I saw you with him. I still think I should have had some idea. I could have stopped it. I know I could.

'But that didn't happen. The surefire way to lose your mind is by making yourself feel responsible for our poor, poor Gracie's death. For her suffering. I've had to force myself to stop thinking that it was all my fault. I know you feel it. I've always known that, but nothing I've said could touch you. He was a monster. He did it. You and I didn't do it. We lived near a paedophile. When it comes down to it, it was geography. It was bad luck. Your father blamed himself, too. He thought he'd failed in his duty to protect his daughters. We had to struggle to make our marriage work, and for a while it didn't look as if it was possible, but we are the best friends in the world, now. I see Grace in him, and he sees her in me, and we both see her in you two.'

She leans forward to top up my wine. I wonder whether to say anything, but can't think exactly what it would be, so I stay quiet. I cup the glass in my hands. I love the smell of this house. I wish my sisters were here, with us.

'Your father and I,' my mother continues, fixing me with her direct gaze; she is beautiful, 'we knew that we had to come to terms with it, for your sake. We obviously had to leave the village, but it was only when we came here that we began to settle down. We've grieved and grieved for her. We still grieve, but the pain is a little bit duller than it was. We've come through it, as much as we're ever going to. You and Emma saved us. We were still responsible for you two, so we couldn't go to pieces. We live, now. For years, we existed.

Baby Maddy . . .' She stops and grins. 'She really is a blessing. She's gorgeous.'

'Did Yasmin tell you much about me when we were in Havana?'

'She'd email us from time to time. I was scared about what you were going to do. I would sometimes get up in the night to switch the computer on, just to make sure nothing had happened. We were grateful to her, because you, young lady, only wrote to us once.'

'I'm sorry. You know, I hated Yasmin so much. She told Libby about Grace.'

'She was trying to help. The poor girl felt completely responsible for you. She needed to talk to someone else.'

'I know. But I didn't want Lib to feel sorry for me.'

'So you gave her nuts.'

'Christ, Mum. I don't know what I was doing. The very first time I listened to her through the monitor, I heard her saying she was allergic to them.'

'You were lucky.'

'I know.'

She touches my arm. 'Maggie, you have to be able to talk about Grace. When you meet someone, like Libby, you have to be able to look them in the eye and say, I had two sisters, but one of them died. Once you can do that, you won't need to mess around with baby monitors.'

I feel it about to overwhelm me. I gaze at my mother's face. I have to be strong, like her.

'I miss her,' I say. I see the tears in her eyes, and I fall into her embrace. 'I miss her so much.'

I choke and sob. I have not spoken those words for ten years. I never thought I would say them again.

'My darling,' she whispers into my hair. 'I miss her too. You're my little girl. It's all right to miss her. It's all okay. You're going to be all right.'

chapter thirty-three

Libby's epilogue – October

Libby oversees the placing of the boxes in the new house.

'That's for upstairs,' she says. 'The front bedroom. That one's baby stuff. That can go in the second bedroom. That's for the kitchen.' She reaches for her hair as she speaks, out of habit, and remembers again that it is no longer there. She loves her sharp haircut, but it still takes her by surprise when she catches herself in the mirror.

The kettle is buried deep in a box somewhere, wrapped in newspaper so it doesn't break anything. The crate of food is still in the van. Libby straps Charlie into his pushchair, to his dismay, and pushes him down the road to buy cups of coffee, bags of crisps and bacon sandwiches for herself, David and the removal men. She attaches the rain cover to his pushchair, even though it is not yet quite raining, and tries to recall the seven weeks when she woke up each morning and cursed the fact that it was relentlessly hot and sunny.

David is making a point of carrying boxes, smiling ingratiatingly, and calling the men 'mate'. He suspects they would prefer it if he stepped back and directed them, but he is embarrassed at the idea. He is dreading the moment when one of them asks him what he does for a living.

'Nice place,' says one of the guys, looking around.

'Yeah, we're pleased with it, mate,' David agrees. He finds it hard to take in. They own a house, a townhouse, with four bedrooms, high ceilings and, in estate agents' parlance, 'oblique sea views'. That is to say, if you look a particular way through the side of the bay windows, you can see a grey smudge of water between some houses. They couldn't have done this without Libby's salary. David smiles. He always wanted Charlie to have a parent at home, because he thought it would give him security and grounding. He still believes that, and Charlie still has a parent at home. He is getting used to being a househusband. He's thought about trying to call himself something else: a consultant, perhaps. A carer. A chef, chauffeur, playground helper; a physical mobility tutor and speech coach. He always ends up giving up and returning to househusband. He says it with a self-deprecating shrug, but he really doesn't mind it, any more.

Charlie has grown a thick crop of golden curls. He is a beautiful boy and David is alternately frustrated, overwhelmed, and exhilarated with looking after him. He took his first unaided steps a month ago. David rang Libby at work, desperate to share the news.

'And I missed it!' she said, distraught. She looked at the papers that covered her desk and wished she could sweep them all into the bin and go home.

'Come back early,' he suggested. 'See him do it again for you before bed.'

And she did. She knows that her progress through the firm is less dazzling now, but she doesn't mind. She would rather share herself between her job and her boys than miss out on Charlie.

For now, she reflects as she balances four cups of coffee in the shopping compartment under the buggy, it is all fitting together reasonably well. She is, naturally, tired, but David looks after Charlie and the house better than she ever imagined he would. He is far better at it than she ever was. And she is gratified by the frequency with which he takes her in his arms, and says 'Lib, I had no idea what it was like. Sorry.' When he does that, she ruffles his hair and reminds him that it was worse for her, because Charlie was too little to be rewarding company.

He is a glorious companion, now. He walks, and chats non-sensically, and runs into his parents' arms to hug them. His first birthday is next week, and Libby has booked a soft play centre for his party. Alfie and Milly are going to come, as are various other babies they have met in their three months back in Brighton. The soft play centre is located inside a pub. It is not the kind of pub she would normally go to, but she has discovered the parameters of acceptability shifting radically in the few weeks since Charlie became a toddler. Libby knows that the children are too young to appreciate the party properly, so it seemed only fair to ensure there would be alcoholic entertainment for the adults.

Libby remembers just in time not to tip the buggy as she descends the kerb to cross the road. She looks up. It has clouded over, but it's still fairly warm, and she doesn't think it's actually going to rain. It would be a good time to go to the park, to get out of the men's way. She pulls her mobile out of her pocket, and starts punching out a text message. She was surprised at how little time it took her to get used to mobile phones, supermarkets, and cars when they came back from Cuba. She was immobilised by her ankle for the first few weeks, and sat in their flat imagining Maggie living beneath them. Then, one afternoon, Maggie's sister appeared at the front door. Libby recognised her at once from the photos Maggie had printed out in Havana. She looked brighter and less stressed in real life, and Libby realised after a while that this was because she had only seen photos of her immediately after she had given birth.

'Hello,' she said, smiling. 'I hope you don't mind me dropping by. My name's Emma Wilson.'

In spite of everything, Libby couldn't be unfriendly. 'And this is Maddy!' she exclaimed, cooing over the baby in her arms.

'Yes,' said Emma, who looked spookily like Maggie, as well as completely different. 'How's your leg? Sorry, you probably shouldn't be standing like this, should you?'

'Not really,' Libby agreed. 'Why don't you two come in? My husband and our baby are out at the park. Would you like a cup of tea?'

'Are you sure? This feels a bit weird. I mean, I'm Maggie's sister, and she . . .'

Libby looked at her. She felt strange as well. She was still covered in bruises. 'It's all right,' she told her firmly. 'None of that's your fault, and from the way Maggie used to talk about you, you're as sorted as she wasn't. Come on in. How is she?'

'She's doing all right. It's a big thing for her, but it's good she's tackling it. We're going out to France in a couple of weeks. Jeremy and I are just here to clear out her flat, because, can you believe, she's been paying rent on it all this time.'

'Wow. Amex must have paid her well.'

'Amex? Oh yes, American Express, that's right. Mmm.'

'What? Did she not really work for them?'

Emma laughed. 'You're very sharp. I thought Yasmin would have told you.'

'Yasmin can be extremely discreet. You wouldn't expect it, would you? But no, she didn't tell me anything. Now you say it, though, it makes sense. So what did Maggie really do for a living?'

Emma sighed. 'You don't want to know. Honestly, you don't.'

She told her, of course. She had several cups of tea and numerous biscuits, and stayed to meet Charlie. Emma and Jeremy and Maddy are coming to Charlie's birthday party next week, before they catch a ferry to France from Newhaven. They have spoken on the phone a few times, and Libby is almost amused to realise that Maggie's sister has become a friend. It is the most unlikely outcome she could have imagined.

Libby gives up on her text message at the moment that she crashes the pushchair into a lamppost, and decides to call Natalie, instead.

'Nat!' she says. 'We're at the house. Do you want to come over? Then I thought we could take the boys to the park. If the weather holds out.' She smiles. 'Great. See you in a bit then.' When she gets back to the house, preparing to call Jenny, she discovers that Jenny is already there.

Charlie struggles to be freed from his pushchair. As soon as Libby lets him out, he runs to Milly and pats her on the head.

'Ullah,' he says.

'Ehoh,' Milly replies. The babies grin at each other. Their mothers are convulsed by their sweetness. Charlie looks so angelic that he is usually mistaken for a girl, but Libby cannot bear to cut off his curls.

'Sorry, Jen,' says Libby, as she hands out the coffees. 'I would have got you one if I'd known. Have mine.'

Jenny smiles. She has become much less frantic recently. She has a new boyfriend, and is calm and happy. She even dresses better. Today she is in a pair of black moleskin trousers and a denim jacket. It is a world away from the droopy skirts she used to wear. 'That's all right,' she says. 'Really. I'm off coffee, to be honest.'

'How's everything? How's Peter?'

'Fantastic. I keep waiting to discover his deep dark secret, because I can't imagine any sane man would want to take on a single mum with a nasty ex lurking, but I'm just beginning to decide that there really are some nice men out there, after all.'

Libby squeezes Jenny's shoulder. 'I'm so pleased. Well done. And you look brilliant.'

The three mothers and their children spend an hour at the playground. There are a few other children there, playing on the slide and the see-saw. Libby is still amazed at the amount of greenery in Brighton. The stretches of grass seem like an enormous luxury, compared with the dusty streets of Havana. Yet the children in Havana improvised baseball games in every corner of the city. They were happy and lively. The children in this park are monitored twenty-four hours a day, and if they tried to play a game in the street, let alone one that involved a ball flying around randomly, they would be told they were stupid and that they would get themselves killed. All these parents live in fear of letting their children out of their sight. Libby knows that she is obsessed with potential danger, that the story of Maggie's other sister, and Maggie's own abduction of Gracia, have made her want to keep Charlie at her side for ever. She knows she cannot do it. She will have to force herself to let him go, sooner or later.

Charlie and Milly run to the sandpit and scoop sand into their mouths. Alfie, who is far more relaxed, is happy to sit in a swing for half an hour.

'When does your long-lost sister arrive?' Jenny asks. 'Is it next week?'

'A week on Monday,' says Libby. 'At least we've got lots of room for her now. God knows how it'll be. Bloody weird for all of us, I'd say.'

'Oh, she's Australian, she'll be all right. She'll be living in a shared house in Neasden before you know it.'

'I know. I can't wait to meet her, but I'm terrified. You know? I don't want to disappoint her.'

Jenny snorts. 'Yeah, right. She gains a big sister with a big house? She gains a beautiful nephew and a hunky brother-in-law? She's going to be over the moon.'

They smile. 'I hope so,' Libby tells her.

Jenny looks across to Natalie, who is standing in front of Alfie's swing and pretending to be thrown backwards every time Alfie's feet touch her. Alfie is roaring with laughter.

'Actually,' Jenny says, 'talking of families, I have, in fact, got something to tell you.'

'Mmm?' says Libby, ready to dart to stop Charlie throwing sand into Milly's face.

'Nat, you can hear us, can't you?'

'Yep.'

'How shall I put this? I've just discovered I'm pregnant again. And Peter's delighted. So it looks like Milly's going to be a big sister.'

Libby and Natalie's jaws drop open.

'Jenny!' they scream. They rush over and fling their arms around her. The children stop what they are doing, and stare.

'We won't be having another for a couple of years,' Libby says, later, in the café. She reaches, again, for her hair. Again, it is not there. 'I know the Cuba experience was traumatic, but that wasn't Cuba's fault.'

'It was because you were there with a madwoman,' says Natalie, helpfully.

'Exactly. And it gave me a taste for adventure. David doesn't know this yet, but last week I booked three weeks off work next month. I thought about taking us all to Australia, but then I thought, sod it, if he wants to see us that much he can come here. So instead I've reserved us flights to Nepal. We're going trekking in the Himalayas! And apparently November is the very best time to go. Charlie can ride in a basket on a porter's back. Won't that be the best thing ever?'

Natalie laughs. 'You are a completely different woman from the one who almost divorced David because she didn't want to go to Havana.'

'I know. I feel different. How about you, Nat? Will you be having another, one day?'

Natalie laughs, mirthlessly. 'It rather depends, don't you think? I'd love more kids, of course I would, but it takes two. When I find my Peter, that's when I'll think about new babies.'

'How have things been with Graham?'

Natalie stares into her mug. 'Mmm,' she says. 'He comes over every weekend for Alfie. In fact he's taking him out tomorrow. I hate that. I miss him so much. Alfie, that is. Graham I do not miss. You know, when it all came out, it turned out your friend did me a favour.'

Libby looks at her and decides to test the water.

'She really is a lovely girl, underneath it all,' she says, uncertainly.

'It took me ages to be able to speak to her, because of you, but when I did . . . It turns out that all that time, all she was doing was looking out for Maggie. She's surprising.'

'What's she up to now?' asks Jenny, casting a nervous glance at Natalie, who seems unconcerned.

'Still looking out for Maggie. After it all blew up in Havana, I thought she was going to carry on travelling, hang out in South America, teach some English, have some sex, all that, but she didn't. She said she felt she'd done it all before, and she needed to settle down. She went to stay with Maggie and her parents for a bit. For months, actually. She emailed us this morning. She's coming back next week and applying for jobs. The current idea seems to be to train as a lawyer.'

Jenny laughs. 'You've bloody gone and got yourself another stalker!'

'I hope not.'

Natalie looks nervous. 'She's not moving to Brighton, is she? I can kind of say she did me a favour, and mean it, but I still don't want to stand next to her in the queue at Waitrose.'

Libby shakes her head. 'London. She's a London kind of girl, at heart. And I know what you mean. I can send Maggie the best wishes in the world via Emma, but that doesn't mean I ever want to set eyes on her again. You know, I think there was a little something between her and David. He's never mentioned it, but he looks so uncomfortable when anyone mentions her. He's transparent. And I *so* don't want to know.'

Jenny stares. 'David wouldn't do that.'

Libby shrugs. 'It was a weird time.'

None of them speak for a while.

'You know,' says Natalie, when they have finished their drinks, 'Graham actually mentioned Yasmin last weekend. He had the bloody nerve to ask whether Libby's friend, the blonde one, was back in Brighton. Can you believe that?'

'My God,' says Libby, 'you are so much better off without him.'

'I know. It's hard work, but it's better than being married.'

They all smile. 'You'll meet someone brilliant,' says Jenny. 'You really will.'

Libby nods. 'And meanwhile you're a wonderful mother.'

They all turn to look at the babies. Charlie has leaned across from his pushchair to Alfie's, and is removing all the toys he can reach. Alfie is watching him with interest. Milly is drinking her milk with intense concentration.

'I know,' says Natalie. 'The children are brilliant, I've got good friends, and right now, for me, that's all that matters.'

chapter thirty-four

Maggie's epilogue – October

Dear Maggie,

Thanks for your email yesterday. It's brilliant to know that you're doing so well. I know it is not my place to say this, but I am proud of you. I love our email correspondence. It is strange to have the old Maggie back, but in an adult form. Every day I check the inbox every half-hour hoping for your messages.

Which brings me, somewhat awkwardly, to what I was going to say. I don't really know how to go about this, particularly when I know you wouldn't actually tell me to fuck off, but you might well think it. And if you thought it I just wouldn't hear from you again, which would frankly be no good at all. Well, here goes. Mel and I split up. There are many reasons why this has happened, and I have to say that you are one of them. Not that I would presume anything could ever happen between us again, but I realised (and so did she) that if we were completely right for each other I wouldn't be so excited every time I heard from you. Neither of us was seeing the wedding as anything other than a major hassle. So we called it off, and I moved out of our flat yesterday. I'm kipping on a friend's sofa for now, but I guess I'll get my own place when I can face it. It feels as if we've done the right thing, although very sad.

Now, here is where you tell me to get lost. Can I come and see you in France? I would stay in a B&B or whatever the equivalent is. I am just dying to see you again, to see what it's like and whether I am projecting a relationship that is long dead on to your emails.

I await your reply with interest. Naturally if you said yes I would wait until Yasmin had left.

Love, Ivan x

I take the stairs two at a time. Ivan wants to come and see me! I know I shouldn't get excited about it, that we are almost certainly falling victim to nostalgia, that we will probably find ourselves sitting opposite each other in a bar casting around desperately for anything to say. But I cannot help myself. At the very least, he can be my friend.

Today is the first real day of autumn. The sun is shining, but the air is crisp and cold. Yasmin is leaving, today, and Emma and Jeremy and Maddy are arriving. And Ivan is coming to see me. Suddenly, my life is crammed with friends and family.

When I walk into the kitchen, Yasmin is sitting at the table, laughing at something my dad just said. She looks healthy and happy, in jeans and a thick cream jumper. Her complexion is perfect, thanks to the combination of excellent genes and fresh Provençal air.

'Hey, Mags,' she says, as I come into the room and sit down. 'Lovely day. I don't want to go back to gloomy old Norwich.'

'So don't,' Mum and I say together. I look at Mum and we both laugh. She pours a cup of coffee, and hands it to me.

'But I have to. I can't hang out here bumming off the Wilsons for ever. I need to get a job. I really ought to have a career by now.'

'Yasmin,' says my father, 'when you say you plan to train as a lawyer, can you really imagine yourself upholding the law? You realise you will spend the vast majority of your waking hours dealing with contracts and clauses and enormous files?'

She shrugs and tears a croissant into pieces. 'Mmm, not really. But what else can I do? What about if I was a barrister? Could I stand up in court and make impressive speeches?'

'Yasi,' I tell her, 'you haven't got a clue, have you, any more than I have?'

'Correct.'

I take a piece of her croissant and dip it into my coffee. 'Let's start a business.'

Mum and Dad exchange glances. 'What kind of business?' Mum asks, indulgently.

'I don't know,' I tell her. 'What about if we ran a holiday company, showing people The Real Provence?'

Dad snorts. 'Using our house as a base, I suppose?'

Yasmin takes up the idea. 'No, they could all stay in hotels, Maggie and I could be like their local friends, and we could tailor itineraries for their needs. We'll buy a battered old 2CV, because they'll love that, and drive them around the ochre cliffs, Aix, the Avignon festival.'

Mum smiles. 'We'll work on the business plan, shall we? Now, I hate to say this, I really do, but Yasmin, you need to get yourself together if you're catching that train today.'

'Which I am. Cheers so much for having me all summer.'

Mum stands up. 'It was the absolute least we could do. Now, Mike'll take you to the station. Mike, remember to come straight back because Emma should be here after lunch. Yasmin, we appreciate so much everything you've done for Maggie. We can't express how much it's meant to us, that she's had such a strong friend.'

I step in. 'I'll take her,' I say. 'Please can I? I know the way. I can drive the car. I'd love to see Yasi off on the platform. Please? Yas and I can talk about our business on the way.'

Dad fumbles in his pocket and throws me the car keys. 'Drive safely, young lady.'

'Thanks!' I grin at them both, and take another croissant. I have put on weight since I've been here, and I feel better for it. I like having soft hips and a little tummy. I don't feel spiky any more. I hadn't realised how seriously underweight I was. Today I'm wearing a pair of jeans I bought in Avignon, and a light brown shirt from the local market. I take a band from my pocket, and tie my hair back. I'm going to have it cut short one of these days. It's too much trouble, the way it is. I will go and meet Ivan at the station, too, when he comes. I wonder whether to invite him to stay in the house, or whether that would put too much pressure on us both. I am not seriously imagining that we will fall into some great romance, so I expect that it would be fine for him to stay with us.

'On your way, sweetheart,' Mum says, 'could you pop to a shop? We need salad veg, and some tea bags. Better get some cakes while you're there. You know your sister and brother-in-law. They eat everything in sight.'

'Cakes? Mmm-hmm. Done.'

Yasmin disappears upstairs to get her bag. I take the fifty-euro note Mum holds out, and sit on the front doorstep, putting my boots on. The air is clean, and there is a light mist. Brown leaves blow around my feet. I'm glad it's autumn. Autumn suits me. Leaves litter the street, and I can smell woodsmoke. I look at the house opposite and see Patrice looking down at me. I give her a wave. She returns it.

The plants by the door are wet. A spider's web runs from the wall of the old house to the step. It glistens in the morning sunlight, illuminated by beads of dew.

Yasmin says goodbye to my parents. There is much gratitude on all sides.

'Won't be long,' I tell them, and give each parent a kiss on each cheek. I have taken to the French way of greeting people.

It seems eminently civilised. Besides, I want to show Mum and Dad my affection for them. I virtually ignored them for years. I have been through various stages of childishness over the past couple of months, and now I am nearly grown up, for the first time in my life. I also have a best friend again. And, potentially, another friend, in the shape of Ivan.

'Drive carefully,' says Dad. 'No speeding. Remember, if you see an amber light, you slow down. You don't speed up.'

I laugh. 'I'll be fine. Honestly, I will. I'll crawl along like an old crone out on a Sunday lunchtime.'

'I'll put a wedge under the accelerator, if you like,' offers Yasmin. 'Make sure she can only do thirty.'

'Take my mobile,' says Mum, handing it to me, 'and ring us if you get held up for any reason. But don't talk while you're driving. Yasmin, dear, have a good journey. You have got a book to read, haven't you?'

I get in the car and wave at them both. They stand in the village square, on top of the hill, and watch us leave.

I know this part of the world better than I ever knew Brighton. The lanes and short cuts are completely familiar, and I drive through villages and beside fields, chatting to Yasmin as I go. I have completely forgiven her for Ivan. I toy with the idea of telling her that he wants to visit me, but I know that it would affect her, and decide to leave it, for now. Yasmin has forgiven me for being overcome by madness in Cuba. I was completely wrong about her. She has always been my best friend.

I overtake lorries full of ripe purple grapes. When we reach the local town, I park on a yellow line and run into the shop. I say hello to everybody. I speak French well enough to shop and chat a little. I love the way everybody smiles at me. No one sees Maggie, the needy girl with no friends. They don't see poor Maggie (her sister died). They just see the English girl from up the hill. They take me at face value, and I am beginning to suspect that I come across quite acceptably.

As we drive along the big road towards Avignon, the mist lifts and the sky clears. Yasmin switches the radio on, and Schubert's Unfinished Symphony fills the car. Emma, Jeremy and Maddy will be at the house for two weeks. I will be there when they arrive. I am going to see my niece for the first time. We are a family. I see no reason to leave France, for now.

With some wonderment, I realise what is happening to me. I am beginning to grow up. I know there is a long way to go yet: the thought of moving out of my parents' house is not an appealing one, and I don't feel ready to cope by myself. But I am moving in the right direction. I am able to accept that Grace was my sister, and that now she is dead. I'm still glad she was once alive.

I look at my best friend, who is twiddling a strand of hair around a finger. She is humming along to the music. She will not desert me. I have people who care for me. That support structure was there all along, but I chose to ignore it.

'Say hi to Libby and David for me,' I tell her.

She smiles. 'Okay.'

'And you have to email me every day. Talk to someone about our business plan. You can always come back out and we can make a go of it. You never know.'

Yasmin laughs. 'You're going faster than your dad would like. And no, you never do know, do you? It might work.'